Praise for the *New York Times* bestselling series
The Secrets of the Immortal Nicholas Flamel

THE NECROMANCER

"Unrelenting forward momentum . . . This book will thrill fans."

—*School Library Journal*

THE SORCERESS

"Master yarnspinner that he is, Scott expertly cranks up the suspense while keeping his now-large cast in quick motion. . . . This page-turner promises plenty of action to come." —*Kirkus Reviews*

THE MAGICIAN

★ "Readers will be swept up by a plot that moves smartly along, leaving a wide trail of destruction and well-timed revelations."

—*Kirkus Reviews*, Starred

"An exciting and impeccably thought-out fantasy, well suited for those left in the lurch by Harry Potter's recent exeunt." —*Booklist*

THE ALCHEMYST

★ "[A] riveting fantasy. While there is plenty here to send readers rushing to their encyclopedias . . . those who read the book at face value will simply be caught up in the enthralling story. A fabulous read." —*School Library Journal*, Starred

"The plot zings along at a satisfying pace with enough battles and magic to satisfy the most jaded teen fantasy fans."

—*Voice of Youth Advocates*

ALSO BY MICHAEL SCOTT

The Magician

The Sorceress

The Necromancer

The Warlock

The Enchantress

THE ALCHEMYST

{ *The Secrets of* THE IMMORTAL NICHOLAS FLAMEL }

Michael Scott

EMBER

Text copyright © 2007 by Michael Scott
Cover art copyright © 2007 by Michael Wagner

All rights reserved. Published in the United States by Ember, an imprint of Random House Children's Books, a division of Random House, Inc., New York. Originally published in hardcover in the United States by Delacorte Press, an imprint of Random House Children's Books, New York, in 2007.

Ember and the E colophon are registered trademarks of Random House, Inc.

Visit us on the Web! randomhouse.com/teens

Educators and librarians, for a variety of teaching tools, visit us at randomhouse.com/teachers

The Library of Congress has cataloged the hardcover edition of this work as follows:
Scott, Michael.
The alchemyst : the secrets of the immortal Nicholas Flamel / Michael Scott. — 1st ed.
p. cm.
Summary: While working at pleasant but mundane summer jobs in San Francisco, fifteen-year-old twins, Sophie and Josh, suddenly find themselves caught up in the deadly, centuries-old struggle between rival alchemists, Nicholas Flamel and John Dee, over the possession of an ancient and powerful book holding secret formulas for alchemy and everlasting life.
ISBN 978-0-385-73357-1 (trade) — ISBN 978-0-385-90372-1 (glb)
ISBN 978-0-375-84317-4 (ebook)
1. Flamel, Nicholas, d. 1418—Juvenile fiction. 2. Dee, John, 1527–1608—Juvenile fiction.
[1. Flamel, Nicholas, d. 1418—Fiction. 2. Dee, John, 1527–1608—Fiction. 3. Alchemists—Fiction.
4. Magic—Fiction. 5. Supernatural—Fiction. 6. Brothers and sisters—Fiction. 7. Twins—Fiction.
8. San Francisco (Calif.)—Fiction.] I. Title.
PZ7.S42736A1c 2007
[Fic]—dc22
2006024417

ISBN 978-0-385-73600-8 (tr. pbk.)

RL: 5.0

Printed in the United States of America

50 49

For Claudette, of course
iamque opus exegi

I am legend.

Death has no claim over me, illness cannot touch me. Look at me now and it would be hard to put an age upon me, and yet I was born in the Year of Our Lord 1330, more than six hundred and seventy years ago.

I have been many things in my time: a physician and a cook, a bookseller and a soldier, a teacher of languages and chemistry, both an officer of the law and a thief.

But before all these I was an alchemyst. I was *the* Alchemyst.

I was acknowledged as the greatest Alchemyst of all, sought after by kings and princes, by emperors and even the Pope himself. I could turn ordinary metal into gold, I could change common stones into precious jewels. More than this: I discovered the secret of Life Eternal hidden deep in a book of ancient magic.

Now my wife, Perenelle, has been kidnapped and the book stolen.

Without the book, she and I will age. Within the full cycle of the moon, we will wither and die. And if we die, then the evil we have so long fought against will triumph. The Elder Race will reclaim this Earth again, and they will wipe humanity from the face of this planet.

But I will not go down without a fight.

For I am the immortal Nicholas Flamel.

From the Day Booke of Nicholas Flamel, Alchemyst
Writ this day, Thursday, 31st May, in
San Francisco, my adopted city

THURSDAY,
31st May

CHAPTER ONE

"*O*—answer me this: why would anyone want to wear an overcoat in San Francisco in the middle of summer?" Sophie Newman pressed her fingers against the Bluetooth earpiece as she spoke.

On the other side of the continent, her fashion-conscious friend Elle inquired matter-of-factly, "What sort of coat?"

Wiping her hands on the cloth tucked into her apron strings, Sophie moved out from behind the counter of the empty coffee shop and stepped up to the window, watching men emerge from the car across the street. "Heavy black wool overcoats. They're even wearing black gloves and hats. And sunglasses." She pressed her face against the glass. "Even for this city, that's just a little *too* weird."

"Maybe they're undertakers?" Elle suggested, her voice popping and clicking on the cell phone. Sophie could hear something loud and dismal playing in the background—Lacrimosa maybe, or Amorphis. Elle had never quite got over her Goth phase.

"Maybe," Sophie answered, sounding unconvinced. She'd been chatting on the phone with her friend when, a few moments earlier, she'd spotted the unusual-looking car. It was long and sleek and looked as if it belonged in an old black-and-white movie. As it drove past the window, sunlight reflected off the blacked-out windows, briefly illuminating the interior of the coffee shop in warm yellow-gold light, blinding Sophie. Blinking away the black spots dancing before her eyes, she watched as the car turned at the bottom of the hill and slowly returned. Without signaling, it pulled over directly in front of The Small Book Shop, right across the street.

"Maybe they're Mafia," Elle suggested dramatically. "My dad knows someone in the Mafia. But he drives a Prius," she added.

"This is most definitely not a Prius," Sophie said, looking again at the car and the two large men standing on the street bundled up in their heavy overcoats, gloves and hats, their eyes hidden behind overlarge sunglasses.

"Maybe they're just cold," Elle suggested. "Doesn't it get cool in San Francisco?"

Sophie Newman glanced at the clock and thermometer on the wall over the counter behind her. "It's two-fifteen here . . . and eighty-one degrees," she said. "Trust me, they're not cold. They must be dying. Wait," she said, interrupting herself, "something's happening."

The rear door opened and another man, even larger than

4

the first two, climbed stiffly out of the car. As he closed the door, sunlight briefly touched his face and Sophie caught a glimpse of pale, unhealthy-looking gray-white skin. She adjusted the volume on the earpiece. "OK. You should see what just climbed out of the car. A huge guy with gray skin. Gray. That might explain it; maybe they have some type of skin condition."

"I saw a National Geographic documentary about people who can't go out in the sun . . . ," Elle began, but Sophie was no longer listening to her.

A fourth figure stepped out of the car.

He was a small, rather dapper-looking man, dressed in a neat charcoal-gray three-piece suit that looked vaguely old-fashioned but that she could tell had been tailor-made for him. His iron gray hair was pulled back from an angular face into a tight ponytail, while a neat triangular beard, mostly black but flecked with gray, concealed his mouth and chin. He moved away from the car and stepped under the striped awning that covered the trays of books outside the shop. When he picked up a brightly colored paperback and turned it over in his hands, Sophie noticed that he was wearing gray gloves. A pearl button at the wrist winked in the light.

"They're going into the bookshop," she said into her earpiece.

"Is Josh still working there?" Elle immediately asked.

Sophie ignored the sudden interest in her friend's voice. The fact that her best friend liked her twin brother was just a little too weird. "Yeah. I'm going to call him to see what's up. I'll call you right back." She hung up, pulled out the earpiece and absently rubbed her hot ear as she stared, fascinated, at the small man. There was something about him . . . something *odd*. Maybe he was a fashion designer, she thought, or a movie producer, or maybe he was an author—she'd noticed that some authors liked to dress up in peculiar outfits. She'd give him a few minutes to get into the shop, then she'd call her twin for a report.

Sophie was about to turn away when the gray man suddenly spun around and seemed to stare directly at her. As he stood under the awning, his face was in shadow, and yet for just the briefest instant, his eyes looked as if they were glowing.

Sophie knew—*just knew*—that there was no possible way for the small gray man to see her: she was standing on the opposite side of the street behind a pane of glass that was bright with reflected early-afternoon sunlight. She would be invisible in the gloom behind the glass.

And yet . . .

And yet in that single moment when their eyes met, Sophie felt the tiny hairs on the back of her hands and along her forearms tingle and felt a puff of cold air touch the back of her neck. She rolled her shoulders, turning her head slightly from side to side, strands of her long blond hair curling across her cheek. The contact lasted only a second before the small man looked away, but Sophie got the impression that he had looked directly at her.

In the instant before the gray man and his three overdressed companions disappeared into the bookshop, Sophie decided that she did not like him.

Peppermint.

And rotten eggs.

"That is just vile." Josh Newman stood in the center of the bookstore's cellar and breathed deeply. Where *were* those smells coming from? He looked around at the shelves stacked high with books and wondered if something had crawled in behind them and died. What else would account for such a foul stink? The tiny cramped cellar always smelled dry and musty, the air heavy with the odors of parched curling paper, mingled with the richer aroma of old leather bindings and dusty cobwebs. He loved the smell; he always thought it was warm and comforting, like the scents of cinnamon and spices that he associated with Christmas.

Peppermint.

Sharp and clean, the smell cut through the close cellar atmosphere. It was the odor of new toothpaste or those herbal teas his sister served in the coffee shop across the street. It sliced though the heavier smells of leather and paper, and was so strong that it made his sinuses tingle; he felt as if he was going to sneeze at any moment. He quickly pulled out his iPod earbuds. Sneezing with headphones on was not a good idea: made your ears pop.

Eggs.

Foul and stinking—he recognized the sulfurous odor of rotten eggs. It blanketed the clear odor of mint . . . and it was disgusting. He could feel the stench coating his tongue and lips, and his scalp began to itch as if something were crawling through it. Josh ran his fingers through his shaggy blond hair and shuddered. The drains must be backing up.

Leaving the earbuds dangling over his shoulders, he checked the book list in his hand, then looked at the shelves again: *The Complete Works of Charles Dickens,* twenty-seven volumes, red leather binding. Now where was he going to find that?

Josh had been working in the bookshop for nearly two months and still didn't have the faintest idea where anything was. There was no filing system . . . or rather, there *was* a system, but it was known only to Nick and Perry Fleming, the owners of The Small Book Shop. Nick or his wife could put their hands on any book in either the shop upstairs or the cellar in a matter of minutes.

A wave of peppermint, immediately followed by rotten eggs, filled the air again; Josh coughed and felt his eyes water. This was impossible! Stuffing the book list into one pocket of his jeans and the headphones into the other, he maneuvered his way through the piled books and stacks of boxes, heading for the stairs. He couldn't spend another minute down there with the smell. He rubbed the heels of his palms against his eyes, which were now stinging furiously. Grabbing the stair rail, he pulled himself up. He needed a breath of fresh air or he was going to throw up—but, strangely, the closer he came to the top of the stairs, the stronger the odors became.

He popped his head out of the cellar door and looked around.

And in that instant, Josh Newman realized that the world would never be the same again.

CHAPTER TWO

*J*osh peered over the edge of the cellar, eyes watering with the stink of sulfur and mint. His first impression was that the usually quiet shop was crowded: four men facing Nick Fleming, the owner, three of them huge and hulking, one smaller and sinister-looking. Josh immediately guessed that the shop was being robbed.

His boss, Nick Fleming, stood in the middle of the bookshop, facing the others. He was a rather ordinary-looking man. Average height and build, with no real distinguishing features, except for his eyes, which were so pale that they were almost completely colorless. His black hair was cropped close to his skull and he always seemed to have stubble on his chin, as if he hadn't shaved for a couple of days. He was dressed as usual in simple black jeans, a loose black T-shirt advertising a concert that had taken place twenty-five years earlier and a pair of battered cowboy boots. There was a cheap

9

digital watch on his left wrist and a heavy silver-link bracelet on his right, alongside two tatty multicolored friendship bracelets.

Facing him was a small gray man in a smart suit.

Josh realized that they were not speaking . . . and yet something was going on between them. Both men were standing still, their arms close to their bodies, elbows tucked in, open palms turned upward. Nick was in the center of the shop, while the gray man was standing close to the door, his three black-coated companions around him. Strangely, both men's fingers were moving, twitching, dancing, as if they were typing furiously, thumb brushing against forefinger, little finger touching thumb, index and little finger extended. Tendrils and wisps of green mist gathered in Fleming's palms, then curled in ornate patterns and drifted onto the floor, where they writhed like serpents. Foul, yellow-tinged smoke coiled and dripped from the gray man's gloved hands, spattering onto the wooden floor like dirty liquid.

The stench rolled off the smoke, thickening the atmosphere with the scent of peppermint and sulfur. Josh felt his stomach twist and lurch and he swallowed hard; the rotten-egg smell was enough to make him gag.

The air between the two men shimmered with tendrils of green and yellow smoke, and where they touched, sparks hissed and sizzled. Fleming's fingers moved, and a long fist-thick coil of green smoke appeared in the palm of his hand. He blew on it, a quick hissing breath, and it spun up into the air, twisting and untwisting at head height between the two men. The gray man's short, stubby fingers tapped out their

10

own rhythm and a yellow ball of energy spun from his hands and bobbed away. It touched the coil of green smoke, which immediately wrapped around the ball. There was a sparking *snap* . . . and the invisible explosion blew both men backward across the room, sending them crashing across the tables of books. Lightbulbs popped and fluorescents shattered, raining powdery glass onto the floor. Two of the windows exploded outward, while another dozen of the small square panes shattered and spiderwebbed.

Nick Fleming tumbled to the floor, close to the opening to the cellar, almost landing on top of Josh, who was standing frozen on the steps, wide-eyed with shock and horror. As Nick clambered to his feet, he pushed Josh back down the stairs. "Stay down, whatever happens, stay down," he hissed, his English touched with an indefinable accent. He straightened as he turned and Josh saw him turn his right palm upward, bring it close to his face and blow into it. Then he made a throwing motion toward the center of the room, as if he were lobbing a ball.

Josh craned his neck to follow the movement. But there was nothing to see . . . and then it was as if all the air had been sucked out of the room. Books were suddenly ripped from the nearby shelves, drawn into an untidy heap in the center of the floor; framed prints were dragged from the walls; a heavy woolen rug curled upward and was sucked into the center of the room.

Then the heap exploded.

Two of the big men in black overcoats caught the full force of the explosion. Josh watched as books, some heavy and hard, others soft and sharp, flew around them like angry birds. He winced in sympathy as one man took the full force of a dictionary in the face. It knocked away his hat and sunglasses . . . revealing dead-looking, muddy, gray skin and eyes like polished black stones. A shelf of romance novels battered against his companion's face, snapping the cheap sunglasses in two. Josh discovered that he, too, had eyes that looked like stones.

And he suddenly realized that they *were* stones.

He was turning to Nick Fleming, a question forming on his lips, when his boss glanced at him. "Stay down," he commanded. "He's brought Golems." Fleming ducked as the gray man sent three long spearlike blades of yellow energy across the room. They sliced through bookshelves and stabbed into the wooden floor. Everything they touched immediately started to rot and putrefy. Leather bindings snapped and cracked, paper blackened, wooden floorboards and shelves turned dry and powdery.

Fleming tossed another invisible ball into the corner of the room. Josh Newman followed the motion of his boss's arm. As the unseen ball sailed through the air, a shaft of sunlight caught it, and for an instant, he saw it glow green and faceted, like an emerald globe. Then it moved out of the sunlight and vanished again. This time when it hit the floor, the effect was even more dramatic. There was no sound, but the entire building shook. Tables of cheap paperbacks dissolved into matchwood, and slivers of paper filled the air with bizarre confetti. Two of the men in black—the Golems—were slammed back against the shelves, bringing books tumbling down on top of them, while a third—the biggest—was pushed so hard against the door that he was propelled out onto the street.

And in the silence that followed came the sound of gloved hands clapping. "You have perfected that technique, I see, Nicholas." The gray man spoke English with a curious lilt.

"I've been practicing, John," Nick Fleming said, sliding toward the open cellar door, shoving Josh Newman farther down the stairs. "I knew you would catch up with me sooner or later."

"We've been looking for you for a very long time, Nicholas. You've got something of ours. And we want it back."

A sliver of yellow smoke bit into the ceiling above Fleming's and Josh's heads. Bubbling, rotten black plaster drifted down like bitter snowflakes.

"I burned it," Fleming said, "burned it a long time ago." He pushed Josh even farther into the cellar, then pulled the sliding door closed, sealing them both in. "Don't ask," he warned, his pale eyes shining in the gloom. "Not now." Catching Josh by the arm, Nick pulled him into the darkest corner of the bookstore cellar, caught a section of shelving in both hands and jerked it forward. There was a click, and the shelving swung outward, revealing a set of steps hidden behind it. Fleming urged Josh forward into the gloom. "Quickly now, quickly and quietly," he warned. He followed Josh into the opening and pulled the shelves closed behind him just as the cellar door turned into a foul black liquid and flowed down the stairs with the most appalling stench of sulfur.

"Up." Nick Fleming's voice was warm against Josh's ear. "This comes out in the empty shop next door to ours. We have to hurry. It'll take Dee only a few moments to realize what's happened."

Josh Newman nodded; he knew the shop. The dry cleaner's had been empty all summer. He had a hundred questions, and none of the answers that ran through his mind was satisfactory, since most of them contained that one awful word in them: *magic*. He had just watched two men toss balls and spears of something—of *energy*—at each other. He had witnessed the destruction those energies had caused.

Josh had just witnessed magic.

But of course, everyone knew that magic simply did not and could not exist.

CHAPTER THREE

*W*hat was that disgusting smell?

Sophie Newman was just about to press the Bluetooth headset back into her ear when she breathed deeply and paused, nostrils flaring. She'd just smelled something awful. Closing her phone and pushing her headset into a pocket, she leaned over the open jar of dark tea leaves and inhaled.

She had been working in The Coffee Cup since she and her brother had arrived in San Francisco for the summer. It was an OK job, nothing special. Most of the customers were nice, a few were ignorant and one or two were downright rude, but the hours were fine, the pay was good, the tips were better and the shop had the added advantage of being just across the road from where her twin brother worked. They had turned fifteen last December and had already started to save for their own car. They estimated it would take them at least two years—if they bought no CDs, DVDs, games, clothes or shoes, which were Sophie's big weakness.

Usually, there were two other staff on duty with her, but one had gone home sick earlier, and Bernice, who owned the shop, had left after the lunchtime rush to go to the wholesalers' to stock up on fresh supplies of tea and coffee. She had promised to be back in an hour; Sophie knew it would take at least twice that.

Over the summer, Sophie had grown used to the smells of the different exotic teas and coffee the shop sold. She could tell her Earl Grey from her Darjeeling, and knew the difference between Javanese and Kenyan coffee. She enjoyed the smell of coffee, though she hated the bitter taste of it. But she loved tea. In the past couple of weeks she had been gradually sampling all the teas, particularly the herbal teas with their fruity tastes and unusual aromas.

But now something smelled foul and disgusting.

Almost like rotten eggs.

Sophie brought a tin of loose tea to her face and breathed deeply. The crisp odor of Assam caught at the back of her throat: the stench wasn't coming from there.

"You're supposed to drink it, not inhale it."

Sophie turned as Perry Fleming came into the shop. Perry Fleming was a tall, elegant woman who could have been any age from forty to sixty. It was clear that she had once been beautiful, and she was still striking. Her eyes were the brightest, clearest green Sophie had ever seen, and for a long time she had wondered if the older woman wore colored contact lenses. Perry's hair had once been jet-black, but now it was

16

shot through with strands of silver, and she wore it in an intricate braided ponytail that lay along her back almost to the base of her spine. Her teeth were small and perfect, and her face was traced with tiny laugh lines at the corners of her eyes. She was always much more elegantly dressed than her husband, and today she was wearing a mint green sleeveless summer dress that matched her eyes, in what Sophie thought was probably pure silk.

"I just thought it smelled peculiar," Sophie said. She sniffed the tea again. "Smells fine now," she added, "but for a moment there, I thought it smelled like . . . like . . . like rotten eggs."

She was looking at Perry Fleming as she spoke. She was startled when the woman's bright green eyes snapped wide open and she whirled around to look across the street . . . just as all the little square windows of the bookshop abruptly developed cracks and two simply exploded into dust. Wisps of green and yellow smoke curled out into the street and the air was filled with the stench of rotten eggs. Sophie caught another smell too, the sharper, cleaner smell of peppermint.

The older woman's lips moved, and she whispered, "Oh no . . . not now . . . not here."

"Mrs. Fleming . . . Perry?"

The woman rounded on Sophie. Her eyes were wild and terrified and her usually faultless English now held a hint of a foreign accent. "Stay here; whatever happens, stay here and stay down."

Sophie was opening her mouth to ask a question when she felt her ears pop. She swallowed hard . . . and then the door to the bookshop crashed open and one of the big men Sophie had seen earlier was flung out onto the street. Now he was missing his hat and glasses, and Sophie caught a glimpse of his dead-looking skin and his marble black eyes. He crouched in the middle of the street for a moment, then he raised his hand to shield his face from the sunlight.

And Sophie felt something cold and solid settle into the pit of her stomach.

The skin on the man's hand was moving. It was slowly flowing, shifting viscously down into his sleeve: it looked as if his fingers were melting. A glob of what appeared to be gray mud spattered onto the street.

"Golems," Perry gasped. "My God, he's created Golems."

"Gollums?" Sophie asked, her mouth thick and dry, her tongue suddenly feeling far too large for her mouth. "Gollum, from Lord of the Rings?"

Perry was moving toward the door. "No: Golems," she said absently, "Men of Clay."

The name meant nothing to Sophie, but she watched with a mixture of horror and confusion as the creature—the Golem—on the street crawled out of the sun and under the cover of the awning. Like a huge slug, he left a wet muddy trail behind him, which immediately dried in the fierce sunlight. Sophie caught another glimpse of his face before he staggered into the bookshop. His features had flowed like melted wax and a fine web of cracks covered the skin. It reminded her of the floor of a desert.

Perry dashed out into the street. Sophie watched as the woman pulled her hair free of its intricate braid and shook it loose. But instead of lying flat against her back, her hair flowed out about her, as if it were blown in a gentle breeze. Only there was no breeze.

Sophie hesitated a moment; then, grabbing a broom, she dashed across the road after Perry. Josh was in the bookstore!

The bookshop was in chaos.

The once-neat shelves and carefully stacked tables were scattered and tossed about the room in heaps. Bookcases were shattered, shelves snapped in half, ornate prints and maps lay crushed on the floor. The stench of rot and decay hung about the room: pulped paper and wood turned dry and rotting, even the ceiling was scored and torn, plaster shredded to reveal the wooden joists and dangling electrical wires.

The small gray man stood in the center of the floor. He was fastidiously brushing dust off the sleeve of his coat while two of his Golems explored the cellar. The third Golem, damaged and stiff from exposure to the sun, leaned awkwardly against a crushed bookcase. Flakes of gray mudlike skin were spiraling off what remained of his hands.

The gray man turned as Perry, followed by Sophie, dashed into the bookshop. He gave a neat little bow. "Ah, Madame Perenelle. I was wondering where you were."

"Where is Nicholas?" Perry demanded. She pronounced the name "Nicola." Sophie saw a static charge ripple down the woman's hair, blue and white sparks crackling.

"Downstairs, I believe. My creatures are looking for him."

Clutching the broom tightly in both hands, Sophie slipped

past Perry and crept around to the other side of the room. Josh. Where was Josh? She had no idea what was happening and didn't care. She just needed to find her brother.

"You are looking as lovely as ever," the gray man said, eyes fixed on Perry. "You haven't aged a day." He bowed again, an old-fashioned, courtly movement that he performed effortlessly. "It is always a joy to see you."

"I wish I could say the same for you, Dee." Perry moved farther into the room, eyes darting from side to side. "I recognized your foul stench."

Dee closed his eyes and breathed deeply. "I rather like the smell of brimstone. It is so . . ." He paused. "So dramatic." Then his gray eyes snapped open and the smile faded. "We've come for the Book, Perenelle. And don't tell me you've destroyed it," he added. "Your continued remarkable good health is proof indeed of its existence."

Which book? Sophie wondered, glancing around the room; the shop was *full* of books.

"We are the guardians of the Book," Perry said, and something in her voice made Sophie turn to look at her. The girl stopped, mouth and eyes wide with horror. A silver mist surrounded Perry Fleming, rising off her skin in gossamer threads. Pale and translucent in places, it gathered thick and hard around her hands, making it look as if she were wearing metal gauntlets. "You will never get it," Perry snapped.

"We will," Dee said. "We've accumulated all the other treasures over the years. Only the Book remains. Now, make it easy on yourself and tell me where it is. . . ."

"Never!"

20

"I knew you would say that," Dee said, and then the huge Golem launched himself at Perry. "Humans are so predictable."

Nick Fleming and Josh were opening the door of the dry cleaner's when they saw Perry, followed by Sophie, race across the street and into the bookshop. "Get this door open," Nick snapped as he reached under his T-shirt. From a simple square cloth bag dangling around his neck, he produced what looked like a small book bound in copper-colored metal.

Josh slammed back the bolts and tugged open the door and Nick raced out, quickly thumbing through the rough-edged pages as he ran, looking for something. Josh caught a brief glimpse of ornate writing and geometric patterns on the thick yellowed pages as he followed Nick back into the bookshop.

Nick and Josh arrived in time to see the Golem touch Perry.

And explode.

Fine, gritty powder filled the air, and the heavy black overcoat crumpled to the floor. For a moment, a miniature whirlwind spun there, churning up the dust, then it curled away.

But Nick and Josh's entry diverted Perry's attention. She half turned . . . and in that instant Dee drew his left arm across his eyes and hurled a tiny crystal ball onto the floor.

It was as if the sun had exploded in the room.

The light was incredible. Blinding and harsh, it blanketed

the room in its ghastly flare, and with the light came the smell: the stink of burning hair and overcooked food, smoldering leaves and scorched metal mingled with the acrid fumes of diesel.

Josh caught a glimpse of his sister just as Dee tossed the crystal. He was partially shielded by Nick and Perry, both of whom were battered to the floor by the light. Josh's vision became a kaleidoscope of black-and-white still images as the light seared the rods and cones at the back of his eyes. He saw Nick drop the metal-bound book onto the floor . . . saw two black-clad shapes surround Perry and vaguely heard her scream . . . saw Dee snatch the book with a grunt of triumph while Nick groped blindly on the floor.

"You lose, Nicholas," Dee hissed, "as you have always lost. Now I get to take those things most precious to you: your beloved Perenelle and your book."

Josh was moving even before he was aware of it. He launched himself at Dee, catching the small man by surprise. Although only fifteen, Josh was tall for his age, and heavy: he was big enough to be a linebacker, and the youngest on his football team. He knocked Dee to the ground, sending the book spinning out of his grasp. Josh felt the heavy metal cover beneath his fingertips and caught it—just as he was lifted straight off the floor and tossed into a corner. He landed on a pile of books that cushioned his fall. Black spots and darts of rainbow light moved across his eyes every time he blinked.

Dee's gray shape loomed over Josh, then his gloved hand reached down for the book. "Mine, I think."

Josh's grip tightened, but Dee simply wrenched the book from his hand.

"You. Leave. My. Brother. Alone." Sophie Newman brought the broom down five times on Dee's back, once for every word.

Dee barely glanced at her. Clutching the book in one gloved hand, he caught the broom in the other and muttered a single word, and it immediately withered and turned to ragged pulpy splinters in Sophie's hands. "You're lucky I'm in a good humor today," he whispered, "else I'd do the same to you." Then Dee and his two remaining Golems swept out of the devastated bookshop, carrying Perry Fleming between them, and slammed the door closed. There was a long moment of silence, and then the last remaining undisturbed shelf of books clattered to the floor.

CHAPTER FOUR

"*I* suppose calling the police is out of the question." Sophie Newman leaned against a precariously listing bookcase and wrapped her arms around her body to stop herself from shaking. She was surprised that her voice sounded so calm and reasonable. "We've got to tell them that Perry's been kidnapped. . . ."

"Perry's not in any danger just yet." Nick Fleming was sitting on one of the lower rungs of a short stepladder. He was holding his head in his hands and breathing deeply, coughing occasionally as he tried to clear his lungs of dust and grit. "But you're right, we're not going to the police." He managed a wan smile. "I'm not sure what we could say to the police that would make any sense to them."

"I'm not sure that it makes much sense to us either," Josh said. He was sitting on the only unbroken chair left in the bookshop. Although he'd broken no bones, he was bruised all over and knew he was going to turn several really interesting shades of purple over the next couple of days. The last time he'd felt like this was when he'd been run over by three guys on the football field. Actually, this felt worse. At least then, he knew what was happening.

"I think that perhaps gas escaped into the shop," Nick suggested cautiously, "and what we've all experienced and seen is nothing more than a series of hallucinations." He stopped, looking at Sophie and Josh in turn.

The twins lifted their heads to look at him, identical expressions of disbelief on their faces, bright blue eyes still wide with shock. "Lame," Josh said finally.

"Very lame," Sophie agreed.

Nick shrugged. "Actually, I thought it was a pretty good explanation. It covered the smells, the explosion in the shop and any . . . any *peculiar* things you *thought* you might have seen," he finished hurriedly.

Adults, Sophie had decided a long time before, were really bad at making up good excuses. "We didn't imagine those things," she said firmly. "We didn't imagine the Golems."

"The what?" Josh asked.

"The big guys were Golems; they were made out of mud," his sister explained. "Perry told me."

"Ah, she did, did she?" Fleming murmured. He looked around the devastated shop and shook his head. It had taken less than four minutes to completely trash it. "I'm surprised he brought Golems. They are usually so unreliable in warmer countries. But they served his purpose. He got what he came for."

"The book?" Sophie asked. She had caught a glimpse of it in Josh's hand before the small man pulled it free. Although she was standing in a shop full of books, and their father owned a huge library of antiquarian books, she had never seen anything like that particular one before. It looked as if it was bound in tarnished metal.

Fleming nodded. "He's been looking for that for a long time," he said softly, his pale eyes lost and distant. "A very long time."

Josh rose slowly to his feet, his back and shoulders aching. He held out two crumpled pages to Nick. "Well, he didn't get all of it. When he pulled the book out of my hand, I guess I must have been holding on to these."

Fleming snatched the pages from Josh's hand with an inarticulate cry. Dropping to the floor, he brushed away shredded books and shattered shelving and laid the two pages on the floor side by side. His long-fingered hands were trembling slightly as he smoothed the pages flat. The twins knelt on the floor on either side of him, staring intently at the pages . . . and trying to make sense of what they were seeing. "And we're certainly not imagining *that*," Sophie whispered, tapping the page with her index finger.

The thick pages were about six inches across by nine inches long and were composed of what looked like pressed bark. Tendrils of fibers and leaves were clearly visible in the surface, and both were covered with jagged, angular writing.

26

The first letter at the top left-hand corner of each page was beautifully illuminated in gold and red, while the rest of the words were written in reddish black ink.

And the words were moving.

Sophie and Josh watched as the letters shifted on the page like tiny beetles, shaping and reshaping themselves, becoming briefly almost legible in recognizable languages like Latin or Old English, but then immediately dissolving and re-forming into ancient-looking symbols not unlike Egyptian hieroglyphs or Celtic Ogham.

Fleming sighed. "No, you're not imagining that," he said finally. He reached down the neck of his T-shirt and pulled out a pair of pince-nez on a length of black cord. The pince-nez were old-fashioned glasses without arms, designed to perch on the bridge of the nose. Using the spectacles as magnifying glasses, Nick moved them across the wriggling, shifting words. *"Ha!"*

"Good news?" Josh asked.

"Excellent news. He's missing the Final Summoning." He squeezed Josh's bruised shoulder, making him wince. "If you had wanted to take two pages from the book, rendering it useless, then you could not have chosen better than these." The broad smile faded from his face. "And when Dee finds out, he'll be back, and I guarantee you he will not just bring Golems with him next time."

"Who *was* the gray man?" Sophie asked. "Perry also called him Dee."

Gathering up the pages, Nick stood. Sophie turned to look at him and realized that he suddenly looked old and tired, incredibly tired. "The gray man was Dr. John Dee, one of the most powerful and dangerous men in the world."

"I've never heard of him," Josh said.

"To remain unknown in this modern world: that, indeed, is real power. Dee is an alchemist, a magician, a sorcerer and a necromancer, and they are not all the same thing."

"Magic?" Sophie asked.

"I thought there was no such thing as magic," Josh said sarcastically, and then immediately felt foolish, after what he'd just seen and experienced.

"Yet you have just fought creatures of magic: the Golems are men created of mud and clay, brought to life by a single word of power. In this century, I'll wager there are less than half a dozen people who have even seen a Golem, let alone survived an encounter with one."

"Did Dee bring them to life?" Sophie asked.

"Creating Golems is easy; the spell is as old as humanity. Animating them is a little harder and controlling them is practically impossible." He sighed. "But not for Dr. John Dee."

"Who is he?" she pressed.

"Dr. John Dee was Court Magician during the reign of Queen Elizabeth I in England."

Sophie laughed shakily, not entirely sure whether to believe Nick Fleming. "But that was centuries ago; the gray man couldn't have been older than fifty."

Nick Fleming crawled around on the floor, pushing through books until he found the one he wanted. *England in the Age of Elizabeth*. He flipped it open: on the page facing an image of Queen Elizabeth I was an old-fashioned etching of a sharp-faced man with a triangular beard. The clothes were different, but there was no doubt that this was the man they had encountered.

Sophie took the book from Nick's hands. "It says here that Dee was born in 1527," she said very softly. "That would make him nearly five hundred years old."

Josh came to stand beside his sister. He stared at the picture, then looked around the room. If he breathed deeply, he could still smell the peculiar odors of . . . magic. That was what he had been smelling—not mint and rotten eggs, but the scent of magic. "Dee knew you," he said slowly. "He knew you well," he added.

Fleming moved about the shop, picking up odd items and dropping them to the floor again. "Oh, he knows me," he said. "He knows Perry, too. He's known us for a long time . . . a very long time." He looked over at the twins, his almost colorless eyes now dark and troubled. "You're involved now, more's the pity, so the time for lies and subterfuge is past. If you are to survive, you will need to know the truth."

Josh and Sophie looked at one another. They had both picked up the phrase "If you are to survive . . ."

"My real name is Nicholas Flamel. I was born in France in the year 1330. Perry's real name is Perenelle: she is ten years older than me. But don't ever tell her I said that," he added hastily.

Josh felt his stomach churn and rumble. He was going to say "Impossible!" and laugh and be irritated with Nick for telling them such a stupid story. But he was bruised and aching from being flung across the room by . . . by what? He remembered the Golem that had reached for Perry—*Perenelle*—and how it had dissolved into powder at her touch.

"What . . . what are you?" Sophie asked the question that was forming on her twin's lips. "What *are* you and Perenelle?"

Nick smiled, but his face was cold and humorless, and for an instant, he almost resembled Dee. "We are legend," he said simply. "Once—a long time ago—we were simple people, but then I bought a book, the Book of Abraham the Mage, usually called the Codex. From that moment on, things changed. Perenelle changed. I changed. I became the Alchemyst.

"I became the greatest alchemyst of all time, sought after by kings and princes, by emperors and even the Pope himself. I discovered the secret of the philosopher's stone hidden deep in that book of ancient magic: I learned how to turn ordinary metal into gold, how to change common stones into precious jewels. But more than this, much more, I found the recipe for a formulation of herbs and spells that keeps disease and death at bay. Perenelle and I became virtually immortal." He held up the torn pages in his hand. "This is all that remains of the Codex. Dee and his kind have been seeking the Book of the Mage for centuries. Now they have it. And Perenelle, too," he added bitterly.

"But you said the Book is useless without these pages," Josh reminded him quickly.

"That is true. There is enough in the Book to keep Dee

busy for centuries, but these pages are vital," Nick agreed. "Dee will be coming back for them."

"There's something else, though, isn't there?" Sophie asked quickly. "Something more." She knew he was holding something back; adults always did. Their parents had taken months to tell Josh and her that they would be spending the summer in San Francisco.

Nick glanced at her sharply, and once again she was reminded of the look Dee had given her earlier: there was something cold and inhuman in it. "Yes . . . there is something more," he said hesitantly. "Without the Book, Perenelle and I will age. The formulation for immortality must be brewed afresh every month. Within the full cycle of the moon, we will wither and die. And if we die, then the evil we have so long fought against will triumph. The Elder Race will claim this earth again."

"The Elder Race?" Josh asked, his voice rising and cracking. He swallowed hard, conscious now that his heart was thumping in his chest. What had started out as just another ordinary Thursday afternoon had turned into something strange and terrible. He played a lot of computer games, read some fantasy novels, and in those, *elder* always meant ancient and dangerous. "Elder, as in old?"

"Very old," Flamel agreed.

"You mean there are more like Dee, like you?" Josh said, then winced as Sophie kicked his shins.

Flamel turned to look at Josh, his colorless eyes now clouded with anger. "There are others like Dee, yes, and others like me, too, but Dee and I are not alike. We were never alike," Flamel added bitterly. "We chose to follow different paths, and his has led him down some very dark roads. He too is immortal, though even I am not sure how he retains his youth. But we are both human." He turned to the cash register, which was lying broken open on the floor, and started scooping out the money as he spoke. When he turned to look at the twins, they were startled by the grim expression on his face. "Those whom Dee serves are not and never were from the race of man." Shoving the money into his pockets, he grabbed a battered leather jacket off the floor. "We've got to get out of here."

"Where will you go? What will you do?" Sophie asked.

"What about us?" Josh finished the thought for her, as she often did for him.

"First I have to get you to a place of safety before Dee realizes that the pages are missing. Then I'll go in search of Perenelle."

The twins looked at each other. "Why do you have to get us to a safe place?" Sophie asked.

"We don't know anything," Josh said.

"Once Dee discovers that the Book is incomplete, he will return for the missing pages. And I guarantee you, he will leave no witnesses on this earth."

Josh started to laugh, but the sound died in his throat when he realized that his sister was not even smiling. "You're . . ." He licked suddenly dry lips. "You're saying that he would kill us?"

Nicholas Flamel tilted his head to one side, considering. "No," he said finally, "not kill you."

Josh heaved a sigh of relief.

"Believe me," Flamel continued. "Dee can do much worse to you. Much worse."

CHAPTER FIVE

$\mathcal{T}$he twins stood on the sidewalk outside the bookshop, glass from the broken windows crunching under their feet, watching as Nick produced a key. "But we can't just leave," Sophie said firmly.

Josh nodded. "We're not going anywhere."

Nick Fleming—or Flamel, as they were beginning to think of him—turned the key in the lock of the bookshop and rattled the door. Within the shop, they could hear books sliding onto the floor. "I really loved this shop," Flamel muttered. "It reminded me of my very first job." He glanced at Sophie and Josh. "You have no choice. If you want to survive the rest of the day, you have to leave now." Then he turned away, pulling on his battered leather jacket as he hurried across the road to The Coffee Cup. The twins looked at each other, then hurried after him.

"You've got keys to lock up?"

Sophie nodded. She produced the two keys on their Golden Gate Bridge key ring. "Look, if Bernice comes back and finds the shop closed, she'll probably call the police or something. . . ."

"Good point," Flamel said. "Leave a note," he told Sophie, "something short—you had to leave suddenly, some sort of emergency, that sort of thing. Say that I accompanied you. Scribble it; make it look as if you left in a hurry. Are your parents still on that dig in Utah?" The twins' parents were archaeologists, currently on loan to the University of San Francisco.

Sophie nodded. "For another six weeks at least."

"We're still staying with Aunt Agnes in Pacific Heights," Josh added. "Aunt Agony."

"We can't just disappear. She'll be expecting us home for dinner," Sophie said. "If we're even five minutes late, she gets in a tizzy. Last week, when the trolley car broke down and we were an hour late, she'd already phoned our parents by the time we got there." Aunt Agnes was eighty-four, and although she drove the twins to distraction with her constant fussing, they were very fond of her.

"Then you'll need to give her an excuse too," Flamel said bluntly, sweeping into the coffee shop with Sophie close behind him.

Josh hesitated before stepping into the cool, sweet-smelling gloom of The Coffee Cup. He stood on the sidewalk, his backpack slung over his shoulder, looking up and down. If you ignored the sparkling glass littering the sidewalk in front of the bookshop, everything looked perfectly normal, an ordinary weekday afternoon. The street was still and silent, the air was heavy with just a hint of the ocean. Across the bay, beyond Fisherman's Wharf, a ship's horn sounded, the deep noise lost and lonely in the distance. Everything looked more or less as it had half an hour earlier.

And yet . . .

And yet it was not the same. It could never be the same again. In the last thirty minutes, Josh's carefully ordered world had shifted and altered irrevocably. He was a normal high school sophomore, not too brilliant, but not stupid either. He played football, sang—badly—in his friend's band, had a few girls he was interested in, but no real girlfriend yet. He played the occasional computer game, preferred first-person shooters like Quake and Doom and Unreal Tournament, couldn't handle the driving games and got lost in Myst. He loved *The Simpsons* and could quote chunks of episodes by heart, really liked *Shrek,* though he'd never admit it, thought the new Batman was all right and that X-Men was excellent. He even liked the new Superman, despite what other people said. Josh was ordinary.

But ordinary teens did not find themselves in the middle of a battle between two incredibly ancient magicians.

There was no magic in the world. Magic was movie special effects. Magic was stage shows with rabbits and doves and sometimes tigers, and David Copperfield sawing people in half and levitating over the audience. There was no such thing as real magic.

But how then could he explain what had just happened in the bookshop? He had watched shelves turn to rotten wood, seen books dissolve into pulp, smelled the stink of rotten eggs from Dee's spells and the cleaner scent of mint when Fleming—*Flamel*—worked his magic.

Josh Newman shivered in the bright afternoon sunshine and ducked into The Coffee Cup, pulling open his backpack and reaching in for his battered laptop. He needed to use the café's wireless Internet connection; he had names he wanted to look up: Doctor John Dee, Perenelle and especially Nicholas Flamel.

Sophie scribbled a quick note on the back of a napkin, then chewed the end of the pencil as she read it.

Mrs. Fleming unwell. Gas leak in the shop. Gone to hospital. Mr. Fleming with us. Everything else OK. Will phone later.

When Bernice came back and found the shop closed just before the late-afternoon rush, she was not going to be happy. Sophie guessed that she might even lose her job. Sighing, she signed the note with a flourish that tore through the paper, and stuck it to the cash register.

Nicholas Flamel peered over her shoulder and read it. "That's good, very good, and it explains why the bookshop is closed too." Flamel glanced over his shoulder to where Josh was tapping furiously at his keyboard. "Let's go!"

"Just checking my mail," Josh muttered, powering off the machine and closing it.

"At a time like this?" Sophie asked incredulously.

"Life goes on. E-mail stops for no man." He attempted a smile, and failed.

Sophie grabbed her bag and vintage denim jacket, taking

a last look around the coffee shop. She had the sudden thought that she would not be seeing it again for a long time, but that was ridiculous, of course. She turned out the lights, ushered her brother and Nick Fleming—Flamel—through the door ahead of her and hit the alarm. Then she pulled the door shut, turned the key in the lock and dropped the key chain through the letter box.

"Now what?" she asked.

"Now we get some help and we hide until I figure out what to do with you both." Flamel smiled. "We're good at hiding; Perry and I have been doing it for more than half a millennium."

"What about Perry?" Sophie asked. "Will Dee . . . harm her?" She'd come to know and like the tall, elegant woman over the past few weeks as she came into the coffee shop. She didn't want anything to happen to her.

Flamel shook his head. "He can't. She's too powerful. I never studied the sorcerous arts, but Perry did. Right now all Dee can do is contain her, prevent her from using her powers. But in the next few days she *will* start to age and weaken. Possibly in a week, certainly within two weeks, he would be able to use his powers against her. Still, he'll be cautious. He will keep her trapped behind Wards and Sigils. . . ." Flamel saw the look of confusion on Sophie's face. "Magical barriers," he explained. "He'll only attack when he is sure of victory. But first he will try to discover the extent of her arcane knowledge. Dee's search for knowledge was always his greatest strength . . . and his weakness." He absently patted his pockets, looking for something. "My Perry can take care of herself. Remind me to tell you the story sometime of how she faced down a pair of Greek Lamiae."

Sophie nodded, though she had no idea what Greek Lamiae were.

As Flamel strode down the street, he found what he was looking for: a pair of small round sunglasses. He put them on, stuck his hands in the pockets of his leather jacket and began to whistle tunelessly, as if he hadn't a care in the world. He glanced back over his shoulder. "Well, come on."

The twins looked at each other blankly, then hurried after him.

"I checked him out online," Josh muttered, looking quickly at his sister.

"So that's what you were doing. I didn't think e-mail could be that important."

"Everything he says checks out: he's there on Wikipedia and there are nearly two hundred thousand results for him on Google. There are over ten million results for John Dee. Even Perenelle is there, and it mentions the book and everything. It even says that when he died, his grave was dug up by people searching for treasure and they found it empty—no body and no treasure. Apparently, his house is still standing in Paris."

"He sure doesn't look like an immortal magician," Sophie murmured.

"I'm not sure I know what a magician looks like," Josh said quietly. "The only magicians I know are Penn and Teller."

"I'm not a magician," Flamel said, without looking at them. "I'm an alchemyst, a man of science, though perhaps not the science you would be familiar with."

Sophie hurried to catch up. She reached out to touch his arm and slow him down, but a spark—like static electricity—snapped into her fingertips. "Aaah!" She jerked her hand back, fingertips tingling. Now what?

"I'm sorry," Flamel explained. "That's an aftereffect of the . . . well, what you would call magic. My aura—the electrical field that surrounds my body—is still charged. It's just reacting when it hits your aura." He smiled, showing perfectly regular teeth. "It also means you must have a powerful aura."

"What's an aura?"

Flamel strode on a couple of steps down the sidewalk without answering, then turned to point to a window. The word TATTOO was picked out in fluorescent lighting. "See there . . . see how there is a glow around the words?"

"I see it." Sophie nodded, squinting slightly. Each letter was outlined in buzzing yellow light.

"Every human has a similar glow around their body. In the distant past, people could see it clearly and they named it the *aura*. It comes from the Greek word for breath. As humans evolved, most lost the ability to see the aura. Some still can, of course."

Josh snorted derisively.

Flamel glanced over his shoulder. "It's true. The aura has even been photographed by a Russian couple called the Kirlians. The electrical field surrounds every living organism."

"What does it look like?" Sophie asked.

Flamel tapped his finger on the shop window. "Just like that: a glow around the body. Everyone's aura is unique—different colors, different strengths. Some glow solidly, others pulse. Some appear around the edge of the body, other auras cloak the body like an envelope. You can tell a lot from a person's aura: whether they are ill or unhappy, angry or frightened, for example."

"And you can see these auras?" Sophie said.

Flamel shook his head, surprising them. "No, I cannot. Perry can, sometimes. I cannot. But I know how to channel and direct the energy. That's what you were seeing earlier today: pure auric energy."

"I think I'd like to learn how to do that," Sophie said.

Flamel glanced at her quickly. "Be careful what you wish for. Every use of power has a cost." He held out his hand. Sophie and Josh crowded around on the quiet side street. Flamel's hand was visibly trembling. And when Sophie looked into his face, she noticed that his eyes were bloodshot. "When you use auric energy, you burn as many calories as if you had run a marathon. Think of it like draining a battery. I doubt I could have lasted very much longer against Dee back there."

"Is Dee more powerful than you?"

Flamel smiled grimly. "Infinitely." Shoving his hands back into the pockets of his leather jacket, he continued down the street, Sophie and Josh now walking on either side of him. In the distance, the Golden Gate Bridge began to loom over the rooftops. "Dee has spent the past five centuries developing his powers; I've spent that same time hiding mine, concentrating only on those few little things I needed to do to keep Perenelle and myself alive. Dee was always powerful, and I dread to think what he is capable of now." At the bottom of the hill he paused, looking left and right, then abruptly turned to the left and headed into California Street. "There'll be time for questions later. Right now, we have to hurry."

"Have you known Dee long?" Josh persisted, determined to get some answers.

Nicholas Flamel smiled grimly. "John Dee was a mature man when I accepted him as my apprentice. I still took apprentices in those days, and so many of them went on to make me proud. I had visions of creating the next generation of alchemists, scientists, astronomers, astrologers and mathematicians: these would be the men and women who would create a new world. Dee was probably the finest student I ever had. So I suppose you could say that I've known him for nearly five hundred years—though our encounters have been somewhat sporadic over the past few decades."

"What turned him into your enemy?" Sophie asked.

"Greed, jealousy . . . and the Codex, the Book of Abraham the Mage," Flamel answered. "He's coveted that for a long time, and now he has it."

"Not all of it," Josh reminded him.

"No, not all of it." Flamel smiled. He walked on, with the twins still on either side of him. "When Dee was my apprentice in Paris, he found out about the Codex. One day I caught him attempting to steal it, and I knew then that he had allied himself with the Dark Elders. I refused to share its secrets with him and we had a bitter argument. That night he sent the first assassins after Perry and me. They were human and we dealt with them easily. The next night, the assassins were decidedly less than human. So Perry and I took the Book, gathered up our few belongings and fled Paris. He's been chasing us ever since."

They stopped at a cross light. A trio of British tourists was waiting for the light to change and Flamel fell silent, a quick glance at Sophie and Josh warning them to say nothing. The light changed and they crossed, the tourists heading to the right, Nicholas Flamel and the twins moving to the left.

"Where did you go when you left Paris?" Josh asked.

"London," Flamel said shortly. "Dee nearly caught us there in 1666," he continued. "He loosed a Fire Elemental after us, a savage, mindless creature that almost devoured the city. History calls it the Great Fire."

Sophie looked over at Josh. They had both heard of the Great Fire of London; they had learned about it in world history. She was surprised by how calm she felt: here she was, listening to a man who claimed to be more than five hundred years old, recounting historical events as if he had been there when they happened. And she believed him!

"Dee came dangerously close to capturing us in Paris in 1763," Flamel continued, "and again in 1835, when we were in Rome working as booksellers, as it happens. That was always my favorite occupation," he added. He fell silent as they approached a group of Japanese tourists listening intently to their guide, who was standing beneath a bright yellow umbrella. When they were out of earshot, he continued, the events of more than a century and a half earlier obviously still fresh and bitter in his memory.

"We fled to Ireland, thinking he would never find us on that island at the edge of Europe. But he pursued us. He had managed to master the control of Wights then, and brought two over with him: the Disease Wight and the Hunger Wight, no doubt intending to set them on our trail. At some point he lost control of the creatures. Hunger and disease ravaged that poor land: a million people died in Ireland's Great Famine in the 1840s." Nicholas Flamel's face hardened into a mask. "I doubt if Dee even paused to think about it. He always had nothing but contempt for humankind."

Sophie glanced at her brother again. She could tell by the expression on his face that he was concentrating hard, trying to keep up with the deluge of information. She knew he would want to go online and check out some of the details. "But he never caught you," she said to Flamel.

"Not until today." He shrugged and smiled sadly. "It was inevitable, I suppose. Throughout the twentieth century, he kept getting closer. He was becoming more powerful, his organization was melding ancient magic and modern technology. Perry and I hid out in Newfoundland for a long time until he loosed Dire Wolves on us, and then we drifted from city to city, starting on the East Coast in New York in 1901 and gradually moving westward. I suppose it was only a matter of time before he caught up with us," he added. "Cameras, videos, phones and the Internet make it so much harder to remain hidden nowadays."

"This book . . . this Codex he was looking for . . . ," Josh began.

"The Book of Abraham the Mage," Flamel clarified.

"What's so special about it?"

Nicholas Flamel stopped in the middle of the sidewalk so suddenly that the twins walked right past him. They turned and looked back. The rather ordinary-looking man spread his arms wide, as if he were about to take a bow. "Look at me. Look at me! I am older than America. *That* is what is so special about the book." Flamel lowered his voice and continued urgently. "But you know something—the secret of life eternal is probably the *least* of the secrets in the Codex."

Sophie found herself slipping her hand into her brother's. He squeezed lightly and she knew, without his saying a word, that he was as frightened as she was.

"With the Codex, Dee can set about changing the world."

"Changing it?" Sophie's voice was a raw whisper, and abruptly, the May air felt chilly.

"Changing it how?" Josh demanded.

"Remaking it," Flamel said softly. "Dee and the Dark Elders he serves will remake this world as it was in the unimaginably ancient past. And the only place for humans in it will be as slaves. Or food."

45

CHAPTER SIX

*A*lthough there were other ways he could have used to communicate, Dr. John Dee preferred this century's method of choice: the cell phone. Settling back into the cool leather interior of the limousine, he flipped open the phone, pointed it to where Perenelle Flamel was slumped unconscious between two dripping Golems and took a quick picture.

Madame Perenelle Flamel. His prisoner. Now, *that* was certainly something for the photo album.

Dee keyed in a number and hit Send, then he tilted his head, looking at the graceful woman across from him. Capturing Perenelle had been an extraordinary stroke of good fortune, but he knew he'd only managed it because she'd used up so much energy destroying his Golem. He stroked his small triangular beard. He was going to have to make more Golems soon. He looked at the two opposite: in the brief time they had been outside in the early-afternoon sun, they had started to crack and melt. The big one on Perenelle's left was dripping black river mud across the leather seat.

Perhaps he would choose something other than Golems next time. The brutish creatures worked fine in damper climates, but were especially unsuited to a West Coast summer. He wondered if he still had the recipe to create a ghoul.

It was Perenelle who presented him with a problem, however—a serious problem: he simply wasn't sure how powerful she was.

Dee had always been rather in awe of the tall, elegant Frenchwoman. When he'd first apprenticed himself to Nicholas Flamel, the Alchemyst, he'd made the mistake of underestimating her. He'd quickly found that Perenelle Flamel was at least as powerful as her husband—in fact, there were some areas in which she was even more powerful. Those traits that made Flamel such a brilliant alchemyst—his attention to detail, his knowledge of ancient languages, his infinite patience— made him a poor sorcerer and a terrible necromancer. He simply lacked the imaginative spark of pure visualization that was needed for that work. Perenelle, on the other hand, was one of the most powerful sorceresses he had ever encountered.

Dee pulled off one of his gray leather gloves and dropped it onto the seat beside him. Leaning toward Perenelle, he dipped his finger in the puddle of mud dripping from one of the Golems and traced a curling symbol on the back of the woman's left hand. Then he painted a mirror image of the symbol on her right hand. He dipped his hand in the sticky black mud again and was inscribing three wavy lines on her forehead when she suddenly opened her bright green eyes. Dee abruptly sat back in his seat.

"Madame Perenelle, I cannot tell you what a pleasure it is to see you again."

Perry opened her mouth to speak, but no words would form. She tried to move, but not only were the Golems gripping her arms tightly, her muscles refused to obey.

"Ah, you must excuse me, but I've taken the liberty of placing you under a warding spell. A simple spell, but it will suffice until I can organize something more permanent." Dee smiled, but there was nothing humorous in his expression. His cell phone trilled, playing the theme from *The X-Files,* and he flipped it open. "Excuse me," he said to Perenelle.

"You got the photo?" Dee asked. "Yes, I thought that would amuse you: the legendary Perenelle Flamel in our hands. Oh, I'm quite sure Nicholas will come after her. And we'll be ready. This time he will not escape."

Perenelle could clearly hear the cackle of laughter on the other end.

"Yes, of course." Dee reached into an inside pocket and took out the copper-bound book. "We have the Codex. Finally." He began to turn the thick rough-edged pages as he spoke. His voice fell, and it was unclear whether he was talking to the caller or to himself. "Ten thousand years of arcane knowledge in one place . . ."

Then his voice trailed away. The phone dropped from his hand and bounced across the floor of the car.

At the back of the book, two pages were missing, roughly torn out.

Dee closed his eyes and then licked his lips with a quick flicking movement of his tiny tongue. "The boy," he rasped, "the boy, when I pulled it from his hand." He opened his eyes and began to scan the preceding pages carefully. "Maybe they're not important . . . ," he murmured, lips moving as he followed the shifting, moving words. He concentrated on the bright illuminated letters at the top of every page, which gave a clue to what followed. Then he stopped abruptly, clutching the book in trembling fingers. When he raised his head, his eyes were blazing. "I'm missing the Final Summoning!" he howled. Yellow sparks danced around his head, and the rear window behind him bloomed a spiderweb of white cracks. Tendrils of yellow-white power dripped from his teeth like saliva. "Go back!" he roared to the driver. "Go back now. No, stop, cancel that order. Flamel's no fool. They'll be long gone." He snatched the phone off the floor and, avoiding Perenelle's eyes, took a moment to compose himself. He drew in a deep shuddering breath and visibly calmed himself, then dialed. "We have a slight problem," he said crisply into the phone, voice calm and unemotional. "We seem to be missing a couple of pages from the back of the book. Nothing important, I'm sure. Perhaps you would do me a courtesy," he said very casually. "You might convey to the Morrigan that I am in need of her services."

Dee noticed that Perenelle's eyes had widened in shock at the mention of the name. He grinned in delight. "Tell her

I need her special talents and particular skills." Then he snapped the phone shut and looked over at Perenelle Flamel. "It would have been so much easier if they had just given me the Codex. Now the Morrigan is coming. And you know what that means."

CHAPTER SEVEN

Sophie spotted the rat first.

The twins had grown up in New York and had spent most of their summers in California, so encountering a rat was nothing new. Living in San Francisco, a port city, one quickly got used to seeing the creatures, especially early in the morning and late at night, when they came out of the shadows and sewers. Sophie wasn't especially frightened of them, though like everyone else she had heard the horror stories, urban legends and FOAF—friend of a friend—stories about the scavengers. She knew they were mostly harmless unless cornered; she thought she remembered reading somewhere that they could jump to great heights. She'd also read an article in the *New York Times* Sunday magazine that said that there were as many rats in the United States as there were people.

But this rat was different.

Sleek and black, rather than the usual filthy brown, it

crouched, unmoving, at the mouth of the alleyway, and Sophie could have sworn that its eyes were bright red. And watching them.

Maybe it was an escaped pet?

"Ah, you've noticed," Flamel murmured, catching her arm, urging her forward. "We're being watched."

"Who?" Josh asked, confused, turning quickly, expecting to see Dee's long black car cruising down the street. But there was no sign of any car, and no one seemed to be paying them any special attention. "Where?"

"The rat. In the alleyway," Nicholas Flamel said quickly. "Don't look."

But it was too late. Josh had already turned and looked. "By a rat? A rat is watching us: you cannot be serious." He stared hard at the rat, expecting it to turn and scuttle away. It just raised its head and looked at him, its mouth opening to reveal pointed teeth. Josh shuddered. Snakes and rats: he hated them equally . . . though not as much as he hated spiders. And scorpions.

"Rats don't have red eyes, do they?" he asked, looking at his sister, who, as far as he knew, was afraid of nothing.

"Not usually," she said.

When he turned back, he discovered that there were now two jet-black rats standing still in the alleyway. A third scuttled out of the gloom and settled down to watch them.

"OK," Josh said evenly, "I've seen men made of mud, I guess I can accept spying rats. Do they talk?" he wondered aloud.

"Don't be ridiculous," Flamel snapped. "They're rats."

Josh really didn't think it was such a ridiculous suggestion.

"Has Dee sent them?" Sophie asked.

"He's tracking us. The rats have followed our scent from the shop. A simple scrying spell allows him to see what they see. They are a crude but effective tool, and once they have our scent they can follow us until we cross water. But I'm more concerned about those." He tilted his chin upward.

Sophie and Josh looked up. Gathering on the rooftops of the surrounding buildings were an extraordinary number of black-feathered birds.

"Crows," Flamel said shortly.

"That's bad?" Sophie guessed. From the moment Dee had stepped into the shop, there hadn't been a whole lot of good news.

"It could be very bad. But I think we'll be OK. We're nearly there." He turned to the left and led the twins into the heart of San Francisco's exotic Chinatown. They passed the Sam Wong Hotel, then turned right into a cramped back-street, then immediately left into an even narrower alleyway. Off the relatively clean main streets, the alleyways were piled high with boxes and open bins that stank with that peculiarly sweet-sour odor of rotten food. The narrow alley they had turned into was especially foul-smelling, the air practically solid with flies, and the buildings on either side rose so high that the passage was in gloomy shadow.

"I think I'm going to be sick," Sophie muttered. Only the day before, she'd said to her twin that the weeks working in the coffee shop had really heightened her sense of smell.

She'd boasted that she was able to distinguish odors she'd never smelled before. Now she was regretting it: the air was rancid with the stink of rotten fruit and fish.

Josh just nodded. He was concentrating on breathing through his mouth, though he imagined that every foul breath was coating his tongue.

"Nearly there," Flamel said. He seemed unaffected by the rank odors whirling about them.

The twins heard a rasping, skittering sound and turned in time to see five jet-black rats scramble across the tops of the open bins behind them. A huge black crow settled on one of the wires that crisscrossed the alleyway.

Nicholas Flamel suddenly stopped outside a plain, unmarked wooden door so encrusted with grime that it was virtually indistinguishable from the wall. There was no handle or keyhole. Spreading his right hand wide, Flamel placed his fingertips at specific locations and *pressed*. The door clicked open. Grabbing Sophie and Josh, he pulled them into the shadow and eased the door shut behind them.

After the bitter stench of the alleyways, the hallway smelled wonderful: sweet with jasmine and other subtle exotic odors. The twins breathed deeply. "Bergamot," Sophie announced, identifying the orange odor, "and Ylang-Ylang and patchouli, I think."

"I'm impressed," Flamel said.

"I got used to the herbs in the tea shop. I loved the odors of the exotic teas." She stopped, suddenly realizing that she was talking as if she would never go back to the shop and smell its gorgeous odors again. Right about now, the first of

the early-afternoon crowd would be coming in, ordering cap-
puccinos and lattes, iced tea and herbal infusions. She blinked
away the sudden tears that prickled at her eyes. She missed
The Coffee Cup because it was ordinary and normal and *real*.

"Where are we?" Josh asked, looking around now that his
eyes had become accustomed to the dim light. They were
standing in a long, narrow, spotlessly clean hallway. The walls
were covered in smooth blond wood, and there were intri-
cately woven white reed mats on the floor. A simple doorway
covered in what looked like paper stood at the opposite end
of the corridor. Josh was about to take a step toward the door
when Flamel's iron hand clamped onto his shoulder.

"Don't move," he murmured. "Wait. Look. Notice. If
you keep those three words in mind, you just might survive
the next few days." Digging into his pocket, he picked out a
quarter. Positioning it on his thumb, he flicked it into the air.
It spun over and over and began to fall toward the middle of
the hallway. . . .

There was a barely perceptible hiss—and a needle-tipped
dart punched right through the metal coin, impaling it in
midair and pinning it to the opposite wall.

"You've left the safe and mundane world you once knew,"
Nicholas Flamel said seriously, looking at each twin in turn.
"Nothing is as it seems. You must learn to question everything. To wait before moving, to look before stepping and to
observe everything. I learned these lessons in alchemy, but
you will find them invaluable in this new world you've unwit-
tingly wandered into." He pointed down the corridor. "Look
and observe. Tell me: what do you see?"

Josh spotted the first tiny hole in the wall. It was camouflaged to look like a knot in the wood. Once he found the first one, he realized that there were dozens of holes in the walls. He wondered if each hole held a tiny dart that was powerful enough to punch through metal.

Sophie noticed that the floor did not join neatly with the wall. In three separate places—on both the left- and right-hand sides, close to the skirting—there was a definite gap.

Flamel nodded. "Well done. Now watch. We've seen what the darts can do, but there is another defense. . . ." He took a tissue out of his pocket and tossed it onto the floor, close to one of the narrow openings. There was a single metallic clink—and then a huge half-moon-shaped blade popped out from the wall, sliced the tissue into confetti and slid back into hiding.

"So if the darts don't get you . . . ," Josh began.

"The blades will," Sophie finished. "Well, how do we get to the door?"

"We don't," Flamel said, and turned to push on the wall to the left. An entire section clicked open and swung back, allowing the trio to step into a huge, airy room.

The twins recognized the room immediately: it was a dojo, a martial arts school. Since they were little, they had studied tae kwon do in dojang like this across the United States as they traveled with their parents from university to university. Many schools had martial arts clubs on campus, and their parents always enrolled them in the best dojo they could find. Both Sophie and Josh were red belts, one rank below a black belt.

Unlike other dojos, however, this one was plain and un-adorned, decorated in shades of white and cream, with white walls and black mats dotted across the floor. But what imme-diately caught their attention was the single figure dressed in a white T-shirt and white jeans sitting with its back to them in the center of the room. The figure's spiky bright red hair was the only spot of color in the entire dojo.

"We've got a problem," Nicholas Flamel said simply, ad-dressing the figure.

"*You've* got a problem; that's nothing to do with me." The figure didn't turn, but the voice was surprisingly both fe-male and young, the accent soft and vaguely Celtic: Irish or Scottish, Sophie thought.

"Dee found me today."

"It was only a matter of time."

"He came after me with Golems."

There was a pause. Still the figure didn't turn. "He always was a fool. You don't use Golems in a dry climate. That's his arrogance."

"He has taken Perenelle prisoner."

"Ah. That's tough. He'll not harm her, though."

"And he has the Codex."

The figure moved, coming slowly to her feet and turn-ing to face them. The twins were shocked to discover that they were looking at a girl not much older than them-selves. Her skin was pale, dappled with freckles, and her round face was dominated by grass green eyes. Her red hair was so vibrant that Sophie wondered if she had dyed it that color.

"The Codex?" The accent was definitely Irish, Sophie decided. "The Book of Abraham the Mage?"

Nicholas Flamel nodded.

"Then you're right, we do have a problem."

Flamel reached into his pocket and pulled out the two pages Josh had torn from it. "Well, nearly all of the book. He's missing the Final Summoning."

The young woman hissed, the sound like that of water boiling, and a quick smile flickered across her face. "Which he will want, of course."

"Of course."

Josh was watching the red-haired young woman intently, noting how she stood perfectly still, like most of the martial arts teachers he knew. He glanced sidelong at his sister and raised his eyebrows in a silent question as he inclined his chin slightly toward the girl. Sophie shook her head. They were curious why Nicholas Flamel treated her with such obvious respect. Sophie had also come to the conclusion that there was something *wrong* about the girl's expression, but she couldn't quite put her finger on it. It was an ordinary face—perhaps the cheekbones were a little too prominent, the chin a little too pointed—but the emerald-colored eyes caught and held one's attention . . . and then Sophie realized with a start that the girl didn't blink.

The young woman suddenly threw back her head and breathed deeply, her nostrils flaring. "Is that why I can smell Eyes?"

Flamel nodded. "Rats and crows everywhere."

"And you brought them here?" There was a note of accusation in her voice. "I've spent years building this place."

"If Dee has the Codex, then you know what he will do with it."

The young woman nodded. She turned her wide green eyes on the twins. "And these two?" she asked, finally acknowledging their presence.

"They were there when Dee attacked. They fought for me, and this young man managed to tear the pages from the book. This is Sophie and this is her twin, Josh."

"Twins?" The young woman stepped forward, and looked at each of them in turn. "Not identical, but I can see the resemblance now." She turned to Flamel. "You're not thinking . . . ?"

"I'm thinking it's an interesting turn of events," Flamel said mysteriously. He looked at the twins. "I would like to introduce you to Scathach. She'll probably not tell you much about herself, so I'll tell you that she is of the Elder Race and has trained every warrior and hero of legend for the past two thousand years. In mythology she is known as the Warrior Maid, the Shadow, the Daemon Slayer, the King Maker, the—"

"Oh, just call me Scatty," the young woman said, her cheeks turning the same color as her hair.

CHAPTER EIGHT

Dr. John Dee crouched in the back of the car and attempted, not entirely successfully, to control his temper. The air was heavy with the odor of sulfur, and thin tendrils of yellow-white fire crackled around his fingertips and puddled on the floor. He had failed, and while his masters were particularly patient—they often instigated plans that took centuries to mature—their patience was now beginning to run out. And they were definitely not known for their compassion.

Unmoving, held by the warding spell, Perenelle Flamel watched him, eyes blazing with a combination of loathing and what might even have been fear.

"This is becoming complicated," Dee muttered, "and I hate complications."

Dee was holding a flat silver dish in his lap, into which he had poured a can of soda—the only liquid he had available.

60

He always preferred to work with pure water, but technically any fluid would do. Crouched over the dish, he stared into the liquid and allowed a little of his own auric energy to trickle across the surface as he muttered the first words of the spell of scrying.

For a single moment there was just his own reflection in the dark liquid, then it shuddered and the soda began to bubble and boil furiously. When the liquid settled, the image in the bowl no longer reflected Dee's face, but showed a curiously flat image, rendered in shades of purple-gray and greenish black. The viewpoint was close to the ground, shifting and moving with sickening rapidity.

"Rats," Dee murmured, thin lips curling with distaste. He hated using rats as Eyes.

"I cannot believe you led them here," Scatty said, shoving handfuls of clothes into a backpack.

Nicholas Flamel stood in the doorway of Scatty's tiny bedroom, arms folded across his chest. "Everything happened so fast. It was bad enough when Dee got the Codex, but when I realized there were pages missing, I knew the twins would be in trouble."

At the mention of the word *twins,* Scatty looked up from her packing. "They're the real reason you're here, aren't they?"

Flamel suddenly found something very interesting to stare at on the wall.

Scatty strode across the small room, glanced out into the

hall, to make sure Sophie and Josh were still in the kitchen, and then pulled Flamel into the room and pushed the door closed.

"You're up to something, aren't you?" she demanded. "This is about more than just the loss of the Codex. You could have taken Dee and his minions on your own."

"Don't be so sure. It's been a long time since I fought, Scathach," Flamel said gently. "The only alchemy I do now is to brew a little of the philosopher's stone potion to keep Perenelle and myself young. Occasionally, I'll make a little gold or the odd jewel when we need some money."

Scatty coughed a short humorless laugh, and spun back to her packing. She had changed into a pair of black combat pants, steel-toed Magnum boots and a black T-shirt, over which she wore a black vest covered in pockets and zippers. She pushed a second pair of trousers into her backpack, found one sock and went looking for its match under her bed.

"Nicholas Flamel," she said, her voice muffled by the blankets, "you are the most powerful alchemyst in the known world. Remember, I stood beside you when we fought the demon Fomor, and you were the one who rescued me from the dungeons of An Chaor-Thanach and not the other way around." She came out from under the bed with the missing sock. "When the Rusalka were terrorizing St. Petersburg, you alone turned them back, and when Black Annis raged across Manitoba, I watched you defeat her. You alone faced down the Night Hag and her Undead army. You've spent more than half a millennium reading and studying the Codex, no one is more familiar with the stories and legends it holds—"

Scatty stopped suddenly and gasped, green eyes widening. "That's what this is about," she said. "This is to do with the legend. . . ."

Flamel reached out and pressed his forefinger to Scatty's lips, preventing her from saying another word. His smile was enigmatic. "Do you trust me?" he asked her eventually.

Her response was immediate. "Without question."

"Then trust me. I want you to protect the twins. And train them," he added.

"Train them! Do you know what you're asking?"

Flamel nodded. "I want you to prepare them for what is to come."

"And what is that?" Scathach asked.

"I have no idea"—Flamel smiled—"except that it is going to be bad."

"We're fine, Mom, honestly, we're fine." Sophie Newman tilted the cell phone slightly so that her brother could listen in. "Yes, Perry Fleming was feeling sick. Something she ate, probably. She's fine now." Sophie could feel the beads of sweat gathering in the small hairs at the back of her neck. She was uncomfortable lying to her mother—even though her mother was so wrapped up in her work that she never bothered to check.

Josh and Sophie's parents were archaeologists. They were known worldwide for their discoveries, which had helped reshape modern archaeology. They were among the first in their field to discover the existence of the new species of small hominids that were now commonly called Hobbits in

Indonesia. Josh always said that their parents lived five million years in the past and were only happy when they were up to their ankles in mud. The twins knew that they were loved unconditionally, but they also knew that their parents simply didn't understand them . . . or much else about modern life.

"Mr. Fleming is taking Perry out to their house in the desert and they've asked us if we'd like to go with them for a little break. We said we had to ask you first, of course. Yes, we spoke to Aunt Agnes; she said so long as it was OK with you. Say yes, Mom, please."

She turned to her brother and crossed her fingers. He crossed his too; they had talked long and hard about what to say to their aunt and their mother before they made the calls, but they weren't entirely sure what they were going to do if their mother said they couldn't go.

Sophie uncrossed her fingers and gave her brother a thumbs-up. "Yes, I've got time off from the coffee shop. No, we won't be a bother. Yes, Mom. Yes. Love to you, and tell Dad we love him too." Sophie listened, then moved the phone away from her mouth. "Dad found a dozen *Pseudoarctolepis sharpi* in near-perfect condition," she reported. Josh looked blank. "A very rare Cambrian crustacean," she explained.

Her brother nodded. "Tell Dad that's great. We'll keep in touch," he called out.

"Love you," Sophie said, cutting the conversation short, then hung up. "I hate lying to her," she said immediately.

"I know. But you couldn't really tell her the truth, now, could you?"

64

Sophie shrugged. "I guess not."

Josh turned back to the sink. His laptop was perched precariously on the draining board next to his cell phone. He was using the cell to go online because, shockingly, there was no phone line or Internet connection in the dojo.

Scatty lived above the dojo in a small two-room apartment with a kitchen at one end of the hall and a bedroom with a tiny bathroom at the other. A little balcony connected the two rooms and looked down directly onto the dojo below. The twins were standing in the kitchen while Flamel brought Scatty up to date on the events of the past hour in her bedroom at the other end of the hall.

"What do you think of her?" Josh asked casually, concentrating on his laptop. He'd managed to get online, but the connection speed was crawlingly slow. He called up Altavista and typed in a dozen versions of *Scathach* before he finally got a hit with the correct spelling. "Here she is: twenty-seven thousand hits for Scathach, the shadow or the shadowy one," he said, then added offhandedly, "I think she's cool."

Sophie picked up on the too-casual tone immediately. She smiled broadly and her eyebrows shot up. "Who? Oh, you mean the two-thousand-year-old warrior maid. Don't you think she might be a little too old for you?"

A wash of color rose from beneath the neck of Josh's T-shirt, painting his cheeks bright red. "Let me try Google," he muttered, fingers rattling across the keyboard. "Forty-six thousand hits for Scathach," he said. "Looks like she's real too. Let's see what Wiki has to say about her," he went on, and then realized that Sophie wasn't even looking at him. He turned to her and discovered that she was staring fixedly through the window.

There was a rat standing on the rooftop of the building across the alley, staring at them. As they watched, it was joined by a second and then a third.

"They're here," Sophie whispered.

Dee concentrated on keeping his lunch down.

Looking through the rat's eyes was a nauseating experience. Because of their tiny brain, it required a huge effort of will to keep the creature focused . . . which, in an alleyway filled with rotten food, was no easy task. Dee was momentarily grateful that he had not used the full force of the scrying spell, which would have allowed him to hear, to taste and—this was a terrifying thought—to smell everything the rat encountered.

It was like looking at a badly tuned black-and-white television. The image shifted, pitched and lurched with the rat's every movement. The rat could go from running horizontally on the ground, to running vertically up a wall, then upside-down across a rope, all within a matter of seconds.

Then the image stabilized.

Directly in front of Dee, outlined in purple-tinged gray and glowing in grayish black, were the two humans he had seen in the bookshop. A boy and a girl—in their midteens, perhaps—and similar enough in appearance for them to be related. A sudden thought struck him hard enough to break his concentration: brother and sister, possibly . . . or could they be something else? Surely not!

He looked back into the scrying dish and concentrated with his full will, forcing the rat he was controlling to stand absolutely still. Dee focused on the young man and woman, trying to decide if one was older than the other, but the rat's vision was too clouded and distorted for him to be sure.

But if they *were* the same age . . . that meant they were twins. That was curious. He looked at them again and then shook his head: they were humans. Dismissing the thought, he unleashed a single command that rippled through every rat within a half-mile radius of the twins' position. "Destroy them. Destroy them utterly."

The gathering crows took to the air, cawing raucously, as if applauding.

Josh watched openmouthed as the huge rat leapt from the roof opposite, effortlessly bridging the six-foot space. Its mouth was wide and its teeth were wickedly pointed. He managed a brief "Hey!" and jerked away from the window . . . just as the rat hit the glass with a furry, wet thump. It slid down to the alley one floor below, where it staggered around in stunned surprise.

Josh grabbed Sophie's hand, and dragged her out of the kitchen and onto the balcony. "We've got a problem," he shouted. And stopped.

Below them, three huge Golems, trailing flaking dried mud, were pushing their way through the wide-open alley door. And behind them, in a long sinuous line, came the rats.

CHAPTER NINE

*T*he three Golems moved stiffly into the corridor, spotted the open door at the far end of the hallway and moved toward it. The finger-length metal darts hissed from the walls and stuck deeply into their hardened mud skin, but didn't even slow the creatures down.

The half-moon blades close to the floor were a different matter altogether. The blades clicked out of their concealed sheaths in the walls and sliced into the ankles of the clay men. The first creature crashed to the floor, hitting it with the sound of wet mud. The second tottered on one foot before it slowly toppled forward, hit the wall and slid down, leaving a muddy smear in its wake. The semicircular blades click-clacked again, slicing the creatures completely in two, and then the Golems abruptly reverted to their muddy origin. Thick globules of mud spattered everywhere.

The third Golem, the largest of the creatures, stopped. Its

black stone eyes moved dully over the remains of its two companions, and then it turned and punched a huge fist directly into the wall, first to the right, then to the left. A whole section of the wall on the left-hand side gave way, revealing the space beyond. The Golem stepped into the dojo and looked around, black eyes still and unmoving.

The rats meanwhile raced toward the open door at the end of the corridor. Most of them survived the scything blades. . . .

In the speeding limousine, Dr. John Dee released his control of the rats, and now concentrated his attention on the surviving Golem. Controlling the artificial creature was much easier. Golems were mindless beings, created of mud mixed with stones or gravel to give their flesh consistency, and brought to life by a simple spell written on a square of parchment and pressed into their mouths. Sorcerers had been building Golems of all shapes and sizes for thousands of years: they were the source of every zombie and walking-dead story ever created. Dee himself had told the story of the greatest of all the Golems, the Red Golem of Prague, to Mary Shelley one cold winter's evening when she, Lord Byron, the poet Percy Bysshe Shelley and the mysterious Dr. Polidori were visiting his castle in Switzerland in 1816. Less than six months later, Mary created the story of *The Modern Prometheus,* the book that became more commonly known as *Frankenstein*. The monster in her book was just like a Golem: created of spare parts and brought to life by magical science. Golems were impervious to most weapons, though a sudden fall or blow could shatter their mud skin, especially if it was dry and hardening. In a damp climate, their skins rarely dried out and could absorb incredible punishment, but this warm climate made them brittle—which was why they had fallen so easily to the concealed blades. Some sorcerers used glass or mirrors for their eyes, but Dee preferred highly polished black stones. They enabled him to see with almost razor-sharp clarity, albeit in monochrome.

Dee caused the Golem to tilt his head upward. Directly above him, on a narrow balcony overlooking the dojo, were the pale and terrified faces of the teens. Dee smiled and the Golem's lips mimicked the movement. He'd deal with Flamel first; then he'd take care of the witnesses.

Suddenly, Nicholas Flamel's head appeared, followed, a moment later, by the distinctive spiky hair of the Warrior Maid, Scathach.

Dee's smile faded and he could feel his heart sink. Why did it have to be Scathach? He'd had no idea that the red-haired warrior was in this city, or even on this continent, for that matter. Last he'd heard of her, she was singing in an all-girl band in Berlin.

Through the Golem's eyes, Dee watched both Flamel and Scathach leap over the railing and float down to stand directly in front of the mud man. Scathach spoke directly to Dee—but this particular Golem had no ears and couldn't hear, so he had no idea what she had just said. A threat probably, a promise certainly.

Flamel drifted away, moving toward the door, which was

now dark and heaving with rats, leaving Scatty to face him and the Golem alone.

Maybe she wasn't as good as she'd once been, he thought desperately, maybe time had dulled her powers.

"We should help," Josh said.

"And do what?" Sophie asked, without a trace of sarcasm. They were both standing on the balcony, looking down into the dojo. They had watched openmouthed as Flamel and Scatty leaped over the edge and drifted far too slowly to the ground. The red-haired girl faced the huge Golem, while Flamel hurried to the door where the rats were gathering. The vermin seemed reluctant to enter the room.

Without warning, the Golem swung a huge fist, then followed it up with a massive kick.

Josh opened his mouth to shout a warning, but he didn't get a chance to say anything before Scatty moved. One moment she was standing directly in front of the creature, then she was throwing herself forward, moving under the blows, closing right in on it. Her hand moved, blurringly fast, and she delivered a flat open-handed blow to the point of the Golem's jaw. There was a liquid squelch, and then its jaw unhinged and its mouth gaped open. In the blackness of its maw, the twins could clearly see a yellow rectangle of paper.

The creature struck out wildly and Scatty danced back out of range. It lashed out a kick, which missed and struck the polished floorboards, shattering them to splinters.

"We've got to help!" Sophie said.

"How?" Josh shouted, but his twin had run into the kitchen, desperately looking for a weapon. She emerged a moment later carrying a small microwave oven. "Sophie," Josh murmured, "what are you going to do with . . . ?"

Sophie heaved the microwave over the edge of the railing. It struck the Golem full in the chest—and stuck, globules of mud spattering everywhere. The Golem stopped, confused and disorientated. Scatty took advantage of its disorientation and moved in again, feet and hands striking blows from all angles, further confusing the creature. Another blow from the Golem came close enough to ruffle Scatty's spiky red hair, but she caught its arm and used it as leverage to spin the creature to the floor. Floorboards cracked and snapped as it hit them. Then her hand shot out . . . and almost delicately plucked the paper square from the Golem's mouth.

Instantly, the Golem returned to its muddy origins, splashing foul, stinking water and dirt across the once-pristine dojo floor. The microwave rattled to the ground.

"I guess no one's cooking anything in that," Josh murmured.

Scatty waved the square of paper at the twins. "Every magical creature is kept animated by a spell that is either in or on its body. All you have to do is remove it to break the spell. Remember that."

Josh glanced quickly at his sister. He knew she was thinking the same thing he was: if they ever came up against a Golem again, there was no way they were getting close enough to stick their hands in its mouth.

72

Nicholas Flamel approached the rats warily. Underestimating them would be deadly indeed, but while he had no difficulty fighting and destroying magical creatures, which were never properly alive in the first place, he was reluctant to destroy living creatures. Even if they were rats. Perry would have no such compunction, he knew, but he had been an alchemyst for far too long: he was dedicated to preserving life, not destroying it. The rats were under Dee's control. The poor creatures were probably terrified . . . though that would not stop them from eating him.

Flamel crouched on the floor, turned his right hand palm up and curled the fingers inward. He blew gently into his hand, and a tiny ball of green mist immediately formed. Then he suddenly turned his hand and plunged it straight into the polished floorboards, his fingers actually penetrating the wood. The tiny ball of green energy splashed across the room like a stain. Then the Alchemyst closed his eyes and his aura flared around his body. Concentrating, he directed his auric energy to flow through his fingers into the floor.

The wood started to glow.

Still watching from the landing, the twins were unsure what Flamel was doing. They could see the faint green glow around his body, rising off his flesh like mist, but they couldn't work out why the furry mass of rats gathered in the doorway had not burst into the room.

"Maybe there's some sort of spell keeping them from coming in," Sophie said, knowing instinctively that her twin was thinking the same thing.

Scatty heard her. She was systematically shredding the yellow square of paper she'd taken from the Golem's mouth to tiny pieces. "It's just a simple warding spell," she called up, "designed to keep bugs and vermin off the floor. I used to come in here every morning and find bug droppings and moths all over the place; it took ages to sweep it clean. The warding spell is keeping the rats at bay . . . but all it takes is one to break through and the spell will be broken. Then they'll all come."

Nicholas Flamel was fully aware that John Dee could probably see him though the eyes of the rats. He picked out the largest, a cat-sized creature that remained unmoving while the rest of the vermin scuttled and heaved about it. With his right hand still buried in the floorboard, Flamel pointed his left hand directly at the rat. The creature twitched and, for a single instant, its eyes blazed with sickly yellow light.

"Dr. John Dee, you have made the biggest mistake of your long life. I will be coming for you," Flamel promised aloud.

Dee glanced up from his scrying bowl to see that Perenelle Flamel was wide awake and watching him intently. "Ah, Madame, you are just in time to see my creatures overpower your husband. Plus, I'll finally have an opportunity to deal with that pest Scathach, *and* I'll have the pages of the book." Dee didn't notice that Perenelle's eyes had widened at the mention of Scathach's name. "All in all, a good day's work, I think." He focused his full attention on the biggest rat and issued two simple commands: "Attack. Kill."

Dee closed his eyes as the rat uncoiled and launched itself into the room.

The green light flowed out from Flamel's fingers and ran along the floorboards, outlining the planks in green light. Abruptly, the wooden floor sprouted twigs, branches, leaves and then a tree trunk . . . then another . . . and a third. Within a dozen heartbeats a thicket of trees sprouted out of the floor and were visibly climbing toward the ceiling. Some of the trunks were no thicker than a finger, others were wrist thick and one, close to the door, was so wide it almost filled the opening.

The rats turned and scattered, squealing as they raced down the corridor, desperately attempting to leap over the click-clacking blades.

Flamel scrambled back and climbed to his feet, brushing off his hands. "One of the oldest secrets of alchemy," he announced to the wide-eyed twins and Scatty, "is that every living thing, from the most complex creatures right down to the simplest leaf, carries the seeds of its creation within itself."

"DNA," Josh murmured, staring at the forest sprouting and growing behind Flamel.

Sophie looked around the once-spotless dojo. It was now filthy, spattered and splashed with muddy water, the smoothly polished floorboards broken and cracked with the trees growing from them, more foul-smelling mud in the hallway. "Are you saying that alchemists knew about DNA?" she asked.

The Alchemyst nodded delightedly. "Exactly. When Watson and Crick announced that they had discovered what they called 'the secret of life' in 1953, they were merely rediscovering something alchemists have always known."

"You're telling me that you somehow woke the DNA in those floorboards and forced trees to grow," Josh said, choosing his words carefully. "How?"

Flamel turned to look at the forest that was now taking over the entire dojo. "It's called magic," he said delightedly, "and I wasn't sure I could do it anymore . . . until Scatty reminded me," he added.

CHAPTER TEN

"So let me get this straight," Josh Newman said, trying to keep his voice perfectly level, "you don't know how to drive? Neither of you?"

Josh and Sophie were sitting in the front seats of the SUV Scatty had borrowed from one of her martial arts students. Josh was driving, and his sister had a map on her lap. Nicholas Flamel and Scathach were sitting in the back.

"Never learned," Nicholas Flamel said, with an expressive shrug.

"Never had the time," Scatty said shortly.

"But Nicholas told us you're more than two thousand years old," Sophie said, looking at the girl.

"Two thousand five hundred and seventeen, as you humani measure time with your current calendar," Scatty mumbled. She looked into Flamel's clear eyes. "And how old do I look?"

"Not a day over seventeen," he said quickly.

"Couldn't you have found time to learn how to drive?" Sophie persisted. She'd wanted to learn how to drive since she was ten. One of the reasons the twins had taken summer jobs this year, rather than go on the dig with their parents, was to get the money for a car of their own.

Scathach shrugged, an irritated twitch of her shoulders. "I've been meaning to, but I've been busy," she protested.

"You do know," Josh said to no one in particular, "that I'm not supposed to be driving without a licensed driver with me."

"We're nearly fifteen and a half and we can both drive," Sophie said. "Well, sort of," she added.

"Can either of you ride a horse?" Flamel asked, "or drive a carriage, or a coach-and-four?"

"Well, no . . . ," Sophie began.

"Handle a war chariot while firing a bow or launching spears?" Scatty added. "Or fly a lizard-nathair while using a slingshot?"

"I have no idea what a lizard-nathair is . . . and I'm not sure I want to know either."

"So you see, you are experienced in certain skills," Flamel said, "whereas we have other, somewhat older, but equally useful skills." He shot a sidelong glance at Scathach. "Though I'm not so sure about the nathair flying anymore."

Josh pulled away from a stop sign and turned right, heading for the Golden Gate Bridge. "I just don't know how you could have lived through the twentieth century without being able to drive. I mean, how did you get from place to place?"

"Public transportation," Flamel said with a grim smile. "Trains and buses, mainly. They are a completely anonymous method of travel, unlike airplanes and boats. There is far too much paperwork involved in owning a car, paperwork that could be traced directly to us, no matter how many aliases we used." He paused and added, "And besides, there are other, older methods of travel."

There were a hundred questions Josh wanted to ask, but he was concentrating furiously on controlling the heavy car. Although he knew *how* to drive, the only vehicles he'd actually driven were battered Jeeps when they accompanied their parents on a dig. He'd never driven in traffic before, and he was terrified. Sophie had suggested that he pretend it was a computer game. That helped, but only a little. In a game, when you crashed, you simply started again. Here, a crash was for keeps.

Traffic was slow across the famous bridge. A long gray stretch limo had broken down in the inside lane, causing a bottleneck. As they approached, Sophie noticed that there were two dark-suited figures crouched under the hood on the passenger's side. She realized she was holding her breath as they drew close, wondering if the figures were Golems. She heaved a sigh as they pulled alongside and discovered that the men looked like harassed accountants. Josh glanced at his sister and attempted a grin, and she knew he had been thinking the same thing.

Sophie twisted in her seat, and turned to look back at Flamel and Scatty. In the darkened, air-conditioned interior of the SUV, they seemed so ordinary: Flamel looked like a fading hippy, and Scatty, despite her rather military dress sense, wouldn't have looked out of place behind the counter at The Coffee Cup. The red-haired girl had propped her chin on her fist and was staring through the darkened glass across the bay toward Alcatraz.

Nicholas Flamel dipped his head to follow the direction of her gaze. "Haven't been there for a while," he murmured.

"We did the tour," Sophie said.

"I liked it," Josh said quickly. "Sophie didn't."

"It was creepy."

"And so it should be," Flamel said quietly. "It is home to an extraordinary assortment of ghosts and unquiet spirits. Last time I was there, it was to put to rest an extremely ugly Snakeman."

"I'm not sure I even want to know what a Snakeman is," Sophie muttered, then paused. "You know, a couple of hours ago, I could never have imagined myself saying something like that?"

Nicholas Flamel sat back in the comfortable seats and folded his arms across his chest. "Your lives—yours and your brother's—are now forever altered. You know that, don't you?"

Sophie nodded. "That's beginning to sink in now. It's just that everything's happening so fast that it's hard to take it all in. Mud men, magic, books of spells, rats . . ." She looked at Scathach. "Ancient warriors . . ."

Scatty dipped her head in acknowledgment.

"And of course, a six-hundred-year-old alchemyst . . ." Sophie stopped, a sudden thought crossing her mind. She looked from Flamel to Scatty and back again. Then she took a moment to formulate her question. Staring hard at the man, she asked, "You *are* human, aren't you?"

Nicholas Flamel grinned. "Yes. Perhaps a little more than human, but yes, I was born and will always be one of the human race."

Sophie looked at Scathach. "But you're . . ."

Scathach opened her green eyes wide, and for a single instant, something ancient was visible in the planes and angles of her face. "No," she said very quietly. "I am not of the race of humani. My people were of different stock, the Elder Race. We ruled this earth before the creatures who became humani climbed down from the trees. Nowadays, we are remembered in the myths of just about every race. We are the creatures of legend, the Were clans, the Vampire, the Giants, the Dragons, the Monsters. In stories we are remembered as the Old Ones or the Elder Race. Some stories call us gods."

"Were you ever a god?" Sophie whispered.

Scatty giggled. "No. I was never a god. But some of my people allowed themselves to be worshipped as gods. Others simply became gods as humani told tales of their adventures." She shrugged. "We were just another race, an older race than man, with different gifts, different skills."

"What happened?" Sophie asked.

"The Flood," Scatty said very softly, "amongst other things."

"The earth is a lot older than most people imagine," Flamel said quietly. "Creatures and races that are now no more than myth once walked this world."

Sophie nodded slowly. "Our parents are archaeologists. They've told us about some of the inexplicable things that archaeology sometimes reveals."

"Remember that place we visited in Texas, Taylor something . . . ," Josh said, carefully easing the heavy SUV into the middle lane. He'd never driven anything so big before, and was terrified he was going to hit something. He'd had a couple of near misses and was convinced he'd actually clipped someone's side mirror, but he'd kept going, saying nothing.

"The Taylor Trail," Sophie said, "at the Paluxy River in Texas. There are what look like dinosaur footprints and human prints in the same fossilized piece of stone. And the stone is dated to one hundred million years old."

"I have seen them," Flamel replied, "and others like them all across the world. I have also examined the shoe print that was found in Antelope Springs in Utah . . . in rock about five hundred million years old."

"My dad says things like that can be easily dismissed as either fakes or misinterpretation of the facts," Josh said quickly. He wondered what his father would say about the things they had seen today.

Flamel shrugged. "Yes, that is true. But what science cannot understand, it dismisses. Not everything can be so easily brushed aside. Can you dismiss what you've seen and experienced today as some sort of misinterpretation of the facts?"

Sophie shook her head.

Beside her, Josh shrugged uncomfortably. He didn't like the direction this conversation was taking. Dinosaurs and humans living together at the same time was simply inconceivable. The very idea went against everything his parents had taught them, everything they believed. But somewhere at the back of his mind, a small voice kept reminding him that every year archaeologists—including his parents—kept making extraordinary discoveries. A couple of years earlier, it was *Homo floresiensis,* the tiny people in Indonesia, nicknamed Hobbits; then there was the species of dwarf dinosaur discovered in Germany, and the hundred-and-sixty-five-million-year-old dinosaur tracks found in Wyoming and, only recently, the eight new prehistoric species discovered in a cave in Israel. But what Flamel was suggesting was staggering in its implications. "You're saying that humans and dinosaurs existed on the earth at the same time," Josh said, surprised that he sounded so angry.

"I'm saying that humans have existed on the earth with creatures far stranger, and much older than the dinosaurs," Flamel said seriously.

"How do you know?" Sophie demanded. He claimed to have been born in 1330, he couldn't have seen dinosaurs . . . could he?

"It's all written down in the Codex . . . and, in the course of my long life, I've seen beasts that are considered myths, I've fought beings from legend, I've faced down creatures that looked like they crawled from a nightmare."

"We did Shakespeare in school last term. . . . There's a line from *Hamlet*." Sophie frowned, trying to remember. "There are more things in heaven and earth . . ."

Nicholas Flamel nodded delightedly. ". . . than are dreamt of in your philosophy," he finished the quotation. "*Hamlet,* act one, scene five. I knew Will Shakespeare, of course. Now, Will could have been an alchemist of extraordinary talent . . . but then he fell into Dee's clutches. Poor Will; do you know that he based the character of Prospero in *The Tempest* on Dee?"

"I never liked Shakespeare," Scatty muttered. "He smelled."

"You knew Shakespeare?" Josh was unable to keep the disbelief out of his voice.

"He was my student briefly, very briefly," Flamel said. "I've lived a long time; I've had a lot of students—some made famous by history, most forgotten. I've met a lot of people, human and unhuman, mortal and immortal. People like Scathach," Flamel finished.

"There are more like you . . . more of the Elder Race?" Sophie asked, looking at the red-haired girl.

"More than you might think, though I try not to associate with them," Scatty said uneasily. "There are those amongst the Elders who cannot accept that our time is past, that this age belongs to the humani. They want to see a return to the old ways, and they believe that their puppet Dee and others like him are in a position to bring that about. They are called the Dark Elders."

"I don't know if anyone has noticed," Josh interrupted

suddenly, "but would you say there are a lot of birds gathering?"

Sophie turned to stare through the windshield, while Flamel and Scatty peered through the back window.

The spars and pylons, the braces, ropes and wires of the Golden Gate Bridge were slowly filling with birds: thousands of them. Mainly blackbirds and crows, they covered all available surfaces, with more arriving every moment.

"They're coming from Alcatraz," Josh said, dipping his head to look across the choppy waters toward the island.

A dark cloud had gathered above Alcatraz. It rose out of the abandoned prison in a dark curl and hung in the air looking like smoke, but this smoke didn't dissipate: it moved and circled in a solid mass.

"Birds." Josh swallowed hard. "There must be thousands of them."

"Tens of thousands," Sophie corrected him. She turned to look at Flamel. "What are they?"

"The Morrigan's children," he said enigmatically.

"Trouble," Scatty added. "Big trouble."

Then, as if driven by a single command, the huge flock of birds moved away from the island and headed across the bay, directly toward the bridge.

Josh hit his window button and the tinted glass hummed down. The noise of the birds was audible now, a raucous cawing, almost like high-pitched laughter. Traffic was slowing, some people even stopping to get out of their cars to take photographs with digital cameras and cell phones.

Nicholas Flamel leaned forward and placed his left hand

on Josh's shoulder. "You should drive," he said seriously. "Do not stop . . . whatever happens, even if you hit something. Just drive. As fast as you can. Get us off this bridge."

There was something in Flamel's unnaturally controlled voice that frightened Sophie even more than if he had shouted. She glanced sidelong at Scatty, but the young woman was rummaging through her backpack. The warrior pulled out a short bow and a handful of arrows and placed them on the seat beside her. "Roll up your window, Josh," she said calmly. "We don't want anything getting in."

"We're in trouble, aren't we?" Sophie whispered, looking at the Alchemyst.

"Only if the crows catch us," Flamel said with a tight smile. "Could I borrow your cell phone?"

Sophie pulled her cell out of her pocket and flipped it open. "Aren't you going to work some magic?" she asked hopefully.

"No, I'm going to make a call. Let's hope we don't get an answering service."

CHAPTER ELEVEN

Security gates opened, and Dee's black limousine swerved into the driveway, the Golem chauffeur expertly maneuvering the car through barred gates into an underground parking garage. Perenelle Flamel lurched sideways and fell against the sodden Golem sitting on her right-hand side. Its body squelched with the blow, and spatters of foul-smelling mud squirted everywhere.

Dr. John Dee, sitting directly opposite, grimaced in disgust and scooted as far away from the creature as he could. He was on his cell phone, talking urgently in a language that had not been used on earth in more than three thousand years.

A drop of Golem mud splashed onto Perenelle's right hand. The sticky liquid ran across her flesh . . . and erased the curling symbol Dee had drawn on her skin.

The binding spell was partially broken. Perenelle Flamel

dipped her head slightly. This was her chance. To properly channel her auric powers she really needed both hands, and unfortunately, the ward Dee had drawn on her forehead prevented her from speaking.

Still . . .

Perenelle Delamere had always been interested in magic, even before she met the poor bookseller who later became her husband. She was the seventh daughter of a seventh daughter, and in the tiny village of Quimper in the northwest corner of France, where she had grown up, she was considered special. Her touch could heal—not only humans, but animals, too—she could talk to the shades of the dead and she could sometimes see a little of the future. But growing up in an age when such skills were regarded with deep suspicion, she had learned to keep her abilities to herself. When she first moved to Paris, she saw how the fortune-tellers working in the markets that backed onto the great Notre Dame Cathedral made a good and easy living. Adopting the name Chatte Noire—Black Cat—because of her jet-black hair, she set herself up in a little booth in sight of the cathedral. Within a matter of weeks she built a reputation for being genuinely talented. Her clients changed: no longer were they just the tradespeople and stall holders, now they were also drawn from the merchants and even the nobility.

Close to where she had her little covered stall sat the scriveners and copiers, men who made their living writing letters for those who could neither read nor write. Some of them, like the slender, dark-haired man with startling pale eyes, occasionally sold books from their tables. And from the first moment she saw that man, Perenelle Delamere knew that she would marry him and that they would live a long and happy life together. She just never realized quite how long.

They were married less than six months after they first met. They'd been together now for over six hundred years.

Like most educated men of his time, Nicholas Flamel was fascinated with alchemy—a combination of science and magic. His interest was sparked because he was occasionally offered alchemical books or charts for sale or asked to copy some of the rarer works. Unlike many other women of her time, Perenelle could read and knew several languages—her Greek was better than her husband's—and he would often ask her to read to him. Perenelle quickly became familiar with the ancient systems of magic and began to practice in small ways, developing her skills, concentrating on how to channel and focus the energy of her aura.

By the time the Codex came into their possession, Perenelle was a sorceress, though she had little patience for the mathematics and calculations of alchemy. However, it was Perenelle who recognized that the book written in the strange, ever-changing language was not just a history of the world that had never been, but a collection of lore, of science, of spells and incantations. She had been poring over the pages one bitter winter's night, watching the words crawl on the page, when the letters formed and re-formed, and for a heartbeat she had seen the initial formula for the philosopher's stone, and realized instantly that here was the secret to life eternal.

The couple spent the next twenty years traveling to every country in Europe, heading east into the land of the Rus, south to North Africa, even into Araby in an attempt to decipher and translate the curious manuscript. They came into contact with magicians and sorcerers of many lands, and studied many different types of magic. Nicholas was only vaguely interested in magic; he was more interested in the science of alchemy. The Codex, and other books like it, hinted that there were very precise formulas for creating gold out of stone and diamonds out of coal. Perenelle, on the other hand, learned as much as she could about all the magical arts. But it had been a long time since she had seriously practiced them.

Now, trapped in the limo, she recalled a trick she had learned from a strega—a witch—in the mountains of Sicily. It was designed for dealing with knights in armor, but with a little adjustment . . .

Closing her eyes and concentrating, Perenelle rubbed her little finger in a circle against the car seat. Dee was absorbed in his phone call and didn't see the tiny ice white spark that snapped from her fingertip into the fine-grained leather. The spark ran through the leather and coiled around the springs beneath. It shot, fizzing and hissing, along the springs and into the metal body of the car. It curled into the engine, buzzing over the cylinders, circled the wheels, spitting and snapping. A hubcap popped off and bounced away . . . and then abruptly, the car's electrics went haywire. The windows started opening and closing of their own accord; the sunroof hummed open, then slammed shut; the wipers scraped across the dry windshield, then beat so fast they snapped off; the horn began to sound out an irregular beat. Interior lights flickered on and off. The small TV unit in the left-hand wall popped on and cycled dizzyingly through all its channels.

The air tasted metallic. Tendrils of static electricity now danced around the interior of the car. Dee flung his cell phone away, nursing suddenly numb fingers. The phone hit the carpeted floor and exploded into shards of melted plastic and hot metal.

"You . . . ," Dee began, turning to Perenelle, but the car lurched to a halt, completely dead. Flames leapt from the engine, filling the back of the car with noxious fumes. Dee pushed the door, but the electric locks had engaged. With a savage howl, he closed his hand into a fist and allowed his rage to boil through him. The stench of smoke, burning plastic and melting rubber was abruptly concealed beneath the stink of sulfur, and his hand took on the appearance of a golden metal glove. Dee punched straight through the door, practically ripping it off its hinges, and flung himself out onto the cement floor.

He was standing in the underground car park of Enoch Enterprises, the huge entertainment company he owned and ran in San Francisco. He scrambled back as his hundred-and-fifty-thousand-dollar custom-made car was quickly consumed by fire. Intense heat fused the front of the car into irregular clumps of metal, while the windshield flowed like candle wax. The Golem driver was still sitting at the wheel, unaffected by the intense heat, which did nothing but bake its skin to iron hardness.

Then the garage's overhead sprinkler system came on, and bitterly cold water sprayed down onto the fire.

Perenelle!

Soaked through, doubled over and coughing, Dee wiped tears from his eyes, straightened and used both hands to douse the flames with a single movement. He called up a tiny breeze to clear the smoke, then ducked his head to peer into the blackened interior of the car, almost afraid of what he would find.

The two Golems that had been sitting on either side of Perenelle were now nothing more than ash. But there was no sign of the woman—except for the rent in the opposite door that looked as if it had been hacked by an axe.

Dee folded to the ground with his back to the ruined car and beat both hands into the filthy mixture of mud, oil, melted plastic and burnt rubber. He hadn't secured the entire Codex, and now Perenelle had escaped. Could this day get any worse?

Footsteps tip-tapped.

From the corner of his eye, Dr. John Dee watched as pointy-toed, stiletto-heeled black boots came into view. And he knew then the answer to his question. The day was about to get worse: much worse. Fixing a smile on his lips, he rose stiffly to his feet and turned to face one of the few of the Dark Elders who genuinely terrified him.

"Morrigan."

The ancient Irish had called her the Crow Goddess, and she was worshipped and feared throughout the Celtic kingdoms as the Goddess of Death and Destruction. Once there had been three sisters: Badb, Macha and the Morrigan, but the others had disappeared over the years—Dee had his own suspicions about what had happened to them—and the Morrigan now reigned supreme.

She stood taller than Dee, though most people stood taller than the doctor, and was dressed from head to foot in black leather. Her jerkin was studded with shining silver bolts, giving it the appearance of a medieval breastplate, and her leather gloves had rectangular silver studs sewn onto the back of the fingers. The gloves had no fingertips, allowing the Morrigan's long, spearlike black nails to show. She wore a heavy leather belt studded with small circular shields around her waist. Draped over her shoulders, with its full hood pulled around her face and sweeping to the ground behind her, was a cloak made entirely of ravens' feathers.

In the shadow of the hood, the Morrigan's face seemed even paler than usual. Her eyes were jet-black, with no white showing; even her lips were black. The tips of her overlong incisors were just visible against her lower lip.

"This is yours, I believe." The Morrigan's voice was a harsh whisper, her voice ragged and torn, like a bird's caw.

Perenelle Flamel came forward, moving slowly and carefully. Two enormous ravens were perched on her shoulders, and both held their razor-sharp beaks dangerously close to her eyes. She had barely scrambled out of the burning car, desperately weakened by her use of magic, when she'd been attacked by the birds.

"Let me see it," the Morrigan commanded eagerly.

Dee reached into his coat and produced the metal-bound Codex. Surprisingly, the Crow Goddess did not reach for it.

"Open it," she said.

Puzzled, Dee held the book in front of the Morrigan and turned the pages, handling the ancient object with obvious reverence.

"The Book of Abraham the Mage," she whispered, leaning forward, but not approaching the book. "Let me see the back."

Reluctantly, Dee turned to the back of the book. When the Morrigan saw the damaged pages, she hissed with disgust. "Sacrilege. It has survived ten thousand years without suffering any damage."

"The boy tore it," Dee explained, closing the Codex gently.

"I'll make sure he suffers for this." The Crow Goddess closed her eyes and cocked her head to one side, as if listening. Her black eyes glittered and then her lips moved in a rare smile, exposing the rest of her pointed teeth. "He will suffer soon; my children are almost upon them. They will all suffer," she promised.

CHAPTER TWELVE

*J*osh spotted an opening between two cars—a VW Beetle and a Lexus. He pushed his foot to the floor and the heavy car shot forward. But the gap wasn't quite wide enough. The SUV's grill struck the side mirrors on the other two cars and snapped them off. "Oops . . ." Josh immediately took his foot off the gas.

"Keep going," Flamel ordered firmly. He had Sophie's phone in his hand and was talking urgently in a guttural, rasping language that sounded like nothing the twins had ever heard before.

Deliberately not looking in the rearview mirror, Josh roared across the bridge, ignoring the honks and shouts behind him. He shot along the outside lane, then cut into the middle lane, then back out again.

Sophie braced herself against the dashboard, peering through half-closed eyes. She saw the car hit another side mirror; it came spinning, almost slowly, up onto the hood of their SUV, scoring a long scrape in the black paint before it bounced away. "Don't even think about it," she muttered as a tiny open-topped Italian sports car spotted the same gap in the traffic that Josh was aiming for. The driver, an older man with far too many gold chains around his neck, put his foot down and raced for the gap. He didn't make it.

The heavy SUV caught the right front edge of the little car, just tapping it on the bumper. The sports car was flung away, spinning in a complete 360-degree turn on the crowded bridge, bouncing off four other cars in the process. Josh tore through the opening.

Flamel twisted around in the seat, looking through the rear window at the chaos they had left in their wake. "I thought you said you could drive," he murmured.

"I *can* drive," Josh said, surprised that his voice sounded so calm and steady, "I just didn't say I was good at it. Do you think anyone got our license plates?" he asked. This was nothing like one of his driving games! The palms of his hands were slick and wet and beads of sweat were running down the sides of his face. A muscle twitched in his right leg from the effort of keeping the accelerator pressed hard to the floor.

"I think they've got other things to worry about," Sophie whispered.

The crows had descended on the Golden Gate Bridge. Thousands of them. They came in a black wave, cawing and screaming, wings cracking and snapping. They hovered over the cars, darting low, occasionally even landing on car roofs

96

and hoods to peck at the metal and glass. Cars crashed and sideswiped one another along the entire length of the bridge.

"They've lost focus," Scathach said, watching the birds' behavior. "They're looking for us, but they've forgotten our description. They have such tiny brains," she said dismissively.

"Something distracted their dark mistress," Nicholas Flamel said. "Perenelle," he said delightedly. "I wonder what she did. Something dramatic, no doubt. She always did have a sense of the theatrical."

But even as he was speaking, the birds rose into the air again, and then, as one, their black eyes turned in the direction of the fleeing black SUV. This time when they cawed, it sounded like screams of triumph.

"They're coming back," Sophie said quickly, breathlessly. She realized that her heart was pumping hard against her rib cage. She looked at Flamel and the Warrior for support, but their grim expressions gave her no comfort.

Scathach looked at her and said, "We're in trouble now."

In a huge black-feathered mass, the crows took off after the car.

Most of the traffic on the bridge was now stalled. People sat frozen in terror in their cars as the birds flowed, foul and stinking, over the roofs. The SUV was the only car moving. Josh had his foot pressed flat to the floor, and the needle on the speedometer hovered close to eighty. He was becoming more comfortable with the controls—he hadn't hit anything for at least a minute. The end of the bridge was in sight. He grinned; they were going to make it.

And then the huge crow landed on the hood.

Sophie screamed and Josh jerked the wheel, attempting to knock the evil-looking creature off, but it had hooked its feet into the raised ridges on the hood. It cocked its head to one side, looking first at Josh, then Sophie, and then, in two short hops, it came right up to the windshield and deliberately peered inside, black eyes glittering.

It pecked at the glass . . . and a tiny starred puncture mark appeared.

"It shouldn't be able to do that," Josh said, trying to keep his eyes on the road.

The crow pecked again and another hole appeared. Then there was a thump, followed by a second and a third, and three more crows landed on the roof of the car. The metal roof pinged as the birds began to peck at it.

"I hate crows." Scathach sighed. She rooted through her bag and pulled out a set of nunchaku—two twelve-inch lengths of ornately carved wood linked by four and a half inches of chain. She tapped the sticks in the palm of her hand. "Pity we haven't got a sunroof," she said. "I could get out there and give them a little taste of this."

Flamel pointed to where a long shaft of sunlight was coming through a pinhole in the roof. "We may soon have. Besides," he added, "these are not normal crows. The three on the roof and the one on the hood are Dire-Crows, the Morrigan's special pets."

The huge bird on the hood tapped the windshield again, and this time, its beak actually penetrated the glass.

"I'm not sure what I can do . . . ," Scathach began, and

then Sophie leaned over and hit the windshield wiper switch. The heavy blades activated . . . and simply swept the bird off the hood in a flurry of feathers and a shrill croak of surprise. The red-haired warrior grinned. "Well, there is that, of course."

Now the rest of the birds had reached the SUV. They settled on the vehicle in a great blanket. First dozens, then hundreds gathered on the roof, the hood, the doors, clutching every available opening. If one fell off or lost its grip, dozens more fought for its place. The noise inside the car was incredible as thousands of birds pecked and tapped at the metal, the glass, the doors. They tore into the rubber molding around the windows, ripped into the spare tire on the back of the SUV, tearing it to shreds. There were so many on the hood, pressed up against the windshield, that Josh couldn't see where he was going. He took his foot off the accelerator and the car immediately started to slow.

"Drive!" Flamel shouted. "If you stop, we are truly lost."

"But I can't see!"

Flamel leaned through the seats and stretched out his right hand. Sophie suddenly saw the small circular tattoo on the underside of his wrist. A cross ran through the circle, the arms of the cross extending over the edges of the circle. For a single instant it glowed . . . and then the Alchemyst snapped his fingers. A tiny ball of hissing, sizzling flame appeared on his fingertips. "Close your eyes," he commanded. Without waiting to see if they obeyed, he flicked it toward the glass.

Even through their closed lids, the twins could see the searing light that lit up the interior of the car.

"Now drive," Nicholas Flamel commanded.

When the twins opened their eyes, most of the crows were gone from the hood, and those few that remained looked dazed and shocked.

"That's not going to hold them for long," Scatty said. She looked up as a razor-sharp beak punched a hole straight through the metal roof. She snapped out the nunchaku. She held one stick in her hand, while the other, attached to the short chain, shot out with explosive force and cracked against the beak embedded in the roof. There was a startled shriek and the beak—slightly bent—disappeared.

Sophie turned her head to peer in her side mirror. It was dangling off the car, barely held on by a shred of metal and some wire. She could see more birds—thousands of them—flying in to replace those that had been swept away, and she knew then that they were not going to make it. There were simply too many of them.

"Listen," Nicholas Flamel said suddenly.

"I don't hear anything," Josh said grimly.

Sophie was just about to agree with him when she heard the sound. And she suddenly felt the hairs on her arms prickle and rise. Low and lonely, the noise hovered just at the edge of her hearing. It was like a breeze, one moment sounding soft and gentle, the next louder, almost angry. A peculiar odor wafted into the car.

"What is that smell?" Josh asked.

"Smells like spicy oranges," Sophie said, breathing deeply.

"Pomegranates," Nicholas Flamel said.

And then the wind came.

It howled across the bay, warm and exotic, smelling of cardamom and rosewater, lime and tarragon, and then it raced along the length of the Golden Gate Bridge, plucking the birds off the struts, lifting them off the cars, pulling them out of the air. Finally the pomegranate-scented wind reached the SUV. One moment the car was surrounded by birds; the next, they were gone, and the car was filled with the scents of the desert, of dry air and warm sand.

Sophie hit a button and the scarred and pitted window jerked down. She craned her neck out the SUV, breathing in the richly scented air. The huge flock of birds was being pulled high into the sky, borne aloft on the breeze. When one escaped—one of the big Dire-Crows, Sophie thought—it was quickly caught by a tendril of the warm breeze and pushed back into the rest of the flock. From underneath, the mass of birds looked like a dirty cloud . . . and then the cloud dispersed as the birds scattered, leaving the sky blue and clear again.

Sophie looked back along the length of the bridge. The Golden Gate was completely impassable; cars were pointed in every direction, and there had been dozens of minor accidents, which blocked the lanes . . . and of course, effectively prevented anyone from following them, she realized. Every vehicle was spattered and splotched with white bird droppings. She looked at her brother and saw with a shock that there was a tiny smear of blood on his bottom lip. She pulled a tissue from her pocket. "You're cut!" she said urgently, licking the edge of the tissue and dabbing at her twin's face.

Josh pushed her hand away. "Stop. That's disgusting." He touched his lip with his little finger. "I must have bit it. I didn't even feel it." He took the tissue from his sister's hand and rubbed his chin. "It's nothing." Then he smiled quickly. "Did you see the mess the birds left back there?" Sophie nodded. He made a disgusted face. "Now, *that* is going to smell!"

Sophie leaned back against the seat, relieved that her brother was fine. When she'd seen the blood she'd been truly frightened. A thought struck her and she turned around to look at Flamel. "Did you call up the wind?"

He smiled and shook his head. "No, I've no control over the elements. That skill rests solely with the Elders and a very few rare humans."

Sophie looked at Scatty, but the Warrior shook her head. "Beyond my very limited abilities."

"But you *did* summon the wind?" Sophie persisted.

Flamel handed Sophie back her phone. "I just phoned in a request," he said, and smiled.

CHAPTER THIRTEEN

"Turn here," Nicholas Flamel instructed.

Josh eased his foot off the accelerator and turned the battered and scarred SUV down a long narrow track that was barely wide enough to accommodate the car. They had spent the last thirty minutes driving north out of San Francisco, listening to the increasingly hysterical radio reports as a succession of experts gave their opinions about the bird attack on the bridge. Global warming was the most commonly cited theory: the sun's radiation interfering with the birds' natural navigation system.

Flamel directed them north, toward Mill Valley and Mount Tamalpais, but they quickly left the highway and stuck to narrow two-lane roads. Traffic thinned out until there were long stretches where they were the only car in sight. Finally, on a narrow road that curved and turned with sickening complexity, he had Josh slow almost to a crawl. He rolled down his window and peered out into a thick forest that came right up to the edge of the road. They had actually driven past the unmarked path before Flamel spotted it. "Stop. Go back. Turn here."

Josh looked at his sister as he eased the car onto the rough, unpaved and rutted track. Her hands were folded in her lap, but he could see that her knuckles were white with tension. Her nails, which had been neat and perfect only a few hours previously, were now rough and chewed, a sure sign of her stress. He reached over and squeezed her hand; she squeezed tightly in return. As with so much of the communication between them, there was no need for words. With their parents away so much, Sophie and Josh had learned from a very early age that they could only really depend on themselves. Moving from school to school, neighborhood to neighborhood, they often found it difficult to make and keep friends, but they knew that whatever happened, they would always have each other.

On either side of the overgrown path, trees rose high into the heavens and the undergrowth was surprisingly thick: wild brambles and thorn bushes scraped at the side of the car, while furze, gorse, and stinging nettles, wrapped through with poison ivy, completed the impenetrable hedge.

"I've never seen anything like it," Sophie murmured. "It's just not natural." And then she stopped, realizing what she'd just said. She swiveled around in the seat to look at Flamel. "It's *not* natural, is it?"

He shook his head, suddenly looking old and tired. There were dark rings under his eyes, and the wrinkles on his forehead and around his mouth seemed deeper. "Welcome to our world," he whispered.

"There's something moving through the undergrowth," Josh announced loudly. "Something big . . . I mean really big." After everything he'd seen and experienced so far today, his imagination started working overtime. "It's keeping pace with the car."

"So long as we stay on the track, we shall be fine," Flamel said evenly.

Sophie peered into the dark forest floor. For a moment she saw nothing, then she realized that what she'd first taken for a patch of shadow was, in fact, a creature. It moved, and sunlight dappled its hairy hide. She caught a glimpse of a flat face, a pug nose and huge curling tusks.

"It's a pig—a boar," she corrected herself. And then she spotted three more, flanking the right-hand side of the car.

"They're on my side too," Josh said. Four of the hulking beasts were moving through the bushes to his left. He glanced in the rearview mirror. "And behind us."

Sophie, Scatty and Nicholas turned in their seats to stare through the rear window at the two enormous boars that had slipped through the undergrowth and were trotting along on the path behind them. Sophie suddenly realized just how big the creatures were—each one was easily the size of a pony. They were hugely muscled across the shoulders, and the tusks jutting up from their lower jaws were enormous, starting out as thick as her wrist before tapering to needle-sharp points.

"I didn't think there were any wild boars in America," Josh said, "and certainly not in Mill Valley, California."

"There are wild boars and pigs all over the Americas," Flamel said absently. "They were first brought over by the Spanish in the sixteenth century."

Josh shifted gears, eased off the accelerator and allowed the car to move forward at a crawl. The road had come to a dead end. The barrier of bushes, thorns and trees now stretched across the path. "End of the road," he announced, putting the car into park and setting the emergency brake. He looked left and right. The boars had also stopped moving, and he could see them, four to a side, watching. In the rearview mirror, he could see that the two larger boars had stopped too. They were boxed in. What now, he wondered, what now? He looked at his sister and knew she was thinking exactly the same thing.

Nicholas Flamel leaned forward between the seats and looked at the barrier. "I believe this is here to discourage the foolhardy who have traveled this far. And if one were exceptionally foolish, one might be tempted to get out of one's vehicle."

"But we are neither foolhardy nor foolish," Scatty snapped. "So what do we do?" She nodded at the boars. "I haven't seen this breed in centuries. They look like Gaulish war boars, and if they are, then they are virtually impossible to kill. For every one we can see, there are probably at least three more in the shadows, and that's not counting their handlers."

"These are not Gaulish; this particular breed has no need of handlers," Flamel said gently, the merest hint of his French accent surfacing. "Look at their tusks."

Sophie, Josh and Scatty turned to look at the tusks of the

huge creatures standing in the middle of the track behind them. "They've got some sort of carvings on them," Sophie said, squinting in the late-afternoon light. "Curls."

"Spirals," Scatty said, a touch of wonder in her voice. She looked at Flamel. "They are Torc Allta?"

"Indeed they are," Flamel said. "Wereboars."

"By wereboars," Josh said, "do you mean like were-wolves?"

Scatty shook her head impatiently. "No, not like werewolves . . ."

"That's a relief," Josh said, "because for a second there I thought you were taking about humans who changed into wolves."

"Werewolves are Torc Madra," Scatty continued, as if she hadn't heard him. "They're a different clan altogether."

Sophie stared hard at the nearest boar. Beneath its piglike features, she thought she could begin to see the shapes and planes of a human face, while the eyes—cool and bright, bright blue—regarded her with startling intelligence.

Josh turned back to the steering wheel, gripping it tightly. "Wereboars . . . of course they are different from werewolves. Different clan entirely," he muttered, "how silly of me."

"What do we do?" Sophie asked.

"We drive," Nicholas Flamel said.

Josh pointed at the barrier. "What about that?"

"Just drive," the Alchemyst commanded.

"But . . . ," Josh began.

"Do you trust me?" Flamel asked for the second time that day. The twins looked at each other, then back at Flamel, and nodded, heads bobbing in unison. "Then drive," he said gently.

Josh eased the heavy SUV into gear and released the emergency brake. The vehicle crept forward. The front bumper touched the seemingly impenetrable barrier of leaves and bushes . . . and vanished. One moment it was there; the next, it was as if the bushes had swallowed the front of the car.

The SUV rolled into the bushes and trees, and for a single instant everything went dark and chill, and the air was touched with something bittersweet like burnt sugar . . . and then the path appeared again, curving off to the right.

"How . . . ," Josh began.

"It was an illusion," Flamel explained. "Nothing more. Light twisted and bent, reflecting the images of trees and bushes in a curtain of water vapor, each drop of moisture acting as a mirror. And just a little magic," he added. He pointed ahead with a graceful motion. "We're still in North America, but now we've entered the domain of one of the oldest and greatest of the Elder Race. We'll be safe here for a while."

Scatty made a rude sound. "Oh, she's *old*, all right, but I'm not so sure about *great*."

"Scathach, I want you to behave yourself," Flamel said, turning to the young-looking but ancient woman sitting beside him.

"I don't like her. I don't trust her."

"You've got to put aside your old feuds."

"She tried to kill me, Nicholas," Scatty protested. "She abandoned me in the Underworld. It took me centuries to find my way out."

108

"That was a little over fifteen hundred years ago, if I remember my mythology," Flamel reminded her.

"I've got a long memory," Scatty muttered; for an instant she looked like a sulky child.

"Who are you talking about?" Sophie demanded, and then Josh hit the brakes, bringing the heavy car to a halt.

"Wouldn't be a tall woman with black skin, would it?" Josh asked.

Sophie spun around to look through the cracked windshield, while Flamel and Scatty leaned forward.

"That's her," Scatty said glumly.

The figure stood in the path directly in front of the car. Tall and broad, the woman looked as if she had been carved from a solid slab of jet-black stone. The merest fuzz of white hair covered her skull like a close-fitting cap, and her features were sharp and angular: high cheekbones; straight, pointed nose; sharply defined chin; lips so thin they were almost nonexistent. Her pupils were the color of butter. She was wearing a long, simple gown made of a shimmering material that moved gently in a wind that didn't seem to touch anything around her. As it shifted, rainbow colors ran down its length, like oil on water. She wore no jewelry, though Sophie noticed that each of her short blunt fingernails was painted a different color.

"Doesn't look a day over ten thousand years old," Scatty muttered.

"Be nice," Flamel reminded her.

"Who is it?" Sophie asked again, staring hard at the woman. Although she looked human, there was something *different,* something otherworldly about her. It showed in the way she stood absolutely still and in the arrogant tilt of her head.

"This," Nicholas Flamel said, a note of genuine awe in his voice, "is the Elder known as Hekate." He pronounced the name slowly, *"HEH-ca-tay."*

"The Goddess with Three Faces," Scatty added bitterly.

CHAPTER FOURTEEN

"Stay in the car," Nicholas Flamel directed, opening the door and stepping outside onto the short-cropped grass.

Scatty folded her arms over her chest and glared out through the cracked windshield. "Fine by me."

Flamel ignored her jibe and slammed the door before she could say anything else. Taking a deep breath, he attempted to compose himself as he stepped toward the tall, elegant woman surrounded by the tall leafless trunks of sequoia trees.

The undergrowth rustled and one of the enormous Torc Allta appeared directly in front of the Alchemyst, its massive head level with his chest. Flamel stopped and bowed to the creature, greeting it in a language that had not been designed for human tongues. Abruptly, the boars were everywhere, ten of them, eyes bright and intelligent, the coarse red hair on their backs and shoulders bristling in the late-afternoon light, long strings of ropey saliva dribbling from their ornately carved tusks.

Flamel took care to bow to each one in turn. "I did not think there were any of the Torc Allta clan left in the Americas," he said to no one in particular, dropping back into English.

Hekate smiled, the merest movement of her lips. "Ah, Nicholas, you of all people should know that when we are gone, when the Elder Race is no more, when even the humani have gone from this earth, then the Allta clans will reclaim it for themselves. Remember, this world belonged to the Were clans first." Hekate spoke in a deep, almost masculine voice, touched with an accent that had all the hissing sibilants of Greece and the liquid consonants of Persia.

Nicholas bowed again. "I understand that the clans are strong in Europe—the Torc Madra particularly, and I hear that there are Torc Tiogar in India again, and two new clans of Torc Leon in Africa. All thanks to you."

Hekate smiled, her teeth tiny and straight in her mouth. "The clans still worship me as a goddess. I do what I can for them." The unseen, unfelt wind touched her robe, swirling it around her body, so that it ran with green and gold threads. "But I doubt you have come all this way to talk to me about my children."

"I have not." Flamel glanced back at the battered and scarred SUV. Josh and Sophie were staring intently at him, eyes wide in wonder, while Scathach's face was just visible in the backseat. She had her eyes closed and was pretending to

112

be asleep. Flamel knew the Warrior had no need of sleep. "I want to thank you for the Ghost Wind you sent us."

Now it was Hekate's turn to bow. Her right hand moved and opened, revealing a tiny cell phone cupped in her palm. "Such useful devices. I can remember a time when we entrusted our messages to the winds or trained birds. Seems like only yesterday," she added. "I am glad the ruse was successful. Unfortunately, you have probably revealed your ultimate destination to the Morrigan and Dee. They will know who sent the Ghost Wind, and I am sure they are aware that I have an enclave here."

"I know that. And I apologize for drawing them down on you."

Hekate shrugged, a slight movement of her shoulders that sent a rainbow of light down her robe. "Dee fears me. He will bluster and posture, threaten me, possibly even try a few minor spells and incantations, but he will not move against me. Not alone . . . not even with the Morrigan's assistance. He would need at least two or more of the Dark Elders to stand against me . . . and even then he would not be assured of success."

"But he is arrogant. And now he has the Codex."

"But not all of it, you said on the phone."

"No, not all of it." Nicholas Flamel drew the two pages from under his T-shirt and went to hand them to Hekate. But the woman abruptly backed away, throwing up her hand to shield her eyes, a sound like hissing steam bubbling from her lips. In an instant the boars were around Flamel, crowding him, mouths open, tusks huge and deadly against his skin.

Sophie drew breath to scream and Josh shouted and then Scathach was out of the SUV, an arrow notched to her bow, leveled at Hekate. "Call them off," she shouted.

The Torc Allta didn't even glance in her direction.

Hekate deliberately turned her back on Flamel and folded her arms, then she glanced over her shoulder at Scathach, who immediately pulled the bowstring taut. "You think that can harm *me*?" the goddess laughed.

"The arrow was dipped in the blood of a Titan," Scathach said quietly, her voice carrying on the still air. "One of your parents, if I remember correctly? And one of the few ways left to slay you, I do believe."

The twins watched as the Elder's eyes turned cold and became, for a split second, gold mirrors, reflecting the scene before her. "Put the pages away," Hekate commanded the Alchemyst.

Flamel immediately tucked the two pages back under his T-shirt. The older woman muttered a word and the Torc Allta stepped back from the Alchemyst and trotted into the undergrowth, where they immediately disappeared, though everyone knew they were still there. Hekate then turned to face Flamel again. "They would not have harmed you without a command from me."

"I'm sure," Nicholas said shakily. He glanced down at his jeans and boots. They were covered with dribbles and strings of white Torc Allta saliva, which he was sure was going to leave a stain.

"Do not produce the Codex—or any portion of it—in my presence . . . nor in the presence of any being of the Elder Race. We have an . . . *aversion* to it," she said, choosing the word carefully.

"It doesn't affect me," Scathach said, loosening her bow.

"You are not one of the First Generation of the Elder Race," Hekate reminded her. "Like the Morrigan, you are of the Next Generation. But I was there when Abraham the Mage set down the first words of power in the Book. I saw him trap the Magic of First Working, the oldest magic, in its sheets."

"I apologize," Flamel said quickly. "I did not know."

"There is no reason you should have known." Hekate smiled, but there was nothing humorous in it. "That eldritch magic is so strong that most of my people cannot even bear to look upon the letters. Those who came after the original Elder Race, though still of our blood"—and here she gestured toward Scathach—"can look upon the Codex, though even they cannot touch it. The ape descendents—the humani—can. It was Abraham's ultimate joke. He married one of the first humani, and I believe he wanted to ensure that only his children could handle the book."

"We're the ape descendents," Josh said, his voice unconsciously dropping to little more than a whisper.

"The humani . . . the human race," Sophie said, then fell silent as Flamel continued talking.

"Is that why the Book was given into my keeping?"

"You are not the first of the humani to . . . to care for the Codex," Hekate said carefully. "It should never have been created in the first place," she snapped, threads of red and green running like live wires on her robe. "I advocated that every single page should be separated from the others and dropped into the nearest volcano, and Abraham along with it."

"Why wasn't it destroyed?" Nicholas asked.

"Because Abraham had the gift of Sight. He could actually see the curling strands of time, and he prophesied that there would come a day when the Codex and all the knowledge it contained would be needed."

Scatty stepped away from the SUV and approached Flamel. She was still holding the bow loosely by her side, and she noted how Hekate's butter-colored eyes watched her closely.

"The Book of the Mage was always assigned a guardian," Scathach explained to Flamel. "Some, history recalls as the greatest heroes of myth, while others were less well known, like yourself, and a few remained completely anonymous."

"And if I—a human—was chosen to caretake this precious Codex, because your people cannot even look upon it, much less touch it, then it is obvious that another human must have been chosen to find it," Flamel said. "Dee."

Hekate nodded. "A dangerous enemy, Dr. John Dee."

Flamel nodded. He could feel the cool, dry pages against his skin beneath his T-shirt. Although he had possessed the Codex for more than half a millennium, he knew he had barely even begun to scratch the surface of its secrets. He still had no real idea just how old it was. He kept pushing the date of its creation back further and further. When the Book first came to him in the fourteenth century, he believed it to be five hundred years old. Later, when he started to do his research, he thought it might be eight hundred years old, then a thousand years, then two thousand years old. A century ago, in light of the new discoveries coming out of the tombs of Egypt, he had reassessed the age of the Book at five thousand years. And now, here was Hekate, who was ten thousand and more years old, saying she had been around when the mysterious Abraham the Mage had composed the Book. But if the Elder Race—the gods of mythology and legend—could neither handle nor look upon the book, then what was Abraham, its creator? Was he of the Elder Race, a humani or something else, one of the many other mythical races that walked the earth in those first days?

"Why are you here?" Hekate asked. "I knew the Codex had been taken as soon as it left your presence, but I cannot help you recover it."

"I have come to you for another reason," Flamel continued, stepping away from the car and lowering his voice, forcing Hekate to lean close to listen to him. "When Dee attacked me, stole the Book and snatched Perry, two humani came to our aid. A young man and his sister." He paused and then added, "Twins."

"Twins?" she said, her voice as flat and expressionless as her face.

"Twins. Look at them: tell me what you see."

Hekate's eyes flickered toward the car. "A boy and a girl, dressed in the T-shirts and denim that are the shabby uniform of this age. That is all I see."

"Look closer," Flamel said. "And remember the prophecy," he added.

"I know the prophecy. Do not presume to teach me my own history!" Hekate's eyes flared and, for an instant, changed color, becoming dark and ugly. "Humani? Impossible." Striding past Flamel, she peered into the interior of the car, looking first at Sophie, and then at Josh.

The twins noticed simultaneously that the pupils of her eyes were long and narrow, like a cat's, and that behind the thin line of her lips, her teeth were pointed, like tiny needles.

"Silver and gold," Hekate whispered abruptly, glancing at the Alchemyst, her accent thickening, small pointed tongue darting at her thin lips. She turned back to the twins. "Step out of the vehicle."

They looked at Flamel, and when he nodded, both climbed out. Sophie went around the car to stand next to her brother.

Hekate reached out first toward Sophie, who hesitated momentarily before she stretched out her hand. The goddess took Sophie's left palm in her right hand and turned it over, then she reached for Josh's hand. He placed his hand in hers without hesitation, trying to act nonchalant, as if stretching out to touch a ten-thousand-year-old goddess were something he did every day. He thought her skin felt surprisingly rough and coarse.

Hekate spoke a single word in a language that predated the arrival of the earliest human civilization.

"Oranges," Josh whispered, suddenly smelling—and then tasting—the fruit.

"No, it's ice cream," Sophie said, "freshly churned vanilla ice cream." She turned to look at her brother . . . and discovered that he was staring at her in wonder.

A silver glow had appeared around Sophie. Like a thin second skin, it hovered just above the surface of her flesh, winking in and out of existence. When she blinked, her eyes turned to flat reflective mirrors.

The glow that covered Josh was a warm golden hue. It was concentrated mainly around his head and hands, throbbing and pulsing in sync with his heartbeat. The irises of his eyes were like golden coins.

But although the twins could see the glow that hovered around each other and their own bodies, they *felt* no different. There were only the smells in the air—oranges and vanilla ice cream.

Without a word, Hekate pulled away from the twins, and immediately the glow faded. Striding back to Flamel, she caught him by the arm and moved him farther down the path, out of earshot of the twins and Scatty.

"Do you have any idea what that was all about?" Sophie asked the Warrior. There was a distinct tremble in her voice, and she could still taste vanilla ice cream in her mouth and smell it on the air.

"The goddess was checking your auras," Scathach said.

"That was the golden glow around Josh?" Sophie asked, looking at her brother.

"Yours was silver," Josh said immediately.

Scathach picked up a flat pebble and tossed it into the bushes. It hit something solid, which immediately lumbered away through the undergrowth. "Most auras are a mixture of colors. Very, very, very few people have pure colors."

"Like ours?" Sophie asked.

"Like yours," Scatty said glumly. "Last person I knew to have a pure silver aura was the woman you know as Joan of Arc."

"What about the gold aura?" Josh said.

"Even rarer," Scatty said. "The last person I can recall having that color was . . ." She frowned, remembering. "The boy king, Tutankhamen."

"Was that why he was buried with so much gold?"

"One of the reasons," Scathach agreed.

"Don't tell me you knew King Tut," Josh teased.

"Never met him," Scathach said, "though I did train dear Joan and fought by her side at Orléans. I told her not to go to Paris," she added very softly, pain in her eyes.

"My aura is rarer than yours," Josh deliberately teased his sister to break the somber mood. He looked at the Warrior Maid. "But what exactly does it mean to have pure-colored auras?"

When Scathach turned to look at him, her face was expressionless. "It means you have extraordinary powers. All of the great magicians and sorcerers of the past, the heroic leaders, the inspired artists, have had pure-color or single-color auras."

The twins looked at one another, suddenly uncertain. This was just a little *too* weird, and there was something in Scathach's lack of expression that was frightening. Sophie's eyes suddenly widened in shock. "I just realized that both of those people, Joan of Arc and Tutankhamen, died young."

"Very young," Josh said, sobering, recalling his history. "They both died when they were nineteen."

"Yes, they did, didn't they?" Scathach agreed, turning away to look at Nicholas Flamel and the Goddess with Three Faces.

"Humani," Hekate snarled. "Humani with silver and gold auras." She sounded both puzzled and angry.

"It has happened before," Flamel said mildly.

"You think I don't know that?"

They were standing at the edge of a bubbling brook that cut through the trees and fed into an octagonal pond dappled with white water lilies. Huge red and albino koi moved through the perfectly clear water.

"I've never come across the two auras together, and never in twins. They possess enormous untapped power," Flamel said urgently. "Do I have to remind you of the Codex? 'The two that are one and the one that is all'—the very first prophecy Abraham speaks of."

"I know the prophecy," Hekate snapped, her dress now shot through with red and black veins. "I was there when the old fool made it."

Flamel was about to ask a question, but kept his mouth shut.

"He was never wrong either," Hekate muttered. "He knew that Danu Talis would sink beneath the waves and that our world would end."

"He also predicted it would come again," Flamel reminded her. "When 'the two that are one and the one that is all' have arrived, when the sun and moon are united."

Hekate tilted her head and her slit-pupiled eyes flickered toward Josh and Sophie. "Gold and silver, sun and moon." She turned back to Flamel. "Do you believe them to be the basis of the prophecy?"

"Yes," he said simply, "I do. I have to."

"Why?"

"Because with the Codex now gone, Dee can begin to bring back the Dark Elders. If the twins are those mentioned in the prophecy, then, with proper training, I might be able to use them to prevent that . . . and to help me rescue Perry."

"And if you are mistaken?" Hekate wondered aloud.

"Then I have lost the love of my life, and this world and all the humani on it are lost. But if we are to have any chance of success, I need your help."

Hekate sighed. "It's been a long time . . . a very long time since I took a student." She turned to look at Scathach. "And that didn't turn out too well."

"This is different. This time you would be working with raw talent, pure, untainted power. And we don't have a lot of time." Flamel drew in a deep breath and spoke formally in the ancient language of the sunken island of Danu Talis. "Daughter of Perses and Asteria, you are the Goddess of Magic and Spells, I ask you to Awaken the twins' magical powers."

"And if I do it—what then?" Hekate demanded.

"Then I will teach them the Five Magics. Together we will retrieve the Codex and save Perenelle."

The Goddess with Three Faces laughed, the sound bitter and angry. "Have care, Nicholas Flamel, Alchemyst, lest you create something that will destroy us all."

"Will you do it?"

"I will have to think upon it. I will give you my answer later."

Sitting in the car on the other side of the clearing, Sophie and Josh suddenly became aware that Flamel and Hekate had turned to stare at them. The twins shivered simultaneously.

CHAPTER FIFTEEN

"*There* is something very wrong with this house." Sophie strode into her brother's room, holding her expensive cell phone up to her face. "I can't get a signal anywhere." She moved around the room, watching the screen, but the signal bar remained flat.

Josh looked blankly at his sister. "Wrong with this house?" he repeated incredulously. Then he spoke very slowly. "Sophie, we're inside a tree! I'd say there's something wrong with that, wouldn't you?"

When Hekate had finished speaking with Flamel, she had turned and disappeared into the woods without saying a word to them, and it had been left to Flamel to bring them to the goddess's home. Instructing them to leave the car, he led them down a narrow winding pathway that cut through the overgrown woods. They had been so intent on the strange flora—huge bruise-colored flowers that turned to track their movements, vines that slithered and squirmed like snakes as they followed them, grasses that had not existed since the Oligocene era—that they failed to notice that the path had opened out, and that they were facing Hekate's home. Even when they looked up, it took them several moments to make sense of what they were seeing.

Directly ahead of them, in the center of a broad, gently sloping plain sprinkled with vast swathes of multicolored flowers, was a tree. It was the height and circumference of a large skyscraper. The topmost branches and leaves were wreathed in wisps of white cloud, and the roots that burst from the ground like clawing fingers were as tall as cars. The tree itself was gnarled and twisted, its bark scored and deeply etched with cracks and lines. Long vines, like huge pipes, wrapped around the tree and dangled from the branches.

"Hekate's home," Flamel explained. "You are the only living humani in the last two thousand years to see it. Even I've only ever read about it."

Scatty smiled at the looks on the twins' faces. She nudged Josh. "Where exactly did you expect her to live? A trailer?"

"I wasn't . . . I mean, I don't know . . . I didn't think . . . ," Josh began. The sight was incredible, and from the little he had studied about biology, he knew that no living thing could grow so huge. No *natural* thing, he corrected himself.

Sophie thought the tree looked like an ancient woman, bent over with age. It was all very well for Flamel to talk about the distant past and a two-thousand-year-old warrior or a ten-thousand-year-old goddess: the numbers meant almost nothing. Seeing the tree was different. Both she and

Josh had seen ancient trees before. Their parents had taken them to see the three-thousand-year-old giant redwoods, and they had spent a week camping with their father in the White Mountains in the north of California as he investigated the Methuselah Tree, which, at nearly five thousand years old, was supposed to be the oldest living thing on the planet. Standing before the Methuselah Tree, a gnarled and twisted bristlecone pine, it was easy to accept its great age. But now, seeing Hekate's tree house, Sophie had no doubt that it was incredibly ancient, millennia older than the Methuselah Tree.

They followed a smoothly polished stone path that led to the tree. As they got closer, they realized that it was more like a skyscraper than they'd first thought: there were hundreds of windows cut into the bark, with lights flickering in the rooms beyond. But it was only when they reached the main entrance that they appreciated just how vast the tree was. The smoothly polished double doors towered at least twenty feet tall, and yet they opened at the merest touch of Flamel's fingers. The twins stepped into an enormous circular foyer.

And stopped.

The interior of the tree was hollow. From just inside the entrance, they could look straight up to where wispy clouds gathered *inside* the tree. A gently curving staircase curled up along the inside of the trunk, and every few steps brought them to an open doorway spilling out light. Dozens of tiny waterfalls spouted from the walls and splashed down onto the floor far below, where the water gathered in a huge circular pool that took up most of the foyer. The interior walls were smooth and unadorned, except for the twists and knots of vines that broke through the surface. Josh thought they looked like veins.

And it was completely deserted.

No one moved within the tree, nothing—human or inhuman—climbed the countless stairs, no winged creature flew in the moist air.

"Welcome to the Yggdrasill," Nicholas Flamel said, stepping back and allowing them to enter. "Welcome to the World Tree."

Josh held up his phone. The screen was blank. "And have you noticed," he asked, "there are no power sockets?"

"There have to be," Sophie said decisively. She walked over to the bed and dropped to her knees. "There are always sockets beside the beds. . . ."

There were none.

The twins stood in the center of Josh's room and looked around. His room was a mirror image of his sister's. Everything around them was composed of a honey-colored blond wood, from the highly polished floors to the smooth walls. There was no glass in the windows, and the door was a wafer-thin rectangle of wood that looked and felt like the papery bark of a tree. The only item of furniture in the room was the bed, a low wooden futon covered with heavy fur throws. A thick fur rug lay on the floor beside the bed. It was dappled with an intricate pattern of spots that resembled no animal either of the twins had ever seen.

There was also a tree growing out of the center of the floor.

Tall, thin and elegant, the red-barked tree rose straight out of the wooden floor. No limbs protruded from the trunk until it came close to the ceiling, and then the branches burst out into a canopy that covered the roof. The leaves were a deep, luxuriant green on one side, ash white on the other. Every so often, some spiraled to the floor, and covered it in a soft, almost furry carpet.

"Where are we?" Sophie asked finally, unaware that she had spoken the thought aloud.

"California?" Josh said softly, but in a voice that suggested he didn't quite believe what he was saying.

"After all we've seen today?" Sophie asked. "I don't think so. We're *inside* a tree. A tree big enough to house the whole University of San Francisco campus, a tree so old it makes the Methuselah Tree look like it was just planted. And don't try to tell me it's a building shaped to look like a tree. Everything here is made from natural materials." She drew a breath and looked around. "Do you think it could still be alive?"

Josh shook his head. "Can't be. The whole inside is scooped out. Maybe it was alive a long time ago; but now it's just a shell."

Sophie was not so sure. "Josh, there is nothing modern and nothing artificial in this room, no plastics, no metals, no paper; everything looks hand carved. There aren't even candles or lanterns."

"It took me a while to realize what those bowls of oil were," Josh said. He didn't tell his sister that he'd been about to drink what he thought was some sort of sweet-smelling fruit juice when he'd seen the wick floating in it.

"My room is identical to yours," Sophie continued. She lifted her phone again. "There's no signal, and look"—she pointed—"you can actually *see* the battery draining away."

Josh brought his head close to his twin's, their blond hair mingling, and stared at the rectangular screen. The battery indicator on the right-hand side was visibly falling, bar by bar. "You think that's why my iPod has no power either?" Josh asked, pulling it from his back pocket. "It was fully charged this morning. And my computer is dead." He suddenly looked at his watch, and then he lifted his arm to allow his sister to see it. The face of the chunky military-style digital watch he wore was blank.

Sophie looked at her own watch. "Mine is still working," she said in surprise. "Because it winds up," she said, answering her own question aloud.

"So something is draining the power," he muttered. "Some energy in the air?" He'd never heard of anything that could draw energy from batteries.

"It is this place," Scathach said, appearing in the doorway. She had changed from her black military-style combats and T-shirt into green and brown camo pants, high-top combat boots and a cut-off camo T-shirt that exposed her muscular arms. She was wearing a short sword strapped to her leg and there was a bow over her left shoulder, with a quiver of arrows just visible over the top of her head. Sophie noticed that there was a Celtic-looking spiral design etched into Scatty's right shoulder; Sophie had always wanted a tattoo, but she knew her mother would never let her get one. "You have gone beyond your world into a Shadowrealm," the Warrior added. "The Shadowrealms exist partially in your world and partially in another time and space." The Warrior remained standing by the door.

"Are you not going to come in?" Sophie asked.

"You have to invite me," Scatty said, with a peculiarly shy smile.

"Invite you in?" Sophie turned to her twin, eyebrows raised in a question.

"You have to invite me in," Scatty repeated, "else I'll not be able to cross the threshold."

"Just like vampires," Josh said, abruptly feeling as if his tongue were too thick for his mouth. After today, he was quite prepared to believe in vampires, though he really didn't want to run into one. He turned to his twin. "The only way a vampire can enter a house is if he or she is invited. Then they can drink your blood. . . ." He turned to look at Scatty, eyes suddenly wide. "You're not a . . ."

"I don't like that term," Scatty snapped.

"Scathach, please enter," Sophie said, before her brother could protest further.

The Warrior hopped lightly over the threshold and entered the room. "And yes," she said, "I am what you would call a vampire."

"Oh," Sophie whispered. Josh tried to stand in front of his sister to protect her, but she pushed him out of the way.

Although she loved her brother, there were times when he could be too protective.

"Don't believe everything you've read about my race," Scathach said, moving around the room, peering through the windows into the lush gardens. An enormous yellow-white butterfly fluttered past the opening. It was the size of a dinner plate and had not existed on the earth since the Jurassic period. "Hekate created and maintains this place by an extraordinary use of magic," she continued. "But magic, like everything else, follows certain natural laws. Magic needs energy, and it takes that energy wherever it can find it, even from the tiny batteries in your electrical toys. If no other source of energy is available, it will take the life force of the magician who created it. That is why every use of magic weakens the magician."

"Are you saying nothing electrical works in this Shadowrealm?" Sophie wondered aloud, and then she shook her head quickly. "But Hekate used a phone. I saw her showing it to Flamel earlier. Why doesn't its battery drain?"

"Hekate is immensely powerful and is more or less immune to the effects of the magic she generates. I would imagine that she keeps the phone on her person so it doesn't drain, or possibly she keeps it in the real world with a servant. Many members of the Elder Race have human servants."

"Like Flamel and Dee?" Sophie asked.

"Nicholas serves no Elder," Scathach said slowly. "The Book is his master. Dee, on the other hand . . . well, no one knows exactly who, or what, he serves." She glanced over her shoulder, her gaze lingering on each of them. "You'll probably find yourself feeling exhausted in about an hour, muscles sore, maybe even a little headachy. That's the magical field feeding off your auras. Don't be too concerned, however: your particular auras are exceptionally strong. Just drink plenty of liquids." Scatty moved from window to window and leaned forward, peering out. "I know they are out there, but I cannot see them," she said suddenly.

"Who?" Sophie wondered.

"The Torc Allta."

"Are they really wereboars? I mean, men who change into boars?" Sophie asked. She was conscious that her twin hadn't spoken since Scathach had entered the room. He was staring at her, eyes wide in horror, mouth drawn into a thin line. She knew that expression well: he was scared, and she guessed that he was thinking about all the vampire novels he'd read and movies he'd seen.

"No, not really," Scatty said. "I know Nicholas has told you that before the humani claimed the earth, this world belonged to other creatures, other races. But even amongst the Elder Race, the Torc clans were special. They could transform from beast shape to man shape and back again." Scatty sat on the edge of the low bed and stretched her legs straight out in front of her. "When the earliest humani first appeared, the Torc clans taught them how to work wood and stone and how to create fire. The humani worshipped the Torc clans as gods—why do you think so many of the earliest gods have animal shapes? Think of the cave paintings of creatures that are neither man nor beast but something in between. You must have seen statues of the Egyptian gods Sobek, Bastet and Anubis: humani bodies, but with animal heads. Think of the dances where humani pretend to be animals: they are just memories of the time when the Torc clans lived side by side with the humani."

"Therianthropes," Sophie said absently.

Scatty looked at her blankly.

"Figures that are made from animal and human shapes mixed together," Josh explained. "I told you that our parents are archaeologists," he added. Then he looked quickly at the red-haired woman. "Do you drink blood?" he asked suddenly.

"Josh!" Sophie whispered.

"No, I don't drink blood," Scathach said quietly. "Not now. Not ever."

"But a vampire—"

Scathach surged to her feet and two steps brought her directly in front of Josh. She was not quite as tall as he was, but in that moment, she seemed huge. "There are many types of vampires, many clans, just as there are many Were clans. Some of my race are blood drinkers, it is true."

"But not you," Sophie said hastily, before her brother could ask any further awkward questions.

"No, not my clan. Those of my clan . . . well, we feed in . . . other ways," Scatty said with a wry smile. "And we rarely need to feed," she added. She spun away. "Everything you have been taught, all the myths and legends of your world, have a kernel of truth in them. You've seen wonders today. You will see more in the days to come."

133

"What do you mean, in the days to come?" Josh interrupted, voice rising in alarm. "We're going home, aren't we?" But even as he was asking the question, he knew the answer.

"Eventually," the Warrior Maid said, "but not today, and definitely not tomorrow."

Sophie laid her hand on her brother's arm, silencing the question he was about to ask. "What were you saying about myths and legends?" she asked.

Somewhere deep in the house a bell chimed, the sound high and pure. It lingered in the still air.

Scathach ignored it. "I want you to remember that everything you know—or think you know—about myth and legend is not necessarily false, nor is it entirely true. At the heart of every legend there is a grain of truth. I suspect that much of your knowledge comes from movies and TV. Xena and Dracula have a lot to answer for. All minotaurs are not evil, the Gorgon Medusa did not turn every man to stone, not all vampires are blood drinkers, the Were clans are a proud and ancient race."

Josh attempted a laugh; he was still shaken by the revelation that Scathach was a vampire. "You'll be telling us next that ghosts exist."

Scathach's expression remained serious. "Josh, you have entered the Shadowrealm, the world of ghosts. I want you both to trust your instincts from now on: forget what you know—or think you know—about the creatures and races you will encounter. Follow your hearts. Trust no one. Except each other," she added.

"We can trust you and Nicholas, though, right?" Sophie said.

The bell rang again, flat and piercing in the distance.

"Trust no one," Scathach repeated, and the twins realized that she was not answering the question. She turned toward the door. "I think that's the dinner bell."

"Can we eat the food?" Josh asked.

"Depends," Scatty said.

"Depends on what?" he asked in alarm.

"Depends on what it is, of course. I don't eat the meat myself."

"Why not?" Sophie said, wondering if there was some particular ancient creature they should avoid.

"I'm a vegetarian," Scatty answered.

CHAPTER SIXTEEN

Perenelle Flamel sat in a corner of the tiny windowless room and drew her knees up to her chest, then wrapped her arms around her shins. She rested her chin on her knees. She could hear voices—angry, bitter voices.

Perry concentrated on the sound. She allowed her aura to expand a little as she murmured a small spell she had learned from an Inuit shaman. The shaman used it to listen to the fish moving under the arctic ice sheets and the bears crunching across the distant ice fields. The simple spell worked by shutting down all other senses and concentrating exclusively on hearing. Perry watched as the color faded from her surroundings and darkness closed in until she went blind. She gradually lost her sense of smell and felt the pins-and-needles tingle in her fingertips and toes as her sense of touch dulled, then faded completely. She knew that if there were anything in her mouth, she would no longer be able to taste it. Only her hearing remained, but it was enhanced and supersensitive. She heard beetles crawling in the walls behind her, heard the scritch-scratch as a mouse gnawed through wood somewhere above her, knew that a colony of termites was munching their way through distant floorboards. She also heard two voices, high and thin, as if they were being picked up on a badly tuned radio, and coming from a great distance. Perry tilted her head, homing in on the sound. She heard wind whistling, the flap of clothing, the high crying of birds. She could tell that the voices she was hearing were coming from the roof of the building. They strengthened, warbled and bubbled, and then abruptly clarified: they belonged to Dee and the Morrigan, and Perry could clearly hear the fear in the gray man's voice and the rage in the Crow Goddess's shrill cries.

"She must pay for this! She must!"

"She is an Elder. Untouchable by the likes of you and me," Dee said, trying unsuccessfully to calm the Morrigan.

"*No one* is untouchable. She has interfered where she was not wanted. My creatures had almost overwhelmed the car when her Ghost Wind swept them away."

"Flamel, the warrior Scathach and the two humani have now disappeared," Dee's voice echoed, and Perry frowned, concentrating hard, trying to follow every word. She was delighted to discover that Nicholas had sought the assistance of Scathach: she was a formidable ally. "It's as if they have vanished off the face of the earth."

"They *have* vanished off the face of the earth," the Morrigan snapped. "He's taken them into Hekate's Shadow-realm."

Unconsciously, Perry nodded. Of course! Where else would Nicholas have gone? The entrance to Hekate's Shadowrealm in Mill Valley was closest to San Francisco, and while the Elder was no friend to the Flamels, she was not allied to Dee and his Dark Elders either.

"We must follow them," the Morrigan stated flatly.

"Impossible," Dee said reasonably. "I have neither the skills nor the powers to penetrate Hekate's realm." There was a pause, and then he added, "Nor do you. She is a First Generation Elder, you are of the Next Generation."

"But she is not the only Elder on the West Coast." The Morrigan's voice was a snap of triumph.

"What are you suggesting?" Fear had touched Dee's voice with a hint of his original English accent.

"I know where Bastet sleeps."

Perenelle Flamel sat back against the cold stone and allowed her senses to return. Feeling came first—pins and needles racing through her fingers and toes—then her sense of smell, and finally sight. Blinking, waiting for the tiny colored spots of light to fade, Perry tried to make sense of what she had just discovered.

The implications were terrible. The Morrigan was prepared to awaken Bastet and attack Hekate's Shadowrealm to retrieve the pages of the Codex.

Perry shuddered. She had never met Bastet—she didn't know anyone who had in the last three centuries and had lived to tell the tale—but she knew her by reputation. One of the most powerful members of the Elder Race, Bastet had been worshipped in Egypt since the earliest ages of man. She had the body of a beautiful young woman with the head of a cat, and Perry had absolutely no idea of the magical forces she controlled.

Events were moving surprisingly swiftly. Something big was happening. Many years before, when Nicholas and Perry had first discovered the secret of immortality, they had realized that their extra-long lives allowed them to view the world from a different perspective. They no longer planned events days or weeks in advance; often they would make plans decades into the future. Perry had come to understand that the Elders, whose lives were infinitely longer, could make plans that encompassed centuries. And that often meant that events moved with an extraordinarily deliberate slowness.

But now the Morrigan was abroad. The last time she had walked in the World of Men, she had been spotted in the bitter, mud-filled trenches of the Somme; before that she had prowled the bloodstained battlefields of the American Civil War. The Crow Goddess was drawn to death; it hung around her like a foul stench. She was also one of the Elders who believed that humans had been placed on this earth to serve them.

Nicholas and the twins were safe in Hekate's Shadowrealm, but for how long? Bastet was a First Generation Elder. Her powers had to be at least equal to Hekate's . . . and if the Cat Goddess and the Crow Goddess, combined with Dee's alchemical magic, attacked Hekate, would her defenses hold? Perry didn't know.

And what of Nicholas, Scathach and the twins?

139

Perelle felt tears prickle the back of her eyes, but blinked them away. Nicholas would be six hundred and seventy-seven years old on the twenty-eighth of September, in three months' time. He was well able to take care of himself, though his mastery of practical spells was very limited, and he could be remarkably forgetful at times. Only the summer before, he had forgotten how to speak English and had reverted to his native archaic French. It had taken her nearly a month to coach him back to speaking English. Before that he had gone through a period when he had signed his checks in Greek and Aramaic characters. Perelle's lips curled in a smile. He spoke sixteen languages well and another ten badly. He could read and write in twenty-two of them—though there wasn't much chance to practice his Linear B, cuneiform or hiero-glyphics these days.

She wondered what he was doing right now. He would be looking for her, of course, but he would also need to protect the twins and the pages that Josh had torn from the Codex. She needed to get a message to him, she had to let him know that she was fine and to warn him about the danger they were in.

One of the earliest gifts the young woman known as Perelle Delamere had discovered when she was growing up was her ability to talk to the shades of the dead. It wasn't until her seventh birthday that she realized that not everyone could see the flickering black-and-white images she encoun-tered daily. On the eve of her seventh birthday, her beloved grandmother, Mamom, died. Perelle watched as the with-ered body was gently lifted from the bed where she had spent

140

the last ten years of her life and laid in the coffin. The small girl had followed the funeral procession through the tiny town of Quimper and out into the graveyard that overlooked the sea. She had watched the little rough-hewn box as it was lowered into the earth, and then she had returned to her home.

And Mamom was sitting up in the bed, eyes bright with their usual mischief. The only difference was that Perenelle could no longer see her grandmother clearly. There was no color to her—everything was in black-and-white—and her image kept flickering in and out of focus.

In that instant Perenelle realized she could see ghosts. And when Mamom turned in her direction and smiled, she knew that they could see her.

Sitting in the small windowless cell, Perenelle stretched her legs out in front of her and pressed both hands to the cold concrete floor. Over the years she had developed a series of defenses to protect herself from the unwanted intrusions of the dead. If there was one thing she had learned early on about the dead—particularly the old dead—it was that they were extraordinarily rude, popping up at the most inopportune and inappropriate moments. The dead particularly liked bathrooms—it was a perfect location for them: quiet and still, with lots of reflective surfaces. Perenelle recalled a time she'd been brushing her teeth when the ghost of an American president had appeared in the mirror in front of her. She'd almost swallowed the toothbrush.

Perenelle had quickly come to understand that ghosts could not see certain colors—blues and greens and some tints of yellow—and so she deliberately encouraged those colors into her aura, carefully creating a shield that rendered her invisible in the particular Shadowrealm where the shades of the dead gathered.

Opening her eyes wide, Perenelle concentrated on her own aura. Her natural aura was a pale ice white, which acted like a beacon for the dead, drawing them to her. But over it, like layers of paint, she had created auras of bright blue, emerald green, and primrose yellow. Now, one by one, Perenelle shut off the colors—yellow first, then green, then the final blue defense.

The ghosts came then, drawn to her ice white aura like moths to a flame. They flickered into existence around her: men, women and children, wearing clothes from across the decades. Perenelle moved her green eyes over the glistening images, not entirely sure what she was looking for. She dismissed women and girls in the flowing skirts of the eighteenth century and men in the boots and gun belts of the nineteenth and concentrated on those ghosts wearing the clothing of the twentieth century. She finally picked out an elderly man wearing a modern-looking security guard's uniform. Gently easing the other shades aside, she called the figure closer.

Perenelle understood that people—particularly in modern, sophisticated societies—were frightened of ghosts. But she knew that there was no reason to fear them: a ghost was nothing more than the remnants of a person's aura that remained attached to a particular place.

"Can I help you, ma'am?" The shade's voice was strong,

with a touch of the East Coast in it: Boston perhaps. Standing tall and straight, like an old soldier, the ghost looked about sixty, though he could have been older.

"Could you tell me where I am?" Perenelle asked.

"You're in the basement of the corporate headquarters of Enoch Enterprises, just to the west of Telegraph Hill. We got Coit Tower almost directly overhead," he added proudly.

"You seem very sure."

"Should be. I worked here for thirty years. Wasn't always Enoch Enterprises, of course. But places like this always need security. Never one break-in on my watch," he informed her.

"That's an achievement to be proud of, Mr. . . . ."

"It surely is." The ghost paused, his image flickering wildly. "Miller. That was my name. Jefferson Miller. Been a while since anyone asked for it. How can I help you?" he asked.

"Well, you've been of great assistance already. At least I know I am still in San Francisco."

The ghost continued to look at her. "Did you expect not to be?"

"I think I may have slept earlier; I was afraid I might have been moved out of the city," she explained.

"Are you being held against your will, ma'am?"

"I am."

Jefferson Miller drifted closer. "Well, that's just not right." There was a long pause while his image flickered. "But I'm afraid I can't help you—I'm a ghost, you see."

Perenelle nodded. "I know that." She smiled. "I just wasn't sure if you knew." She knew that one of the reasons ghosts often remained attached to certain places was because they simply did not know that they were dead.

The old security guard wheezed a laugh. "I've tried to leave . . . but something keeps pulling me back. Maybe I just spent too much time here when I was alive."

Perenelle nodded again. "I can help you leave, if you would like to. I can do that for you."

Jefferson Miller nodded. "I think I would like that very much. My wife, Ethel, she passed on ten years before me. Sometimes I think I hear her voice calling me across the Shadowrealms."

Perenelle nodded. "She is trying to call you home. I can help you cut the ties that bind you to this place."

"Is there anything I can do for you in return?"

Perenelle smiled. "Well, there is one thing. . . . Perhaps you could get a message to my husband."

CHAPTER SEVENTEEN

Sophie and Josh followed Scathach through Hekate's house. There were reminders everywhere that they were inside a tree: everything—floors, walls and ceilings—was wooden, and in places, little buds and shoots of green leaves dappled the walls, as if the wood was still growing.

With her hand resting lightly on her brother's shoulder, Sophie looked around. The house seemed to be composed of a series of circular rooms that flowed, almost imperceptibly, into one another. She caught glimpses as she and Josh passed them; almost all the rooms were bare, and most of them had tall red-barked trees growing through the center of the floor. One room, off to the side and much larger than the rest, had a large oval-shaped pool in the middle of the floor. Startlingly large white-flowered water lilies clustered in the center of the pool, giving it the appearance of a huge unblinking eye. Another room was filled entirely with wooden wind chimes dangling from the branches of its red tree. Each set of chimes was a different size and shape, some etched and carved with symbols, others unadorned. They hung still and quiet until Sophie looked into the room, and then they slowly, melodically began to rattle together. It sounded like distant whispers. Sophie squeezed Josh's shoulder, trying to attract his attention, but he was staring straight ahead, forehead creased in concentration.

"Where is everyone?" Josh finally asked.

"There is only Hekate," Scathach said. "Those of the Elder Race are solitary creatures."

"Are there many still alive?" Sophie wondered aloud.

Scathach paused by an open door and turned to look back over her shoulder. "More than you might think. The majority of them want nothing to do with the humani and rarely venture from their individual Shadowrealms. Others, like the Dark Elders, want a return to the old ways, and work through agents like Dee to make it happen."

"And what about you?" Josh demanded. "Do you want to return to these old ways?"

"I never thought they were that great," she said, then added, "especially for the humani."

They found Nicholas Flamel sitting outside on a raised wooden deck set into a branch of the tree. Growing horizontally from the tree trunk, the branch was at least ten feet across, and sloped down to plunge into the earth close to a crescent-shaped pool. Walking across the branch, Sophie glanced down and was startled to see that beneath the green weeds that curled and twisted in the pool, tiny almost-human faces peered upward, mouths and eyes open wide. On the deck, five high-backed chairs were arranged around a circular table, which was set with beautifully hand-carved wooden bowls and elegant wooden cups and goblets. Warm, rough-cut bread and thick slices of hard cheese were arranged on platters, and there were two huge bowls of fruit—apples, oranges and enormous cherries—in the center of the table. The Alchemyst was carefully slicing the skin off an emerald green apple with a triangular sliver of black stone that looked like an arrowhead. Sophie noticed that he had arranged the green skin into shapes that resembled letters.

Scatty slid into the seat beside the Alchemyst. "Is Hekate not joining us?" she asked, picking up a piece of cut skin and chewing on it.

"I believe she is changing for dinner," Flamel said, slicing off another curl of skin to replace the piece Scatty was chewing. He looked over at Sophie and Josh. "Sit, please. Our hostess will join us shortly and then we'll eat. You must be exhausted," he added.

"I am tired," Sophie admitted. She'd become aware of the exhaustion a little earlier, and now she could barely keep her eyes open. She was also a little frightened, realizing that the tiredness was caused by the magic of the place feeding off her energy.

"When can we go home?" Josh demanded, unwilling to admit that he too was worn out. Even his bones ached. He felt as if he was coming down with a cold.

Nicholas Flamel cut a neat slice from the apple and

popped it in his mouth. "I'm afraid you will not be able to return for a little while."

"Why not?" Josh snapped.

Flamel sighed. He put down the stone arrowhead and the apple and placed his hands flat on the table. "Right now, neither Dee nor the Morrigan knows who you are. It's only because of that, that you and your family are safe."

"Our *family*?" Sophie asked. The sudden thought that her mother or father might be in danger made her feel queasy. Josh reacted with the same shock, his lips drawing into a thin white line.

"Dee will be thorough," Flamel said. "He is protecting a millennia-old secret, and he will not stop with killing you. Everyone you know or have come in contact with will have an *accident*. I'd hazard a guess that even Bernice's Coffee Cup will burn to the ground . . . simply because you once worked in it. Bernice might even perish in the fire."

"But she has nothing to do with anything," Sophie protested, horrified.

"Yes, but Dee doesn't know that. Nor does he care. He has worked with the Dark Elders for a long time, and now he has come to regard humans as they do: as little more than beasts."

"But we won't tell anyone what we've seen . . . ," Josh began, "and no one would believe us anyway. . . ." His sentence trailed away.

"And if we don't tell anyone, then no one will ever know," Sophie said. "We'll never speak of this again. Dee will never find us." But even as the words were leaving her mouth, she was beginning to realize that it was hopeless. She and Josh were as trapped by their knowledge of the Codex's existence as Nicholas and Perry had been.

"He would find you," Flamel said reasonably. He glanced at the Warrior Maid. "How long do you think it would it take for Dee or one of the Morrigan's spies to find them?"

"Not long," she said, munching on the apple skin. "A couple of hours maybe. The rats or birds would track you, then Dee would hunt you down."

"Once you have been touched by magic, you are forever changed." Flamel moved his right hand in front of him, leaving the faintest hint of pale green smoke dangling in the air. "You leave a trail." He huffed a breath at the green smoke and it curled away and disappeared.

"Are you saying we smell?" Josh demanded.

Flamel nodded. "You smell of wild magic. You caught a whiff of it earlier today when Hekate touched you both. What did you smell then?"

"Oranges," Josh said.

"Vanilla ice cream," Sophie replied.

"And earlier still, when Dee and I fought: what did you smell then?"

"Mint and rotten eggs," Josh said immediately.

"Every magician has his or her own distinctive odor; rather like a magical fingerprint. You must learn to heed your senses. Humans use but a tiny percentage of theirs. They barely look, they rarely listen, they never smell, and they think that they can only experience feelings through their skin. But they talk, oh, do they talk. That makes up for the lack of use of their other senses. When you return to your own world, you will be able to recognize people who have some taint of magical energy." He cut out a neat cube of apple and popped it into his mouth. "You may notice a peculiar scent, you might even taste it or see it as a shimmer around their bodies."

"How long will the feeling last?" Sophie asked, curious. She reached out and took a cherry. It was the size of a small tomato. "Will it fade?"

Flamel shook his head. "It will never fade. On the contrary, it will get stronger. You have to realize that nothing will ever be the same for either of you from this day forth."

Josh bit into an apple with a satisfying crunch. Juice ran onto his chin. "You make that sound like a bad thing," he said with a grin, wiping his mouth with his sleeve.

Flamel was about to respond, but glanced up and suddenly came to his feet. Scathach also rose smoothly, silently. Sophie immediately stood, but Josh remained sitting until Sophie caught his shoulder and pulled him up. Then she turned to look at the Goddess with Three Faces.

But this wasn't Hekate.

The woman she had seen earlier had been tall and elegant, middle-aged maybe, her hair cut in a tight white helmet close to her head, her black skin smooth and unwrinkled. This woman was older, much, much older. The resemblance to Hekate was there, and Sophie guessed that this was her mother or grandmother. Although she was still tall, she stooped forward, picking her way around the branch, leaning into an ornately carved black stick that was at least as tall as Sophie. Her face was a mass of fine wrinkles, her eyes deeply sunken in her head, glittering with a peculiar yellow cast. She was completely bald, and Sophie could see where her skull was tattooed in an intricate curling pattern. Although she was wearing a dress similar to the one Hekate had worn earlier, the metallic-looking fabric ran black and red with her every movement.

Sophie blinked, squeezed her eyes shut and then blinked again. She could see the merest hint of an aura around the woman, almost as if she were exuding a fine white mist. When she moved, she left tendrils of this mist behind her.

Without acknowledging anyone's presence, the old woman settled into the seat directly facing Nicholas Flamel. Only when she was seated did Flamel and Scathach sit. Sophie and Josh sat down also, glancing from Nicholas to the old woman, wondering who she was and what was going on.

The woman raised a wooden goblet from the table, but didn't drink. There was movement in the trunk of the tree behind her, and four tall, muscular young men appeared, carrying trays piled high with food, which they set down in the center of the table before backing away silently. The men looked so alike that they had to be related, but it was their faces that drew the twins' attention: there was something *wrong* with the planes and angles of their skulls. Foreheads sloped down to a ridge over their eyes, their noses were short and splayed, their cheekbones pronounced, and their chins receded sharply. The hint of yellow teeth was visible behind thin lips. The men were bare-chested and barefoot, wearing

151

only leather kilts, onto which rectangular plates of metal had been sewn. And their chests, legs and heads were covered with coarse red hair.

Sophie suddenly realized that she was staring, and deliberately turned away. The men looked like some breed of primitive hominid, but she knew the differences between Neanderthal and Cro-Magnon, and her father had plaster skulls of *Australopithecus,* Peking man and the great apes in his study. These men were none of those. And then she noticed that their eyes were blue: bright blue, and incredibly intelligent-looking.

"They're Torc Allta," she said, and then froze in surprise when everyone turned to look at her. She hadn't realized she had spoken aloud.

Josh, who'd been staring suspiciously at what might have been a chunk of fish he'd forked out of a big bowl of stew, glanced at the backs of the four young men. "I knew that," he said casually.

Sophie kicked him under the table. "You did not," she muttered. "You were too busy checking out the food."

"I'm hungry," he said, then leaned across to his twin. "It was the red hair and piggy noses that gave it away," he murmured. "I thought you'd realized that."

"It would be a mistake to let them hear you say that," Nicholas Flamel interrupted quietly. "It would also be a mistake to judge by appearances or to comment on what you see. In this time, in this place, different standards, different criteria apply. Here words can kill—literally."

"Or get you killed," Scathach added. She had piled her

152

plate high with an assortment of vegetables, only some of which were familiar to the twins. She nodded in the direction of the tree. "But you are right: they are Torc Allta in their humani form. Probably the finest warriors of any time," she said.

"They will accompany you when you leave here," the old woman said suddenly, her voice surprisingly strong coming from such a frail-looking body.

Flamel bowed. "We will be honored by their presence."

"Don't be," the old woman snapped. "They'll not accompany you solely for your protection: they're to ensure that you really do leave my realm." She spread her long-fingered hands on the table, and Sophie noticed that her fingernails were each painted a different color. Strangely, the pattern was identical to the one she'd noticed on Hekate's nails earlier. "You cannot stay here," the woman announced abruptly. "You must go."

The twins glanced at each other; why was she being so rude?

Scathach opened her mouth to speak, but Flamel reached over and squeezed her arm. "That was always our intention," he said smoothly. The late-afternoon sunlight slanting through the trees dappled his face, turning his pale eyes into mirrors. "When Dee attacked my shop and snatched the Codex, I realized that I had nowhere else to go."

"You should have gone south," the old woman said, her dress almost completely black now, the red threads looking like veins. "You would have been more welcome there. I want you to leave."

"When I began to suspect that the prophecy was beginning to come about, I knew I had to come to you," Flamel continued, ignoring her. The twins, who were following the exchange closely, noticed how his eyes had flickered briefly in their direction.

The old woman turned her head and looked at the twins with her butter-colored eyes. Her wizened face cracked in a humorless smile that showed her tiny yellow teeth. "I have thought about this; I am convinced that the prophecy does not refer to humani—and especially not humani children," she added with a hiss.

The contempt in the woman's voice made Sophie speak out. "I wish you wouldn't talk about us as if we weren't here," she said.

"Besides," Josh said, "your daughter was going to help us. Why don't we wait and see what she has to say."

The elderly woman blinked at him, and her almost-invisible eyebrows raised in a silent question. "My daughter?"

Sophie saw Scathach's eyes widen in surprise or warning, but Josh pressed on.

"Yes, the woman we met this afternoon. The younger woman—your daughter? Or maybe she's your granddaughter? She was going to help us."

"I have neither a daughter nor a granddaughter!" The old woman's dress flared black and red in long sheets of color. Her lips drew back from her teeth and she snarled some incomprehensible words. Her hands curled into claws, and the air was suddenly filled with the citrus scent of lime. Dozens of tiny spinning balls of green light gathered in the palms of her hand.

And then Scathach slammed a double-edged dagger into the center of the table. The wood split in two with a thunderous snap that spewed splinters into the air, and the bowls of food shattered on the ground. The old woman reared back, the green light dribbling from her fingers like liquid. It ran hissing and spitting down the branch before sinking into the wood.

The four Torc Allta were immediately behind the old woman, curved, scythelike swords in their hands, and three more of the creatures in their boar shape burst through the undergrowth and raced up the branch to assume positions behind Flamel and Scatty.

The twins froze, terrified, unsure what had just happened. Nicholas Flamel hadn't moved, he merely continued to cut and eat the apple. Scathach calmly sheathed her dagger and folded her arms. She spoke quickly to the old woman. Sophie and Josh could see Scathach's lips moving, but all they could hear was a tinny, mosquito-like buzz.

The old woman didn't respond. Her face was an expressionless mask as she stood and swept away from the table, surrounded by the Torc Allta guards. This time neither Flamel nor Scathach stood.

In the long silence that followed, Scathach stooped down to gather some of the fallen fruits and vegetables from the ground, dusted them off and popped them into the only remaining unbroken wooden bowl. She started to eat.

Josh was opening his mouth to ask the same question Sophie wanted an answer to, but she reached under the table and squeezed his arm, silencing him. She was aware that something terribly dangerous had just occurred, and that somehow Josh was involved.

"I think that went well, don't you?" Scathach asked eventually.

Flamel finished the apple and cleaned the edge of the black arrowhead on a leaf. "It depends on how you define the word *well*," he said.

Scathach munched on a raw carrot. "We're still alive and we're still in the Shadowrealm," she said. "Could be worse. The sun is going down. Our hostess will need to sleep, and in the morning, she'll be a different person. Probably won't even remember what happened tonight."

"What did you say to her?" Flamel asked. "I've never mastered the Elder Tongue."

"I simply reminded her of the ancient duty of hospitality and assured her that the slight to her was unintentional and made through ignorance and was, therefore, no crime under the Elder Laws."

"She is fearful . . . ," Flamel murmured, glancing toward the huge tree trunk. The Torc Allta guards could be seen moving inside, while the largest of the boars had remained outside, blocking the doorway.

"She is always fearful when the evening draws in. It is when she is at her most vulnerable," Scathach said.

"It would be nice," Sophie interrupted, "if someone told us exactly what just happened." She hated it when adults talked among themselves and ignored any children present. And that was exactly what was happening now.

Scathach smiled, and suddenly, her vampire teeth looked very long in her mouth. "Your twin managed to insult one of the Elder Race and was very nearly turned into green slime for his crime."

Josh shook his head. "But I didn't say anything . . . ," he protested. He looked at his twin for support as he quickly thought over his conversation with the old woman. "All I said was that her daughter or granddaughter had promised to help us."

Scathach laughed softly. "There is no daughter or grand-daughter. The mature woman you saw this afternoon was Hekate. The old woman you saw this evening is also Hekate, and in the morning, you will meet a young girl who is Hekate as well."

"The Goddess with Three Faces," Flamel reminded them.

"Hekate is cursed to age with the day. Maiden in the morning, matron in the afternoon, crone in the evening. She is incredibly sensitive about her age."

Josh swallowed hard. "I didn't know. . . ."

"No reason why you should have—except that your igno-rance could have gotten you killed . . . or worse."

"But what did you do to the table?" Sophie asked. She looked at the ruin of the circular table: it was split down the middle where Scatty had cut it with her knife. The wood on either side of the split looked dry and dusty.

"Iron," Scatty said simply.

"One of the surprising side effects of the artificial metal,"

Flamel said, "is its ability to nullify even the most powerful magics. The discovery of iron really signaled the end of the Elder Race's power in this world." He held up the black stone arrowhead. "That's why I was using this. The Elders get nervous in the presence of iron."

"But *you're* carrying iron," Sophie said to Scatty.

"I'm Next Generation—not pure Elder like Hekate. I can bear to be around iron."

Josh licked his dry lips. He was still remembering the green light buzzing in Hekate's palms. "When you said 'turned into green slime,' you didn't really mean . . ."

Scathach nodded. "Sticky green slime. Quite disgusting. And I understand the victim retains some measure of consciousness for a while." She glanced at Flamel. "I cannot remember the last person to cross one of the Elders and live, can you?"

Flamel stood. "Let's hope she doesn't remember in the morning. Get some rest," he said to the twins. "Tomorrow is going to be a long day."

"Why?" Sophie and Josh asked simultaneously.

"Because tomorrow, I'm hoping I can convince Hekate to Awaken your magical potential. If you are going to have any chance of surviving the days to come, I will have to train you to become magicians."

CHAPTER EIGHTEEN

*N*icholas Flamel watched Sophie and Josh follow Scathach into the tree. Only when the door had closed behind them did his colorless eyes betray the worry he felt. That had been close: another heartbeat or two and Hekate would have reduced Josh to bubbling liquid. He wasn't sure if she would have been able to reconstitute him in the morning when she had taken on her maiden form. He had to get the twins away from her before their ignorance got them into trouble.

Flamel walked away from the ruined table and followed the slope of the tree limb down to the pool. He stepped off the branch and onto a narrow unpaved path. There were a multitude of marks in the mud—some were boar tracks, others looked more like human feet . . . and some were a curious mixture of both. He knew he was being followed, that his every movement was being tracked by creatures he couldn't see, and he guessed that the Torc Allta were probably the least of Hekate's guards.

Crouching by the water's edge, he took a deep breath and allowed himself a moment to relax. It would be true to say that this had been one of the more eventful days in his long life, and he was exhausted.

From the moment Dee had snatched Perry and the Codex and the twins had appeared, Flamel knew that one of the first prophecies he had read in the Book half a millennium previously was beginning to come true.

"The two that are one, the one that is all."

The Codex was full of cryptic phrases and incomprehensible sayings. Most of them were concerned with the annihilation of Danu Talis, the ancient homeland of the Elder Race, but there was also a series of prophecies that had to do with the return of the Dark Elders and the destruction and enslavement of the humani.

"There will come a time when the Book is taken . . ."

Well, that was fairly self-explanatory.

". . . And the Queen's man is allied with the Crow. . . ."

That had to refer to Dr. John Dee. He had been Queen Elizabeth's personal magician. And the Crow was clearly the Crow Goddess.

"Then the Elder will step out of the Shadows . . ."

Flamel knew that Dee had been working for centuries with the Dark Elders to bring about their return. He had heard unconfirmed reports that more and more of the Dark Elders had left their Shadowrealms and begun to explore the world of the humani again.

". . . And the immortal must train the mortal. The two that are one must become the one that is all."

Nicholas Flamel was the immortal of the prophecy. He was sure of it. The twins—"the two that are one"—must be the mortal who needed to be trained. But he had no idea what the last phrase referred to: "the one that is all."

Circumstances had placed the twins in his care, and he was determined that no harm should come to them, especially now that he believed they were destined to play a critical role in the war against the Dark Elders. Nicholas knew that bringing Josh and Sophie to the Goddess with Three Faces had been an incredible risk—especially in the company of Scathach. The Warrior's feud with the goddess was older than most civilizations. Hekate was one of the most dangerous of the Elders. Immensely powerful, one of her many skills enabled her to Awaken the magical powers that existed in every sentient creature. However, like many of the Elders, her metabolism was linked to a solar or lunar cycle. She aged during the day, and effectively died when the sun went down, but was then reborn with the sunrise as a young woman. This peculiar trait clouded and colored her thinking, and sometimes, as had happened earlier, the older Hekate forgot the promises her younger selves had made. Flamel was hoping he would be able to reason with the maiden Hekate in the morning and convince her to Awaken the twins' extraordinary potential.

The Alchemyst knew that everyone had the possibility for magic within them. Once it had been sparked into life, it tended to become increasingly powerful of its own accord.

Sometimes—very rarely—children suddenly exhibited extraordinary powers, usually either telepathy or telekinesis or a combination of both. Some children realized what was happening and managed to control their growing powers, while others never fully understood it. Left untrained and unchecked, magical energy radiated off the children in waves, moving furniture around, knocking people to the ground, gouging marks in walls and ceilings. This was often reported as poltergeist activity. He knew that if Hekate Awakened the twins' dormant magical powers, then he could use what he had learned over six hundred years of study to increase their skills. Not only would he give them the means of protecting themselves, but he would also be able to begin preparing them for whatever lay ahead.

Still crouching by the pool, he stared into the green-tinged water. Red and white koi moved just below the surface, while deeper down, humanlike faces peered up, eyes huge and blank, mouths filled with needle-pointed teeth. He decided against dipping his fingers into the water.

It was commonly held in all the ancient magical books that there were four elements of magic: Air and Water, Earth and Fire. But centuries of study had revealed to Nicholas that there were, in fact, five elemental forces of magic. The fifth force was the magic of Time, the greatest of all magics. The Elders could control all the other elements, but the secret of the fifth was contained only in the Codex . . . and that was one of the many reasons why Dee, and the Dark Elders he sided with, wanted the Codex. With it in their possession, they would be able to control time itself.

Along with Perenelle, Nicholas Flamel had spent most of his long life studying the elemental forces. While Perry had trained herself in different styles of magic, he had concentrated on the formulae and theorems from the Codex. These formed the basis of the study of alchemy, which was a type of science. Using the formulae, he had learned how to turn base metal into gold and coal into diamonds, but there was very little magic involved. True, it was a remarkably complex formula and required months of preparation, but the process itself was almost ridiculously simple. One day he had been poor, the next wealthy beyond his wildest dreams. Taking Perry's advice, he had founded hospitals, established orphanages and funded schools in his native Paris. Those had been good times . . . no, more than that—they had been great times. Life had been so much simpler then. They had not known about the Elder Race, had not begun to suspect even the tiniest portion of dark knowledge the Codex contained.

In recent years, Nicholas would sometimes awaken at the quietest hour of night with a single thought spinning round and round in his head: if he had known then what he knew now about the Codex, would he have continued his research into the philosopher's stone? That path had ultimately brought him into contact with the Elder Race—notably the Dark Elders—and had brought Dr. John Dee into his life. It had forced Perry and him to fake their own deaths and flee Paris and ultimately to spend the next half millennium in hiding. But the study of the Codex had also made them both immortal. Most nights he answered yes: even knowing all he knew now, he would still have continued his studies and become the Alchemyst.

But there were rare occasions, like today, when the answer was no. Now he stood to lose Perenelle, probably the lives of the innocent twins and the not-so-innocent Scathach— though she would not be so easy to kill—and there was also a chance that he had doomed the world.

Nicholas felt himself grow cold at the thought. The Book of Abraham was full of what he had first assumed to be stories, legends, myths and tales. Over the centuries, his research had revealed that all the stories were true, all the tales were based on fact, and what he believed to be legends and myths were simply reports of real beings and actual events.

The Elder Race existed.

They were creatures that looked human—sometimes— but had the powers of gods. They had ruled for tens of thousands of years before the creatures they called the humani—humankind—appeared on the earth. The first primitive humani worshipped the Elder Race as gods and demons and over generations had constructed whole mythologies and belief systems based around an individual or a collection of Elders. The gods and goddesses of Greece and Egypt, of Sumeria and the Indus Valley, of the Toltec and the Celt, existed. They weren't different gods, however; they were simply the same Elders called by different names.

The Elder Race divided into two groups: those who worked with the humani and those who regarded them as little better than slaves—and, in some cases, food. The Elders warred against one another in battles that took centuries to complete. Occasionally humani would fight on one side, and their exploits were recalled in great legends like those of Gilgamesh and Cuchulain, Atlas and Hippolytus, Beowulf and Ilya of Murom.

Finally, when it became clear that these wars might destroy the planet, the mysterious Abraham, using a powerful collection of spells, forced all of the Elder Race—even those who supported the humani—to retreat from the earth. Most were like Hekate and went willingly, settling into a Shadowrealm of their own creation, and afterward had little or no contact with the humani. Others, like the Morrigan, though she was greatly weakened, continued to venture out into the humani world and worked to restore the old ways. Others still, like Scathach, lived anonymously among humankind. Flamel eventually came to understand that the Codex, which contained the spells that had driven the Elder Race from this world and into their Shadowrealms, also contained the spells that would allow them to return.

And if the Dark Elders returned, then the civilization of the twenty-first century would be wiped away in a matter of hours as the godlike creatures warred among themselves. It had happened before; mythology and history recorded the event as the Flood.

Now Dee had the Book. All he needed were the two pages Flamel could feel pressed against his flesh. And Nicholas Flamel knew that Dee and the Morrigan would stop at nothing to get those pages.

Flamel hung his head and wished he knew what to do. He wished Perenelle were with him; she would surely have a plan.

A bubble burst on the surface of the water. *"The lady asks me to tell you . . ."* Another bubble popped and burst. *". . . that she is unharmed."*

Flamel scrambled back from the pool's edge. Tendrils of mist were rising from the surface of the water, tiny bubbles popping and snapping. A shape began to form out of the mist cloud—a surprising shape: that of an elderly man in a security guard's uniform. The shape hovered, twisting and curling over the pond. The late-evening sunshine shone through the water drops, turning each one into a brilliant rainbow of light. "You are a ghost?" Nicholas asked.

"Yes, sir, I am. Or I was until Mrs. Flamel freed me."

"Do you know me?" Nicholas Flamel asked. He wondered quickly if this might be a trick of Dee's, but then he dismissed the idea: the sorcerer was powerful, but there was no way he could penetrate Hekate's defenses.

The mist shifted and thickened. "Yes, sir, I believe I do: you are Nicholas Flamel, the Alchemyst. Mrs. Flamel asked me to go in search of you. She suggested that I would find you here, in this particular Shadowrealm. She overheard Dee mention that you were here."

"She is unharmed?" Flamel asked eagerly.

"She is. The small man they call John Dee is terrified of her, though the other woman is not."

"What woman?"

"A tall woman, wearing a cloak of black feathers."

"The Morrigan," Flamel said grimly.

"Aye, and that's the message . . ." A fish leapt out of the pond and the figure dissolved into a thousand water droplets that hung frozen in the air, each one a tiny portion of a jig-saw that made up the ghost. "Mrs. Flamel says you have to leave . . . and leave now. The Crow Goddess is gathering her forces to invade the Shadowrealm."

"She'll not succeed. She is Next Generation; she has not the power."

The fish leapt again, scattering the water droplets, and the ghost's voice drifted and whispered away, dying with each bursting bubble. "Mrs. Flamel instructed me to tell you that the Crow Goddess intends to awaken Bastet."

CHAPTER NINETEEN

Scathach stood by the door to Sophie's room and regarded the twins with her grass green eyes. "Get some rest," she said, repeating Flamel's advice. "Stay in your rooms," she added. "You may hear strange sounds from outside—just ignore them. You are completely safe so long as you remain within these walls."

"What sort of sounds?" Josh asked. His imagination was working overtime, and he was beginning to regret all those hours he'd spent playing Doom and Quake, scaring himself silly.

Scathach took a moment to consider. "Screams, maybe. Animal howls. Oh, and laughter." She smiled. "And believe me, you don't want to find out what's laughing," she said, and added, without a trace of irony, "Sleep tight."

Josh Newman waited until Scathach had rounded the end

of the corridor before turning to his sister. "We've got to get out of here."

Sophie chewed her bottom lip hard enough to leave the impression of her two front teeth in the flesh, and then nodded. "I've been thinking the same thing."

"I think we're in some pretty serious danger," Josh said urgently.

Sophie nodded again. Events had moved so fast that afternoon that she'd barely had time to catch her breath. One moment she'd been working in the coffee shop, the next they were racing across San Francisco in the company of a man who claimed to be a six-hundred-year-old alchemyst and a girl who looked no older than herself and yet who Flamel swore was a two-and-a-half-thousand-year-old female warrior. And a vampire. "I keep looking for the hidden cameras," she muttered, glancing around the room.

"Cameras?" Josh looked startled. He immediately picked up on his twin's thoughts. "You mean like *Candid Camera?*" He looked uncomfortable and felt color flood his face: what if he'd managed to make an idiot of himself in front of the entire nation? He'd never be able to show his face at school again. He peered up into the corners of the room, looking for the cameras. They were usually behind mirrors. There were no mirrors in the room, but Josh knew that didn't mean anything; the new generation of cameras were so small that they were virtually invisible. A sudden thought struck him. "What about the birds?"

Sophie nodded once more. "I keep coming back to the

birds. Everything else could be special effects: the Torc Allta could be trained animals and men in prosthetic makeup, what happened in Scathach's dojo could be some sort of effect and the rats could have been trained. But not the birds: there were too many of them, and they ripped the car to shreds." The birds were what had finally convinced her that she and Josh were in very real danger . . . because if the birds were real, then everything else was real too.

Josh dug his hands into the back pockets of his jeans and stood by the open window. The dense foliage came right up to the window ledge, and although there was no glass in the opening, none of the myriad bugs that flitted through the late-evening air entered the room. He recoiled as a bright blue snake as thick as his wrist appeared out of the canopy of leaves and flickered a tongue that was easily six inches long in his direction. The snake vanished as a ball of tiny buzzing lights appeared, darting smoothly through the trees. As they shot past the window, Josh could have sworn that the entire swarm was composed of about a dozen tiny winged women, none of them bigger than his forefinger. The lights came from within their bodies. He licked dry lips. "Okay, let's assume that this is real . . . all of it—the magic, the ancient races—then that brings me back to my original thought: we've got to get out of here."

Sophie walked to the window, stood behind her brother and put her arm on his shoulder. She was older than he was by twenty-eight seconds—less than half a minute, Josh always reminded her—but with their mother and father away so much, she had assumed the role of a much older sister.

Although he was already a good two inches taller than she was, he would always be her baby brother. "I agree," she said tiredly. "We should try and make a run for it."

Something in his sister's voice made Josh turn to look at her. "You don't think we'll get away," he said evenly.

"Let's try," she said, not answering his question. "But I'm sure they'll come after us."

"Flamel said that Dee would be able to track us. I'm sure Flamel—or Scathach—can do that too."

"Flamel has no reason to follow us," Sophie pointed out.

"But Dee does," Josh said. "What happens if we go home and Dee and his people follow us there?" he wondered aloud.

Sophie frowned. "I've been thinking about that. Flamel said that we'll be able to see the magical aura that surrounds people."

Josh nodded.

"Hekate hasn't Awakened our magical powers." She frowned again, trying to remember exactly what Nicholas Flamel had said. "Flamel said we smelled of wild magic."

Josh sniffed deeply. "But I can't smell anything. No fruit or oranges or vanilla ice cream. Maybe we don't smell until that happens."

"If we managed to make it back home, we could head out to Utah to Mom and Dad. We could stay with them for the rest of the summer until all this blows over."

"That's not a bad idea," Josh said. "No one would find us in the desert. And right now, the hot, boring, sandy desert sounds really attractive."

Sophie turned to look at the door. "There's only one problem. This place is a maze. Do you think you can find the way back to the car?"

"I think so." He nodded. "Actually, I'm sure of it."

"Let's go, then." She checked her pocket for her dead cell phone. "Let's get your stuff."

The twins paused by the door of Sophie's room and peered up and down the corridor. It was deserted and in almost total darkness except where irregular clumps of arm-length crystals emitted a milky white light.

Somewhere in the distance, a sound that was caught between laughter and screaming echoed down the corridors. With their rubber-soled sneakers making no sound on the floor, they darted across the corridor into Josh's room.

"How did we ever get into this mess?" Josh wondered out loud.

"I guess we were just in the wrong place at the wrong time," Sophie said. She had remained standing by the door, watching the corridor. But even as she was saying the words, she was beginning to suspect that there was more to it than that. There was something else going on, something to do with the prophecy that Flamel had referred to, something to do with them. And the very idea terrified her.

The twins slipped into the corridor and moved through the circular rooms, taking their time, peering into each one before entering. They kept stopping, listening as snatches of conversations in almost recognizable languages or music played on unidentifiable instruments floated down the corridor. Once, a high-pitched howl of maniacal laughter sent them ducking into the nearest room as it seemed to approach, then disappear again. When they crept back out of the room, they noticed that all the light crystals in the corridor had dimmed to a bloodred glow.

"I'm glad we didn't see what passed by," Josh said shakily.

Sophie grunted a response. Her brother was in the lead; she followed two steps behind, her hand on his shoulder. "How do you know where we're going?" she whispered, bringing her mouth close to his ear. All the rooms looked identical to her.

"When we first came into the house, I noticed that the walls and floor were dark, but as we moved down the corridors, they became lighter and paler in color. Then I realized that we were walking through different shades of wood, like the rings of a tree trunk. All we have to do is to follow the corridor that leads to the dark wood."

"Smart," Sophie said, impressed.

Josh glanced over his shoulder and grinned. "Told you those video games weren't a waste of time. The only way not to get lost in the maze games is to watch for clues, like patterns on the walls or ceilings, and to keep a note of your steps so you can retrace them if you need to." He stepped out into a corridor. "And if I'm right, the main door should be . . . there!" he finished triumphantly.

The twins fled across the vast open field in front of the huge tree house, and made their way to the tree-lined pathway that led back to the car. Even though night had fallen, they had no problem seeing. The moon hung bright and low in the heavens, and the sky was filled with an extraordinary number of brilliant stars, which combined with a swirling band of silvery dust high in the sky to give the night a peculiar grayish luminescence. Only the shadows remained pitch black.

Although it wasn't cold, Sophie shivered: the night *felt* wrong. Josh pulled off his hooded sweatshirt and draped it over his sister's shoulders. "The stars are different," she muttered. "They're so bright." Craning her neck, she looked up into the heavens, trying to peer through the branches of the Yggdrasill. "I can't see the Big Dipper, and the North Star is missing."

"And there was no moon last night," Josh said, nodding to where the full moon was rising huge and yellow-white over the treetops. "No moon in our world," he added solemnly.

Sophie stared hard at the moon. There was something about it . . . something *wrong*. She tried to identify the familiar craters, and then felt her stomach lurch with a sudden realization. Her hand, when she pointed upward, was trembling. "That's not our moon!"

Josh looked hard, squinting against the glare. Then he saw what his sister was talking about. "The surface is . . . *different*. Smoother," he said softly. "Where are the craters? I can't see Kepler, Copernicus or even Tycho."

"Josh," Sophie said quickly, "I think we're looking at the night sky as it was thousands of years ago, maybe hundreds of thousands of years ago." Sophie tilted her head and looked up. Josh was startled to see that the moonlight gave her face a skeletal appearance, and he quickly looked away, disturbed.

He had always been close to his sister, but the last few hours had served to remind him just how important she was to him.

"Didn't Scathach say that Hekate had created this Shadowrealm?" Josh asked. "I bet it's modeled on the world she remembered."

"So this *is* the night sky and the moon as they were thousands of years ago," Sophie said in awe. She wished she had her digital camera with her, just to capture the extraordinary image of the smooth-faced moon.

The twins were looking into the heavens when a shadow flickered across the face of the moon, a speck that might have been a bird . . . except that the wingspan was too wide, and no bird had that serpentlike neck and tail.

Josh grabbed his sister's hand and pulled her toward the car. "I'm really beginning to hate this place," he grumbled.

The SUV was where they had left it, parked in the center of the path. The moon washed yellow light across the shattered windshield, the broken patterns in the starred glass picked out in shadow. The brilliance also highlighted the scars on the car's body, the scratches and gouges in sharp relief. The roof was studded with hundreds of tiny holes where the birds had pecked through the metal, the rear window wiper dangled by a thread of rubber and the two side mirrors were completely missing.

The twins regarded the SUV silently, the full realization of the bird attack beginning to sink in. Sophie ran a finger down a series of scratches in the window on the passenger side of the car. Those few millimeters of glass were all that had protected her flesh from the birds' claws.

"Let's go," Josh said, pulling open the door and sliding into the driver's seat. The keys were where he had left them, in the ignition.

"I feel a little bad, running out on Nicholas and Scatty without saying anything," Sophie said as she pulled open the door and climbed in. But the immortal Alchemyst and the Warrior would be better off without them, she reckoned. They were more than able to defend themselves; the last thing they needed was two teenagers slowing them down.

"We'll apologize if we ever see them again," Josh said. He privately thought he would be happy never to see either of them again. Playing video games was all fine and well. When you were killed in a game, you just started again. In this Shadowrealm, though, there were no second chances, and a lot more ways to die.

"Do you know how we get out of here?" Sophie asked.

"Sure." Her brother grinned, his teeth white in the moonlight. "We reverse. And we don't stop for anything."

Josh turned the key in the ignition. There was a metallic click and a whining sound, which quickly descended into silence. He turned the key again. This time there was only the click.

"Josh . . . ?" Sophie began.

It took him just a moment to figure out what had happened. "The battery's dead. Probably drained by the same force that drained our phones," Josh murmured. He swiveled around in the seat to stare through the scarred rear window. "Look, we came down that path behind us; we didn't turn left or right. Let's make a run for it. What do you think?" He turned back to look at his sister, but she wasn't looking at him, she was staring through the windshield in front of her. "You're not even listening to me."

Sophie reached over, took her twin's face in her hand and turned his head toward the windshield. He looked, blinked, swallowed hard, then reached over to push down the locks on the doors. "What now?" he asked.

Crouching directly in front of them was a creature that was neither bird nor serpent, but something caught in between. It stood about the size of a tall child. Moonlight dappled its snakelike body and shone weakly through outstretched batlike wings, the tiny bones and veins etched in black. Clawed feet dug deeply into the soft ground, and a long tail lashed to and fro behind it. But it was the head that held their attention. The skull was long and narrow, eyes huge and round, the gaping mouth filled with hundreds of tiny white teeth. The head tilted first to one side and then the other, and then the mouth snapped open and closed. The creature took a hop closer to the car.

There was movement in the air behind it, and a second creature, even bigger than the first, dropped from the night skies. It folded its wings and stood upright as it turned its hideous head toward the car.

"Maybe they're vegetarians," Josh suggested. Leaning over the driver's seat, he rummaged in the back of the car, looking for something he could use as a weapon.

"Not with those teeth," his sister said grimly. "I think

they're pterosaurs," she said, remembering the huge suspended skeleton she had seen in the Texas Natural Science Center.

"Like pterodactyls?" Josh asked, turning back. He had found a small fire extinguisher.

"Pterosaurs are older," Sophie said.

A third pterosaur dropped from the night sky, and like three hunched old men, the creatures began to advance on the car.

"We should have stayed in the tree," Sophie muttered. They'd been warned, hadn't they? Stay in your rooms, don't leave . . . and after everything they'd seen so far, they should have guessed that Hekate's Shadowrealm at night was a dangerous and deadly place. Now they were facing something out of the Cretaceous period.

Josh opened his mouth to reply, then closed it again. He pulled the retaining pin out of the fire extinguisher, arming it. He wasn't sure what would happen if he fired off a blast of the gas at them.

The three creatures split up. One approached from the front of the car; the remaining two moved toward the driver and passenger windows.

"Wish we knew some magic now," Sophie said fervently. She could feel her heart tripping in her chest and was aware that her tongue seemed far too large for her mouth. She felt breathless and light-headed.

The largest pterosaur leaned across the hood of the car, resting its huge wings on the scarred metal to support itself. Its long, snakelike head darted forward to peer into the body of the car, and it slowly looked from Sophie to Josh and then back to Sophie. Seen this close, its mouth was enormous, its teeth endless.

Josh positioned the nozzle of the fire extinguisher against one of the many holes in the windshield and aimed it at the pterosaur. His eyes were darting left and right, watching the approach of the other two creatures, and his hands were sweating so heavily that he was finding it difficult to hold the fire extinguisher.

"Josh," Sophie whispered, "do something. Do something now!"

"Maybe the gas in the extinguisher will scare them away," Josh replied, unconsciously lowering his voice to a whisper. "Or poison them or something . . ."

"And why would you want to do that?" The pterosaur tilted its head to look at Josh, mouth working, teeth glinting. The words were full of clicking pops and stops, but the language was English. *"We are not your enemy."*

CHAPTER TWENTY

*E*ven for Bel Air, the area of L.A. renowned for its extravagant properties, the house was extraordinary. Vast and sprawling, built entirely of white travertine marble, and accessible only by a private road, it occupied a sixty-acre estate surrounded by a twelve-foot wall topped by an electric fence. Dr. John Dee had to wait for ten minutes outside the closed gates while an armed security guard checked his identity and another guard examined every inch of the car, even scanned beneath it with a small camera. Dee was glad he'd chosen a commercial limousine service, with a human driver; he wasn't sure what the guards would have made of a mud Golem.

Dee had flown in from San Francisco late in the afternoon on his private jet. The limousine, booked by his office, had picked him up from Burbank—now renamed Bob Hope Airport, he noted—and driven him down to Sunset Boulevard through some of the most appalling traffic he had encountered since he'd lived in Victorian London.

For the first time in his very long life, Dee felt as if events were slipping out of his control. They were moving too quickly, and in his experience, that was when accidents happened. He was being rushed by people—well, not *people,* exactly, more *beings*—too eager for results. They had made him move against Flamel today, even though he'd told them he needed another few days of preparation. And he'd been right. Twenty-four more hours of planning and surveillance would have enabled him to snatch Nicholas as well as Perenelle, and the entire Codex. Dee had warned his employers that Nicholas Flamel could be tricky indeed, but they hadn't listened to him. Dee knew Flamel better than anyone. Over the centuries he had come close to catching him—very close—but on every occasion, Flamel and Perenelle had managed to slip away.

Sitting back in the air-conditioned car while the guards continued their inspections, he recalled the first time he had met the famous Alchemyst, Nicholas Flamel.

John Dee was born in 1527. His was the world of Queen Elizabeth I, and he had served the Queen in many capacities: as an advisor and a translator, a mathematician and an astronomer, and a personal astrologer. It had been left to him to choose the date of her coronation, and he had picked noon on January 15, 1559. He promised the young princess that hers would be a long reign. It lasted for forty-five years.

Dr. John Dee was also the Queen's spy.

Dee spied for the English Queen across Europe and was her most influential and powerful agent operating on the Continent. As a renowned scholar and scientist, magician and alchemist, he was welcomed at the courts of kings and the palaces of nobles. He professed to speak only English, Latin and Greek—though in actuality, he spoke a dozen languages well, and understood at least a dozen more, even Arabic and a smattering of the language of Cathay. He learned early on that people were often indiscreet when they didn't know that he understood their every word, and he used that to his fullest advantage. Dee signed his confidential and coded reports with the numbers 007. He thought it wonderfully ironic that hundreds of years later when Ian Fleming created James Bond, he gave Bond the same code name.

John Dee was one of the most powerful magicians of his age. He had mastered necromancy and sorcery, astrology and mathematics, divination and scrying. His journeys across Europe brought him into contact with all the great magicians and sorcerers of that time . . . including the legendary Nicholas Flamel, the man known as the Alchemyst.

Dee discovered the existence of Nicholas Flamel—who had supposedly died in 1418—entirely by accident. That encounter was to shape the rest of his life and, in so many ways, influence the history of the world.

Nicholas and Perenelle had returned to Paris in the first decade of the sixteenth century, and were working as physicians, tending to the poor and sick in the very hospitals the Flamels had founded more than a hundred years earlier. They were living and working virtually in the shadow of the great

Cathedral of Notre Dame. Dee was in Paris on a secret mission for the Queen, but the moment he saw the slender dark-haired man and his green-eyed wife working together in the high-ceiling wards of the hospital, he knew who they were. Dee was one of the few people in the world who had a copy of Flamel's masterwork, *The Summary of Philosophy*, which included an engraving of the famous Alchemyst opposite the title page. When Dee had introduced himself to the doctor and his wife, calling them by their true names, neither had denied it. Of course, they also knew of the famous Dr. John Dee by reputation. Although Perenelle had had some reservations, Nicholas had been delighted with the opportunity to take on the English magician as a new apprentice. Dee had immediately left England and spent the next four years training with Nicholas and Perenelle in Paris.

And it was in Paris, in the year 1575, that he had first learned of the existence of the Elder Race.

He had been studying late at night in his tiny attic room in Flamel's house when a creature out of a nightmare had slithered down the chimney, scattering coal and wood as it crawled out onto the scorched mat. The creature was a gargoyle, one of the ancient breed of ghouls that infested the sewers and graveyards of most European cities. Similar to the crude shapes carved in stone that decorated the cathedral almost directly opposite the house, this was a living creature of veined, marble-like flesh and cinder black eyes. Speaking in an archaic form of Greek, the gargoyle invited him to a meeting on the roof of the Cathedral of Notre Dame. Recognizing that this invitation was not one he could refuse, Dee followed the creature into the night. Loping along, sometimes on two legs, often on four, the gargoyle led him through increasingly narrow alleys, then down into the sewers, and eventually into a secret passageway that took him deep within the great cathedral's walls. He followed the gargoyle up the thousand and one steps carved into the interior of the wall that finally led onto the roof of the Gothic cathedral.

"Wait," it had commanded, and then said no more. Its mission accomplished, the gargoyle ignored Dee and settled down on the parapet, hunched forward, wings folded over its shoulders, tail curled tightly against its back, tiny horns visible as they jutted from its forehead. It peered over the square far below, tracking the movements of the late-night stragglers or those who had no homes to go to, looking for a suitable meal. If anyone had chanced to glance up, the gargoyle would have been indistinguishable from any of the countless stone carvings on the building.

Dee had walked to the edge of the roof and looked across the city. All of nighttime Paris was laid out below him, thousands of winking lights from cooking fires, oil lamps and candles, the smoke rising straight up into the still air, the countless dots of light split by the black curve of the Seine. From this height, Dee could hear the buzz of the city—a low drone, like a beehive settling down for the night—and smell the noxious stench that hung over the streets—a combination of sewers, rotting fruit and spoiled meat, human and animal sweat and the stink of the river itself.

Perched over the cathedral's famous rose window, Dee waited. The study of magic had taught him many things—

especially the value of patience. The scholar in him enjoyed the experience of standing on the roof of the tallest building in Paris, and he wished he'd brought his sketch pad with him. He contented himself with looking around, committing everything he saw to his incredible memory. He recalled a recent visit to Florence. He had gone there to examine the diaries of Leonardo da Vinci. They were written in a strange cipher which no one had been able to break: it had taken him less than an hour to crack the code—no one had realized that Leonardo had written his diaries not only in code, but in mirror image. The diaries were full of many amazing drawings for proposed inventions: guns that fired many times, an armored coach that moved without the need of horses, and a craft that could sail beneath the sea. There was one, however, that particularly interested Dee: a harness that da Vinci claimed would allow a man to take to the air and fly like a bird. Dee had not been entirely convinced that the design would work, though he wanted nothing more in the world than to fly. Looking out over Paris now, he began to imagine what it would be like to strap da Vinci's wings to his arms and sail out over the roofs.

His thoughts were interrupted as a flicker of movement caught his attention. He turned to the north, where a shape was moving in the night sky, a black shadow trailing scores of smaller dots. The smaller shapes looked as if they could be birds . . . except that he knew that birds rarely fly at night. Dee knew immediately and without question that this was what he had been brought up here to meet. He concentrated on the larger shape as it came closer, trying to make sense of

185

what he was seeing, but it was only when the figure dropped onto the roof that he realized he was looking at an ashen-faced woman dressed entirely in black, wearing a long cloak of crow's wings.

That night, Dr. John Dee first met the Morrigan. That night, he learned of the Elder Race and how they had been forced from the world of men by the magic in the Book of Abraham the Mage, a book that was currently in the possession of Nicholas Flamel. That night, Dee learned that there were those among the Elders who wanted to return to their rightful place as the rulers of mankind. And that night, the Crow Goddess promised Dee that he would one day control the entire world, he would be master of an empire that stretched from pole to pole, from sunrise to sunset. All he had to do was to steal the Book from Flamel and hand it over.

That night, Dr. John Dee became the champion of the Dark Elders.

It was a mission that had taken him across the world, and into the many Shadowrealms that bordered it. He had fought ghosts and ghouls, creatures that had no right to exist outside of nightmares, others that were left over from a time predating the arrival of the humani. He had gone to battle at the head of an army of monsters and had spent at least a decade wandering lost in an icy Otherworld. Many times, he had been concerned for his safety, but he had never been truly frightened . . . until this moment, sitting before the entrance to a Bel Air estate in twenty-first-century Los Angeles. In those early days he had not been fully aware of the powers of the creatures he served, but nearly four and a half centuries in their service had taught him many things . . . including the fact that death was probably the least of all the punishments they could inflict on him.

The armed security guard stepped back and the high metal gates clicked open, allowing Dee's car to sweep in on the long white stone driveway toward the sprawling marble mansion that was just visible through the trees. Although night had fallen, no lights were showing in the house, and for a moment Dee imagined that no one was at home. Then he remembered that the person—the *creature*—he had come to meet preferred the hours of darkness and had no need of lights.

The car turned into the circular drive in front of the main entrance, where the headlights picked up a trio of people standing on the bottom step. When the car finally crunched to a halt on the white gravel, a figure stepped up to the door and pulled it open. It was impossible to make out any details in the gloom, but the voice that came out of the darkness was male, and spoke to him in heavily accented English. "Dr. Dee, I presume. I am Senuhet. Please, come in. We've been expecting you." Then the figure turned away and strode up the steps.

Dee climbed out of the car, brushed off his expensive suit and, conscious that his heart was fluttering, followed Senuhet into the mansion. The other two figures fell into step on either side of him. Although no one said anything, Dee knew they were guards. And he wasn't entirely sure they were human.

The magician recognized the heavy, cloying scent as soon

as he stepped into the house: it was frankincense, the rare and incredibly expensive aromatic gum from the Middle East, used in ancient times in Egypt and Greece and as far to the east as China. Dee felt his eyes water and his nose twitch. Those of the Elder Race were particularly fond of frankincense, but it gave him a headache.

As the three shadowy figures led Dee into the great hallway, he caught a glimpse of Senuhet: a small, slender man, bald and olive skinned. He looked as if he was of Middle Eastern origin, from Egypt or Yemen. Senuhet pushed closed the heavy front door, spoke two words—"Stay here"—and then disappeared into the darkness, leaving Dee in the company of the two silent guards.

Dee looked around. Even in the shadowy half-light, he could see that the hallway was bare. There was no furniture on the tiled floor, there were no pictures or mirrors on the walls, no curtains on the windows. He knew that there were houses like this scattered across the world, homes to those few Dark Elders who liked to walk in the world of men, usually creating mischief. Though they were extraordinarily skilled and dangerous, their powers were extremely limited because of the proliferation of iron in the modern world, which served to dull their magical energies. In the way that lead was poisonous to humans, iron, the metal of mankind, was deadly to the Elder Race. Dee knew, even without looking, that there would not be a scrap of that particular metal in this house. Everything would be made of gold or silver, even down to the door handles and the taps in the bathrooms.

The Dark Elders valued their privacy; their preference was

for quiet, out-of-the-way places—small islands, patches of desert, countries like Switzerland, portions of the former Soviet Union, the arctic reaches of Canada, Himalayan temples and the Brazilian jungle. When they chose to live in cities like this one, their houses were secured behind walls and wire, the grounds patrolled by armed guards and dogs. And if anyone was lucky or foolish enough to actually reach the house, they would encounter older, darker and more lethal guards.

"This way."

Dee was pleased that he'd managed to control his fright at the sound of Senuhet's voice; he hadn't heard the man return. Would they go up or down? he wondered. In his experience those of the Elder Race fell into two neat categories: those who preferred to sleep on roofs and those who preferred basements. The Morrigan was a creature of attics and roofs.

Senuhet stepped into a puddle of light and Dee noted now that his eyes were painted with black kohl, the top lid completely blackened, two horizontal lines running from the corners of his eyes to his ears. Three vertical white lines were painted on his chin, beneath his lips. He led Dee to a concealed door directly under the broad staircase and opened it with a password in the language that the boy king Tutankhamen would have spoken. Dee followed the figure into a pitch-black corridor and stopped when the door clicked shut behind them. He heard the man moving ahead of him, then his footsteps clicking on stairs.

Down. Dee should have guessed that the Dark Elder the Morrigan had sent him to see would be a creature of basements and tunnels. "I'll need light," he said aloud. "I don't want to fall down the stairs in the dark and break my neck." His voiced echoed slightly in the confined space.

"There is no electricity in this house, Dr. John Dee. But we have heard that you are a magician of note. If you wish to create light, then you are permitted to do so."

Without a word, Dee stretched out his hand. A blue spark snapped to life in his palm. It buzzed and hissed, spinning about, then it started to grow, from the size of a pea to that of a grape. It gave off a cold blue-white light. Holding his hand out in front of him, Dee started down the stairs.

He began to count the steps as he descended, but quickly gave up, distracted by the decorations on the walls, the ceiling and even the floor. It was like stepping into an Egyptian tomb, but, unlike any of the countless tombs he had seen, where the artwork was faded, chipped and broken and everything was coated in a fine layer of gritty sand, here the decorations were pristine, brilliant and complete. The colors, slightly distorted by the blue light he was carrying, looked as if they had just been laid down, the pictographs and hieroglyphs were vivid and crisp, the names of gods picked out in thick gold leaf.

A sudden updraft caused the blue-white ball of light to flicker and dance in his hand, sending the shadows leaping and darting. Dee's nostrils flared: the wind carried the stench of something old . . . old and long dead.

The stairs ended in a wide, vaulted cellar. Dee felt something crunch and snap beneath his feet with his first step. He lowered his hand and the blue-white light shone across the floor . . . which was covered with countless tiny white bones, blanketing the ground in an ivory carpet. It took Dee a long moment before he recognized the bones as those of rats and mice. Some of them were so old that they crumbled into white powder when he disturbed them, but others were much newer. Unwilling to ask a question to which he really did not want an answer, Dee followed his silent guide, bones crunching and crackling with every step. He lifted his hand high, shedding light across the chamber. Unlike the stairwell, however, this room was unadorned, the walls streaked black with moisture, green mold gathering close to the floor, sprouting fungi dappling the ceiling.

"Looks like you have a problem with damp," Dee said unnecessarily, simply to break the growing silence.

"It is of no matter," Senuhet said quietly.

"Have you been here long?" Dee wondered, glancing around.

"In this place?" The other man paused, considering. "Less than a hundred years. No time at all, really."

A shape moved in the shadows. "And we will not be here much longer. That is why you are here, isn't it, Dr. Dee?" The voice was a cross between a sultry growl and a purr, shaping the English words with difficulty. Almost against his will, Dee raised his hand, allowing the light in his palm to illuminate the tall, slender figure that moved in the gloom. The light moved over bare feet, toenails black and pointed like claws, then up a heavy white kiltlike skirt studded with stones and precious jewels, and a chest crisscrossed with wide straps etched with Egyptian characters—and finally reached the head.

Although he knew what he was going to see, Dee couldn't prevent the gasp of shock from escaping his lips as he looked at Bastet. The body was that of a woman, but the head that brushed the arched ceiling belonged to a cat, sleek and furred, with huge yellow slit-pupiled eyes, a long pointed snout and high triangular ears. The mouth opened and Dee's cold light ran across gleaming yellow teeth. This was the creature that had been worshipped for generations throughout the land of Egypt.

Dee licked dry lips as he bowed deeply. "Your niece, the Morrigan, sends her regards and has asked me to relay the message that it is time to take your revenge on the three-faced one."

Bastet surged forward and wrapped razor-tipped claws in the folds of Dee's expensive suit coat, punching holes in the silk. "Precisely . . . tell me *precisely* what my niece said," she demanded.

"I've told you," Dee said, looking up into the terrifying face. Bastet's breath smelled of rotten meat. He tossed the blue-white ball of light into the air, where it hung, suspended and whirling, then he carefully removed Bastet's claws from his jacket. The coat was a shredded ruin.

"The Morrigan wants you to join her in an attack on Hekate's Shadowrealm," Dee said simply.

"Then it *is* time," Bastet announced triumphantly.

The ancient magician nodded, shadows racing and dancing on the walls with the movement. "It is time," he agreed, "time for the Elder Race to return and reclaim this earth."

Bastet howled, the sound high-pitched and terrifying,

192

and then the darkness behind her boiled and shifted as thousands of cats of every breed, of all shapes and sizes, poured into the cellar and gathered around her in an ever-widening circle. "It is time to hunt," she announced, "time to feed."

The cats threw back their heads and mewled and howled. Dee found the din utterly terrifying: it sounded like countless lost babies crying.

CHAPTER TWENTY-ONE

Scathach was waiting by the enormous open doors when Sophie and Josh returned to the tree. The pterosaur hopped along behind them, and the other two circled low in the sky over their heads, the downdraft of their wings setting eddies of dust circling and dancing around them. Although nothing was said, the twins knew they were being gently—but firmly—herded back toward the house.

In the gloom, Scathach's face was unnaturally pale, her cropped red hair black in the shadows. Although her lips were set in a grim line, her voice, when she spoke, was carefully neutral. "Do you really want me to tell you just how stupidly dangerous that was?"

Josh opened his mouth to reply, but Sophie caught his arm, silencing him. "We just wanted to go home," she said simply, tiredly. She already knew what the Warrior was going to say.

"You cannot," Scathach said, and turned away.

The twins hesitated at the door, then turned to look back at the pterosaur. It tilted its snakelike head and regarded them with a huge slit-pupiled eye, and its voice echoed flatly in their heads. *"Don't worry too much about Scathach; her bark is much worse than her bite."* The creature opened its mouth to show hundreds of triangular teeth in what might have been a smile. *"I do believe she was worried about you,"* it added, then turned away, ran in a series of short hops and took to the air with a crack of wings.

"Don't say a word," Sophie warned her brother. Josh's quips and comments were always getting him into trouble. Whereas Sophie had the ability to see something and keep her mouth shut, her brother always had to make a comment or observation.

"You're not the boss of me," Josh snapped, but his voice was shaky. Josh had a fear of snakes going back to the time he'd gone camping with their father and had fallen into a rattlcsnake nest. Luckily, the deadly serpent had just fed and had chosen to ignore him, giving him the seconds he'd needed to scramble away. He'd had nightmares about snakes for weeks after that, and still did occasionally, when he was particularly stressed—usually at exam time. The huge, serpent-like pterosaurs belonged to his darkest nightmares, and when they'd come hopping out of the night, he'd felt his heart hammering so powerfully that the skin on his chest had actually pulsed. When that long-toothed face had leaned toward him, he'd been sure he was going to faint. Even now, he could feel the icy sweat trickling along the length of his spine.

Sophie and Josh followed Scathach through Hekate's house. The twins were aware now of movement in the shadows, floorboards creaking underfoot, wooden walls popping and cracking as if the house were moving, shifting, growing. They were also conscious that the voices, the screams and shouts of earlier, had fallen silent.

Scathach led them to an empty circular room where Nicholas Flamel was waiting. He stood facing away from them, hands clasped tightly against the small of his back, and stared out into the shadowed night. The only light in the room came from the huge moon now starting to dip toward the horizon. One side of the room was bathed in harsh silver-white light, the other was in darkness. Scatty crossed the room to stand beside the Alchemyst. She folded her arms across her chest and turned to the twins, her face an expressionless mask.

"You could have been killed," Flamel said very softly, without turning around. "Or worse."

"You can't keep us here," Josh said quickly, his voice sounding too loud in the silence. "We're not your prisoners."

The Alchemyst glanced over his shoulder. He was wearing his tiny round glasses and, in the gloom, his eyes were hidden behind the silver circles. "No, you're not," he said very quietly, his French accent suddenly pronounced. "You are the prisoners of circumstance, of coincidence and chance . . . if you believe in such things."

"I don't," Scathach muttered.

"Neither do I," Nicholas said, turning around. He took off his glasses and squeezed the bridge of his nose. There were dark circles under his pale eyes, and his lips were pinched in a thin line. "We are all prisoners of a sort here—prisoners of circumstance and events. Nearly seven hundred years ago, I bought a battered secondhand book written in an incomprehensible language. That day I too became a prisoner, trapped as securely as if I were behind bars. Two months ago, Josh, you should never have asked me for a job, and you, Sophie, should never have started working in The Coffee Cup. But you did, and because you made those decisions you are both standing here with me tonight." He paused and glanced at Scathach. "Of course, there is a school of thought that suggests that you were fated to take the jobs, to meet Perenelle and me and to come on this adventure."

Scathach nodded. "Destiny," she said.

"You're saying that we have no free will," Sophie asked, "that all this was meant to happen?" She shook her head. "I don't, for one minute, believe that." The very idea went against everything she believed; the idea that the future could be foretold was simply ludicrous.

"Neither do I," Josh said defiantly.

"And yet," Flamel said very softly, "what if I were to tell you that the Book of the Mage—a book written more than ten thousand years ago—speaks of you?"

"That's impossible," Josh blurted, terrified by the implications.

"Ha!" Nicholas Flamel spread his arms wide. "And is this not impossible? Tonight you encountered the nathair, the winged guardians of Hekate's realm. You heard their voices in your heads. Are they not impossible? And the Torc Allta—

197

are they not equally impossible? These are creatures that have no right to exist outside of myth."

"And what about us?" Scathach asked. "Nicholas is nearly seven hundred years old, and I am so old I have seen empires rise and fall. Are we not equally impossible?"

Neither Josh nor Sophie could deny that.

Nicholas stepped forward and put a hand on Josh's and Sophie's shoulders. He was no taller than they were and looked directly into their eyes. "You must accept that you are trapped in this impossible world. If you leave, you will bring destruction onto your family and friends, and in all probability, you will bring about your own deaths."

"Besides," Scathach added bitterly, "if you're mentioned in the Book, then you're supposed to be here."

The twins looked from Scatty to Flamel. He nodded. "It's true. The book is full of prophecies—some of which have certainly come true, others which may yet come to pass. But it does specifically mention 'the two that are one.'"

"And you believe . . . ?" Sophie whispered.

"Yes, I believe you may be the prophecy. In fact, I am convinced of it."

Scathach stepped forward to stand beside Flamel. "Which means that you are suddenly much more important—not only to us, but also to Dee and the Dark Elders."

"Why?" Josh licked dry lips. "Why are we so important?"

The Alchemyst glanced at Scatty for support. She nodded. "Tell them. They need to know."

The twins looked from Scatty back to the Alchemyst. There was a sense that what he was about to tell them was of immense importance. Sophie slipped her hand into her brother's, and he squeezed her fingers tightly.

"The Codex prophesies that the two that are one will come either to save or to destroy the world."

"What do you mean, *either* save or destroy?" Josh demanded. "It's got to be one or the other, right?"

"The word used in the Codex is similar to an ancient Babylonian symbol that can mean either thing," Flamel explained. "Actually, I've always suspected that it means that one of you has the potential to save the world, while the other has the power to destroy it."

Sophie nudged her brother in the ribs. "That would be you."

Flamel stepped back from the twins. "In a couple of hours, when Hekate arises, I will ask her to Awaken your magical potential. I believe she will do it; I hope and pray that she does," he added fervently. "Then we will leave."

"But where are we going?" Josh asked at the same time that Sophie said, "Will Hekate not allow us to stay here?"

"I'm hoping some of the other Elders or immortal humans might be persuaded to help train you. And no, we cannot stay here. Dee and the Morrigan have contacted one of the most fearsome of the Elders: Bastet."

"The Egyptian cat goddess?" Sophie asked.

Flamel blinked in surprise. "I'm impressed."

"Our parents are archaeologists, remember? While other children were being read bedtime stories, our parents told us myths and legends."

The Alchemyst nodded. "Even as we speak, Bastet and

the Morrigan are gathering their forces for an all-out attack on Hekate's Shadowrealm. I suspected that they would try and attack during the hours of darkness, when Hekate is sleeping, but so far there is no sign of them, and it will be dawn soon. I'm sure they know that they will only get one chance, and they need all their forces in place before they attack. At the moment, they believe we are still ignorant of their intentions; more importantly, they do not know that we are aware of Bastet's involvement. But we will be ready for them."

"How *do* we know?" Sophie asked.

"Perenelle told me," Flamel said, and waved away the next obvious question. "She is a resourceful woman, she enlisted a disembodied spirit to pass on a message to me."

"A disembodied spirit?" Sophie said. "You mean like a ghost?" She realized that now it was quite easy to believe in ghosts.

"Just so," Flamel said.

"What will happen if they attack here? I mean, what kind of attack are we talking about?" Josh asked.

Flamel looked at Scatty. "I was not alive the last time beings of the Elder Races warred with one another."

"I was," Scatty said glumly. "The vast majority of humani will not even know anything is happening." She shrugged. "But the release of magical energies in the Shadowrealms will certainly have an effect on the climate and local geology: there may be earthquakes, a tornado or two, hurricanes and rain, lots of rain. And I really hate the rain," she added. "One of the reasons I left Hibernia."

"There must be something we can do," Sophie said. "We have to warn people."

"And what form would that warning take?" Flamel asked. "That there is about to be a magical battle that may cause earthquakes and flooding? Not something you can phone in to your local news or weather station, is it?"

"We have to—"

"No, we don't," the Alchemyst said firmly. "We have to get you and the pages from the Book away from here."

"What about Hekate?" Josh asked. "Will she be able to defend herself?"

"Against Dee and the Morrigan, yes. But with Bastet as their ally, I simply don't know," Scatty answered. "I don't know how powerful the goddess is."

"More powerful than you can imagine."

They all turned toward the door, where a girl who looked no older than eleven stood blinking and yawning widely. She rubbed a hand against her bright yellow eyes and stared at them, then smiled, her teeth startlingly white against her jet-black skin. She was wearing a short togalike robe of the same iridescent material that the crone Hekate had worn, but this time the dress was streaked with golds and greens. Her ice-white hair curled down to her shoulders.

The Alchemyst bowed. "Good morning. I did not think you rose before the dawn."

"How could I sleep with all this activity?" Hekate demanded. "The house awakened me."

"The house . . . ," Josh began.

"The house," Hekate said flatly, "is alive."

There were a dozen comments Josh could have made, but remembering the green slime from the previous night, he wisely decided to keep his mouth shut.

"I understand that the Morrigan and my Elder sister Bastet are planning an assault on my Shadowrealm," the girl said grimly.

Nicholas glanced quickly at Scathach, who shifted her shoulders slightly in a shrug. She had no idea how Hekate knew.

"I am sure you understand that everything that happens in this house, every word said or whispered—or even thought," Hekate added, glancing sidelong at Josh, "I hear." The girl smiled and, in that instant, looked like the older versions of herself. The smiled curled her lips, but did not light up her eyes. She walked into the room, and Sophie noticed that as she moved, the house reacted to her presence. Where she had stood in the doorway, green shoots had sprouted, and the lintel and doorsill had blossomed tiny green flowers. The Goddess with Three Faces stopped before Nicholas Flamel and looked up into his troubled eyes. "I would have preferred that you not come here. I would have preferred that you not bring trouble into my life. I would have preferred not to go to battle with my sister and my niece. And I would most certainly have preferred not to be forced to choose sides."

Scathach folded her arms across her chest and regarded the goddess grimly. "You never did like to choose sides, Hekate—no wonder you have three faces."

Sophie was watching Hekate as Scathach spoke, and for an instant she glimpsed something dark and immeasurably old behind the girl's eyes. "I have survived the millennia because I heeded my own counsel," Hekate snapped. "But I have chosen sides when the struggle was worth it."

"And now," Nicholas Flamel said very softly, "I think it is time to choose again. Only you can decide, however: is this a worthy struggle?"

Hekate ignored the question and spun around to face Sophie and Josh. Her tiny hand moved in the air and immediately the auras around the twins flared to silver and golden light. She tilted her head to one side, looking at them, watching the silver bubbles crawling along the cocoon that enveloped Sophie, and following the tracery of golden veins that moved up and down Josh's aura. "You may be right," she said eventually, "these may indeed be the ones spoken of in the cursed Codex. It has been many centuries since I've encountered auras so pure. They possess incredible untapped potential."

Flamel nodded. "If I had the time, I would take them to be properly trained, gradually Awaken their dormant powers . . . but events have conspired against me, and time is that one precious commodity I do not have. It is within your power to unlock their potential. You can do something in an instant that it would normally take years to do."

Hekate glanced over her shoulder at the Alchemyst. "And there are good reasons why it should take many years," she said dismissively. "The humani barely use their senses. Yet you are proposing to Awaken these two to their full potential.

I will not do it: the sensory overload could destroy them, drive them mad."

"But—" Flamel began.

"I will not do it." She turned back to the twins. "What he is asking me to do could kill you—if you are lucky," she said, and then turned and swept from the room, leaving little grassy footprints in her wake.

CHAPTER TWENTY-TWO

$\mathcal{T}$he twins were speechless for a moment. Then Josh began, "What did she mean . . . ?"

But Nicholas hurried past him, following Hekate out into the hallway. "She's exaggerating," he called back over his shoulder. "Trying to frighten you."

"Well, it worked," Josh muttered. He looked at Scathach, but she turned her back and walked into the garden. "Hey," he called, hurrying after her, "come back. I've got questions." He felt a quick surge of anger; he was tired of being treated like a child. He—and his sister—deserved some answers.

"Josh," Sophie warned.

But her brother darted past her and reached for Scathach's shoulder. His fingers never even touched her. Suddenly, he was caught, twisted, turned and then spun through the air. He hit the ground hard enough to drive the breath from

205

his lungs, and he found himself staring down the length of Scathach's sword, the tip of which she held rock steady between his eyes. When she spoke, her voice was little more than a whisper. "Last night you insulted a goddess of the Elder Race; today you've managed to irritate one of the Next Generation—and it's not even dawn yet," she added. The Warrior Maid sheathed her sword and looked over at a stunned Sophie. She hadn't even seen Scathach move. "Is he always like this?" Scatty asked.

"Like what?" Sophie asked.

"Foolish, ill-advised, reckless . . . ? Shall I go on?"

"No need. And yes, he's usually like this. Sometimes worse." When they were growing up, she used to tease Josh that he got all the "doing" genes, whereas she got the "thinking" genes. Her brother was both impulsive and reckless, but to be fair, she thought, he was also loyal and trustworthy.

Scathach pulled Josh to his feet. "If you continue at this rate, you'll not last long in this world."

"I just wanted to ask you a few questions."

"You're lucky. A couple of centuries ago, I probably would have killed you. I used to have a bit of a temper," she admitted, "but I've been working on my self-control."

Josh rubbed the small of his back. If Scathach had smashed him down on the stones, he could really have been hurt, but he recognized that she'd been careful to drop him onto the grass and moss. "That felt like a judo throw," he said shakily, attempting to sound casual and change the subject.

"Something like that . . ."

"Where did you learn judo, anyway?"

"I didn't learn judo. I created the distant ancestor of most of the martial arts that are studied today," the red-haired warrior said, bright green eyes flashing wickedly. "In fact, it would do neither of you any harm if I were to show you a few simple moves."

"I think we can do better than simple," Josh said. "We studied tae kwon do for two years when our parents were teaching in Chicago, and we did a year of karate in New York . . . or was that Boston?"

"You created judo?" Sophie asked, keeping her voice carefully neutral.

"No, Kano Jigoro created modern judo, but he based his fighting system on jujitsu, which is related to aikido, which evolved around the fourteenth century. I believe I was in Japan around then. All martial arts have a common root. And that's me," Scatty said modestly. "Come, if you know a little tae kwon do and karate, that's useful. Let me show you some basic moves while we're waiting for Nicholas."

"Where is he?" Sophie asked, looking back over her shoulder at the house. What was going on in there? "Is he asking Hekate to Awaken our magical potential?"

"He is," Scatty affirmed.

"But Hekate said that could kill us!" Josh said in alarm. He was beginning to suspect that Flamel's agenda was about more than just protecting him and his sister. The Alchemyst was up to something.

"She was only guessing," Scatty said. "She's always been a bit of a drama queen."

"Then Nicholas is sure we're in no danger?" Josh said.

"No, he's not really sure." Scatty smiled. "But believe me, you are in danger. The only difference is if Hekate Awakens you, then you'll be in *grave* danger."

Nicholas Flamel followed Hekate through the house. The young woman's fingers trailed along the walls, leaving streaks of bright wood touched with leaves and flowers in her wake. "I need your help, Hekate. I cannot do this alone," he called after her.

The goddess ignored him. She turned down a long, straight corridor and darted ahead. Her feet left little puddles of green grass that grew even as Flamel hurried after her. By the time he was halfway down the corridor it was knee high, then waist high, and suddenly, the entire corridor was covered in the tall, razor-sharp grass. Its blades whispered softly together, sounds that might almost have been words.

Nicholas Flamel allowed a little of his growing anger to seep into his aura. Closing his right hand into a fist, he suddenly splayed his fingers and the air was touched with the rich, tart odor of mint. The grass directly ahead of him flattened as if it had been hit with a strong wind, and the Alchemyst was just in time to see the young woman step into a room set slightly apart from the rest of the house. If he had delayed a moment longer, he would have walked right past the opening.

"Enough of these games," Flamel snapped, stepping into the room.

Hekate spun to face him. She had aged in the few moments she had spent running down the corridor. She now looked about fifteen. Her face was set in an ugly mask and her yellow eyes were bitter. "How dare you speak to me that way!" She raised her hands threateningly. "You know what I can do to you."

"You would not dare," Flamel said with a calm that he did not feel.

"And why not?" Hekate asked, surprised. She was not used to being contradicted.

"Because I am the Guardian of the Book."

"The book you lost . . ."

"I am also the Guardian who appears in the prophecies in the Book," Flamel snapped. "The next-to-last Guardian," he added. "The twins also appear in the book. You say you knew Abraham—you know then how accurate his prophecies and foretellings were."

"He was often wrong," Hekate muttered.

"As Guardian, I am asking you to do something I believe to be essential to the survival of not only the Elder Race, but humani, too: I want you to Awaken the twins' magical potential."

"It could kill them," the goddess stated flatly. She didn't really care if the humani cattle lived or died.

"That is a possibility," Flamel admitted, feeling something icy settle in the pit of his stomach, "but if you do not help us, then their deaths are a certainty."

Hekate turned and walked to the window. Across the sloping lawn, Scathach was demonstrating a series of punches for the twins. They were smoothly mimicking her moves. Flamel went to join Hekate by the window.

"What a world we live in," he commented, sighing, "when everything—possibly even the continuance of the human race—lies on the shoulders of those teenagers."

"You know why the humani triumphed and the Elder Race was ultimately banished?" Hekate asked suddenly.

"Because of iron, wasn't it?"

"Yes, because of iron. We survived the Fall of Danu Talis, we survived the Flood, and the Age of Ice. And then, about three thousand years ago, a single metalworker, who had been crafting in bronze, began to experiment in the new metal. He was just one man—and yet he managed to wipe out an entire race of people and a way of life. Great change always comes down to the actions of a single person." Hekate fell silent, watching the twins punch and kick next to Scathach. "Silver and gold. The rarest of all auras," she muttered, and for a single heartbeat, the auras bloomed around the twins. "If I do this and it kills them, will you be able to live with it on your conscience?"

"I am old now, so old," Nicholas said very softly. "Do you know how many friends I've buried over the centuries?"

"And did you feel their loss?" There was a note of genuine curiosity in Hekate's voice.

"Every one."

"Do you still?"

"Yes. Every day."

The goddess reached out and placed her hand on his shoulder. "Then you are still human, Nicholas Flamel. The day you stop caring is the day you become like Dee and his kind." She turned back to the garden and looked at the

210

twins. They were both trying, and failing, to land blows on Scathach, who was ducking and weaving, though not moving from the one spot. From the distance they looked like three ordinary teenagers practicing a new dance, but Hekate knew that there was nothing ordinary about any of them.

"I'll do it," she said eventually, "I'll Awaken their powers. The rest is up to you. You will have to train them."

Flamel bowed his head so she would not see the tears in his eyes. If the twins survived the Awakening, then there was a chance, albeit a slim one, that he would get to see Perenelle again. "Tell me," he began, then coughed to clear his throat. "The man who discovered how to process iron—that blacksmith three thousand years ago. What happened to him?"

"I killed him," Hekate said, her yellow eyes wide and innocent. "His actions destroyed us. What else could I do? But it was too late. The secret of iron had been introduced into the world."

Flamel looked at the twins, watched Josh haul his sister to her feet, watched her hook a leg behind his and drop him to the ground. Their laughter hung bright and clear in the predawn air. He prayed that they were not too late this time.

CHAPTER TWENTY-THREE

The cats of San Francisco left the city in the dead of night.

Singly and in pairs, feral and scarred street cats, plump, smooth-coated house cats, all shapes, every size, purebred and mixed, long-haired and short-haired, they moved through the shadows in a silent feline wave. They surged across the bridges, boiled through alleys, raced through the tunnels beneath the streets, leapt across roofs.

All heading north.

They darted past shocked and terrified late-night revelers, skirted rats and mice without stopping to feed, ignored birds' nests. And although they moved in complete silence, their passage was marked by an extraordinary sound.

That night the city of San Francisco echoed with the primeval howls of a hundred thousand dogs.

Dr. John Dee was unhappy.

And just a little bit frightened. It was all very well to talk about attacking Hekate in her own Shadowrealm, but it was another thing entirely to sit at the entrance to her invisible kingdom and watch the cats and birds arrive, called by their respective mistresses, Bastet and the Morrigan. What could those small creatures do against the ancient magic of Hekate of the Elder Race?

Dee sat in a huge black Hummer alongside Senuhet, the man who acted as Bastet's servant. Neither of them had spoken during the short flight in Dee's private jet from L.A. to San Francisco earlier, though there were a thousand questions Dee wanted to ask the older man. Over the years he had come to recognize that the servants of the Dark Elders—like himself—did not like to be questioned.

They had reached the entrance to Hekate's Shadowrealm close to two o'clock, and were in time to see the first of the Morrigan's creatures arriving. The birds swooped in from the north and east in long, dark flocks, the only sound the snapping of their wings, and settled in the trees in Mill Valley, gathering so thickly that some of the branches cracked beneath the strain.

Over the next few hours, the cats arrived.

They poured out of the darkness in a never-ending stream of fur, and then stopped—all facing the hidden opening to the Shadowrealm. Dee looked out his car window: he couldn't see the ground. It was covered, as far as he could see in every direction, with cats.

Finally, just as the eastern horizon began to pale with

salmon-colored light, Senuhet lifted a small black statue from a bag he wore around his neck and placed it on the dashboard. It was a beautifully carved Egyptian cat no bigger than his little finger. "It is time," he said softly.

The eyes of the black statue glowed red.

"She is coming," Senuhet said.

"Why didn't we attack earlier, when Hekate slept?" Dee asked. Despite several hundred years of study about the Dark Elders, he realized that, in truth, he knew very little. But that gave him some comfort, because he realized that they knew equally little about humans.

Senuhet waved his hand, gesturing to the gathered birds and cats. "We needed our allies," he said shortly.

Dee nodded. He guessed that Bastet was even now moving through the various Shadowrealms that bordered the human world. The Elder Race's aversion to iron meant that certain modern conveniences—like cars and planes—were off limits to them. His thin lips curled in a humorless smile; that was why they needed people like him and Senuhet to act as their agents.

He felt, rather than saw, the birds move in the trees: half a million—maybe more—heads turned to the west. He followed their gaze, looking toward the darkest spot in the sky. At first, he could see nothing, but then a shape appeared high in the heavens, noticeable only because it blotted out the stars. The Morrigan was coming.

Dee knew that at the heart of every legend there is a grain of truth. Looking up into the night sky, watching the pale-faced creature appear out of the west, her feathered cloak spread behind her like enormous wings, Dee believed he knew where the legends of the Nosferatu vampires originated. Over the course of his long life, he had met vampires—real ones—and none of them were as terrifying as the Crow Goddess.

The Morrigan settled to the ground directly in front of the Hummer, cats scattering at the last moment as she folded her cloak and landed. In the gloom, only the white oval of her face was visible; her eyes were as black as night, looking like holes burned in paper.

Then the cats growled, a low rumbling that trembled through the very air, and Bastet stepped out of the shadows. The Cat Goddess was wearing the white cotton robes of an Egyptian princess and holding a spear that was as tall as she was. She strode through the sea of cats, which parted before her and closed in behind. Towering over the Morrigan, she bowed deeply to the Crow Goddess. "Niece, is it time?" she purred.

"It is," the Morrigan replied, returning the bow. Shrugging back her cloak, she revealed a longbow strapped across her shoulders. She unslung the bow and notched an arrow from the quiver at her hip.

Then, turning as one, the two Dark Elders raced toward the seemingly impenetrable hedge and leapt through.

The cats and birds flowed after them.

"Now it begins," Senuhet said gleefully, gathering his weapons—two curved Egyptian bronze swords—and climbing out of the car.

Or ends, Dee thought, but he kept his fears to himself.

FRIDAY, *1st June*

CHAPTER TWENTY-FOUR

$\mathcal{J}$osh stood at the edge of the ancient forest with his sister and watched a trio of tiny winged creatures that looked astonishingly like dragons whirl and dance through the first shafts of dawn sunlight. Josh glanced at her, then looked quickly away. "I don't want you to do this," he said quickly.

Sophie laid her hand on her brother's arm. "Why not?" she said. She moved in front of her twin, forcing him to look at her. Over his left shoulder, in front of the entrance to the incredible Yggdrasill, she could see Flamel, Scatty and Hekate watching them. All around, thousands of Torc Allta, both in their human and wereboar forms, were scurrying about, preparing for battle. The boars wore plates of leather armor across their haunches and backs, and the human Torc Allta were carrying bronze spears and swords. Huge flocks of nathair swooped across the skies and the bushes, and tall grasses were alive with unseen crawling, slithering, scuttling creatures. Guards were taking up positions all around the Yggdrasill, clambering out onto the huge branches, standing guard with bows and spears in every window.

Sophie looked into her brother's bright blue eyes. She could see herself reflected there, and she abruptly realized that his eyes were magnified behind unshed tears. She reached for him, but he caught her hand and squeezed her fingers gently. "I don't want anything to happen to you," he said simply.

Sophie nodded, unwilling to trust herself to speak. She felt exactly the same way about her twin.

Three of the enormous pterosaur-like nathair flew overhead, the downdraft of their wings sending plumes of dust along the ground below. Neither Sophie nor Josh looked up.

"Nicholas said that there are risks," Josh continued, "but Hekate said that it's dangerous, possibly even deadly. I don't want you to go through with this Awakening in case something goes wrong," he finished quickly.

"We have to do it. Nicholas said—"

"I'm not entirely sure I trust him," Josh interrupted. "I have a feeling he's up to something. He's too eager for Hekate to Awaken our powers despite the dangers."

"He said it's our only chance," Sophie persisted.

"Yesterday, he said he had to get us away from the shop to keep us safe . . . now, all of a sudden, we have to be trained so that we can protect ourselves from Dee and these Dark Elders. Trust me, Sophie, Nicholas Flamel is playing his own game."

Sophie's gaze drifted to the Alchemyst. She'd known him for a couple of months, and she remembered writing in her blog that she thought he was *cool*. Of course, now she realized that she didn't really know him at all. The man she'd thought of as Nick Fleming was an imposter. A lie. Flamel was staring intently at her, and for the briefest of moments, she imagined that he knew what they were talking about.

"Both of us don't have to go through this Awakening," Josh continued. "Let me do it."

Again, Sophie looked into his eyes. "And how do you think I'd feel if something happened to you?"

This time it was Josh who found he couldn't speak. The idea that something terrible could happen to his sister had only occurred to him a little while before. But the very thought of it terrified him.

Sophie took her brother's hands in hers. "From the moment we were born, we've done everything together," she said, her voice low and serious. "And with Mom and Dad away so much, it's really always been just you and me. You've always looked after me, I've always looked out for you. I'm not going to allow you to go through this . . . process by yourself. We'll do this—just like we've done everything else—together."

Josh looked long and hard at his sister. "Are you sure?" he asked. He was beginning to see a new Sophie.

"I've never been more sure."

They both knew what remained unsaid: neither wanted to be left behind if anything happened during the Awakening.

Josh finally nodded. He then squeezed his sister's hand and they both turned to face the Alchemyst, Hekate and Scatty.

"We're ready," the twins said.

"The Morrigan is here," Scatty informed them as they followed Nicholas and Hekate through the huge door into the heart of the tree. She had changed into black pants, a high-necked black T-shirt that left her arms bare and thick-soled combat boots. She wore two short swords strapped to her back, the hilts protruding slightly over her shoulders, and had daubed her eyes and cheekbones with a black dye that gave her face a startlingly skull-like appearance. "She's brought Bastet with her. They're already surging into the Shadow-realm."

"Hekate can hold them back, can't she?" Sophie asked. She only had an inkling of the goddess's powers, but the thought that there was something more powerful than her was terrifying.

Scatty shrugged. "I have no idea. They've arrived in force; they've brought their armies with them."

"Armies?" Josh echoed. "What kind of armies? More mud people?"

"No Golems this time. They have brought the birds of the air and the cats of the earth with them."

Sophie laughed shakily. "Birds and cats . . . what can *they* do?"

Scatty glanced at the girl, the whites of her eyes startling against the black war paint. "You saw what the birds did to the car on the way here."

Sophie nodded, suddenly feeling sick in the pit of her stomach. Images of the filthy black crows battering the windshield and pecking holes in the metal hood would haunt her to her dying day.

"Well, imagine what would happen if tens of thousands of birds gathered."

"Tens of thousands," Sophie whispered.

"More like hundreds of thousands," Scatty said, turning into a narrow corridor. "The nathair scouts estimate maybe half a million."

"And didn't you say something about cats?" Josh asked.

"Yes, I did. More than we can count."

Josh looked at his sister, the realization of the terrible danger they faced really beginning to sink in now. They could die in this strange Shadowrealm and no one would ever know. He felt tears prickling his eyes and blinked them away; their parents would spend the rest of their lives wondering what had happened to them.

The corridor they were following turned into another, even narrower passageway. The ceiling was so low that both twins had to walk with their heads ducked down. There were no steps or stairs, but the corridor circled down and down in a long, slow spiral. The twins realized that they were going into the ground deep beneath the tree. The walls became darker, the smooth wood now scarred with straggling roots that curled out and pulled at their hair with clutching fingers.

The air turned damp, perfumed with loam and fresh earth, rotting leaves and new growth.

"The house *is* alive," Sophie said in wonder as they turned into another twisting, spiraling corridor that was completely composed of the gnarled and bulbous roots of the great tree that rose above them. "Even with us moving around inside, with the rooms and the windows and the pools—it's still a living tree!" She found the idea both astonishing and frightening at the same time.

"This tree was grown from a seed of the Yggdrasill, the World Tree," Scatty said quietly, rubbing the palm of her hand against the exposed roots. She brought her palm to her face and breathed deeply, drawing in the aroma. "Millennia ago, when Danu Talis sank beneath the waves, a few of the Elders were able to rescue some of the flora and fauna and transplant it to other lands. But only two of the Elders, Hekate and Odin, managed to nurture their Yggdrasill seeds to life. Odin, like Hekate, had power over magic."

Josh frowned, trying to remember what little he knew about Odin. Wasn't he the one-eyed Norse god? But before he could ask, Hekate disappeared into an opening framed by knots of twisted roots. Nicholas Flamel stopped and waited for the twins and Scatty to catch up. His pale eyes were deeply shadowed, and a thin vertical crease showed between his eyebrows. When he spoke, he chose his words with care, his nervousness making his French accent even more pronounced. "I wish you did not have to do this," he said, "but you must believe me when I say that there is no other way." He reached out and put one hand on Sophie's right shoulder and one on Josh's left shoulder. Their auras—silver and gold—flared briefly, and the heavy air was touched with the scents of vanilla ice cream and oranges. "I'm afraid that when you helped Perenelle and me, you placed yourselves in the most dreadful danger. If—*when* Hekate Awakens your magical potential, I will teach you some protective spells, and there are others I will take you to, specialists in the five ancient forms of magic. I'm hoping they will complete your training."

"We're going to be trained as magicians?" Sophie asked. She guessed she should be more excited, but she kept remembering Scatty's words, that once Hekate Awakened their powers, they would be in *grave* danger.

"As magicians and sorcerers, as necromancers, warlocks and even enchanters." Flamel smiled. He glanced over his shoulder, then turned back to the twins. "Now go inside and do whatever she tells you. I know you are afraid, but try not to be. Let me tell you, there is no shame in fear." He smiled, his lips curling upward, but the smile never reached his troubled eyes. "When you come out of that room, you will be different people."

"I don't want to be a different person," Sophie whispered. She wanted everything to be just as it had been a couple of hours earlier, when everything was ordinary and boring. Right now, she would give anything to go back to a boring world.

Flamel stepped back from the doorway and ushered the twins inside. "From the moment you laid eyes on Dee, you started to change. And once begun, change cannot be reversed."

✧ ✧ ✧

It was dark inside the chamber, whose walls were composed entirely of knotted and twisted roots. Sophie could feel her brother's hand in hers and she squeezed his fingers slightly. His hand tightened in return.

As the twins moved deep into the hollow, which was obviously larger than it had first seemed, their eyes gradually adjusted to the gloom and the room took on a greenish glow. Thick, furry moss covered the twisted roots and radiated a watery jade green light, making it appear as if everything were underwater. The air was heavy with moisture, and drops of liquid gathered on their hair and skin like tiny beads of sweat. Although it wasn't cold, they both shivered.

"You should consider yourselves honored." Hekate's voice came from the green gloom directly ahead of them. "I have not Awakened a humani for many generations."

"Who . . . ," Josh began, and then his voice cracked. He gave a dry cough and tried again. "Who was the last human you Awakened?" He was determined not to let his fear show.

"It was some time ago—in the twelfth century, as you humani measure time—a man from the land of the Scots. I do not remember his name."

Both Sophie and Josh instinctively knew that Hekate was lying.

"What happened to him?" Sophie asked.

"He died." There was a peculiar high-pitched giggle. "He was killed by a hailstone."

"Must have been some hailstone," Josh whispered.

"Oh, it was," Hekate murmured. And in that moment, they both knew that she had something to do with the mysterious man's death. To Josh the goddess suddenly seemed like a vindictive child.

"So what happens now?" Josh asked. "Do we stand or sit or lie down?"

"You do nothing," Hekate snapped, "and this is not something to be done lightly. For thousands of generations, you humani have deliberately distanced yourselves from what you laughingly call magic. But magic is really only the utilization of the entire spectrum of the senses. The humani have cut themselves off from their senses. Now they see only in a tiny portion of the visible spectrum, hear only the loudest of sounds, their sense of smell is shockingly poor and they can only distinguish the sweetest and sourest of tastes."

The twins were aware that Hekate was moving about them now. They couldn't hear her move, but were able to track her by the sound of her voice. When she spoke from behind them, they both jumped.

"Once, mankind needed all those senses simply to survive." There was a long pause, and when she spoke again, she was so close that her breath ruffled Sophie's hair. "Then the world changed. Danu Talis sank beneath the waves, the Age of the Lizards passed, the Time of Ice came, and the humani grew . . . *sophisticated*." She made the word into a curse. "The humani grew indolent and arrogant. They found they did not need all their senses, and gradually, they lost them."

"You're saying we lost the powers of magic because we grew lazy," Josh said.

Sophie suppressed a groan; one of these days her brother was going to get them into real trouble.

But when Hekate replied, her voice was surprisingly soft, almost gentle. "What you call magic is nothing more than an act of the imagination fired by the senses, then given shape by the power of your aura. The more powerful the aura, the greater the magic. You two have extraordinary potential within you. The Alchemyst is correct: you could be the greatest magicians the world has ever known. But here's the problem," Hekate continued, and now the room grew a little lighter, and they could see the shape of the woman standing in the center of the room, directly beneath a tangle of roots that looked exactly like a clutching hand reaching down from the roof. "The humani have learned to live without their senses. The brain filters so much data from your consciousness that you live in a type of fog. What I can do is Awaken your dormant powers, but the danger—the very real danger—is that it will overload your senses." She stopped, then asked, "Are you prepared to take that risk?"

"I am," Sophie said immediately, before her brother could protest. She was afraid that if he made a quip, the goddess would do something to him. Something ugly and lethal.

The goddess turned to look at Josh.

He sought out his sister in the gloom. The green light lent her face a sickly cast. The Awakening was going to be dangerous, possibly even deadly, but he could not allow Sophie to go through it on her own. "I'm ready," he said defiantly.

"Then we will begin."

CHAPTER TWENTY-FIVE

Dee waited until the last of the birds and cats had disappeared into Hekate's Shadowrealm before he left the car and strolled toward the hidden opening. Senuhet, Bastet's servant, had left earlier, eagerly following his mistress into the Shadowrealm, but Dee had not been quite so enthusiastic. It was always a bad idea to be first into battle. The soldiers in the rear were the ones who tended to survive. He was guessing that Hekate's guards had massed just beyond the invisible wall, and he had no inclination to be first through the opening. It didn't make him a coward, he reasoned; it just made him careful, and being careful had kept him alive for many hundreds of years. But he couldn't hang around out there forever; his inhuman masters would expect to see him on the battlefield. The small man drew his two-thousand-dollar leather coat tightly around his shoulders the moment before he stepped into the opening, leaving behind the chill early-morning air and stepping into . . .

. . . a battlefield.

There were bodies everywhere, and none of them were human.

The Morrigan's birds had changed when they entered Hekate's Shadowrealm: they had become almost human . . . though not entirely so. They were now tall and thin like their mistress; their wings had stretched, becoming long and bat-like, connected to human-shaped bodies by translucent skin and tipped with deadly claws. Their heads were still those of birds.

There were a few cats scattered among the field of feathers. They too had become almost human when they stepped into the Shadowrealm, and like Bastet, they had retained their cat heads. Their paws were a cross between human hands and cat claws, tipped with curved, razor-sharp nails, and their bodies were covered in a fine down of hair.

Looking around, Dee could see no sign that any of Hekate's guards had fallen in battle, and was suddenly frightened: what did the goddess have guarding her realm? He reached under his coat, pulled out the sword that had once been called Excalibur and set off down the path to where the huge tree rose out of the morning mist. The sunrise ran blood-red along the ancient black blade.

"Birdmen," Scathach muttered, and then added a curse in the ancient Celtic language of her youth. She hated birdmen; they gave her hives. She was standing at the entrance to the

Yggdrasill, watching the creatures appear out of the forest. The mythologies of every race included stories of men who turned into birds, or birds who transformed into half-human creatures. In her long life Scatty had encountered many of the creatures and had once come perilously close to death when she'd fought a Sirin, an owl with the head of a beautiful woman. Since that encounter, she'd been allergic to bird feathers. Already her skin was starting to itch and she could feel a sneeze building at the back of her nose. The Morrigan's creatures moved awkwardly, like hunched-over humans, dragging their knuckles on the ground. They were poor warriors, but they often succeeded by sheer force of numbers.

Then Bastet's cat-people appeared. They moved slowly, stealthily, some standing on two feet, but most moving on all fours. Here, Scatty knew, was the basis of the great cat legends of Africa and India. Unlike the birds, the cat-people were deadly fighters: they were lightning fast, and their claws were capable of inflicting terrible damage. Scathach sneezed; she was also allergic to cats.

The strange army came to a halt, perhaps awed by the incredible building-sized tree or just confused by the sight of a single warrior standing framed in the open doors. They milled about; then, as if driven by a single command, they surged forward in a long ragged line.

The Warrior twisted her head from side to side and rolled her shoulders, and then her two short swords appeared in her hands. She raised them above her head in an *X*.

It was the signal the Torc Allta and the nathair had been waiting for. Seemingly from nowhere, hundreds of the terrifying lizards hurtled out of the sky, with the sun at their backs, and swooped over the advancing army. They flew in great sweeping circles, their huge wings raising enormous plumes of gritty dust that blinded and confused the birds and cats. Then the Torc Allta, who had been lying concealed in the tall grass and behind the twisting roots of the Yggdrasill, rose in the middle of the attackers. As Scatty hurried back into the depths of the house, she realized how closely the noises of the battle resembled feeding time at the San Francisco Zoo.

"We're running out of time," Scathach yelled to Flamel as she raced into the corridor.

"How many?" Nicholas asked grimly.

"Too many," Scatty replied. She paused briefly and then added, "The Torc Allta and nathair will not be able to hold them for long."

"And the Morrigan and Bastet?"

"I didn't see them. But you can be sure they're coming, and when they do . . ." She left the sentence unfinished. With Hekate busy Awakening the twins, nothing would be able to stand against the two Dark Elders.

"They'll come," he said grimly.

Scatty stepped closer to Flamel. They had known each other for over three hundred years, and although she was his senior by nearly two millennia, she had come to regard him as the father she no longer remembered. "Take the twins and flee. I'll hold them here. I'll buy you as much time as possible."

The Alchemyst reached out and placed his hand on the Warrior's shoulder and squeezed. A tiny pop of energy snapped between them and they both briefly glowed. When he spoke, he unconsciously reverted to the French language of his youth. "No, we'll not do that. When we leave here, we go together. We need the twins, Scatty—not just you and me, but the entire world. I believe that only they will be able to stand against the Dark Elders and keep them from achieving their ultimate aim and reclaiming the earth."

Scatty looked over his shoulder into the gloomy chamber. "You're asking a lot of them. When are you going to tell them the whole truth?" she asked.

"In time . . . ," he began.

"Time is something you do not have," Scatty murmured. "You've started to age. I can see it in your face, around your eyes, and there's more gray in your hair."

Flamel nodded. "I know. The immortality spell is breaking down. Perenelle and I will begin to age a year for every day we go without the formulation for immortality. We will be dead by the end of the month. But by then it will not matter. If the Dark Elders succeed, the world of the humani will have already ceased to exist."

"Let's make sure that doesn't happen." Scatty turned her back on Flamel, then sank to the ground, back straight, her legs folded, feet turned high on her thighs in a full lotus position, arms outstretched, palms wrapped around the hilts of the swords that were lying across her lap. If the cats or birds broke into the house and found the corridor, they would have to get past her to find Hekate—and the Warrior would make them pay dearly.

Hekate had given Flamel a short staff made of a branch of the Yggdrasill, and now, holding it in both hands, he took up a position directly outside the door to the chamber where the goddess was working with the twins. If any of the invaders did manage to get past Scathach, they would then face him. Scatty would fight with her swords, hands and feet, but his weapons were potentially even more destructive. He held up his hand and the narrow space grew heavy with the smell of mint as his aura flickered and sparked into green life around him. Though he was still powerful, every use of magic weakened him and drew on his life force. Scatty was right; he had started to age. He could feel tiny aches and vague pains where there had been none before. Even his eyesight was no longer as sharp as it had been only the day before. If he was forced to use his powers, it would speed the aging process, but he was determined to give Hekate all the time she needed. He turned to look over his shoulder, trying to penetrate the gloom. What was happening in there?

"We will start with the elder," Hekate announced.

Sophie could feel her brother drawing a breath to protest, but she squeezed his fingers so tightly that she could actually feel his bones grinding together. He kicked her ankle in response.

"It is traditional," the goddess continued. "Sophie . . ." She paused, then said, "What is your family name, your parents' names?"

"Newman . . . and my mother's name is Sara, my father is Richard." It felt odd calling her parents anything other than Mom and Dad.

The green light in the chamber brightened and they could see Hekate outlined against the glowing walls. Although her face was in darkness, her eyes reflected the green light like chips of polished glass. She reached out and placed the palm of her hand against Sophie's forehead. "Sophie, daughter of Sara and Richard, of Clan Newman, of the race humani . . ."

She began in English, but then drifted into a lyrically beautiful language that predated humanity. As she spoke, Sophie's aura began to glow, a misty silver light outlining her body. A cool breeze wafted across her skin and she was suddenly conscious that she was no longer hearing Hekate. She could see the goddess's mouth moving, but she could not make out the words over the sounds of her own body—the breath hissing in and out of her nose, the rush of blood in her ears, the solid beat of her heart in her chest. There was a pressure on her temples, as if her brain were expanding inside her skull, and an ache ran the length of her spine and spread outward into all her bones.

Then the room began to lighten. Hekate—looking older now—was standing outlined in shifting streams of sparkling lights. Sophie suddenly realized that she was seeing the goddess's aura. She watched as the lights twisted and curled around Hekate's arm and flowed down into her fingers, and then, with a tingling shock, Sophie could actually feel it penetrating her skull. For an instant she was dizzy, disorientated, and then, through the buzzing in her ears, Hekate's words abruptly started to make sense. ". . . I Awaken this terrible power within you. . . ." The goddess moved her hands over Sophie's face, her touch like ice and fire. "These are the senses the humani have abandoned," Hekate continued. She pressed her thumbs lightly against Sophie's eyes.

"To see with acuity . . ."

Sophie's vision bloomed, and the darkened chamber came to blazing light, every shadow picked out in exquisite detail. She could see each thread and stitch on Hekate's robe, could pick out individual hairs on her head and follow the map of tiny wrinkles that were visibly growing at the corners of her eyes.

"To hear with clarity . . ."

It was as if cotton had been pulled from Sophie's ears. Suddenly, she could *hear*. It was like the difference between listening to music on her iPod headphones and then to the same track on her bedroom stereo. Every sound in the room magnified and intensified: the wheezing of her brother's breath through his nostrils, the tiny shifting creaks of the huge tree above them, the scritch-scratching of invisible creatures moving through the roots. Tilting her head slightly, she could even hear the distant sounds of battle: the screeching of birds, the roars of cats and the bellowing of boars.

"To taste with purity . . ."

Hekate's fingers brushed Sophie's lips and suddenly the girl was conscious that her tongue was tingling. She licked her lips, finding traces of the fruit she had eaten earlier and discovering that she could actually taste the air—it was rich

236

and earthy—and even distinguish the water droplets in the atmosphere.

"To touch with sensitivity . . ."

Sophie's skin came alive. The fabrics against her skin—the soft cotton of her T-shirt, the stiff denim of her jeans, the gold chain with her birth sign around her neck, her warm cotton socks—all left different and distinct impressions on her flesh.

"To smell with intensity . . ."

Sophie actually rocked backward with the sudden eye-watering explosion of scents that invaded her: the spicy otherworldly odors of Hekate, the cloying earthiness of her surroundings, her brother's twenty-four-hour deodorant, which was plainly not working, the supposedly unscented gel in his hair, the mint of the toothpaste she had used earlier.

Sophie's aura began to glow, silver mist rising off her skin like fog off a lake. It surrounded her body in a pale oval. She closed her eyes and threw her head back. Colors, smells and sounds were rushing at her: and they were brighter, stronger, louder than any she had ever experienced before. The effect from her heightened senses was almost painful . . . no, it *was* painful. It hurt. Her head throbbed, her bones ached, even her skin itched—everything was just too much. Sophie's head tilted back, and then, almost of their own accord, her arms shot out to either side . . . and she rose four inches off the dirt floor.

"Sophie?" Josh whispered, unable to keep the terror from his voice. "Sophie . . ." His sister, wrapped in an undulating silver glow, was floating in the air directly before him. The light from her body was so strong that it painted the circular chamber in shades of silver and black. It was like a scene from a terrifying horror movie.

"Don't touch her," Hekate commanded sternly. "Her body is attempting to assimilate the wash of sensations. This is the most dangerous time."

Josh's mouth went dry and his tongue was suddenly too big for it. "Dangerous . . . what do you mean, dangerous?" Something in his mind clicked and he felt as if his worst fears were about to be realized.

"In most cases, the brain cannot cope with the heightened sensations of Awakening."

"In *most* cases?" he whispered, appalled.

"In almost every case," Hekate said, and he heard the regret in her voice. "That is why I was unwilling to do this."

Josh asked the question he really didn't want answered: "What happens?"

"The brain effectively shuts down. The person is left in a coma from which they never awaken."

"And Flamel *knew* this could happen?" Josh asked, feeling a great surge of anger begin in the pit of his stomach. He felt sick. The Alchemyst had known the Awakening could, in all likelihood, send him and Sophie into a coma, and yet had still been prepared to let them go through with it. The rage burned within him, fueled in equal parts by fear and a terrible sense of betrayal. He'd thought Flamel was his friend. He'd been wrong.

"Of course," Hekate said. "He told you there were dangers, didn't he?"

"He didn't tell us everything," Josh snapped.

"Nicholas Flamel never tells anyone everything." One side of Hekate's face was touched with the silver light radiating from Sophie, the other was sheathed in black shadow. Suddenly, Hekate's nostrils flared and her eyes widened. She looked up at the ceiling of roots. "No," she gasped. "No!"

Sophie's eyes snapped open and then she opened her mouth and screamed. "Fire!"

"They're burning the World Tree!" Hekate howled, her face contorted into a savage mask. Shoving Josh to one side, she darted out into the corridor, leaving him alone with the person who had once been his twin. He stared at the girl floating in the air before him, unsure what to do, afraid to even touch her. All he knew was that for the first time in their lives, they were different in ways he could not even begin to comprehend.

CHAPTER TWENTY-SIX

"*We* need to go." Nicholas Flamel caught Josh's shoulder and shook him, bringing him back to the present.

Josh turned to look at the Alchemyst. There were tears on his cheeks, but he was unaware of them. "Sophie . . . ," he whispered.

". . . is going to be fine," Nicholas said firmly. Shouts echoed in the corridor outside, the sudden clash of weapons mingling with the roars of humans and animals. Above it all rose Scathach's delighted laughter. Flamel reached for Sophie, who was still floating four inches above the earth, and his aura flared white-green when he took her hand. Gently he pulled her back to the ground. As soon as her feet touched the earth, it was as if all the strength had left her body, and he caught her before she crumpled to the floor, unconscious.

Josh was immediately at his sister's side. He pushed Flamel away and held his twin in his arms. Crackling energy darted from Sophie's fading aura to his flesh, but he didn't even register the tiny stings. When he looked up at Flamel, his face was an angry mask. "You *knew*," he accused, "you knew how dangerous this was. My sister could have been left in a coma."

"I knew that was not going to happen," Nicholas said calmly, crouching down beside Josh. "Her aura—your aura—is too strong. I knew you would both survive. I would never have deliberately placed either of you in danger. I swear that." He reached for Sophie's wrist to check her pulse, but Josh pushed his hand away. He didn't believe him; he wanted to, but somehow Flamel's words rang false.

They both jumped as an agonized, catlike squeal came from the corridor outside. It was followed by Scatty's voice. "We really should be leaving. And right now would be a good time!"

The smell of burning wood was stronger, and tendrils of gray smoke begun to curl into the chamber.

"We've got to go. We can talk about this later," Flamel said firmly.

"You better believe we will," Josh promised.

"I'll help you carry her," the Alchemyst offered.

"I can do it myself," Josh said, and gathered his sister into his arms. He wasn't going to trust Sophie to anyone else. He was surprised by how light she felt, and he was suddenly thankful for all those painful months of football practice that had made him stronger than he looked.

The Alchemyst picked up the short staff he'd left propped against the wall and spun it in the air before him. The tip glowed green and it left the faintest of smoking emerald trails in the air. "Ready?" Flamel asked.

Josh, his sister held tightly against his chest, nodded.

"Whatever happens, whatever you see, don't stop, don't turn back. Just about everything outside this doorway will not hesitate to kill you."

Josh followed Flamel through the door . . . and immediately stopped, frozen in shock. Scatty was standing in the center of the narrow corridor, her two short swords a blur before her. Behind the swords, crowding the corridor, were some of the most terrifying creatures he had ever seen. He'd been expecting monsters; what he had not been expecting were creatures even more terrifying. Creatures that were neither beast nor human, but something caught in between. Humans with the heads of cats snarled and slashed at Scatty, their claws striking sparks off her swords. Others with the bodies of men but with the huge peaked skulls of ravens jabbed at her, attempting to gouge and stab her.

"Scatty—down!" Flamel shouted. Without waiting to see if she even heard him, he stretched out his arm and leveled the short staff. His aura flared green and the air was suddenly bitter with the odor of mint. An emerald-colored globe of spinning light gathered at the tip of the staff and then shot forward with an audible pop. Scatty barely managed to duck before the ball sizzled through the air and shattered against the ceiling almost directly over her head. It left a bright mark, like a stain, which started to dribble and drip sticky green light. The scarred head of a tabby cat pushed through the opening, mouth gaping, fangs glinting. It spotted Scatty and lunged for her—and a drop of the gooey light splashed off the top of its head. The cat-headed human went wild. It threw itself back into the corridor, where it immediately attacked everything in its path. A birdman stepped up to the opening, and was doused in the dripping green light. Its black wings abruptly developed holes and tears, and it fell back with a hideous chattering cawing. Josh noticed that although the green light, which had the consistency of honey, burned the creatures, it had no effect on the wood. He knew he should be paying more attention, but all his concern was focused on his sister. She was breathing quickly, and behind her closed eyelids her eyes were dancing.

Scatty scrambled to her feet and darted back to Flamel and Josh. "Very impressive, I'm sure," she muttered. "I didn't know you could do that."

Flamel spun the staff like a baton. "This focuses my power."

Scatty looked around. "We seem to be trapped."

"Hekate went this way," Nicholas said, turning to the right and pointing to what looked like an impenetrable barrier of knotted roots. "I saw her come running out of the chamber and walk straight through this." He stepped up to the knotted wood and stretched out his arm. It disappeared right up to the elbow.

"I'll go first," Scatty said. Josh noticed that although she had been fighting the deadly combination of birds and cats, there was neither a scratch on her body nor a hair out of place. She wasn't even breathing hard—though if she really was a vampire, then maybe she didn't need to breathe at all, he thought. Scatty darted forward, and in the last moment before she reached the wall of roots, she dived straight into the opening, swords crossed over her chest.

Flamel and Josh looked at one another in the brief moment that followed . . . and then Scatty's head poked through the solid-looking tangle of roots. "All clear."

"I'll take the rear," Flamel said, stepping back to allow Josh to go ahead of him. "I'll deal with anything that follows us."

Josh nodded, unwilling to trust himself to talk to Flamel. He was still furious with the Alchemyst for endangering his sister's life, but he also recognized that Flamel was now fighting for them, placing himself in very real danger to protect them. Josh stepped up to the wall of twisted roots and packed earth, closed his eyes . . . and walked right through. There was an instant of damp chill and then he opened his eyes to see Scatty directly in front of him. He was standing in a low, narrow chamber created entirely from the Yggdrasill's gnarled roots. Clumps of green moss leaked a dim green light into the chamber, and he could see that Scatty was standing at the bottom of a set of narrow, irregular steps that led upward into the gloom. Scatty's head was tilted to one side, but before Josh could ask what she was hearing, Flamel stepped through the wall. He was smiling, and the top of his staff emitted traces of green gas. "That should hold them for a while."

"Let's go," Scatty called as soon as the Alchemyst appeared.

The stairway was so narrow that Josh was forced to move in a sideways crab-crawl, head ducked low, with Sophie held close to his body to prevent her head and legs from cracking against the rough wooden walls. He tested every step before he took it; he didn't want to risk falling and dropping his sister. He suddenly realized that these steps were cut into the space between the inner and outer bark of the great tree, and couldn't help wondering if a tree the size of Yggdrasill was riddled with secret passages, hidden rooms, forgotten chambers and lost stairways. It must be, he decided. Did Hekate even know where they all were? And then, his mind racing, he wondered who had created these steps. Somehow he could not imagine the goddess carving them out of the living wood herself.

As they climbed, they could smell the bitter stench of burning wood, and the sounds of battle came clearer. The cat shrieks became even more human, the bird screeches were completely terrifying, and they mingled with the bellowing roars of the boars and the hissing of the nathair. Now that the group was no longer underground, the heat and smoke intensified and they began to hear another sound—a deep bass groaning rumble.

"We need to hurry." Scatty's voice drifted back out of the gloom. "We *really* need to hurry now. . . ." And somehow the forced calm in the Warrior's voice frightened Josh more than if she had screamed. "Careful now; we've reached an opening. We're at the end of a thick root, about thirty yards away from the main body of the tree. We're well clear of the fighting," she added.

Josh rounded a corner and discovered Scatty standing bathed in shafts of early-morning sunshine that shone through a curtain of vines directly ahead of her. She turned to face him, sunlight turning her red hair golden and running along the blades of her short swords, and in that moment, Josh saw her as the ancient and terrifying Warrior she was. The sounds of battle were all around them, but louder than all the other noises was the groaning rumble that seemed to vibrate deep in the ground. "What is that sound?" he asked.

"The cries of the Yggdrasill," Scatty answered grimly. "Hekate's enemies have set light to the World Tree."

"But why?" He found the very idea horrifying—this ancient living tree had harmed no one. But the action gave him an insight into the contempt with which the Dark Elders held life.

"Her powers are inextricably linked to it; her magic brought it to towering life, its life force keeps her strong. They believe that by destroying it, they will destroy her."

Flamel came panting up the steps to stand behind Josh. The Alchemyst's thin face was bright red and beaded with sweat. "Getting old," he said with a wry smile. He looked at Scatty. "What's the plan?"

"Simple," she began, "we get away from here as quickly as possible." Then she spun the sword in her left hand so that the blade was lying flat against the length of her arm. She pointed with the hilt. Flamel and Josh stood close to her and peered out through the curtain of vines. On the opposite side of the field, Dr. John Dee had appeared, moving cautiously through the undergrowth. The black-bladed short sword that he held in both hands glowed and flickered with a cold blue light.

"Dee," Flamel said. "Never in my life would I have imagined being delighted to see him. This is good news indeed."

Both Scatty and Josh looked at him in surprise.

"Dee is human . . . which means that he came here via human transportation," the Alchemyst explained.

"A car"—Scatty nodded in agreement—"that he would probably have left just outside the Shadowrealm."

Josh was about to ask how she knew he would have left it outside when he suddenly realized he knew the answer. "Because he knew if he drove it in here, the battery would be drained."

"Look," Scatty murmured.

They watched one of the huge, boarlike Torc Alltas emerge from the long grass behind Dee. Although it was still in its beast shape, it rose on its hind legs, until it reached nearly three times the height of the man.

"It's going to kill him," Josh murmured.

Dee's sword flared bright blue, and then the small man threw himself backward, *toward* the Torc Allta, bringing the sword around in a short arc. The sudden movement seemed to surprise the creature, but it easily batted aside the blade . . . and then it froze. Where the blade had touched it, a thin sheath of ice grew up the beast's arm, tiny crystals sparkling in the early-morning sunshine. The ice coated the Torc Allta's chest and flowed down its massive legs and up his shoulders and head. Within a matter of heartbeats the creature was encased in a block of blue-veined ice. Dee picked himself up off the ground, dusted off his coat and then, without warning, hammered on the ice with the hilt of his sword.

The block shattered into millions of tinkling pieces, each one containing a fragment of the Torc Allta.

"One of the elemental swords," Scatty remarked grimly, "Excalibur, the Sword of Ice. I thought it was lost ages past, thrown back into the lake when Artorius died."

"Looks like the doctor found it," Flamel murmured.

Josh discovered that he wasn't even surprised to hear that King Arthur had been real, and he found himself wondering which other legendary figures had really existed.

They watched as Dee hurried back into the undergrowth, heading for the other side of the huge tree house, where the sounds of battle were loudest. The smell of smoke was stronger now. Sharp and bitter, it curled and twisted around the tree, carrying with it the reek of ancient places and long-forgotten spices. Wood snapped and cracked, sap boiled and popped and the deep bass thrumming was now strong enough to set the entire tree vibrating.

"I'll clear the way," Scatty said as she darted through the vines. Almost immediately a trio of the birdmen came winging toward her, followed by two of the cat-people, running on all fours.

"We've got to help her!" Josh said desperately, though he'd no idea what he could do.

"She is Scathach; she doesn't need our help," Flamel said. "She'll lead them away from us first. . . ."

Scathach raced into the undergrowth, running lightly, her heavy boots making no sound on the soft earth. The birds and cats followed.

"She'll back herself up against something, so that they can

only come at her from one side, then she'll turn to face them."

Josh watched as Scatty spun and faced her attackers, with her back to a gnarled oak tree. The cat creatures reached her quickly, claws flashing, but her short swords were quicker, and struck sparks from their claws. A bird-creature swung in low, huge wings flapping, talons extended. Driving the sword in her left hand into the ground, she caught the creature's extended wrist and yanked it out of the air, then tossed it into the middle of the snarling cats. The bird instinctively lashed out at the cats, and suddenly, the animals were fighting among themselves. Two more bird-people immediately dropped onto the cats with a hideous squalling. Scatty yanked her sword out of the ground and used it to beckon to Flamel and Josh.

Flamel tapped Josh's shoulder. "Go. Get to Scathach."

Josh turned to look at the Alchemyst. "What about you?"

"I'll wait a moment, then follow and protect you."

And even though Josh knew Flamel had placed them in terrible danger, he had no doubts that the Alchemyst would watch his back. He nodded, then turned and burst through the curtain of vines and ran, clutching his sister tightly to his chest. Away from the shelter of the tree, the noise of battle was incredible, but he concentrated on the ground directly ahead of him, watching for roots or other irregularities in the earth that could trip him. In his arms, Sophie stirred; her eyes flickered, and she started to move. Josh tightened his grip. "Stay still," he said urgently, though he wasn't sure if she could hear him. He shifted direction, moving to the right, away from the struggling creatures, but he couldn't help noticing that when they were badly injured, they reverted to their original bird and cat shapes. Two bemused-looking cats and three ragged crows picked themselves out of the dirt and watched him run past. Josh could hear Flamel running behind him, could smell the mint on the morning air as the Alchemyst worked his magic. Another ten or fifteen footsteps would take him to Scatty, and Josh knew that once he was with her, he was safe. But when he reached Scatty, he was just in time to see her eyes widen in horror. He looked over his shoulder and saw a tall woman with the head and claws of a sleek feline, wearing the robes of ancient Egypt, leap at least twenty feet and land squarely on Nicholas Flamel's back, driving him into the ground. A curved, sicklelike claw shot out and sliced his short staff neatly in two, then the creature threw back her head and hissed and spat triumphantly.

CHAPTER TWENTY-SEVEN

*P*erenelle Flamel was moved from her tiny underground cell by four small guards dressed entirely in black leather, their heads and faces concealed behind motorcycle helmets. She wasn't entirely sure they were human—certainly she could detect no trace of an aura, a heartbeat or even breathing from the figures. As they crowded around her, she caught the faintest hint of something old and dead, like rotten eggs and overripe fruit. She thought they might be simulacra, artificial creatures grown in vats of putrid bubbling liquid. Perenelle knew that Dee had always been fascinated by the idea of creating his own followers and had spent decades experimenting with Golems, simulacra and homunculi.

Without saying a word, and with jerky gestures, the four figures ushered her out of the cell and down a long, narrow, dimly lit corridor. Perenelle deliberately moved slowly, giving herself time to gather her strength and absorb impressions of the place. Jefferson Miller, the ghost of the security guard, had told her that she was in the basement of Enoch Enterprises, west of Telegraph Hill, close to the famous Coit Tower. She knew she was deep underground: the walls ran with moisture, and the air was so cold that it plumed in clouds before her face. Now that she was out of the cell and away from its protective spells and charms, she felt a little of her strength begin to return. Perenelle desperately tried to think of a spell she could use on the guards, but contact with the ghost of Mr. Miller had left her exhausted, and she had a headache pulsing at the back of her eyes that made it hard to concentrate.

A shape suddenly flickered into existence directly ahead of her. Her breath, a foggy white in the chilly air, had briefly formed a face.

Perenelle glanced at her guards on either side, but they hadn't reacted. She drew in a deep lungful of breath, held it, allowing her body to warm it, and then breathed out in a long, slow exhalation. A face formed in the white mist: that of Jefferson Miller.

Perenelle frowned; his ghost should be long gone by now. Unless . . . unless he had come back to tell her something.

Nicholas!

Instantly, she knew her husband was in danger. Perenelle breathed in another great lungful of air and held it. She concentrated hard on Nicholas, seeing him clearly in her mind's eye, with his narrow, rather mournful-looking face, pale eyes and closely cropped hair. She smiled, remembering him when he'd been younger and his hair, thick and dark, had been longer than hers. He'd always worn it tied back at the nape of his neck with a purple velvet ribbon. She breathed out and the air turned into a white cloud that instantly formed into Jefferson Miller's face again. Perenelle stared into the ghost's eyes, and there, reflected in his pupils, she could see her husband trapped beneath the paw of the cat-headed goddess.

Rage and terror blossomed within her, and suddenly, her headache and exhaustion left her. Her silver-threaded black hair rose from her head as if blown in a strong breeze, sparks of blue and white static snapping along its length. Her ice-white aura flared around her body like a second skin. Too late the guards realized that something was wrong. They reached for her, but the moment their hands touched the glowing edges of her aura, they were catapulted away as if they'd received an electric shock. One guard even threw himself onto her body, but before he could lay a finger on her, Perenelle's aura caught him and propelled him high into the wall with enough force to knock the motorcycle helmet off his head. The figure slid down the wall, arms and legs twisted in awkward positions. When Perenelle looked at his face, she realized that the creatures were indeed simulacra. This one was unfinished: his face and head were simply smooth flesh, bald, without eyes, nose, mouth or ears.

The woman raced down the corridor, only pausing when she came to an oily-looking puddle on the floor. Crouching over the puddle, she concentrated hard and touched the murky water with her index and little fingers. Her white aura sizzled when it touched the liquid, and the water briefly smoked before it cleared and Perenelle found she was looking at the scene she had briefly glimpsed in the ghost's eyes. Her husband was lying under Bastet's claws. Behind them, Scatty was struggling to hold off the attacking cats and birds, while Josh stood with his back to a tree, awkwardly clutching a branch like a baseball bat, striking out at anything that came too close. Sophie lay at his feet, moving slowly, blinking in confusion.

Perenelle glanced up and down the corridor. She could hear noises in the distance, footsteps against stone, and she knew more guards were approaching. She could run and hide or she could fight the guards; she had a little of her strength back. But that wasn't going to help Nicholas and the children.

Perenelle looked back into the puddle. In the distance she could see Hekate withstanding the combined attack of the Morrigan and her birds and Bastet's cats. Perenelle also spotted Dee moving around behind Hekate, the sword in his hand glowing bright, poisonous blue, while behind them the Yggdrasill burned with fierce red and green flames.

There was one other thing she could do. Something desperate and dangerous, and if it succeeded, it would leave her utterly exhausted and completely defenseless. Dee's creatures would simply be able to pick her up and carry her away.

Perenelle didn't think twice.

Crouching over the puddle of dirty water, she placed her right hand, palm up, in her left hand and concentrated fiercely. Perenelle's aura began to shift and move, flowing down her arms like drifting smoke, gathering in the palm of her hand, running like liquid along the creases and lines in her flesh. A tiny speck of silver-white light appeared in the folds of skin. It solidified into a perfect sphere and then it started to spin and grow, and now the ice white threads of her aura flowed more swiftly down her arms. Within a heartbeat the sphere was the size of an egg, and then Perenelle suddenly reversed her palm and thrust the ball of pure auric energy into the water. She uttered three words.

"Sophie. Wake up!"

CHAPTER TWENTY-EIGHT

"*Sophie. Wake up!*"

Sophie Newman's eyes snapped open. And then she squeezed them shut again and pressed her hands against her ears. The lights were so bright, so vivid, the sounds of battle so incredibly clear and distinct.

"*Sophie. Wake up!*"

The shock of hearing the voice again forced her to open her eyes and look around. She could hear Perenelle Flamel as clearly as if she were standing beside her, but there was no one there. She was lying propped against the rough bark of an oak tree, with Josh standing beside her, a thick branch clutched in both hands, desperately beating back terrifying creatures.

Sophie slowly pushed herself to her feet, holding on to the tree for support. The last thing she clearly remembered was the bitter odor of rich green wood burning. She remembered saying "Fire!" and then the rest was a series of confused images—a narrow tunnel, creatures with bird heads and cat skulls—that might have been dreams.

As Sophie's eyes adjusted and she looked around, she realized that they had not been dreams.

They were completely surrounded by birds and cats: hundreds of them. Some of the cat-headed humans lurked in the long grass and attempted to creep toward them on all fours or on their bellies, spitting and clawing. There were bird-men in the branches of the tree overhead, maneuvering to get close enough to drop down, while others kept hopping in, jabbing at Josh with their evil-looking beaks.

On the opposite side of the field, the Yggdrasill burned. The ancient wood snapped and cracked, plumes of white-hot sap boiling up into the pristine air like fireworks. But even as the burnt wood fell away, new growth appeared, fresh and green, in its place. Sophie was conscious of another sound too, and realized she was listening to the Yggdrasill. And now, with her incredibly sensitive hearing, she thought she could make out phrases and words, snatches of songs and fragments of poems within the agonized cries of the burning tree. In the distance, she could see Hekate desperately trying to put out the fires, but she was also fighting the Morrigan, the cats and the birds at the same time. Sophie also noticed that there were no more nathair in the skies, and very few of the Torc Allta remained to guard their ancient mistress.

Closer, Sophie spotted Scatty's bright red hair. She, too, was surrounded by dozens of birds and cats. The Warrior was moving in what looked like an intricate dance, twin swords flashing, sending the creatures howling back from her. Scatty was trying to fight her way over to where Nicholas Flamel was lying facedown on the ground beneath the claws of the most terrifying creature Sophie had ever seen: Bastet, the Cat Goddess. With her incredibly sharp eyesight, the girl could make out the individual whiskers on Bastet's feline face, and she actually saw a droplet of saliva gather on the overlarge fangs and drip onto the man below.

Flamel saw Sophie looking in his direction. He tried to draw a breath, but it was difficult with the heavy creature standing on top of him. "Run," he whispered, "run."

"Sophie, I only have a few moments . . ." Perenelle's voice echoed inside the girl's head, shocking her to full alertness. *"This is what you must do. You must let me speak through you. . . ."*

Josh became aware that his sister was climbing to her feet, swaying slightly, hands pressed to her ears as if the sounds were too much, eyes squeezed tightly shut. He saw her lips move, as if she were talking to herself. He lashed out at a pair of humans with mockingbird heads as they darted forward. The heavy branch caught one of the creatures squarely on the beak, and it staggered back, dazed and stunned. The other continued to circle Josh, who realized that it was not coming for him—it was trying to get to Sophie. He turned and lashed out at it, but at that moment, a tall, slender man with a tabby cat's head came bounding toward him. Josh tried to swing the branch, but he was off balance and the catman ducked under the blow. Then it leapt into the air, mouth gaping, claws extended. With a sour taste at the back of his throat, Josh admitted to himself that he and Sophie were in desperate trouble. He needed to get to his sister, he had to protect her . . . and in that instant, he knew he was not going to make it. He closed his eyes at the last minute as the savage cat-headed creature slammed into his chest, expecting to feel the sting of its claws, to hear its squalling roar in his face . . . but all he heard was a gentle purring. He blinked his eyes open and found he was holding a fluffy kitten in his arms.

Sophie! He turned around . . . and stopped in awe.

Sophie's aura had flared pure silver around her body. It was so dense in places that it even reflected the sunlight, making it appear like a medieval suit of armor. Silver sparks crackled through her hair and dripped from her fingers like liquid.

"Sophie?" Josh whispered, elated. His sister was fine.

And then Sophie slowly turned her head to look at Josh, and he experienced the shocking, sickening realization that she did not recognize him.

The birdman that had been moving in to attack the girl suddenly darted forward, beak stabbing at her eyes. Sophie snapped her fingers: tiny droplets of silver spun away from her hands to splash against the creature. Instantly, it folded and twisted in on itself and became a disorientated hermit thrush.

Sophie walked past her brother and stepped toward Bastet.

"No farther, little girl," Bastet commanded, raising a clawed hand.

Sophie's eyes opened wide and she smiled, and Josh

suddenly found that, for the first time in his life, he was frightened of his own sister. He knew that this wasn't his Sophie; this terrifying creature could not be his twin.

When the girl spoke, her voice was a harsh croak. *"You have no idea what I can do to you."*

Bastet's huge feline eyes blinked in surprise. "You can do nothing to me, little girl."

"I am no girl. You may be ancient, but you have never encountered anything like me. I possess the raw power that can nullify your magic. I can use it to return the birds and cats to their natural forms." Sophie's head tilted to one side, a gesture Josh knew well; his sister did it when she was listening intently to someone. Then she stretched out her hands toward the Dark Elder. *"What do you think would happen if I were to reach out and touch you?"*

Bastet hissed a command, and a trio of huge catmen raced toward the girl. Sophie flung out her arm, and a long, whip-like, snaking coil of silver energy flowed from her hand. It touched each of the cats, crackling across their haunches and shoulders, and they immediately came to stumbling halts, rolling and twisting on the ground as they transformed into ordinary everyday cats, two shorthairs and a ragged-looking Persian. The cats bounded to their feet and streaked off, howling piteously.

Sophie spun the whip above her head, scattering drops of liquid silver in every direction. *"Let me give you a taste of what I can do. . . ."* The silver whip cracked and snapped as she approached.

Scatty suddenly found that three of her adversaries had transformed into an American robin, a house finch, and a song sparrow, while the exotic-looking catman directly in front of her warped into a confused Siamese.

Sophie cracked the silver whip again and again, beating away their attackers, droplets of silver splashing everywhere, and more and more of the cat- and birdmen returned to their natural forms. *"Get away from Nicholas,"* she said, her lips not moving in synch with her words, *"or we will find out what your true shape is, Bastet, who is also Mafdet, Sekhmet and Menhit."*

Bastet slowly stepped away from Flamel and raised herself to her full towering height. Her slit-pupiled eyes were wide, her mouth tightly closed. "It has been a long time since any-one has called me by those names. Who are you—certainly no modern humani girl?"

Sophie's mouth moved, the words taking a moment or two to follow. *"Beware this girl, Bastet. She is your doom."*

Bastet's fur was bristling and her bare arms dimpled with goose bumps. Then she slowly backed away, turned and raced toward the burning Yggdrasill. For the first time in millennia, she was frightened.

Nicholas dragged himself to his feet and staggered toward Sophie, Josh and Scatty. He stepped up to Sophie. "Pere-nelle?" he whispered.

Sophie turned her head to him, eyes blank and unsee-ing. Her mouth worked, and then, as in a badly dubbed movie, the words came. *"I'm in San Francisco, held in the basement of Enoch Enterprises. I'm safe and well. Take the children south, Nicholas.*" There was a long moment of silence; then, when she spoke again, the words came quicker than Sophie's lips could move, and the girl's silver aura began to fade and her eyes started to close. *"Take them to the Witch."*

CHAPTER TWENTY-NINE

Dr. John Dee was becoming frantic. Everything was falling apart, and now there was every possibility that he was going to have to take an active part in the battle.

Flamel, Scatty and the twins had managed to escape from the interior of the Yggdrasill and were now fighting on the opposite side of the field, no more than two hundred yards away, but he couldn't get to them—it would mean crossing a battlefield. The last of the Torc Allta, both in their human and boar form, fought running battles with the cat- and bird-men. The nathair had already been defeated. Initially, the winged serpents had brought chaos and confusion to the cats and birds, but they were lumbering and awkward on the ground, and most had been killed once they'd landed. The massive army of Torc Allta had thinned considerably, and he guessed that within the hour, there would be no more wereboars left in North America.

But he could not afford to wait that long. He had to get to Flamel now. He had to retrieve the pages of the Codex as soon as possible.

From his hiding place behind a clump of bushes, Dee watched the Elders. Hekate was standing in the doorway to her tree home, surrounded by the last of her personal Torc Allta guard. While the boars fought the cats and birds, Hekate alone faced down the combined forces of the Morrigan and Bastet.

The three ignored the half-human animals fighting around them. To the casual observer it would have seemed as if the three Elders were simply staring at one another. Dee, however, noted the purple-gray clouds that gathered only above the Yggdrasill; he saw how the delicate white and gold flowers strewn around the huge tree withered and died, turning to black paste in an instant; he had seen the unsightly sheen of fungus that appeared on the smoothly polished stone path. Dee smiled; surely it would not be long now. How much longer could Hekate stand against the two Elders, aunt and niece?

But the goddess showed no sign of weakening.

And then she struck back.

Although the air, now stinking from the burning tree, was still, Dee watched as an invisible, unfelt breeze whipped the Morrigan's cloak about her shoulders and buffeted the huge Bastet, making her tilt her head and lean forward into the wind. The patterns on Hekate's metallic dress whirled with blinding rapidity, the colors blurred and distorted.

With growing alarm, he saw a dark shadow flowing across the withering grass and then watched as a swarm of tiny black flies settled on Bastet's fur, crawling into her ears and up her nose. The Cat Goddess howled and staggered back, rubbing furiously at her face. She fell to the ground, rolling over and over in the long grass, attempting to free herself from the insects. More and more kept coming, and they were joined by fire ants and recluse spiders, which crawled out of the grass and swarmed over her body. Crouched on all fours, she threw back her head and screamed in agony, then turned and ran across the field, rolling and crawling in the grass, splashing through a little pool, trying to clean the insects from her body. She was more than halfway across the field before the thick, swirling cloud left her. She rubbed furiously at her face and arms, leaving long scratches on her skin, before climbing to her feet and striding back toward the Yggdrasill. And then the swarm of flies, thicker now, re-formed in the air before her.

In that moment, Dee considered that perhaps—just perhaps—Hekate could win. Splitting Bastet and the Morrigan had been a master stroke; ensuring that Bastet could not get back was simply genius.

Realizing that she could not return to the Yggdrasill, Bastet hissed her rage, then turned and raced over to where Flamel, Scatty and the twins were trying to defend themselves. Dee saw her leap an incredible distance and bring the Alchemyst to the ground. That gave him some satisfaction, at least, and he allowed himself a slight smile, which quickly faded—he was still trapped on this side of the field. How was he going to get past Hekate?

Even though the Yggdrasill was burning furiously, with whole sections blazing, burning leaves and blackened strips of branches spiraling down, sticky streamers of sap exploding from collapsing branches, Hekate's powers seemed undiminished. Dee ground his teeth in frustration; all his research indicated that Hekate had brought the tree to life by imbuing it with a little of her own life force. In turn, as it grew, it renewed and replenished her powers. Burning the tree had been his idea. He had imagined that as it burned, she would weaken. But on the contrary: setting the tree alight had only served to enrage the goddess, and her anger had made her all the more deadly. When Dee saw Hekate's lips twitch in what might have been a smile and the Morrigan stagger and then step back, he began to realize that here, in her own Shadowrealm, the Goddess with Three Faces was simply too strong for them.

Dee knew then that he would have to act.

Keeping to the shadows of the trees and tall grasses, he moved around the trunk of the enormous Yggdrasill. He was forced to crouch down and hide as a Torc Allta in its boar shape crashed through the undergrowth directly in front of him with at least a dozen cat-people and twice that number of birdmen clinging to him.

Dee came out of the undergrowth on the opposite side of the tree from where Hekate and the Morrigan fought. To his right, he could see that something was happening with

Flamel's group; birds and cats were scattering in every direction . . . and then he realized that he was seeing *ordinary* birds and *everyday* cats fleeing, not the half-human creatures. The Morrigan's and Bastet's transformation spells were failing: was Hekate that powerful? He had to end this now.

Dr. John Dee lifted the short-bladed sword in his hand. Dirty blue light coiled down its length, and for an instant the ancient stone blade hummed as an invisible breeze moved across the edge. The twisting snakes carved into its hilt came to twisting, hissing life.

Gripping the hilt tightly, Dee pressed the point of the blade against the gnarled bark of the ancient tree . . . and pushed.

Excalibur slid smoothly into the wood, sinking right up to the hilt without resistance. For a long moment nothing happened, and then Yggdrasill began to moan. The sound was like that of an animal in pain: beginning as a deep grumbling, it quickly rose to a high-pitched whimpering. Where the hilt of the sword protruded from the tree, a blue stain appeared. Like dripping ink, it flowed down the tree and seeped into the ground, then the oily blue light ran along the veins and seams of wood. Yggdrasill's cries grew higher and higher, until they were almost beyond human hearing. The surviving Torc Allta fell to the ground, writhing in pain, clutching at their ears; birdmen whirled in confusion and the cat-people began to hiss and howl in unison.

The blue stain raced around the tree, coating everything in a thin veneer of glittering ice crystals that reflected the light. Blue-black and purple-green rainbows shimmered in the air.

The oily stain shot up the length of the tree and out along the branches, turning everything it touched to faceted crystals. Even the fire was not immune to it. Flames froze, fire caught in ornate and intricate patterns, then spiderwebbed, like ice on the surface of a pond, and dissolved to sparkling dust. Where the blue stain touched the leaves, they hardened and broke away from the branches. They did not spiral to the ground: they fell and shattered with tiny tinkling sounds, while the branches, now solid pieces of ice, ripped away from the trunk of the tree and crashed to the earth. Dee threw himself to one side to avoid being impaled by a three-foot length of frozen branch. Catching hold of Excalibur's hilt, he dragged the stone blade free of the ancient tree and ran for cover.

The Yggdrasill was dying. Huge slabs of bark sheared off, like icebergs breaking away from an ice cap, and crashed to the ground, littering the beautiful Shadowrealm landscape with shards of razor-sharp ice.

Keeping his distance and watching for falling branches, Dee raced around the tree; he needed to see Hekate.

The Goddess with Three Faces was dying.

Standing quite still before the crumbling Yggdrasill, Hekate was flickering through her three faces—young, mature and old—in heartbeats. The change was happening so fast that her flesh had no time to adapt and she was caught between phases: young eyes in an old face, a girl's head on a woman's body, a woman's body with a child's arms. Her ever-changing dress had lost all color and was the same solid black as her skin.

Dee stood beside the Morrigan and they watched in silence. Bastet rejoined them, and together the three observed Hekate and Yggdrasill's last moments.

The World Tree was now almost entirely blue, covered with a sheath of ice. Frozen roots had burst through the ground, destroying the perfect symmetry of the earth, cutting thick gouges in the soil. Huge holes had appeared in the massive trunk, revealing the circular rooms within, which were warped and stained with the blue ice.

Hekate's transformations slowed. The changes were taking longer to materialize because now the blue stain was slowly creeping up her body, hardening her skin, turning it to ice crystals.

The Morrigan glanced at the blade in Dee's hand, then quickly looked away. "Even after all these years in our employ, Dr. Dee, you can still surprise us," she said quietly. "I was not aware that you possessed the Sword of Ice."

"I'm glad I brought it," Dee said, not directly answering her. "It seems Hekate's powers were stronger than we suspected. At least my guess—that her strength was connected to the tree—was correct."

What remained of the Yggdrasill was now a solid block of ice. Hekate, too, was completely covered beneath a frozen sheet, though behind the blue crystals, her butter-colored eyes were bright and alive. The top of the tree began to melt, dirty water running down the length of the bark, cutting deep grooves into it.

"When I realized that she had the power to nullify your spells, I knew I had to do something," Dee said. "I saw how the cats and birds were reverting to their natural shapes."

"That was not Hekate's doing," Bastet growled suddenly, her accent thick, her voice beastlike.

The Morrigan and Dee turned to look at the Cat Goddess. The creature raised a furry claw and pointed across the field. "It was the girl. Someone spoke through her, someone who knew my true names, someone who used the girl's aura to wield a whip of pure energy: that's what reversed our spells."

Dee looked across the field where he had seen Flamel, Scatty and the twins gathered around the oak tree. But there was no sign of them. He was turning to order the surviving cats and birds to find them when he spotted Senuhet staggering up. The old man was spattered with mud and blood—though none of the blood seemed to be his—and he had lost one of his curved bronze swords. The second had snapped in half.

"Flamel and the others have escaped," he gasped. "I followed them out of the Shadowrealm. They're stealing our car," he added indignantly.

Howling his rage, Dr. John Dee spun around and flung Excalibur at the Yggdrasill. The stone blade struck the ancient World Tree, which tolled with the solemn sound of a great bell. The single note, high-pitched and serene, hung vibrating on the air . . . and then the Yggdrasill began to crack. Long fractures and tears ran the height of the tree.

They started small, but widened as they raced upward in ragged patterns. Within moments the entire tree was covered in the crazed zigzagging. Then the Yggdrasill shattered and came crashing down on the ice statue of Hekate, crushing it to dust.

CHAPTER THIRTY

*J*osh Newman jerked open the door of the black SUV and felt a wave of relief wash over him. The keys were in the ignition. He pulled open the rear door and held it while Nicholas Flamel hurried toward the car, carrying Sophie in his arms. He reached in and gently stretched her out on the backseat. Scatty burst through the barrier of leaves and came hurtling down the path, a broad smile on her face.

"Now, that," she said as she launched herself into the back of the SUV, "was the most fun I've had in a millennium."

Josh climbed into the driver's seat, adjusted it and turned the key in the ignition. The big V6 engine growled to life.

Flamel hopped into the passenger's seat and slammed the door. "Get us out of here!"

Josh pushed the gearshift into drive, gripped the leather

steering wheel in both hands and pressed the accelerator flat to the floor. The big Hummer lurched forward, kicking up stones and dirt as he spun it in a circle and then set off down the narrow path, rocking and bouncing over the ruts, tree branches and bushes scraping its sides, scoring lines along its pristine paintwork.

Although the sun had risen in both the Shadowrealm and the real world, the road was still in deep shadow, and no matter where Josh looked, he still couldn't find the controls for the lights. He kept glancing in the side and rearview mirrors, expecting at any moment to see the Morrigan or the Cat Goddess step through the wall of vegetation behind them. It was only when the path ended in a burst of sunshine and he wrenched the steering wheel to the right, turning the heavy SUV onto the narrow, winding blacktop, that he eased off the gas. The Hummer immediately lost speed.

"Everyone OK?" he asked shakily.

He tilted the rearview mirror down so that he could see into the back. His twin lay stretched across the wide leather seats, her head on Scatty's lap. The Warrior was using a scrap of cloth torn from her T-shirt to wipe the girl's forehead. Sophie's skin was deathly white, and although her eyes were closed, her eyeballs moved erratically beneath her lids, and she twitched as if she was having a nightmare. Scatty caught Josh looking at them in the glass and she smiled in encouragement. "She's going to be OK," she said.

"Is there anything you can do?" Josh demanded, glancing at Flamel sitting next to him. His feelings for the Alchemyst

273

were completely confused now. On the one hand, he had placed them in terrible danger, and yet Josh had seen how savagely Flamel had fought in their defense.

"There is nothing I can do," Flamel said tiredly. "She is simply exhausted; nothing more." Nicholas also looked worn out. His clothes were streaked with mud and what might have been blood. Bird feathers stuck in his hair, and both hands were scratched from his encounters with the cats. "Let her sleep, and when she awakens in a few hours' time, she will be fine. I promise you."

Josh nodded. He concentrated on the road ahead of him, unwilling to continue the conversation with the Alchemyst. He doubted that his sister would ever be *fine* again. He'd seen how she looked at him, her eyes blank and staring: she hadn't recognized him. He'd listened to the voice that had come out of her mouth: it wasn't a voice he'd known. His sister, his twin, had been utterly changed.

They came up on a sign for Mill Valley, and he turned left. He had no idea where they were going; he just wanted to get away from the Shadowrealm. More than that: he wanted to go home, wanted to go back to a normal life, he wanted to forget that he'd ever come across that ad in the university newspaper his father had brought home.

Assistant Wanted, Bookshop. We don't want readers, we want workers.

He'd sent in a résumé and a few days later he'd been called for an interview. Sophie had had nothing else to do that day and had come along for company. While she'd been waiting, she'd gone to the shop across the road for a chai latte. When Josh had come out of The Small Book Shop, beaming delightedly because he'd been offered the job, he'd discovered that Sophie had found a job as well in The Coffee Cup. They would be working right across the street from each other—it was perfect! And it *had* been perfect—until yesterday, when this madness had begun. He had trouble believing it had only been yesterday. He looked in the mirror at Sophie again. She was resting quietly now, completely still, but he was relieved to see that a little color had come back into her cheeks.

What had Hekate done? No—what had *Flamel* done? It all came back to the Alchemyst. This was all his fault. The goddess hadn't wanted to Awaken the twins—she knew the dangers. But Flamel had pushed, and now, because of the Alchemyst, Hekate's Shadowrealm paradise was under attack, and his sister had become a stranger to him.

When Josh had started working in the bookshop for the man he knew then as Nick Fleming, he'd thought he was a little strange, eccentric, maybe even a little weird. But as he'd gotten to know him, he'd come to genuinely like the man, and to admire him. Fleming was everything Josh's father wasn't. He was funny, and interested in just about everything Josh did, and his knowledge of trivia was incredible. Josh knew that his father, Richard, was really only happy and comfortable when he was standing before a lecture hall full of students or buried up to his knees in dirt.

Fleming was different. When Josh quoted Bart Simpson to him, Fleming countered with Groucho Marx and then went further and introduced Josh to the movies of the Marx

Brothers. They shared a love of music—even though their tastes were widely different; Josh introduced Nick to Green Day, Lamb and Dido. Fleming recommended Peter Gabriel, Genesis and Pink Floyd. When Josh let Fleming listen to some ambient and trance on his iPod, Fleming loaned him CDs of Mike Oldfield and Brian Eno. Josh introduced Nick to the world of blogging and showed him his and Sophie's blog, and they had even started talking about putting the entire shop's stock online.

In time Josh had come to think of Fleming as the older brother he'd always wished he had. And now that man had betrayed him.

In fact, he'd been lying to Josh from the very beginning. He hadn't even been Nick Fleming. And somewhere at the back of Josh's mind, an ugly question was beginning to form. Keeping his voice low and his eyes on the road ahead, he asked, "Did you know all this would happen?"

Flamel sat back into the deep leather seat and turned to look at Josh. The Alchemyst was partially in shadow and he clutched the seat belt across his chest with both hands. "What would happen?" he asked carefully.

"You know, I'm not a kid," Josh said, his voice rising, "so don't talk to me like one." In the rear seat, Sophie muttered a little in her sleep, and he forced himself to lower his voice. "Did your precious Book predict all this?" He caught a glimpse of Scatty moving in the backseat and realized she had eased forward to hear the Alchemyst's answer.

Flamel took a long time before replying. Finally, he said. "There are some things you must know first about the Book of Abraham the Mage." He saw Josh open his mouth and he pressed on quickly. "Let me finish. I always knew the Codex was old," he began, "though I never knew just how old. Yesterday Hekate said she was there when Abraham created it . . . and that would have been at least ten thousand years ago. The world was a very different place then. The commonly held view is that mankind appeared in the middle of the Stone Age. But the truth is very, very different. The Elder Race ruled the earth. We have scraps of the truth in our mythology and legends. If you believe the stories," he continued, "they possessed the power of flight, they had vessels that could cross the oceans, they could control the weather and had even perfected what we would call cloning. In other words, they had access to a science that was so advanced, we would call it magic."

Josh started to shake his head. This was too much to take in.

"And before you say this is all far-fetched, just think how far the human race has come in the past ten years. If someone had told your parents, for example, that they would be able to carry their entire music library in their pocket, would they have believed it? Now we have phones that have more computing power than was used to send the first rockets into space. We have electron microscopes that can see individual atoms. We routinely cure diseases that only fifty years ago were fatal. And the rate of change is increasing. Today we are able to do what your parents would have dismissed as impossible and your grandparents as nothing short of magical."

"You haven't answered my question," Josh said. He was

watching his speed carefully; they couldn't afford to be pulled over.

"What I'm saying to you is that I do not know what the Elder Race was able to do. Was Abraham making predictions in the Codex, or was he simply writing down what he had somehow seen? Was he aware of the future, *could* he actually see it?" He swiveled around in the seat to look at Scatty. "Do you know?"

She shrugged, lips curling into a little smile. "I'm Next Generation; much of the Elder World had vanished before I was even born, and Danu Talis was long sunk beneath the waves. I've no idea what they could do. Could they see through time?" She paused, thinking. "I've known Elders who seemed to have that gift: Sibyl certainly could, and so could Themis and Melampus, of course. But they were wrong more often than they were right. If my travels have taught me anything, it is that we create our own future. I've watched world-shaking events come and go without anyone making predictions about them, and I've also seen prophecies— usually to do with the end of the world—that also failed to happen."

A car overtook them on the narrow country road, the first they had seen so far that morning.

"I'm going to ask you the question one more time," Josh said, struggling to keep his voice even. "And this time, just give me a straight yes-or-no answer: was everything that just happened predicted in the Codex?"

"No," Flamel said quickly.

"I hear a *but* in there somewhere," Scatty said.

The Alchemyst nodded. "There is a little *but*. There is nothing in the book about Hekate or the Shadowrealm, nothing about Dee or Bastet or the Morrigan. But . . ." He sighed. "There are several prophecies about twins."

"Twins," Josh said tightly. "You mean twins in general or specifically to do with Sophie and me?"

"The Codex speaks of silver and gold twins, 'the two that are one, the one that is all.' It is no coincidence that your auras are pure gold and silver. So yes, I am convinced the Codex is referring to you and your sister." He leaned forward to look at Josh. "And if you are asking me how long I've known that, then the answer is this: I began to suspect only yesterday, when you and Sophie came to my aid in the shop. Hekate confirmed my suspicions a few hours later when she made your auras visible. I give you my word that everything I've done has been for your protection."

Josh started to shake his head; he wasn't sure he believed Flamel. He opened his mouth to ask a question, but Scatty put her hand on his shoulder before he could speak. "Let me just say this," she said, her voice low and serious, her Celtic accent suddenly pronounced. "I've known Nicholas Flamel for a very long time. America was barely even colonized when we first met. He is many things—dangerous and devious, cunning and deadly, a good friend and an implacable enemy—but he comes from an age when a man's word was indeed precious. If he gives you his word that he's done all this for your protection, then I am suggesting that you believe him."

Josh eased on the brake and the car slowed as it rounded a corner. Finally, he nodded and let out his breath in a deep sigh. "I believe you," he said aloud. But somewhere in the back of his mind, he kept hearing Hekate's last words to him—"Nicholas Flamel never tells anyone everything"—and he had the distinct impression that the Alchemyst still wasn't telling everything he knew.

Suddenly, Nicholas tapped Josh's arm. "Here—stop here."

"Why, what's wrong?" Scatty demanded, reaching for her swords.

Josh signaled and pulled the Hummer off the road to where a roadside diner sign had flickered into life.

"Nothing's wrong." Flamel grinned. "Just time for some breakfast."

"Great. I'm famished," Scatty said. "I could eat a horse. If I weren't a vegetarian . . . and liked horse, of course."

And you weren't a vampire, Josh thought, but kept his mouth shut.

Sophie woke up while Scatty and Flamel were in the diner ordering breakfast to go. One moment she was asleep, the next she sat bolt upright in the backseat. Josh jumped and was unable to prevent a little startled cry from escaping his lips.

He swiveled around in the driver's seat, kneeling up to lean over the back. "Sophie?" he asked cautiously. He was terrified that something strange and ancient would look through his sister's eyes again.

"You don't want to know what I was dreaming about," Sophie said, stretching her arms wide and arching her back. Her neck cracked as she rotated it. "Ow. I ache everywhere."

"How do you feel?" Well, it sounded like his sister.

"Like I'm coming down with flu." She looked around. "Where are we? Whose car is this?"

Josh grinned, teeth white in the shadows. "We stole it from Dee. We're somewhere on the road out of Mill Valley, heading back into San Francisco, I think."

"What happened . . . what happened back there?" Sophie asked.

Josh's smile broadened into a wide grin. "You saved us, with your newly Awakened powers. You were incredible: you had a silver whip energy thing, and every time it touched one of the cats or birds, it changed them back into their real forms." He trailed off as she started to shake her head. "You don't remember anything?"

"A little. I could hear Perenelle talking to me, telling me what to do. I could actually feel her pouring her aura into me," she said in awe. "I could hear her. I could even see her, sort of." She suddenly drew in a deep, shuddering breath. "Then they came for her. That's all I can remember."

"Who did?"

"The faceless men. Lots of faceless men. I watched them drag her away."

"What do you mean, faceless men?"

Sophie's eyes were wide and terrified. "They had no faces."

"Like masks?"

"No, Josh, not masks. Their faces were smooth—no eyes, no nose, no mouth, just smooth skin."

The image that formed in his head was deeply disturbing,

and he deliberately changed the subject. "Do you feel . . . different?" He chose the word carefully.

Sophie took a moment to consider. What was wrong with Josh, why was he so concerned? "Different? How?"

"Do you remember Hekate Awakening your powers?"

"I do."

"What did it feel like?" he asked hesitantly.

For a moment Sophie's eyes flickered with cold silver light. "It was as if someone had flipped a switch in my head, Josh. I felt alive. For the first time in my life I felt alive."

Josh felt a sudden inexplicable pang of jealousy. From the corner of his eye, he spotted Flamel and Scatty leaving the diner, arms piled high with bags. "And how do you feel now?"

"Hungry," she said. "Extremely hungry."

They ate in silence: breakfast burritos, eggs, sausage, grits and rolls, washed down with soda. Scatty had fruit and water.

Josh finally wiped his mouth with a napkin and brushed bread crumbs off his jeans. It was the first proper meal he'd had since lunchtime the day before. "I feel human again." He glanced sideways at Scatty. "No offense."

"None taken," Scatty assured him. "Believe me—I've never wanted to be human, though there are, I believe, some advantages," she added enigmatically.

Nicholas bundled up the remains of their breakfast and shoved them into a paper bag. Then he leaned forward and tapped the screen of the satellite navigation system set into the dashboard. "Do you know how this works?"

Josh shook his head. "In theory, I guess. We put in a destination and it tells us the best way to get there. I've never used one before, though. My dad's car hasn't got one," he added. Richard Newman drove a five-year-old Volvo station wagon.

"If you looked at it, could you make it work?" Flamel persisted.

"Maybe," Josh said doubtfully.

"Of course he can. Josh is a genius with computers," Sophie said proudly from the backseat.

"This is hardly a computer," her twin muttered, leaning forward and hitting the On button. The large square screen flickered to life, and an incredibly patronizing voice warned them about typing addresses into the system while driving, then instructed Josh to hit the OK button, acknowledging that he'd heard and understood the warning. The screen blinked and immediately showed the position of the Hummer on an unnamed backroad. Mount Tamalpais appeared as a little triangle at the top of the screen, and arrows pointed south to San Francisco. The little track that led to Hekate's Shadowrealm wasn't shown.

"We need to go south," Flamel continued.

Josh experimented with the buttons until he got the main menu. "Okay. I need an address."

"Put in the post office at the corner of Signal Street and Ojai Avenue in Ojai."

In the backseat, Scatty stirred. "Oh, not Ojai. Please tell me we're not going there."

Flamel twisted in his seat. "Perenelle told me to go south."

283

"L.A. is south, Mexico is south, even Chile is south of here. There are *lots* of nice places that lie to the south. . . ."

"Perenelle told me to take the children to the Witch," Flamel said patiently. "And the Witch is in Ojai."

Sophie and Josh looked quickly at each other, but said nothing.

Scatty sat back and sighed dramatically. "Would it make a difference if I told you I didn't want to go?"

"None at all."

Sophie crouched between the seats to stare at the little screen. "How long will it take? How far away are we?" she wondered out loud.

"It's going to take most of the day," Josh said, leaning forward to squint at the screen. Where his hair brushed his sister's, a tiny spark crackled between them. "We need to get to Highway One. We go across the Richmond Bridge . . ." His fingers traced the colored lines. "Then to I-580, which eventually turns into I-5." He blinked in surprise. "We stay on that for over two hundred and seventy miles." He hit another button, which calculated some totals. "The entire trip is just over four hundred miles, and will take at least six and a half hours. Before today, the farthest I've ever driven is about ten miles!"

"Well, this will be great practice for you, then," the Alchemyst said with a smile.

Sophie looked from Flamel to Scatty. "Who is this Witch we're going to see?"

Flamel snapped his seat belt into place. "We're going to see the Witch of Endor."

Josh turned the key in the ignition and started the car. He glanced in the rearview mirror at Scatty. "Someone else you've fought with?" he asked.

Scathach grimaced. "Worse than that," she muttered. "She's my grandmother."

CHAPTER THIRTY-ONE

$\mathcal{T}$he Shadowrealm was breaking down.

In the west, the clouds had vanished and huge patches of the sky had already disappeared, leaving only the blinking stars and the overlarge moon in the black sky. One by one the stars were winking out of existence, and the moon was beginning to fray at the edges.

"We don't have much time," the Morrigan said, watching the sky.

Dee, who was crouching on the ground, gathering as many icy fragments of Hekate as he could find, thought he could hear a note of fear in the Morrigan's voice. "We have time," he said evenly.

"We can't afford to be here when the Shadowrealm disappears," she continued, looking down at him, her face expressionless. But he knew by the way she hugged the cloak of crow feathers about her shoulders that she was nervous.

"What would happen?" Dee wondered aloud. He'd never seen the Crow Goddess like this before, and he took pleasure in her discomfiture.

The Morrigan raised her head to look at the encroaching darkness, her black eyes reflecting the tiny spots of stars. "Why, we'd disappear also. Sucked away into the nothingness," she added softly, watching the mountains in the distance turn to something like dust. The dust then spiraled up into the black sky and vanished. "A true death," the Morrigan murmured.

Dee was crouched among the melting remains of the Yggdrasill, while all around him Hekate's elegant and beautiful world was turning to dust and blowing away on invisible winds. The goddess had created her Shadowrealm out of nothingness, and now, without her presence to hold it together, it was returning to that once more. The mountains had vanished, blown away like grains of sand, whole swathes of the forest were slowly fading and blinking out of existence like lights being turned off and the overlarge moon hanging low in the sky was losing shape and definition. Already it was nothing more than a featureless ball. In the east, the rising sun was a golden orb of light and the sky was still blue.

The Crow Goddess turned to her aunt. "How long before it all disappears?" she asked.

Bastet growled and shrugged her broad shoulders. "Who knows? Even I have never witnessed the death of an entire Shadowrealm. Minutes perhaps . . ."

"That's all I need." Dee laid the sword Excalibur on the ground. The smoothly polished stone blade reflected the blackness creeping in from the west. Dee found three of the largest chunks of ice that had once been Hekate and placed them on the blade.

The Morrigan and Bastet leaned over his shoulders and stared at the sword, their reflections rippling and distorted. "What is so important that you must do it here?" Bastet asked.

"This was Hekate's home," Dee replied. "And here, right here, at the place of her death, the connection to her will be strongest."

"Connection . . . ," Bastet growled, and then nodded. She suddenly knew what Dee was about to attempt: the darkest and most dangerous of all the dark arts.

"Necromancy," Dee whispered. "I'm going to talk to the dead goddess. She spent so many millennia here that it is part of her. I'm wagering her consciousness remains active and attached to this place." He reached out and touched the handle of the sword. The black stone glowed yellow and the carved snakes around the hilt came briefly alive, hissing furiously, tongues flickering, before they solidified once again. As the ice melted, the liquid ran over the black stone, covering it in a thin oily sheen. "Now we shall see what we shall see," he muttered.

The water on the blade began to bubble and pop, sizzling and crackling. And a face appeared in each bubble: Hekate's face. It kept flickering through her three guises, only the eyes—butter-colored and hateful—remaining the same as she glared at him.

"Talk to me," Dee shouted, "I command you. Why did Flamel come here?"

Hekate's voice was a bubbling, watery snap. *To escape you.*

"Tell me about the human children."

The images that appeared on the sword blade were surprisingly detailed. They were all from Hekate's perspective. They showed Flamel arriving with the twins, showed the two children sitting, fearful and pale, in the battered and scratched car.

Flamel believes they are the twins of legend mentioned in the Codex.

The Morrigan and Bastet crowded closer, ignoring the rapidly encroaching nothingness. In the west, there were no longer any stars in the heavens, the moon was gone and huge portions of the sky had completely vanished, leaving just blackness in its wake.

"Are they?" Dee demanded.

The next image on the sword showed the twins' auras flaring silver and gold.

"Moon and sun," Dee murmured. He didn't know whether to be horrified or elated. His suspicions were confirmed. From the first moment he'd seen them together, he'd started to wonder if the teens were, in fact, twins.

"Are these the twins foretold in legend?" he demanded again.

Bastet brought her massive head down next to Dee's. Her foot-long whiskers tickled his face, but he didn't risk brushing them away, not with her teeth so close. She smelled of wet cat and frankincense; Dee felt a sneeze building at the back of his nose. The Cat Goddess reached out for the blade, but Dee caught her hand in his. It was like grasping a lion's paw, and her retracted claws suddenly appeared dangerously close to his fingers. "Please don't touch the blade; this is a delicate spell. There is time for perhaps one or two more questions," he added, nodding toward the western horizon, to where the edges of the earth were crumbling, blowing away like multi-colored dust.

Bastet glared at the black blade, her slit-pupiled eyes flaring. "My sister has—or should I say *had*—a very special gift. She could Awaken powers in others. Ask her if she did that with these humani twins."

Dee nodded in sudden understanding; he had been wondering why Flamel had brought the twins to this place. He remembered now: in the ancient world, it was believed Hekate had power over magic and spells. "Did you Awaken the twins' magical abilities?" he asked.

A single bubble popped. "No."

Dee rocked back on his heels, surprised. He had been expecting her to say yes. Had Flamel failed, then?

Bastet growled. "She's lying."

"She cannot," Dee said. "She answers what we ask."

"I saw the girl with my own eyes," the Egyptian goddess growled. "I saw her wield a whip of pure auric energy. I've never seen such power in my life, not since the Elder Times."

Dr. John Dee glanced at her sharply. "You saw the girl . . . but what of the boy? What was he doing?"

"I did not notice him."

"Ha!" Dee said triumphantly. He turned back to the sword.

The Morrigan's cloak rustled warningly. "Make this your last question, Doctor."

The trio looked up to see that the utter blackness was almost upon them. Less than ten feet ahead of them, the world ended in nothingness. Dee turned back to the sword. "Did you Awaken the girl?"

A bubble popped and the sword ran with images of Sophie rising off the ground, her aura blazing silver. "Yes."

"And the boy?"

The sword showed Josh cowering in a corner of a darkened chamber. "No."

The Morrigan's clawlike hands gripped Dee's shoulders and jerked him to his feet. He caught his sword and shook the bubbling water droplets into the rapidly encroaching void.

The mismatched trio—towering Bastet, dark Morrigan and small human—raced away as the world crumbled into nothingness behind them. The last remnants of their army— the birdmen and cat-people—remained, wandering aimlessly. When they saw their leaders fleeing, they turned to follow. Soon every creature was racing to the east, where the last of the Shadowrealm remained. Senuhet limped after Bastet, calling out her name, begging her to stop and help him.

But the world dissolved too quickly. It swallowed birds and cats, it took the ancient trees and rare orchids, the magical creatures and the mythical monsters. It consumed the last of Hekate's magic.

Then the void claimed the sun and the world went dark and was no more.

CHAPTER THIRTY-TWO

The Morrigan and Bastet burst through the tangled hedges, carrying John Dee between them. In the next instant the wall of foliage vanished and one of the many winding paths leading to Mount Tamalpais appeared. They stumbled, and Dee fell sprawling in the dust.

"What now?" Bastet growled. "Have we lost, have they won? We have destroyed Hekate, but she has Awakened the girl."

John Dee staggered to his feet and brushed off his ruined coat. There were scrapes and tears in the sleeve, and something had ripped a fist-sized hole through the lining. Carefully wiping Excalibur clean, he slid it back into its concealed sheath. "It's not the girl we need to concentrate on now. It's the boy. The boy is the key."

The Morrigan shook her head, feathers rustling. "You talk in riddles." She glanced up into the clear morning skies, and almost directly overhead a wisp of gray cloud appeared.

"He has seen his sister's tremendous magical powers Awakened; how do you think the boy is feeling now? Frightened, angry, jealous? Alone?" He looked from the Morrigan to the Cat Goddess. "The boy is at least as powerful as the girl. Is there anyone else on this continent to whom Flamel could take the boy to have his talents Awakened?"

"Black Annis is in the Catskills," the Morrigan suggested, the note of caution clearly audible in her voice.

"Too unpredictable," Dee said, "she'd probably eat him."

"I heard that Persephone was in northern Canada," Bastet said.

Dee shook his head. "Her years in the Underworld Shadowrealm have driven her insane. She is dangerous beyond belief."

The Morrigan drew her cloak tighter around her shoulders. The cloud above her head thickened and drifted lower. "Then there is no one in North America. I came across Nocticula in Austria, and I know that Erichtho still hides out on Thessaly—"

"You're wrong," Dee interrupted. "There is one other who could Awaken the boy."

"Who?" Bastet growled, frowning, her snout wrinkling.

Dr. John Dee turned to the Crow Goddess. "You could."

The Morrigan stepped away from Dee, black eyes wide with surprise, pointed teeth pressing against the bruise-colored flesh of her thin lips. A ripple ran through her black cloak, ruffling all the feathers.

"You are mistaken," Bastet hissed. "My niece is Next Generation, she hasn't got the powers."

Dee turned to face the Crow Goddess. If he knew he was playing a dangerous—possibly even deadly—game, he showed no sign of it. "At one time, perhaps that would have been true. But the Morrigan's powers are more, much, much more, than they were."

"Niece, what is he talking about?" Bastet demanded.

"Be very, very careful, humani," the Crow Goddess cackled.

"My loyalty is not in question here," Dee said quickly. "I have served the Elders for half a millennium. I am merely looking for a way to achieve our aim." He stepped up to the Morrigan. "Once, like Hekate, you wore three faces: you were the Morrigan, the Macha and the Badb. Unlike Hekate, though, you and your two sisters occupied three bodies. It was your consciousnesses that were linked. Individually you were powerful, but together you were invincible." He paused and seemed to be taking a moment to gather his thoughts, but in actuality, he was ensuring he had a firm grip on Excalibur beneath his coat. "When did you decide to kill your sisters?" he asked casually.

With a terrible screech the Morrigan leapt for Dee.

And stopped.

In a flash Excalibur's black stone blade had appeared at her throat, blue light fizzing and sparking down the blade. The serpent hilt came to life and hissed at her.

"Please"—Dee smiled, a chilling twist of his lips—"I've been responsible for the death of one Elder today. I've no

295

wish to add a second to my total." As he spoke, he watched Bastet, who was moving around behind him. "The Morrigan has the power to Awaken the boy," he said quickly. "She possesses the knowledge and power of her two sisters. If we can Awaken the boy and turn him to our side, we have gained ourselves an extraordinarily powerful ally. Remember the prophecy: 'the two that are one, the one that is all.' One to save the world, one to destroy it."

"And which one is the boy?" Bastet asked.

"Whatever we make him," Dee said, eyes darting from the Morrigan to Bastet and back to the Crow Goddess.

Abruptly, Bastet was beside him, her huge claw around his throat. She lifted him slightly, forcing him to rise on his toes and look into her chilling eyes. For a single heartbeat, he thought about swinging the sword around, but he knew that the Cat Goddess was faster, so much faster than he would ever be. She'd see the twitch of his shoulders and simply snap his head clean off.

Bastet glared at her niece. "Is it true? Are Macha and the Badb dead?"

"Yes." The Morrigan glared at Dee. "But I did not kill them. They died willingly, and live inside me still." For a moment her eyes blazed yellow, then red, then solid black, the colors of the three ancient goddesses.

Dee was tempted to ask how they had gotten inside her, then decided that he really didn't want to know the answer and now probably wasn't a good time to ask anyway.

"Could you Awaken the boy?" Bastet demanded.

"Yes."

"Then do it, Niece," the Cat Goddess ordered. She turned her attention back to Dee. Pressing her thumb under his chin, she pushed his head back. "And if you ever raise a weapon to one of the Elder Race again, I will see that you spend the next millennia in a Shadowrealm of my own special creation. And trust me, you will not like it." She released her grip and flung him away, sending him sprawling in the dirt. He was still clutching the sword.

"Tell me," Bastet commanded, towering over him. "Where are Flamel and the twins now? Where have they gone?"

Dee climbed shakily to his feet. He brushed dirt off his coat, and discovered yet another tear in the soft leather; he was never buying leather again. "He will need to start training the girl. Hekate Awakened her, but didn't get a chance to teach her any protective spells. She'll need to be taught to protect herself and control her powers before the stimuli from the physical world drive her mad."

"So where will they go?" Bastet growled. She wrapped her arms around her body and shivered. The cloud the Morrigan had summoned had grown thick and dark as it drifted-lower, and now hovered just over the treetops. There was moisture in the air, and the hint of unidentifiable spices.

"He'll not stay in San Francisco," Dee continued, "he knows we have too many agents in and around the city."

The Morrigan closed her eyes and turned slowly, then she raised her arm. "They're heading south; I can just about make out the silver traces of her aura. It's incredibly powerful."

"Who is the most powerful Elder south of here?" Dee asked quickly. "Someone proficient in elemental magic?"

297

"Endor," Bastet answered immediately, "in Ojai. The deadly Witch of Endor."

"Mistress of the Air," the Morrigan added.

Bastet leaned down, her breath foul in the small man's face. "You know where you have to go. You know what you have to do. We must have the pages of the Codex."

"And the twins?" he asked tightly, trying not to breathe.

"Capture them if you can—if not, then kill them to prevent Flamel from using their powers." Then both she and the Crow Goddess stepped into the thickening cloud and were gone. The damp grayness swirled away, leaving Dr. John Dee alone on the isolated path.

"How do I get to Ojai?" he called.

But there was no response.

Dee shoved his hands in the pockets of his ruined leather coat and set off down the narrow path. He hated it when they did that, dismissed him as if he were nothing more than a child.

But things would change.

The Elders liked to think that Dee was their puppet, their tool. He had seen how Bastet had abandoned Senuhet, who had been with her for at least a century, without a second glance. He knew they would do exactly the same to him, given the chance.

But Dr. John Dee had plans to ensure that they never got that chance.

CHAPTER THIRTY-THREE

*I*t was late in the afternoon when Josh finally turned the Hummer down the long, curving road that led into the small city of Ojai. The stress of driving four hundred miles in one long trip was etched onto his face, and although the computer had estimated that it would take around six and a half hours, it had taken close to nine. Driving the big Hummer on the highway was surprisingly easy: he'd simply put on the cruise control and let it go. It was boring, but off the highway and on any other type of road, the Hummer was a nightmare to control. It wasn't like any of his computer games. It was just so big, and he was terrified he was going to run over something. The huge jet-black vehicle also attracted a lot of attention—he'd never thought he'd be so happy to have tinted windows. He wondered what people would think if they knew it was being driven by a fifteen-year-old.

The road curved to the right, and Ojai's long, straight main street appeared before him. He slowed as he passed the Psychic Boutique and the Ojai Playhouse; then the lights changed at Signal Street and he stopped, leaned across the steering wheel and peered through the smeared, bug-spattered windshield. His first impression as he looked down the empty street was that Ojai was surprisingly green. It was June in California, that time of year when most things had turned brown and withered, but here there were trees everywhere, contrasting with the white stone of the buildings. Directly in front of him, to his right, a low, ornate white stone tower rose over the post office into the brilliant blue sky, while on the left, a row of shops was set back from the road, sheltered beneath a row of white stone arches.

Glancing in the rearview mirror, he was surprised to find Scatty's eyes on him.

"I thought you were asleep," he said quietly. Sophie, who had moved up into the passenger seat beside him after a few hours of driving, lay curled up asleep, and Flamel snored gently beside Scatty.

"I've no need to sleep," she said simply.

There were a lot of questions he really wanted to ask, but instead, he just said, "Do you know where we're going?"

She leaned forward, rested her arms on the back of his seat and her chin on her arms. "Straight on, past the post office—that's the building with the tower—then turn right after Libbey Park at Fox Street. Find a parking space down there." She nodded to the left, toward a row of shops nestled under the white arches. "We're going there."

"Is that where your grandmother is?"

"Yes," Scatty said shortly.

"And is she really a witch?"

"Not just *a* witch. She is the original Witch."

"How do you feel?" Sophie asked. She stood on the sidewalk and stretched, standing on her toes and arching her back. Something popped in her neck. "That feels good," she added, turning her face and closing her eyes against the sun, which was still high in the cloudless robin's-egg blue heavens.

"I should be asking you that question," Josh said, climbing out of the car. He yawned and stretched, rotating his head from side to side. "I never want to drive again," he added. His voice dropped to little more than a whisper. "I'm glad you're okay." He hesitated. "You are okay, aren't you?"

Sophie reached out to squeeze her brother's arm. "I think so."

Flamel climbed out of the car and slammed his door. Scatty had already moved away from the car to stand beneath the shelter of a tree. She'd dug a pair of mirrored sunglasses from her pocket and popped them onto her face. The Alchemyst went to join her as Josh hit the alarm on the key chain. The car blipped once and its lights flashed.

"We need to talk," Flamel said quietly, though the side street was deserted. He ran his fingers through his close-cropped hair, and strands came away on his fingers. He looked at them for a moment, then brushed them on his jeans. Another year was etched onto his face, subtly deepening the lines around his eyes and the semicircular grooves on either side of his mouth. "This person we're going to see can be . . ." He hesitated and then said, " . . . difficult."

"You're telling me," Scatty muttered.

"What do you mean by difficult?" Josh asked in alarm. After everything they had just encountered, *difficult* could mean just about anything.

"Cranky, cantankerous, irritable . . . and that's when she's in a good mood," Scatty said.

"And when she's in a bad mood?"

"You don't even want to be in the same city as her!"

Josh was puzzled. He turned to the Alchemyst. "Then why are we going to see her?"

"Because Perenelle told me to," he said patiently, "because she is the Mistress of Air, and can teach Sophie the basics of elemental air magic, and because she can give Sophie some advice on how to protect herself."

"From what?" Josh asked, startled.

"From herself," Flamel said matter-of-factly, and turned away, heading back toward Ojai Avenue. Scatty moved out of the shadows and fell into step beside him. "Wish I'd brought sunscreen. I burn easily in this sunshine," she grumbled as they walked away. "And wait till you see my freckles in the morning."

Josh turned back to his sister; he was beginning to have some idea of the huge gulf of understanding that now separated him from his twin. "Do you have any idea what he was talking about? Protecting yourself from yourself? What's that supposed to mean?"

"I think I know." Sophie frowned. "Everything around me is so . . . loud, so bright, so sharp, so intense. It's like someone turned the volume up. My senses are so acute; you wouldn't believe what I can hear." She pointed to a battered red Toyota driving slowly down the road. "The woman in that car is talking on the phone to her mother. She's telling her she doesn't want fish for dinner." She pointed to a truck parked in a yard on the opposite side of the street. "There's a sticker on the back of the truck; do you want me to tell you what it says?"

Josh squinted; he couldn't even read the license plate.

"When we ate earlier today, the taste of the food was so overwhelming it almost made me throw up. I could taste the individual grains of salt on the sandwich." She stooped and picked a jacaranda leaf off the ground. "I can trace each vein in the back of this leaf with my eyes closed. But you know what's worst of all? The smells," she said, looking deliberately at her brother.

"Hey . . ." Ever since he'd hit puberty he'd tried every deodorant on the market.

"No, not just you"—she grinned—"though you've really got to change your deodorant, and I think you're going to need to burn your socks. It's all the scents, all the time. The stink of gas in the air is awful, the smell of hot rubber on the road, of greasy food, even the perfume from these flowers is overwhelming." She stopped in the middle of the street, and her tone abruptly changed. She looked at her brother, and the tears she had no idea were there started to leak from her eyes. "It's too much, Josh. It's just too much. I feel sick and my head is pounding, my eyes hurt, my ears ache, my throat is raw."

Josh awkwardly tried to put his arms around his sister to hug her, but she pushed him away. "Please, don't touch me. I can't bear it."

Josh struggled to find words to respond, but there was nothing he could say or do. He felt so helpless. Sophie was always so strong, always in control; she was the person he went to when he was in trouble. She always had the answers.

Until now.

Flamel! Josh felt the anger flare again. This was Flamel's fault. He would never forgive the Alchemyst for what he'd done. He looked up to see Flamel and Scathach turning back to them.

The Warrior came hurrying over to them. "Dry your eyes," she commanded sternly. "Let's not draw attention to ourselves."

"Don't talk to my sis—" Josh began, but Scatty silenced him with a look.

"Let's get you into my grandmother's shop; she'll be able to help. It's just across the road. Come on."

Sophie obediently ran her sleeve across her eyes and followed the Warrior. She felt so helpless. She rarely cried—she'd even laughed at the ending of *Titanic*—so why was she crying now?

Awakening her magical potential had seemed like a wonderful idea. She'd loved the thought of being able to control and shape her will, of channeling her aura's energy and working magic. But it hadn't turned out like that. It had left her feeling battered and exhausted from the stimulation. It had left her in pain. That was why she was crying.

And she was terrified that the pain was not going to go away. And if it didn't, then what would she do—what *could* she do?

Sophie looked up to find her brother staring hard at her, eyes wide with concern. "Flamel said the Witch will be able to help you," he said.

"What if she can't, Josh? What if she can't?"

He had no answer to that.

Sophie and Josh crossed Ojai Avenue and stepped under the arched promenade that ran the length of the block. The temperature immediately dropped to a bearable level, and Sophie realized that her shirt was sticking to the small of her back, ice cold against her spine.

They caught up with Nicholas Flamel, who had stopped in front of a small antiques shop, a dismayed look on his face. The shop was closed. Without saying a word, he tapped at the paper clock taped to the inside of the door. The hands were set to two-thirty and a handwritten scrawl beneath it said *Gone to lunch, back at 2:30.*

It was now close to three-thirty.

Flamel and Scatty leaned against the door, peering inside, while the twins looked through the window. The small shop seemed to sell only glassware: bowls, jugs, plates, paperweights, ornaments and mirrors. Lots of mirrors. They were everywhere, and in all shapes and sizes from tiny circles to huge rectangles. Much of the glass looked modern, but a few of the pieces in the window were obviously antiques.

"So what do we do now?" Flamel wondered. "Where can she be?"

"Probably wandered out to get lunch and forgot to come back," Scatty said, turning to look up and down the street. "Hardly busy today, is it?" Even though it was late Friday afternoon, traffic was light on the main street, and there were fewer than a dozen pedestrians moving slowly beneath the covered promenade.

"We could check the restaurants," Flamel suggested. "What does she like to eat?"

"Don't ask," Scatty said quickly, "you really do not want to know."

"Maybe if we split up . . . ," Nicholas began.

On impulse Sophie leaned forward and turned the handle: a bell jangled musically and the door swung open.

"Nice one, Sis."

"Saw it done in a movie once," she muttered. "Hello?" she called, stepping into the shop.

There was no response.

The antiques shop was tiny, little more than a long rectangular room, but the effect of the hundreds of mirrors—some of which even dangled from the ceiling—made it look much bigger than it actually was.

Sophie threw back her head and breathed deeply, nostrils flaring. "Do you smell that?"

Her twin shook his head. The number of mirrors was making him nervous; he kept catching reflections of himself from all sides, and in every mirror, his image was different, broken or distorted.

"What do you smell?" Scatty asked.

"It's like . . ." Sophie paused. "Like woodsmoke in the fall."

"So she has been here."

Sophie and Josh looked at her blankly.

"That's the odor of the Witch of Endor. That's the scent of eldritch magic."

Flamel stood by the door looking up and down the street. "She can't have gone far, if she left the shop unlocked. I'm going to go look for her." He turned to Scatty. "How will I recognize her?"

She grinned, eyes bright and wicked. "Trust me; you'll know her when you see her."

"I'll be back shortly."

As Flamel stepped out into the street, a big motorcycle pulled up almost directly outside the shop. The rider sat there for a moment and then gunned his engine and roared away. The noise was incredible: all the glassware in the tiny shop shivered and vibrated with the sound. Sophie pressed both hands to her ears. "I don't know how much more of this I can take," she whispered tearfully.

Josh led his sister to a plain wooden chair and made her sit down. He crouched on one side, wanting to hold her hand, but frightened of touching her. He felt utterly useless.

Scatty knelt down directly in front of Sophie, so that their faces were level. "When Hekate Awakened you, she didn't have a chance to teach you how to turn your Awakened senses on and off. Your senses are stuck *on* at the moment, but it won't be like that all the time, I promise you. With a little training and a few basic protective spells, you'll learn to turn your senses on for just the briefest of periods."

Josh looked at the two girls. Once again, he felt apart from his twin: truly apart. They were fraternal twins, and therefore not genetically identical. They didn't share those feelings that identical twins often spoke about—feeling pain when the other twin was hurt, knowing when they were in trouble—but right now he could feel his sister's distress. He only wished there was something he could do to ease her pain.

Almost as if she could read his mind, Scatty said suddenly, "There is something I can do that might help." The twins picked up on the note of hesitation in her voice. "It will not hurt," she added quickly.

"It can't hurt more than what I'm feeling now," Sophie whispered. "Do it," she said quickly.

"I need your permission first."

"Soph—" Josh began, but his sister ignored him.

"Do it," Sophie repeated. "Please," she begged.

"I've told you I am what you humani call a vampire. . . ."

"You are *not* drinking her blood!" Josh yelled, horrified. His stomach flipped over at the thought.

"I've told you before, my clan do not drink blood."

"I don't care—"

308

"Josh," Sophie interrupted angrily, her aura winking into existence for a second with her anger, filling the interior of the shop with the sudden sweetness of vanilla ice cream. A display of glass wind chimes tinkled and rattled in an unfelt breeze. "Josh, be quiet." She swiveled in the seat to look at Scatty. "What do you want me to do?"

"Give me your right hand."

Sophie immediately stretched out her hand and Scatty took it in both of hers. Then she carefully matched the fingers of her left hand to the girl's fingers, thumb to thumb, index finger to index finger, little finger to little finger. "Blood-drinking vampires," she said absently, concentrating on aligning their hands, "are really the weakest, the lowliest of our clan. Have you ever wondered why they drink blood? They're actually dead—their hearts do not beat, they have no need to eat, so the blood provides no sustenance for them."

"Are you dead?" Sophie asked the question Josh was just about to ask.

"No, not really."

Josh looked into the mirrors, but he could clearly see Scathach's reflection in the glass. She caught him looking and smiled. "Don't believe that old rubbish about vampires not casting a reflection: of course we do; we are solid, after all."

Josh watched intently as Scathach pressed her fingers to his sister's. Nothing seemed to be happening. Then he caught a sparkle of silver in a mirror behind Scatty and he realized that in the glass, Sophie's hand had begun to glow with a pale silver light.

"My race, the Clan Vampire," Scatty continued very softly, staring at Sophie's palm, "were of the Next Generation."

In the mirror Josh saw that the silver light had begun to pool in Sophie's palm.

"We were not Elders. All of us who were born after the fall of Danu Talis were completely unlike our parents; we were *different* in incomprehensible ways."

"You've mentioned Danu Talis before," Sophie murmured sleepily. "What is it, a place?" There was a warm, soothing feeling flowing up her arm, not unlike pins and needles, but tingling and pleasant.

"It was the center of the world in the Elder Times. The Elder Race ruled this planet from an island continent known as Danu Talis. It stretched from what is now the coast of Africa to the shores of North America and into the Gulf of Mexico."

"I've never heard of Danu Talis," Sophie whispered.

"Yes, you have," Scathach said. "The Celts called it the De Danann Isle; this modern world knows it as Atlantis."

In the mirror, Josh could see that Sophie's hand was now glowing silver-white. It looked as if she were wearing a glove. Tiny sparking tendrils of silver wrapped themselves around Scatty's fingers like ornate rings, and she shuddered.

"Danu Talis was ripped apart because the Ruling Twins—the Sun and Moon—fought on top of the Great Pyramid. The incredible magical forces they released upset the balance of nature. I've been told that that same wild magic swirling around the atmosphere caused the changes in the Next Generation. Some of us were born as monsters, others were caught between shapes, a few possessed extraordinary powers of transformation and could become beasts at will. And others, like those of us who eventually formed the Clan Vampire, found that we were unable to feel."

Josh looked sharply at Scathach. "What do you mean, *feel*?"

The Warrior smiled and looked at him. Suddenly, her teeth seemed very long in her mouth. "We had little or no emotion. We lacked the capacity to feel fear, to experience love, to enjoy the sensations of happiness and delight. The finest warriors are not only those who do not know fear, but those who are without anger."

Josh stepped back from Scatty and breathed deeply. His legs were beginning to cramp, and pins and needles were tingling in his toes. But he also needed to get away from the vampire. Now all the mirrors and polished glass surfaces in the shop showed the silver light flowing from Sophie's hand up Scatty's arm. It disappeared into her flesh before it reached her elbow.

Scatty turned her head to look at Josh, and he noticed that the whites of her eyes had turned silver. "Bloodsucking vampires don't need the blood. They need the emotions, the sensations carried in the blood."

"You're stealing Sophie's feelings," Josh whispered, horrified. "Sophie, stop her. . . ."

"No!" his twin snapped, eyes opening wide. The whites of her eyes, like Scatty's, had turned reflective silver. "I can actually feel the pain flowing away."

"The sensations are too much for your sister to bear. They

311

are becoming painful, and this makes her afraid. I'm just taking away that pain and fear."

"Why would anyone want to feel pain or fear?" Josh wondered aloud, both intrigued and repelled by the very idea. It seemed somehow *wrong*.

"So they can feel alive," Scatty said.

CHAPTER THIRTY-FOUR

$\mathcal{E}$ven before she opened her eyes, Perenelle Flamel knew she had been moved to a much more secure prison. Someplace deep and dark and sinister. She could feel the old evil in the walls, could almost taste it on the air. Lying still, she tried to expand her senses, but the blanket of malevolence and despair was too strong, and she found she couldn't use her magic. She listened intently, and only when she was absolutely sure that there was no one in the room with her did she open her eyes.

She was in a cell.

Three walls were solid concrete, the fourth was metal bars. Beyond the bars she could see another row of cells.

She was in a prison block!

Perenelle swung her legs out of the narrow cot and came slowly to her feet. She noticed that her clothes smelled slightly of sea salt, and she thought she could detect the sounds of the not-too-distant ocean.

The cell was bare, little more than an empty box, about ten feet long by four feet wide, with a narrow cot holding a thin mattress and a single lumpy pillow. A cardboard tray lay on the floor just inside the bars. It contained a plastic jug of water, a plastic cup and a thick chunk of dark bread on a paper plate. Seeing the food made her realize just how hungry she was, but she ignored it for the moment and crossed to the bars and peered out. Looking left and right, all she could see were cells, and they were empty.

She was alone in the cell block. But where . . .

And then a ship's horn, plaintive and lost, sounded in the distance. With a shiver, Perenelle suddenly knew where Dee's men had taken her: she was on the prison island of Alcatraz, The Rock.

She looked around the room, paying particular attention to the area around the metal gate. Unlike in her previous prison, she couldn't see any magical wards or protective sigils painted on the lintel or the floor. Perenelle couldn't resist a tiny smile. What were Dee's people thinking? Once she had recovered her strength, she'd charge up her aura, and then bend this metal like putty and simply walk out of here.

It took her a moment before she realized that the *click-click* she'd first assumed to be dripping water was actually something approaching, moving slowly and deliberately. Pressing herself against the bars, she tried to see down the corridor. A shadow moved. More of Dee's faceless simulacra? she wondered. They would not be able to hold her for long.

The shadow, huge and misshapen, moved out of the darkness and stepped down the corridor to stand before her cell. Perenelle was suddenly grateful for the bars that separated her from the terrifying entity.

Filling the corridor was a creature that had not walked the earth since a millennium before the first pyramid rose over the Nile. It was a sphinx, an enormous lion with the wings of an eagle and the head of a beautiful woman. The sphinx smiled and tilted her head to one side, and a long black forked tongue flickered. Perenelle noticed that her pupils were flat and horizontal.

This was not one of Dee's creations. The sphinx was one of the daughters of Echidna, one of the foulest of the Elders, shunned and feared even by her own race, even the Dark Elders. Perenelle suddenly found herself wondering who, exactly, Dee was serving.

The sphinx pressed her face against the bars. Her long tongue shot out, tasting the air, almost brushing Perenelle's lips. "Do I need to remind you, Perenelle Flamel," she asked in the language of the Nile, "that one of the especial skills of my race is that we absorb auric energy?" Her huge wings flapped, almost filling the corridor. "You have no magical powers around me."

An icy shiver ran down Perenelle's spine as she realized just how clever Dee was. She was a defenseless and powerless prisoner on Alcatraz, and she knew that no one had ever escaped The Rock alive.

CHAPTER THIRTY-FIVE

*T*he bell jangled as Nicholas Flamel pushed open the door and stepped back to allow a rather ordinary-looking elderly woman in a neat gray blouse and gray skirt to precede him into the shop. Short and round, her hair tightly permed and touched faintly with blue, only the overlarge black glasses covering much of her face set her apart. A white cane was folded in her right hand.

Sophie and Josh immediately realized that she was blind.

Flamel cleared his throat. "Allow me to introduce . . ." He stopped and looked at the woman. "Excuse me. What do I call you?"

"Call me Dora, everyone else does." She spoke English with a decided New York accent. "Scathach?" she suddenly said. "Scathach!" And then her words dissolved into a language that seemed to consist of a lot of spitting sounds . . . which Sophie was surprised to find she could understand.

"She wants to know why Scatty hasn't come to see her in the past three hundred and seventy-two years, eight months and four days," she translated for Josh. She was staring intently at the old woman and didn't see the fear and envy that flickered across his face.

The old woman moved quickly around the narrow room, head darting left and right, never looking directly at Scatty. She continued to speak, seemingly without stopping for breath.

"She's telling Scatty that she could have been dead and no one would have known. Nor cared. Why, only last century she was desperately ill, and no one called, no one wrote . . ."

"Gran . . . ," Scatty began.

"Don't 'Gran' me," Dora said, dropping into English again. "You could have written—any language would have done. You could have phoned. . . ."

"You don't have a phone."

"And what's wrong with e-mail? Or a fax?"

"Gran, have you got a computer or a fax machine?"

Dora stopped. "No. What would I need one of them for?"

Dora's hand moved and suddenly her white stick extended to its full length with a snap. She tapped against the glass of a simple square mirror. "Have you got one of these?"

"Yes, Gran," Scatty said miserably. Her pale cheeks were flushed red with embarrassment.

"So you couldn't find the time to look in a mirror and talk to me. You're so busy these days? I've got to hear it from your brother. And when was the last time you spoke to your mother!"

317

Scathach turned to the twins. "This is my grandmother, the legendary Witch of Endor. Gran, this is Sophie and Josh. And you've met Nicholas Flamel."

"Yes, such a nice man." She kept turning her head, her nostrils flaring. "Twins," she said finally.

Sophie and Josh looked at each other. How did she know? Did Nicholas tell her?

There was something about the way the woman kept moving her head that intrigued Josh. He tried to follow the direction of her gaze . . . and then he realized why the old woman's head kept moving left and right: she was somehow seeing them *through* the mirrors. Automatically, he touched his sister's hand and nodded to the mirror. She glanced at it, back at the old woman, then back at the mirror, and then she nodded at her brother, silently agreeing with him.

Dora stepped up to Scathach, her head turned to one side as she stared hard at a tall length of polished glass. "You've lost weight. Are you eating properly?"

"Gran, I've looked like this for two and a half thousand years."

"So you're saying I'm going blind now, eh?" the old woman asked, then burst into surprisingly deep laughter. "Give your old Gran a hug."

Scathach carefully hugged the old woman and kissed her cheek. "It's good to see you, Gran. You're looking well."

"I'm looking old. Do I look old?"

"Not a day over ten thousand." Scatty smiled.

The Witch pinched Scathach's cheek. "The last person

who mocked me was a tax inspector. I turned him into a paperweight," she said. "I still have it here somewhere."

Flamel coughed discreetly. "Madame Endor . . ."

"Call me Dora," the old woman snapped.

"Dora. Are you aware what happened in Hekate's Shadowrealm earlier today?" He had never met the Witch before—he knew her only by reputation—but he knew she needed to be treated with the utmost caution. She was the legendary Elder who had left Danu Talis to live with and teach the humani centuries before the island sank beneath the waves. It was believed that she had created the first humani alphabet in ancient Sumeria.

"Get me a chair," Dora said to no one in particular. Sophie pulled up the chair she'd been sitting on and Scatty eased her grandmother into it. The old woman leaned forward, both hands resting on the top of her white cane. "I know what happened. I'm sure every Elder on this continent felt her death." She saw their looks of shocked surprise. "You didn't know?" She turned her head sideways and stared into a mirror, directly facing Scatty. "Hekate is dead and her Shadowrealm is no more. I understand an Elder, one of the Next Generation and an immortal human were responsible for her death. Hekate will need to be avenged. Not now, and maybe not soon: but she was family, and I owe her that. See to it." Scatty bowed.

The Witch of Endor had delivered the death sentence calmly, and Flamel suddenly realized that this woman was even more dangerous than he had imagined.

Dora turned her face in another direction and Flamel found himself looking at her reflection in an ornate silver-framed mirror. She tapped the glass. "I saw what happened this morning a month ago."

"And you didn't warn Hekate!" Scatty exclaimed.

"I watched one thread of a possible-future. One of many. In some of the others, Hekate killed Bastet and the Morrigan slew Dee. In another, Hekate killed you, Mr. Flamel, and was in turn killed by Scathach. All versions of the future. Today I discovered which came to pass." She looked around the room, turning her face from mirror to polished vase to picture-frame glass. "So I know why you're here, I know what you want me to do. And I've thought long and hard about my response. I've had a month to think about it."

"What about us?" Sophie asked. "Were we in your threads?"

"Yes, in some," the Witch said.

"What happened to us in the others?" The question was out of Josh's mouth before he had time to think about it. He *really* didn't want to know the answer.

"Dee and his Golems or the rats and birds killed you in most of the threads. You crashed the car in others. You died with the Awakening or fell with the Shadowrealm."

Josh swallowed hard. "We only survived in one thread?"

"Just one."

"That's not good, is it?" he whispered.

"No," the Witch of Endor stated flatly. "Not good at all." There was a long pause while Dora looked sidelong into the polished surface of a silver pot. Then she spoke suddenly.

"First you should know that I cannot Awaken the boy. That must be left to others."

Josh looked up quickly. "There are others who could Awaken me?"

The Witch of Endor ignored him. "The girl has one of the purest silver auras I've encountered in many an age. She needs to be taught some spells of personal protection if she is to survive the rest of the Awakening process. The fact that she's still sane and whole these many hours later is testament to her strength of will." Her head tilted back and Sophie caught the old woman's face looking at her from a mirror suspended from the ceiling. "This I will do."

"Thank you," Nicholas Flamel said with a deep sigh. "I know how difficult the last few hours have been for her."

Josh found that he could not look at his sister. There was *more* to the Awakening. Did that mean she would have to suffer more pain? It was heartbreaking.

Scathach knelt by her grandmother's chair and laid a hand on her arm. "Gran, Dee and his masters are chasing the two missing pages from the Codex," she said. "I would imagine that by now they know—or at least suspect—that Sophie and Josh are the twins mentioned in the Book of Abraham."

Dora nodded. "Dee knows."

Scathach stole a glance at Flamel. "Then he knows that not only does he have to retrieve the pages, but he has to either capture or kill the twins."

"He knows that, too," Dora confirmed.

"And if Dee succeeds, then this world ends?" Scathach said, turning the simple sentence into a question.

"The world has ended before," the Witch answered, smiling. "I'm sure it will end many times before the sun turns black."

"You know that Dee intends to bring back the Dark Elders?"

"I know."

"The Codex says that the Dark Elders can only be stopped by Silver and Gold," Scatty continued.

"The Codex also says, if my memory serves me true, that apples are poisonous and frogs can turn into princes. You don't want to believe everything you read in that Codex," the witch snapped.

Flamel had read the piece in the Codex about apples. He thought it was possibly referring to apple seeds, which were indeed poisonous—if you ate several pounds of them. He hadn't come across the section about frogs and princes, though he'd read the Book hundreds of times. There were countless questions he wanted to ask the Witch, but that wasn't the reason they were there. "Dora, will you teach Sophie the principles of Air magic? She needs to learn enough to at least be able to protect herself from attack."

Dora shrugged and smiled. "Do I have a choice?"

Flamel had not been expecting that answer. "Of course you have a choice."

The Witch of Endor shook her head. "Not this time." She reached up and took off her dark glasses. Scatty didn't move, and only the muscle twitching in Flamel's jaw betrayed his surprise. The twins, however, backed away in horror, their faces registering their shock. The Witch of Endor had no eyes.

There were just hollow empty sockets where eyes should have been, and nestled in the sockets were perfect ovals of reflective glass. Those mirrors turned directly to the twins. "I gave up my eyes for the Sight, the ability to see the patterns of time—time past, present and possible-future. There are many patterns, many versions of possible-future, though not so many as people think. In the past few years, the patterns have been coming together, weaving ever closer. Now there are only a few possible futures. Most of them are terrifying," she added grimly. "And they are all linked to you two." Her hand moved unswervingly to point to Sophie and Josh. "So what choice do I have? This is my world too. I was here before the humani, I gave them fire and language. I'll not abandon them now. I'll train the girl, teach her how to protect herself and instill in her how to control the magic of Air."

"Thank you," Sophie said carefully into the long silence that followed.

"Do not thank me. This is not a gift. What I give you is a curse!"

CHAPTER THIRTY-SIX

*J*osh stepped out of the antiques shop, cheeks flaming red, the Witch's last words ringing in his ears. "You have to leave. What I teach is not for the ears of a humani."

Looking around the room, at Flamel and Scatty and finally his twin sister, Josh had suddenly realized that he was the last pure human in the room. Obviously, in the Witch of Endor's eyes, Sophie was no longer entirely human.

"No problem. I'll wait . . . ," he began, voice suddenly cracking. He coughed and tried again. "I'll wait in the park across the road." And then, without a backward glance, he left the shop, the jangling of the bell mocking him as he closed the door.

But it was a problem. A huge problem.

Sophie Newman watched her brother leave the shop, and even without her Awakened senses, she knew he was upset and angry. She wanted to stop him, to go after him, but Scatty was standing in front of her, eyes wide in warning, finger raised to her lips, the tiniest shake of her head warning Sophie to say nothing. Catching her shoulder, Scatty led her to stand in front of the Witch of Endor. The old woman raised her hands and ran surprisingly gentle fingers over the contours of Sophie's face. The girl's aura shivered and fizzed with each gentle touch.

"How old are you now?" she asked.

"Fifteen. Well, fifteen and a half." Sophie wasn't sure if the half year made a difference.

"Fifteen and a half," Dora said, shaking her head. "I can't remember back that far." She dipped her chin, then tilted it toward Scatty. "Can you remember back to when you were fifteen?"

"Vividly," Scathach said grimly. "Wasn't that about the time I visited you in Babylon and you tried to marry me off to King Nebuchadnezzar?"

"I'm sure you're wrong," Dora said happily. "I think that was later. Though he would have made an excellent husband," she added. She looked up at Sophie and the girl found herself reflected in the mirrors that were the Witch's eyes. "There are two things I must teach you. To protect yourself—that is simplicity itself. But instructing you in the magic of Air is a little trickier. The last time I instructed a humani in Air magic, it took him sixty years to master the basics, and even then he fell out of the sky on his first flight."

"Sixty years." Sophie swallowed. Did that mean she was destined to spend a lifetime trying to control this power?

"Gran, we haven't got that sort of time. I doubt we've even got sixty minutes."

Dora glared into a mirror and her reflection looked out from the glass of an empty picture frame. "So why don't you do this, you're such an expert, eh?"

"*Gran . . .*" Scathach sighed.

"Don't 'Gran' me in that tone of voice," Dora said warningly. "I'll do this my way."

"We don't have time to do it the traditional way."

"Don't talk to me about tradition. What do the young know about tradition? Trust me, when I'm finished, Sophie will know all that I know about the elemental Air magic." She turned back to Sophie. "First things first: are your parents alive?"

"Yes," she said, blinking in surprise, not sure where this was going.

"Good. And you talk to your mother?"

"Yes, almost every day."

Dora glanced sideways at Scatty. "You hear that? Almost every day." She took one of Sophie's hands in hers and patted the back of it. "Maybe you should be teaching Scathach a thing or two. And have you a grandmother?"

"My Nana, yes, my father's mother. I usually call her on Fridays," she added, realizing with a guilty start that today was Friday and that Nana Newman would be expecting a call.

"Every Friday," the Witch of Endor said significantly, and looked at Scatty again, but the Warrior deliberately turned away and concentrated on an ornate glass paperweight. She put it down when she saw that there was a tiny man in a three-piece suit frozen inside the glass. He had a briefcase in one hand and a sheaf of papers in the other. His eyes were still blinking.

"This will not hurt," the Witch said.

Sophie doubted it could be any worse than what she'd already gone through. Her nose wrinkled at the odor of burnt wood, and she felt a cool breeze wash over her hands. She looked down. A gossamer-thin white spiderweb was twisting and spinning from the Witch of Endor's fingers and wrapping itself like a bandage around each of Sophie's fingers. It curled across her palm, completely covering it, then wrapped around her wrist and crept up her arm. She realized then that the Witch had been distracting her with her questions. Sophie looked into the Witch's mirrored eyes and found that she could not put her questions into words. It was as if she had lost the ability to speak. She was also surprised that instead of feeling frightened, from the moment the Witch had taken her hand, a wave of peace and calm had washed through her body. She glanced sideways at Scatty and Flamel. They were watching the process, wide-eyed with shock and, in Scathach's case, with something like horror on her face.

"Gran . . . are you sure about this?" Scathach demanded.

"Of course I'm sure," the old woman snapped, a note of anger in her voice.

And even though the Witch of Endor was speaking to Scathach, Sophie could hear her voice in her head, talking to her, whispering ancient secrets, murmuring archaic spells, divulging a lifetime of knowledge in the space of heartbeats and breaths.

"This is not a spiderweb," Dora explained to a stunned and silent Flamel, noticing that he was leaning forward, staring intently at the webs spinning around Sophie's arms. "It is concentrated air mixed with my own aura. All my knowledge, my experience, even my lore is gathered in this web of air. Once it touches Sophie's skin, she will begin to absorb that knowledge."

Sophie breathed deeply, drawing the wood-scented air deep into her lungs. Images flashed impossibly fast in her head, times and places long past, cyclopean walls of stone, ships of solid gold, dinosaurs and dragons, a city carved into a mountain of ice and faces . . . hundreds, thousands of faces, from every race of mankind, from every time period, human and half human, werebeast and monster. She was seeing everyone the Witch of Endor had ever seen.

"The Egyptians got it wrong," Dora continued, her hands now moving too fast for Flamel to see. "They wrapped the dead," she continued. "They did not realize I wrapped the living. There was a time when I put a little of myself into my followers and sent them out into the world to teach in my name. Obviously someone saw this process in the ancient past and tried to copy it."

Sophie suddenly saw a dozen people wrapped up like her, and a younger-looking Dora moving among them, dressed in a costume from ancient Babylon. Somehow Sophie understood that these were the priests and priestesses in the cult that worshipped the Witch. Dora was passing on a little of her knowledge to them so that they could go out into the world and teach others.

The white weblike air now flowed down Sophie's legs, binding them together. Unconsciously, she brought her hands up across her chest, right hand on her left shoulder, left hand on her right shoulder. The Witch nodded approvingly.

Sophie closed her eyes and saw clouds. Without knowing how, she knew their names: cirrus, cirrocumulus, altostratus and stratocumulus, nimbostratus and cumulus. All different, each type with unique characteristics and qualities. She suddenly understood how to use them, how to shape and wield and move them.

Images flickered.

Flashed.

She saw a tiny woman under a clear blue sky raise a hand and make a cloud grow directly overhead. Rain irrigated a parched field.

Flashed again.

A tall bearded man standing on the edge of a huge sea raised his hands and a howling wind parting the waters.

And flashed again.

A young woman brought a raging storm to a shuddering stop with a single gesture, freezing it in place, then ran into a flimsy wooden house and grabbed a child. A heartbeat later and the storm ate the house.

Sophie watched the images and learned from them.

The Witch of Endor touched Sophie's cheek and the girl opened her eyes. The whites were dotted with silver sparkles. "There are those who will tell you that the magic of Fire or Water or even Earth is the most powerful magic of all. They are wrong. The magic of Air surpasses all others. Air can extinguish fire. It can churn water to mist and can rip up the earth. But air can also bring fire to life, it can push a boat across still water, can shape the land. Air can clean a wound, can pluck a splinter from a fingertip. Air can kill."

The last of the white cobwebbed air closed across Sophie's face, completely encasing her, wrapping her like a mummy.

"This is a terrifying gift I have given you. Within you now is a lifetime—a very long lifetime—of experience. I hope some will be of use to you in the dire days ahead."

Sophie stood before the Witch of Endor completely encased in the white bandagelike air. This was not like the Awakening. This was a gentler, subtler process. She discovered that she *knew* things—incredible things. She had memories of impossible times and extraordinary places. But mixed with these memories and emotions were her own thoughts. Already she was beginning to find it hard to tell them apart.

Then the smoke began to curl and hiss and steam.

Dora suddenly turned to look for Scatty. "Come and give me a hug, child. I will not see you again."

"Gran?"

Dora wrapped her arms around Scathach's shoulders and put her mouth close to her ear.

Her voice dropped to little more than a whisper. "I have given this girl a rare and terrible power. Make sure this power is used for good."

Scathach nodded, not entirely sure what the old woman was suggesting.

"And call your mother. She worries about you."

"I will, Gran."

The mummylike cocoon suddenly dissolved into steam and mist as Sophie's aura flared brilliant silver. She stretched out her arms, fingers splayed wide, and the merest whisper of a wind rattled through the shop.

"Careful. If you break anything, you pay for it," the Witch warned.

Then, suddenly, Scathach, Dora and Sophie turned to look out into the darkening afternoon. An instant later Nicholas Flamel smelled the unmistakable rotten-egg odor of sulfur. "Dee!"

"Josh!" Sophie's eyes snapped open. "Josh is out there!"

CHAPTER THIRTY-SEVEN

Dr. John Dee finally arrived in Ojai as the last light was fading in spectacular shades of pink over the surrounding Topa Topa Mountains. He'd been traveling all day; he was tired and irritable and looking for an excuse to hurt someone.

Hekate's Shadowrealm had drained his cell battery, and it had taken him over an hour before he could find a phone to contact his office. He'd then been forced to sit, fuming, by the side of the road for another ninety minutes while a team of drivers scoured Mill Valley's backroads looking for him. It was close to nine-thirty before he finally returned to his offices at Enoch Enterprises in the heart of the city.

There he'd learned that Perenelle had already been moved to Alcatraz. His company had recently purchased the island from the state and had closed it to the public while restoration work was being carried out. There was talk in the papers that it was going to be turned into a living history museum. In reality, the doctor intended to return it to its original use as one of the most secure prisons in the world. The doctor briefly thought about flying out to the island to talk to Perenelle, but dismissed the idea as a waste of time. The missing pages from the Codex and the twins were his priorities. Although Bastet had said to kill them if he couldn't kidnap them, Dee had other ideas.

Dee knew of the famous prophecy from the Book of Abraham the Mage. The Elders had known that twins were coming, "the two that are one, the one that is all." One to save the world, one to destroy it. But which one was which? he wondered. And could their powers be shaped and twisted by the instruction they received? Finding the boy was becoming as important as finding the missing pages of the Codex. He had to have that gold aura.

Dr. John Dee had lived in Ojai briefly at the turn of the twentieth century—it was still called the city of Nordhoff then—when he'd been plundering the surrounding Chumash burial grounds for their precious artifacts. He'd hated it: Ojai was too small, too insular and, in the summer months, simply too hot for him. Dee was always happiest in the largest of cities, where it was easier to be invisible and anonymous.

He'd flown from San Francisco down to Santa Barbara in the company helicopter, and rented a nondescript-looking Ford at the small airport. Then he'd driven down from Santa Barbara, arriving in Ojai just as the sun was setting in a spectacular display, painting the town in long, elegant shadows. Ojai had changed dramatically in the hundred or so years since he'd last seen it . . . but he still didn't like it.

He turned the car onto Ojai Avenue and slowed. Flamel and the others were close; he could feel it. But he had to be careful now. If he could sense them, then they—especially the Alchemyst and Scathach—would be able to sense him. And he still had no idea what the Witch of Endor was capable of doing. It was extremely worrying that a very senior Elder had been living in California and he'd been totally unaware of her presence. He thought he knew the locations of most of the important Elders and human immortals in the world. Dee wondered if it was significant that he had not been able to contact the Morrigan throughout the day. He'd phoned her with persistent regularity on the drive down, but she wasn't answering her cell. She was either on eBay or playing one of the interminable online strategy games she was addicted to. He didn't know where Bastet was and didn't care. She frightened him, and Dee tended to destroy those people who scared him.

Flamel, Scathach and the twins could be anywhere in the town. But where?

Dee allowed a little energy to trickle into his aura. He blinked as his eyes blurred with sudden tears, and blinked again to clear them. Suddenly, the people in the car next to his, those crossing the road, and the pedestrians on the sidewalk were outlined in shifting multicolored auras. Some auras were just wisps of diaphanous tinted smoke, others were dark spots and sheets of solid muddy colors.

In the end, he found them entirely by chance: he was driving down Ojai Avenue and had gone past Libbey Park when he spotted the black Hummer parked on Fox Street. He pulled in behind it and parked. The moment he got out of his car, he caught the merest hint of a pure gold aura coming from the park, close to the fountain. Dee's thin lips curled in a humorless smile.

They would not escape this time.

Josh Newman sat by the long, low fountain in Libbey Park directly across from the antiques shop and stared into the water. Two flower-shaped bowls, one larger than the other, were set in the center of a circular pool. Water spouted from the top bowl and flowed over the sides into the larger bowl beneath. This in turn overflowed into the pool. The sound helped drown out the nearby traffic noises.

He felt alone, and more than a little lost.

When the Witch had made him leave the antiques shop, he'd walked beneath the shaded promenade and stopped in front of the ice cream shop, lured there by the odors of chocolate and vanilla. He stood outside, reading the menu of exotic flavors, and wondered why his sister's aura smelled of vanilla ice cream and his of oranges. She didn't even really like ice cream; he was the one who loved it.

His finger tapped the menu: blueberry chocolate chip.

Josh shoved his hand in the back pocket of his jeans . . . and felt a rising moment of panic as realized his wallet was missing. Had he left it in the car, had he . . . ? He stopped.

He knew exactly where he'd left it.

The last place he'd seen his wallet, along with his dead cell, his iPod and his laptop, was on the floor next to his bed in his room in the Yggdrasill. Losing his wallet was bad enough, but losing his computer was a disaster. All his e-mails were on it, along with his class notes, a partially written summer honors project, three years of photos—including the trip to Cancún at Christmas—and at least sixty gigs of MP3s. He couldn't remember the last time he had backed up, but it definitely wasn't recently. He actually felt physically ill, and suddenly, the odors from the ice cream parlor didn't smell so sweet and enticing.

Thoroughly miserable, he walked to the corner and crossed at the lights facing the post office, then turned left, heading toward the park.

The iPod had been a Christmas present from his parents. How was he going to explain to them that he'd lost it? Plus there was close to another thirty gigs of music on the little hard drive.

But worse than losing his iPod, his wallet or even his computer was losing his phone. That was a total nightmare. All his friends' numbers were on it, and he knew he hadn't written them down anywhere. Because their parents traveled so much, the twins were rarely more than one or two semesters at the same school. They made friends easily—especially Sophie—and they were still in touch with friends they'd met years earlier in schools scattered across America. Without those e-mail addresses and phone numbers, how was he supposed to get in touch with them, how would he ever find them again?

There was a water fountain in a little nook before the entrance to the park, and he bent his head to drink. An ornamental metal lion's head was set into the wall over the fountain, and below it there was a small rectangular plaque with the words *Love is the water of life, drink deeply*. He let the icy water splash over his lips and straightened to look over at the shop, wondering what was happening inside. He still loved his sister, but did she love him? *Could* she love him, now that he was . . . *ordinary*?

Libbey Park was quiet. Josh could hear children racing around the nearby playground, but their voices sounded high and very distant. A trio of old men, identically dressed in sleeveless shirts, long shorts, white socks and sandals, gathered on a shady bench. One of the men was feeding bread crumbs to a quartet of fat and lazy pigeons. Josh sat down on the edge of the low fountain and leaned over to trail his hand in the water. After the oppressive heat, it felt deliciously cool, and he ran his wet fingers through his hair, feeling water droplets roll down his neck.

What was he going to do?

Was there anything he could do?

In just over twenty-four hours, his life—and his sister's life too—had changed utterly and incomprehensibly. What he had once believed to be merely stories now turned out to be versions of the truth. Myth had become history, legends had become facts. When Scatty had revealed earlier that the mysterious Danu Talis was also called Atlantis, he had almost laughed in her face. To him, Atlantis had always been a fairy tale. But if Scathach and Hekate and the Morrigan and Bastet were real, then so was Danu Talis. And so his parents' life work—archaeology—was suddenly worthless.

Josh knew deep down that he had also lost his twin, the constant in his life, the one person he could always count on. She had changed in ways he could not even begin to comprehend. Why hadn't he been Awakened too? He should have insisted that Hekate Awaken him first. What would it be like to have those powers? The only thing he could compare it to was being a superhero. Even when Sophie's newly Awakened senses were making her sick, he was jealous of her abilities.

From the corner of his eye, Josh became aware that a man had sat down on one of the other edges of the fountain, but he ignored him. He absently picked at a broken fragment of one of the blue tiles that ran around the fountain.

What was he going to do?

And the answer was always the same: what *could* he do?

"Are you a victim too?"

It took him a moment before he realized that the figure sitting to his right was talking to him. He started to stand up, the golden rule with creeps being that you never responded, and you never—ever—entered into any conversation with them.

"It seems we are all victims of Nicholas Flamel."

Startled, Josh looked up . . . and found he was staring at Dr. John Dee, the man he'd hoped never to see again. The last time he'd seen Dee had been in the Shadowrealm. Then, he'd held the sword Excalibur in his hands. Now he sat facing him, looking out of place in his impeccably tailored gray suit.

Josh looked around quickly, expecting to see Golems or rats, or even the Morrigan lurking in the shadows.

"I am alone," Dee said pleasantly, smiling politely.

Josh's mind was racing. He needed to get to Flamel, he needed to warn him that Dee was in Ojai. He wondered what would happen if he simply got up and ran. Would Dee try to stop him with magic in front of all these people? Josh looked over at the three old men again, and it dawned on him that they probably wouldn't even notice if Dee changed him into an elephant right in the middle of downtown Ojai.

"Do you know how long I've been chasing Nicholas Flamel, or Nick Fleming, or any of the hundreds of other aliases he's used?" Dee continued quietly, conversationally. He leaned back and trailed his fingers through the water. "At least five hundred years. And he's always given me the slip. He's tricky and dangerous that way. In 1666, when I was closing in on him in London, he set a fire that nearly burned the city to the ground."

"He told us you caused the Great Fire," Josh blurted. Despite his fear, he was curious. And now he suddenly remembered one of the first pieces of advice Flamel had given them: "Nothing is as it seems. Question everything." Josh found himself wondering if that advice also applied to the Alchemyst himself. The sun had set, and there was a definite chill in the evening air. Josh shivered. The three old men shuffled away, none of them even glancing in his direction, leaving him alone with the magician. Strangely, he didn't feel threatened by the man's presence.

Dee's thin lips flickered in a smile. "Flamel never tells anyone everything," he said. "I used to say that half of everything he said was a lie, and the other half wasn't entirely truthful either."

"Nicholas says you're working with the Dark Elders. Once you have the complete Codex, you will bring them back into this world."

"Correct in every detail," Dee said, surprising him. "Though no doubt Nicholas has twisted the story somewhat. I *am* working with the Elders," he continued, "and yes, I am looking for the last two pages from the Book of Abraham the Mage, commonly called the Codex. But only because Flamel and his wife stole it from the original Bibliothèque du Roi in the Louvre."

"He *stole* it?"

"Let me tell you about Nicholas Flamel," Dee said patiently. "I'm sure he's told you about me. He has been many things in his time: a physician and a cook, a bookseller, a soldier, a teacher of languages and chemistry, both an officer of the law and a thief. But he is now, and has always been, a liar, a charlatan and a crook. He stole the Book from the Louvre when he discovered that it contained not only the immortality potion, but also the philosopher's stone recipe. He brews the immortality potion each month to keep Perenelle and himself at exactly the same age they were when they first drank it. He uses the philosopher's stone formula to turn cheap copper and lead into gold and chunks of common coal into diamonds. He uses one of the most extraordinary collections of knowledge in the world purely for personal gain. And that's the truth."

"But what about Scatty and Hekate? Are they Elders?"

"Oh, absolutely. Hekate was an Elder and Scathach is Next Generation. But Hekate was a known criminal. She was banished from Danu Talis because of her experiments on animals. I suppose you would call her a genetic engineer: she created the Were clans, for example, and loosed the curse of the werewolf onto humanity. I believe you saw some of her experiments yesterday, the boar people. Scathach is nothing more than a hired thug, cursed for her crimes to wear the body of a teen for the rest of her days. When Flamel knew I was closing in, they were the only people he could go to."

Josh was now hopelessly confused. Who was telling the truth? Flamel or Dee?

He was cold now. Night had not yet fully fallen, but a low mist had crept in over the town. The air smelled of damp earth and just the faintest hint of rotten eggs. "What about you? Are you really working to bring back the Elders?"

"Of course I am," Dee said, sounding surprised. "It is probably the single most important thing I can do for this world."

"Flamel says the Elders—the Dark Elders, he calls them— would destroy the world."

Dee shrugged. "Believe me when I tell you that he's lying to you. The Elders would be able to change this world for the better. . . ." Dee's fingers moved in the water, the ripples languid and mesmerizing. Startled, Josh saw images forming in the water, the pictures matching Dee's soothing words. "In the ancient past, the earth was a paradise. It had an incredibly advanced technology, but the air was clean, the water pure, the seas unpolluted."

There was a rippling image of an island set under cloudless azure skies. Endless fields of golden wheat marched into the distance. Trees were laden with an assortment of exotic fruit.

"Not only did the Elder Race shape this world, they even nudged a primitive hominid on the road to evolution. But the Elders were driven out from this paradise by the foolish superstition of the mad Abraham and the spells in the Codex. The Elders did not die—it takes a lot to kill one of the Elder Race—they simply waited. They knew that someday mankind would come to its senses and call them back to save the earth."

Josh could not take his eyes off the sparkling water. Much of what Dee said sounded plausible.

"If we can bring them back, the Elders have the powers and the abilities to reshape this world. They can make the deserts bloom. . . ."

An image formed in the water: huge windblown desert dunes turning green with lush grass.

Another image appeared. Josh was looking at the earth from space, just like Google Earth. A huge swirl of dense cloud had formed over the Gulf of Mexico, heading toward Texas. "They can control the weather," Dee said, and the storm dissipated.

Dee's fingers moved and there appeared the unmistakable image of a hospital ward with a long row of empty beds.

"And they can cure disease. Remember, these beings were worshipped as gods because of their powers. And these are the ones Flamel is trying to stop us from bringing back to the world."

It took Josh an age to form the single-word question. "Why?" He couldn't work out why Flamel would want to prevent such obvious advances.

"Because he has masters, Elders like Hekate and the Witch of Endor, for example, who want the world to dissolve into chaos and anarchy. When that happens, they can come out of the shadows and declare themselves the rulers of the earth." Dee shook his head sadly. "It pains me to say this, but Flamel does not care about you, nor does he care about your sister. He put her in terrible danger today simply to roughly Awaken her powers. The Elders I work with take three days to bring someone through the Awakening ceremony."

"Three days," Josh mumbled. "Flamel said there was no one else in North America who could Awaken me." He didn't want to believe Dee . . . and yet everything the man said sounded so *reasonable*.

"Another lie. My Elders could Awaken you. And they would do it properly and safely. It is, after all, such a dangerous process."

Dee got up slowly and walked around to crouch beside Josh, bringing his eyes level with the boy's face. Fog was beginning to thicken and swirl around the fountain, shifting and eddying as he moved. Dee's voice was silky smooth, a gentle monotone exactly in sync with the rippling water. "What's your name?"

"Josh."

"Josh," Dee echoed, "where is Nicholas Flamel now?"

Even in his drowsy state, an alarm bell—very faint and very, very distant—went off in Josh's head. He couldn't trust Dee, he *shouldn't* trust Dee . . . and yet so much of what he said had the ring of truth to it.

"Where is he, Josh?" Dee persisted.

Josh started to shake his head. Even though he believed Dee—everything he said made perfect sense—he wanted to talk to Sophie first, he needed to get her advice and opinion.

"Tell me." Dee lifted Josh's limp hand and placed it in the pool. Ripples spun out from it. They settled into the image of a small antiques shop filled with glassware, directly across the road from Libbey Park. Grinning triumphantly, Dee came to his feet and whirled around, staring across the road as he activated his senses.

He located their auras immediately.

The green of Flamel, the gray of Scathach, Endor's brown and the girl's pure silver. He had them—and this time there would be no mistakes, no escape.

"You sit here and enjoy the pretty pictures," Dee murmured, patting Josh on the shoulder. The water bloomed with exotic, fractal-like patterns, mesmerizing and hypnotic.

344

"I'll be back for you shortly." Then, without moving a muscle, he called in his waiting army.

Abruptly, the fog thickened and darkened, stinking of rotten eggs and something else: dust and dry earth, damp and mold.

And horror descended on Ojai.

CHAPTER THIRTY-EIGHT

*N*icholas Flamel's hands were already beginning to glow with green light when he pulled open the door of the small shop, grimacing in annoyance as the bell jangled merrily.

The sun had dipped below the horizon while the Witch worked with Sophie, and a chill fog had rolled down the valley. It swirled and rolled the length of Ojai Avenue, curling and twisting through the trees, leaving everything it touched beaded with moisture. Cars crept along, their headlights outlined in huge halos of light barely able to penetrate the gloom. The street was completely deserted; the people outside had all been dressed for summer weather and had fled indoors away from the damp.

Scatty joined Flamel at the door. She carried a short sword in one hand, a nunchaku in the other, dangling loosely on its chain. "This is not good, not good at all." She breathed deeply. "Smell that?"

Flamel nodded. "Sulfur. The odor of Dee."

Scatty rattled the nunchaku. "He's really starting to annoy me."

Somewhere in the distance there was a metallic bang as two cars collided. A car alarm echoed forlornly behind them. And there was a scream, high-pitched and terrifying, and then another and another.

"It's coming. Whatever it is," Nicholas Flamel said grimly.

"We don't want to be trapped here," Scatty said. "Let's find Josh and get back to the car."

"Agreed. He who retreats lives longer." He turned to look back into the shop. The Witch of Endor had Sophie by the arm and was whispering urgently to her. Wisps of white smoke still curled off the girl, and tendrils of white air dripped from her fingers like unwound bandages.

Sophie leaned forward and kissed the old woman on the cheek, then she turned and hurried down the length of the shop. "We have to go," she said breathlessly, "we have to get away from here." She had no idea what lay outside, but her newfound knowledge enabled her imagination to populate the fog with any number of monstrous creatures.

"And close the door behind you," the Witch called out.

And at that moment all the lights flickered and died. Ojai was plunged into darkness.

The bell jangled as the trio stepped out into the now-deserted street. The fog had become so thick that drivers had been forced to pull off the road and there was no longer traffic moving on the main street. An air of unnatural silence had fallen. Flamel turned to Sophie. "Can you pinpoint Josh?"

"He said he'd wait for us in the park." She squinted, trying to penetrate the fog, but it was so thick that she could barely see a foot in front of her face. With Flamel and Scatty on either side of her, she stepped off the sidewalk and made her way to the middle of the empty road. "Josh?" The fog swallowed her words, muffling them to little more than a whisper. "Josh," she called again.

There was no response.

A sudden thought struck her and she flung out her right hand, fingers splayed. A puff of air curled from her hand, but did nothing to the fog except make it swirl and dance. She tried again, and an icy gale whipped across the street, cutting a neat corridor through the fog, catching the rear wing of an abandoned car in the middle of the road, leaving a ragged indentation in the metal. "Whoops. I guess I have to practice," she muttered.

A shape stepped into the opening in the fog, and then a second and a third. And none of them were alive.

Closest to Sophie, Flamel and Scatty was a complete skeleton, standing tall and straight, wearing the ragged remains of the blue uniform coat of a U.S. cavalry officer. It carried the rusted stump of a sword in bony fingers. When it turned its head toward them, the bones at the base of its skull popped and cracked.

"Necromancy," Flamel breathed. "Dee's raised the dead."

Another figure loomed out of the fog: it was the partially mummified body of a man carrying a huge railroad hammer. Behind it came another dead man, whose remaining flesh was tanned to the consistency of leather. A pair of withered leather gun belts was slung low across his hips, and when he saw the group, he reached for the missing guns with skeletal fingers.

Sophie stood frozen in shock, and the wind died away from her fingers. "They're dead," she whispered. "Skeletons. Mummies. They're all dead."

"Yep," Scathach said matter-of-factly, "skeletons and mummies. It depends on what type of ground they were buried in. Damp soil, you get skeletons." She stepped forward and swept out with a nunchaku, knocking the head clear off another gunslinger, who'd been attempting to raise a rusted rifle to his shoulder. "Dry soil, you get the mummies. Doesn't stop them from hurting you, though." The skeletal cavalry officer with the broken sword lashed out at her, and she parried with her own sword. His rusted blade dissolved into dust. Scatty's sword swung again and separated the head from the body, which then immediately crumpled to the ground.

Although the shambling figures moved in complete silence, there were screams all around now. And even though they were muffled by the fog, fear and abject terror were clearly audible in them. The ordinary citizens of Ojai had become aware that the dead were walking through their streets.

The fog was now thick with the creatures. They came from all sides, crowding in on the trio, encircling them in the center of the road. As the twisting sheets of dampness eddied and flowed, more and more skeletal and mummified remains were revealed in brief glimpses: soldiers in the tattered blues and grays of Civil War uniforms; farmers in rags of

349

old-fashioned overalls; cowboys in worn chaps and torn denim; women in long, sweeping skirts, now moldy and ragged; miners in threadbare buckskins.

"He's emptied a boot hill graveyard from one of the old abandoned towns!" Scatty exclaimed, standing with her back to Sophie, striking out around her. "No one here's in clothes made after 1880." Two skeletal women wearing matching bonnets and the rags of their Sunday best clicked their way on bony feet across Ojai Avenue toward her, arms outstretched. Scatty's sword whipped around, slicing away the arms, but that didn't even slow them down. She shoved her nunchaku back into her belt and pulled out her second sword. She struck out again, both swords forming an X in the middle of the air, and lopped off both heads, sending them bouncing back into the fog. The skeletons crumpled into a disarray of bones.

"Josh," Sophie called again, her voice high in desperation. "Josh. Where are you?" Maybe the mummies and skeletons had gotten to him first. Maybe he was going to loom up out of the fog any minute now, eyes blank and staring, head twisted at an awkward angle. She shook her head, trying to clear the ghoulish thoughts.

Flamel's hands burned with cold green fire, and the damp fog was rich with the odor of mint. He snapped his fingers and sent a sheet of virescent fire blazing into the fog. The fogbanks glowed emerald and aquamarine, but otherwise, the magic had no effect. Flamel next threw a small ball of green light directly in front of two lurching skeletons who loomed up before him. Fire blazed over the creatures, crisping

the remains of their gray Confederate uniforms. They continued forward, bones clacking on the street, closing in on him,
and there were hundreds more behind them.

"Sophie, get the Witch! We need her help."

"But she can't help us," Sophie said desperately. "There's
nothing more she can do. She has no power left: she's given
everything to me."

"Everything?" Flamel gasped, ducking beneath a swinging fist. He placed his hand on the center of the dead man's
rib cage and pushed, sending the skeleton flying back into the
crowd, where it fell in a tangle of bones. "Well then, Sophie,
you do something!"

"What?" she called. What could she do against an army of
the undead? She was a fifteen-year-old girl.

"Anything!"

A mummified arm shot out of the fog and cracked her
across the shoulder. It was like being hit by a wet towel.

Fear, revulsion and anger lent her strength. Right at that
moment, however, she couldn't remember anything the Witch
had taught her, but then her instincts—or maybe the Witch's
imparted knowledge—took over. She deliberately allowed
her anger to surge into her aura. Abruptly, the air was filled
with the richness of creamy vanilla as Sophie's aura blazed
pure silver. Bringing the palm of her right hand up to her
face, she blew into her cupped fingers, then tossed the cap-
tured breath into the middle of the dead. A six-foot-tall whirlwind, a miniature twister, appeared, growing up out of the
ground. It sucked the dead nearest to it into its core, grinding and shattering the bones, then spitting out the splintered

remains. Sophie threw a second and then a third ball of air. The three twisters danced and moved among the skeletons and mummies, cutting a swath of destruction through them. She found she could direct the twisters by simply looking in a particular direction, and they would obediently drift that way.

Suddenly, Dee's voice echoed out of the fog. "Do you like my army, Nicholas?" The fog flattened the sound, making it impossible to locate. "The last time I was in Ojai—oh, over a hundred years ago—I discovered a marvelous little graveyard just below the Three Sisters Peaks. The town it was built alongside is long gone, but the graves and their contents remain."

Flamel was fighting frantically as fists punched, fingernails scratched, feet kicked. There was no real strength to the skeletons' blows or the mummies' slaps, but what they lacked in force they made up for in numbers. There were simply too many of them. There was a bruise beginning to darken beneath his eye and a long scratch on the back of his hand. Scatty moved around Sophie, defending her while she controlled the whirlwinds.

"I don't know how long that graveyard was in use. A couple of hundred years, certainly. I've no idea how many corpses it holds. Hundreds, maybe even thousands. And, Nicholas, I've called them all."

"Where is he?" Flamel said through gritted teeth. "He's got to be close—very close—to be able to control this number of corpses. I need to know where he is to do anything."

Sophie felt a wave of exhaustion wash over her, and

suddenly, one of the twisters wobbled and then vanished. The two that remained were weaving from side to side as Sophie's physical strength ebbed. Another died, and the one that remained was rapidly losing power. This exhaustion was the price of performing magic, she realized. But she needed to keep going for just a little longer; she had to find her brother.

"We've got to get out of here." Scathach caught Sophie and held her upright. The skeletal dead surged forward, and Scatty beat them back with neat, precise movements of her sword.

"Josh," Sophie whispered tiredly. "Where's Josh? We've got to find Josh."

The fog robbed Dee's voice of much of its emotion, but the glee in his tone was evident when he said, "And do you know what else I discovered? These mountains have been luring creatures other than humans for the past millennia. The land here is littered with bones. Hundreds of bones. And remember, Nicholas, I am, first and foremost, a necromancer."

The bear that loomed up out of the gray fogbank was at least eight feet tall. And even though patches of fur remained on its skeleton, it was clear that it had died a long time before. The snow-white bones only emphasized its huge daggerlike claws.

Behind the bear, the skeleton of a saber-toothed tiger appeared. And then a cougar, and another bear—smaller this time, and not quite as decomposed.

"A word from me stops them," Dee's voice boomed. "I want the pages of the Codex."

"No," Flamel said grimly. "Where is he? Where is he hiding?"

"Where's my brother?" Sophie called desperately, and then screamed as a dead hand wrapped itself in her hair. Scathach chopped it off at the wrist, but it still hung tangled in her hair like a bizarre hair clip. "What have you done with my brother?"

"Your brother is considering his options. Yours is not the only side in this battle. And now, since I have the boy, all I need are the pages."

"Never."

The bear and the tiger charged through the crowd of bodies, brushing them aside, trampling them in their eagerness to get to the trio. The saber-toothed tiger reached them first. Its gleaming skeletal head was massive, and the two downward-jutting teeth were at least eight inches long. Flamel placed himself between Sophie and the creature.

"Hand over the pages, Nicholas, or I will loose these undead beasts on the town."

Nicholas frantically hunted through his memory for a spell that would stop the creature. He bitterly regretted now not studying more magic. He snapped his fingers and a tiny bubble of light popped onto the ground in front of the tiger.

"Is that all you can manage, Nicholas? My, you're weakening."

The bubble burst and spread across the ground in a cool emerald stain.

"He's close enough to see us," Nicholas said. "All I need is one glimpse of him."

The skeletal tiger's massive right front paw stepped into the green light. And stuck. It attempted to lift its leg, but thick strands of sticky green threads connected it to the road. And now its left paw stepped into the light and stuck.

"Not quite so weak, eh, Dee?" Flamel shouted.

But the press of bodies behind the saber-toothed tiger kept pushing it forward. Suddenly, its bony legs snapped off, sending the huge beast lunging forward. Flamel managed to throw up his arms before the monster collapsed on top of him, jaw gaping, teeth wide and savage.

"Good-bye, Nicholas Flamel," Dee called. "I'll just take the pages from your body."

"No," Sophie whispered. No, it was not going to end like this. She had been Awakened, and the Witch of Endor had imbued her with all her knowledge. There had to be something she could do. Sophie opened her mouth and screamed, her aura blazing with silver incandescence.

CHAPTER THIRTY-NINE

*J*osh awoke, his sister's scream ringing in his ears.

It took him several seconds before he realized where he was: sitting on the edge of the fountain in Libbey Park, while all around him thick, foul-smelling banks of fog shifted and twisted and crawled with half-glimpsed skeletons and mummified bodies clothed in rags.

Sophie!

He had to get to his sister. To his right, in the middle of the gray-black fog, green light sparkled and silver flared, briefly illuminating the mist from within, casting monstrous shadows. Sophie was there; Flamel and Scathach, too, fighting these monsters. He should be with them.

He came shakily to his feet and discovered Dr. John Dee standing directly in front of him.

Dee was outlined in a sickly yellow aura. It sparked and

spat and hissed like burning fat and gave off the rancid odor of rotten eggs. The man had his back to him. He was leaning both forearms against the low stone wall next to the drinking fountain Josh had used earlier. Dee was staring intently at the events taking place in the street, concentrating so hard he was shaking with the effort of controlling the seemingly endless line of skeletons and mummified humans shuffling past. Now that he was on his feet, Josh noticed that there were other creatures in the fog too. He could see the remains of bears and tigers, mountain cats and wolves.

He heard Flamel shout and Sophie scream, and his first thought was to rush at Dee. But he doubted he'd even get close. What could he do against this powerful magician? He wasn't like his twin: he had no powers.

But that didn't mean he was useless.

Sophie's scream sent out a shock wave of icy air that shattered the saber-toothed tiger to powder and knocked back the nearest skeletons. The huge bear crashed to the ground, crushing a dozen skeletons beneath its bulk. The blast of air had also cleared away a patch of fog, and for the first time, Sophie realized the enormity of what they were facing. There weren't dozens or even hundreds, there were thousands of the Old West's dead marching down the street toward them. Dotted through the mass were the bony remains of the animals that had hunted in the surrounding mountains for centuries. She didn't know what else she could do. The final use of magic exhausted her, and she slumped against Scathach, who caught her in her left arm while holding one sword in her right hand.

Flamel climbed tiredly to his feet. Using magic had drained his reserves of energy as well, and even in the past few minutes he had aged. The lines around his eyes were deeper, his hair thinner. Scathach knew he could not survive much longer.

"Give him the pages, Nicholas," she urged.

He shook his head stubbornly. "I will not. I cannot. I've spent my life protecting the Book."

"He who retreats lives longer," she reminded him.

He shook his head. Flamel was bent over, breathing in great heaving gulps of air. His skin was deathly pale, with two spots of unnaturally bright red on his cheeks. "This is the exception, Scathach. If I give him the pages, then I've condemned all of us—Perry, too, and the entire world—to destruction." He straightened and turned to face the creatures for what they all knew would be the last time. "Could you get Sophie away from here?"

Scathach shook her head. "I cannot fight them and carry her."

"Could you get away on your own?"

"I could fight my way out," she said carefully.

"Then go, Scatty. Escape. Get to the other Elders, contact the immortal humans, tell them what happened here, start fighting the Dark Elders before it is too late."

"I'll not leave you and Sophie here," Scathach said firmly. "We're in this together to the end. Whatever that may be."

"It's time to die, Nicholas Flamel," Dee called out of the

gloom. "I'll make sure to tell Perenelle about this moment in every little detail."

A rustle ran through the mass of skeletal human and animal bodies, and then, as one, they surged forward.

And a monster came out of the fog.

Huge and black, howling savagely, with two huge yellow-white eyes and dozens of smaller eyes blazing, it drove straight through the Libbey Park fountain, crushing it to powder, shattering the ornamental vases, and bore down on Dr. John Dee.

The necromancer managed to fling himself to one side before the black Hummer crashed into the wall, pounding it to dust. It stuck nose-down against the remains of the wall, back wheels caught in the air, engine screaming. The door opened and Josh climbed out and carefully lowered himself to the ground. He was holding his chest where the seat belt had cut into it.

Ojai Avenue was littered with the remains of the long dead. Without Dee to control them, they were just so many bones.

Josh staggered into the street and picked his way through the bones and scraps of cloth. Something crunched beneath his feet, but he didn't even look down.

Suddenly, the dead were gone.

Sophie didn't know what had happened. There had been a tremendous roar, a scream of tortured metal and a crunch of stone and then silence. And in the silence, the dead had fallen down like windblown grass. What had Dee summoned now?

A shape moved in the twisting fog.

Flamel gathered the last of his energy into a solid sphere of green glass. Sophie straightened and tried to muster the dregs of her energy. Scathach flexed her fingers. She'd once been told that she'd die in an exotic location; she wondered if Ojai in Ventura County qualified as exotic enough.

The shape loomed closer.

Flamel raised his hand, Sophie gathered the winds and Scathach lifted her notched sword. Josh stepped out of the night. "I've wrecked the car," he said.

Sophie screamed with delight. She ran to her brother, and then her scream turned to one of horror. The skeletal bear had risen from the ground behind him, paws poised to strike.

Scathach moved, hitting Josh hard, shoving him out of the way, and sent him tumbling into a mess of bones. The Warrior's swords parried the bear's sweeping blow, sparks blinking in the fog. She struck out again, and a bear claw as long as her hand tumbled through the air.

One by one the skeletal animals were climbing to their feet. Two huge wolves, one little more than bones, the other merely shriveled flesh, loomed out of the fog.

"This way. Here! This way." The Witch's voice sounded flatly across the street, and a rectangle of light from an open door lit up the night. With Scatty supporting Flamel and Josh half carrying his twin, they raced across the street toward the shop. The Witch of Endor was standing in the doorway, looking blindly into the night, an old-fashioned oil lantern held high. "We've got to get you out of here." She pulled the door closed and pushed the bolts home. "That won't hold them long," she muttered.

"You said . . . you said you have no powers left," Sophie muttered.

"I don't." Dora flashed a quick grin, revealing perfect white teeth. "But this place has." She led them through the shop and into a tiny back room. "Do you know what makes Ojai so special?" she asked.

Something thumped against the door and all the glassware in the shop rattled and tinkled.

"It is built on an intersection of ley lines."

Josh opened his mouth and was actually forming the word *ley* when his sister spoke. "Lines of energy that crisscross the globe," Sophie whispered in his ear.

"How do you know that?"

"I don't know; I guess the Witch taught me. Many of the most famous buildings and ancient sites across the world are built where the ley lines meet."

"Exactly," Dora said, sounding pleased. "Couldn't have put it better myself." The little storeroom was bare except for a long rectangle propped up against the wall, covered in yellowed back issues of the *Ojai Valley Times*.

More blows shook the shop window, the sound of bone against glass setting them on edge.

Dora swept the papers to the ground to reveal a mirror. It stood seven feet tall, four feet wide, the glass dirty, speckled and warped, the images it showed slightly distorted and blurred. "And do you know what drew me to Ojai in the first place?" she asked. "Seven great ley lines meet here. They form a leygate."

"Here?" Flamel whispered. He knew about ley lines and had heard about the leygates used by the ancients to travel across the world in an instant. He hadn't thought any still existed.

Dora tapped the ground with her foot. "Right here. And do you know how you use a leygate?"

Flamel shook his head.

Dora reached for Sophie. "Give me your hand, child." The Witch took Sophie's hand and put it on the glass. "You use a mirror."

The mirror immediately came to blazing life, the glass flaring silver and then clearing. When they looked into the glass, it no longer showed their reflections, but rather the image of a bare, cellarlike room.

"Where?" Flamel asked.

"Paris," Dora said.

"France." He smiled. "Home." And without hesitation, he stepped right through the glass. Now they could see him within the mirror. He turned and waved them through.

"I hate leygates," Scatty muttered. "Make me nauseous." She hopped through the gate, and rolled to her feet beside Flamel. When she turned back to face the twins, she did look as if she was about to throw up.

The skeletal bear lumbered straight through the shop door, ripping it off its hinges. The wolves and the cougars followed. Glassware tumbled, mirrors cracked, ornaments shattered as the beasts lumbered about.

A bruised and cut Dee raced into the shop, pushing the skeletal beasts aside. A cougar snapped at him and he smacked it on the snout. If it had had eyes, it would have blinked in surprise.

"Trapped," he called gleefully. "Trapped and nowhere to go!"

But when he stepped into the storeroom, he knew they had escaped him once more. It took him a single heartbeat to take in the tall mirror, the two figures *in* the glass staring out, the old woman standing next to the girl, pressing her hand to its surface. The boy stood alone, holding on to the frame. Dee instantly knew what it was. "A leygate," he whispered in awe. Mirrors always acted as the gates. Somewhere at the other end of the ley line was another mirror linking them.

The old woman caught the girl and shoved her *through* the mirror. Sophie tumbled to the ground at Flamel's feet, then crouched to turn and look back. Her mouth moved, but there was no sound. *Josh.*

"Josh," Dee commanded, staring at the boy, "stay where you are."

The boy turned to the glass. Already the image in the mirror had blurred.

"I've told you the truth about Flamel," Dee said urgently. All he had to do was to keep the boy distracted for another moment or two and the mirror would lose its power. "Stay with me. I can Awaken you. Make you powerful. You can help change the world, Josh. Change it for the better!"

"I don't know. . . ." The offer was tempting, so tempting. But he knew if he sided with Dee, he would lose his sister altogether. Or would he? If Dee Awakened him, then they would be alike again. Maybe this was a way he could reconnect with his twin.

"Look," Dee said triumphantly, pointing to the fading image in the glass, "they've left you, deserted you again, because you are not one of them. You're no longer important."

The mirror flared silver . . . and Sophie stepped back through the glass. "Josh? Hurry," she said urgently, not looking at Dee.

"I . . . ," he began. "You came back for me."

"Of course I did! You're my brother. I'll never abandon you." Then, catching his hand, wrapping her fingers around his, she pulled him into the glass.

And Dora pushed the mirror, sending it shattering to the floor. "Whoops." She turned to face Dee and pulled off her dark glasses to reveal the mirrors of her eyes. "You should go now. You've got about three seconds."

Dee didn't quite make it out of the shop before it exploded.

CHAPTER FORTY

MOVIE COMPANY CAUSES MAYHEM IN SCENIC OJAI

The latest in a long line of horror movies from Enoch Studios caused traffic mayhem and more than a little confusion in downtown Ojai yesterday. The special effects were a bit too realistic for some locals, and emergency services were inundated with calls from people who claimed that the dead were walking the streets.

John Dee, chairman of Enoch Films, a division of Enoch Enterprises, apologized profusely for the confusion, blaming it on a power outage and an unseasonable fog that swept in as they were about to shoot a scene from their new movie. "It certainly made the extras look *extra*-scary," his spokesperson said. In a related incident, a drunk driver smashed through the historic Libbey Park fountain and into the recently restored pergola. Dee has promised to restore the fountain and pergola to their former glory.

Ojai Valley News

LOCAL ANTIQUES SHOP DEVASTATED BY EXPLOSION

A gas explosion destroyed the shop of longtime Ojai resident Dora Witcherly late last night. An electrical fault ignited solvents used by the owner to clean, polish and restore her antiques. Miss Witcherly was in the shop's back room when the explosion occurred and was unharmed and apparently unconcerned by her brush with death. "When you've lived as long as I have, nothing much surprises you." She has promised to reopen the shop in time for the holidays.

Ojai Online

CHAPTER FORTY-ONE

Deep beneath Alcatraz, Perenelle Flamel lay on a narrow cot, her face turned toward the back wall of her cell. Behind her, in the corridor outside, she could hear the sphinx click-clacking up and down the cold stone floors, and the air was heavy with the musky odors of snake and lion. Perenelle shivered. The cell was freezing, and green-tinged water was dripping down the wall inches from her face.

Where was Nicholas?

What was happening?

Perenelle was afraid, but not for herself. The fact that she was alive meant that Dee needed her for something, and that sooner or later she would come face to face with him. And if Dee had a failing, it was arrogance. He would underestimate her . . . and then she would strike! There was a particularly nasty little spell she had learned in the foothills of the

Carpathian Mountains in Transylvania that she was saving just for him.

Where was Nicholas?

She was afraid for Nicholas and the children. It was difficult for her to judge just how much time has passed, but by examining the wrinkles forming on the backs of her hands, she guessed she'd aged at least two years, so two days had passed. Without the immortality elixir, she and Nicholas would age at the rate of a year a day. They had less than a month left before they succumbed to old—*very* old—age.

And with no one to stand against them, Dee and the others like him would loose the Dark Elders into the world again. It would be chaos; civilization would fall.

Where was Nicholas?

Perenelle blinked away tears. She wasn't going to give the sphinx the satisfaction of seeing her weep. The Elders had nothing but contempt for human emotion; they considered it their biggest weakness. Perenelle knew it was humankind's great strength.

She blinked again, and it took her a moment to realize what she was seeing.

The foul dripping water running down the walls had briefly curled and formed into a pattern. She focused, trying to make sense of what she was seeing.

The liquid twisted and coiled into a face: Jefferson Miller, the ghost of the security guard. The dribbling water bent into letters on the moss-streaked walls.

Flamel. Children.

The words lasted less than a heartbeat before they flowed away.

Safe.

Now Perenelle had to blink hard to clear her eyes. Flamel and the children were safe!

Ojai. Leygate. Paris.

"Thank you," Perenelle mouthed silently as Jefferson Miller's face dissolved and ran liquid down the wall. She had so many questions—but at least now she had some answers: Nicholas and the children were safe. They had obviously reached Ojai and met the Witch of Endor. She must have opened the leygate to take them to Paris, and that suggested that the Witch had helped them and had most likely instructed Sophie in the Magic of Air.

Perenelle knew that the Witch would not have been able to Awaken Josh's powers—but in Paris and across Europe there were Elders and immortal humans who would be able to help, who could Awaken Josh and train both twins in the five elemental magics.

She rolled over on her back and looked at the sphinx, which was now crouched outside her cell, human head resting on enormous lion's paws, wings folded across its back. The creature smiled lazily, long black forked tongue flickering.

"It is ending, Immortal," the sphinx whispered.

Perenelle's smile was terrifying. "On the contrary," she replied. "It is now only just beginning."

End of Book One

AUTHOR'S NOTE

Nicholas and Perenelle Flamel were real people. So was Dr. John Dee. Indeed, all the characters in *The Alchemyst,* with the exception of the twins, are based on real historical characters or mythological beings.

When I originally conceived the idea for *The Alchemyst,* I thought the hero would be Dr. John Dee.

John Dee has always fascinated me. In the Elizabethan Age, the age of the extraordinary, he was exceptional. He was one of the most brilliant men of his time, and all the details about his life in *The Alchemyst* are true: he was an alchemist, a mathematician, a geographer, an astronomer and an astrologer. He did choose the date for Queen Elizabeth I's coronation, and when he was part of her network of spies, he signed his coded messages "007." The two 0's represented the eyes of the Queen, and the symbol that looked like a 7 was Dee's personal mark. There is evidence to suggest that when Shakespeare created the character of Prospero for *The Tempest,* he modeled him on Dee.

The series of books based on an alchemist had been growing in my head and in piles of notebooks for some years, and it seemed perfectly natural that it should be Dee's series. As I wrote other books, I kept coming back to the idea, adding more material, weaving together all the world mythologies and creating the huge and intricate background for the stories. I continued to research the settings, visiting, revisiting and photographing every location I intended to use in the series.

Every story starts with an idea, but it is the characters that move that idea forward. The characters of the twins came to me first. My story was always about a brother and sister, and in mythological terms, twins are very special. Just about every race and mythology has a twin story. As my story progressed, the secondary characters, such as Scathach and the Morrigan, and then later, Hekate and the Witch of Endor, appeared. But somehow I still hadn't quite gotten the hero, the mentor, the teacher for the twins. Dr. John Dee, despite being a wonderful character, was simply not the *right* character.

Then, one day in the late fall of 2000, I was in Paris on business. It is difficult to get lost in Paris, so long as you know where the river Seine is—you can usually see one or more of the great landmarks, such as the Eiffel Tower, Sacré-Coeur or Notre Dame—but somehow I'd managed to do it. I had left Notre Dame earlier, crossed the Seine on the Pont d'Arcole, heading toward the Centre Pompidou, and somewhere between the Boulevard de Sebastopol and the Rue Beaubourg, I got lost. Not entirely lost; I knew vaguely where I was, but night was beginning to fall. I turned off the Rue Beaubourg into the narrow Rue du Montmorency and found myself looking up at a sign that said AUBERGE NICOLAS FLAMEL: the Nicholas Flamel Hostel. And in front of the building was a sign that said the house, where Flamel and his wife had once lived, dated from 1407, which meant that this had to be one of the oldest houses in Paris.

I went inside and found a charming restaurant, where I had a meal that night. It was a strange experience, eating in the same room where the legendary Nicholas Flamel would have lived and worked. The exposed beams in the ceiling looked original, which meant they would have been the beams Nicholas Flamel himself would have seen. In the cellar below my feet, Nicholas and Perenelle would have stored their food and wine, and their bedchamber would have been in the small room directly over my head.

I knew quite a bit about the famous Nicholas Flamel. Dee, who had one of the largest libraries in England, had Flamel's books and would have studied his works.

Nicholas Flamel was one of the most famous alchemists of his day. Alchemy is a peculiar combination of chemistry, botany, medicine, astronomy and astrology. It has a long and distinguished history and was studied in ancient Greece and China, and there is an argument that it forms the basis for modern chemistry. As with Dee, all of the details in *The Alchemyst* about Nicholas Flamel are true. We know quite a bit about him because not only do his own writings exist, but also many people wrote about him during his own lifetime.

He was born in 1330 and scraped by on a living as a bookseller and a scrivener, writing letters and copying books for clients. One day he bought a very special book: the Book of Abraham. It, too, really existed, and Nicholas Flamel left us with a very detailed description of the copper-bound book, which was written on what looked like bark.

Accompanied by Perenelle, he spent more than twenty years traveling all over Europe, trying to translate the strange language the book was written in.

No one knows what happened to Nicholas Flamel on that journey. What is authenticated is that when he returned to

Paris in the late fourteenth century, he was extraordinarily wealthy. The rumor quickly went around that he had discovered the two great secrets of alchemy in the Book of Abraham: how to create a philosopher's stone, which changed ordinary metal into gold, and how to achieve immortality. Neither Nicholas nor Perenelle would ever confirm the rumors, and they never explained how they had become so rich.

Although Nicholas and Perenelle continued to live quiet, unassuming lives, they gave a lot of their money to charity, and founded hospitals, churches and orphanages.

The records show that Perenelle died first; not long after, in 1418, the death of Nicholas Flamel was recorded. His house was sold and the buyers tore the place apart looking for some of the Flamels' great wealth. Nothing was ever found.

Later, in the dead of night, the tomb of Nicholas and Perenelle Flamel was broken into . . . and that was when it was discovered that the tomb was empty. Had they been buried in secret graves, or had they never died in the first place? Paris buzzed with rumors, and the legend of the immortal Flamels began almost immediately.

In the years to follow, there were sightings of the Flamels across Europe.

When I came out of the Auberge Nicolas Flamel that evening, I looked back at the ancient house. Six hundred years ago, one of the most famous alchemists in the world lived and worked there—a man dedicated to science, who had made and given away a vast fortune and whose house was preserved by the grateful people of Paris, who even have streets named after him and his wife (the Rue Nicolas Flamel and the Rue Perenelle in the 4th Arrondissement).

An immortal.

And in that moment, I knew that the twins' mentor was not Dee: Sophie and Josh would be taught by Nicholas and Perenelle. As I stood outside Nicholas and Perenelle's home on that wet fall evening, all the pieces of the book came together, and the Secrets of the Immortal Nicholas Flamel took shape.

Front entrance to the Auberge Nicolas Flamel (the Nicholas Flamel Hostel) on Rue du Montmorency, Paris.

ACKNOWLEDGMENTS

Only one name usually appears on the cover of a book, but behind that name there are dozens of people involved in the creation of the work. Of equal importance, but in no particular order, I must thank . . .

Krista Marino, the most patient of editors, who said, "A little more perspective . . ."

Frank Weimann, at the Literary Group, who said, "I can sell this." And did.

Michael Carroll, who read it first and last and said, "We need to talk about . . ."

O. R. Melling, who said, "Have you finished it yet?"

Claudette Sutherland, who said, "You really should think about . . ."

And finally, of course: Barry Krost, at BKM, who is surely the Alchemyst's grandfather, which would probably make John Sobanski his nephew!

A Special Preview of

THE
MAGICIAN

Book two of

{ *The Secrets of*
THE IMMORTAL
NICHOLAS FLAMEL }

Published by Delacorte Press
an imprint of Random House Children's Books
a division of Random House, Inc., New York

I am dying.

Perenelle, too, is dying.

The spell that has kept us alive these six hundred years is fading, and now we age a year for every day that passes. I need the Codex, the Book of Abraham the Mage, to re-create the immortality spell; without it, we have less than a month to live.

But much can be achieved in a month.

Dee and his dark masters have my dear Perenelle prisoner, they have finally secured the Book, and they know that Perenelle and I cannot survive for much longer.

But they cannot be resting easy.

They do not have the complete Book yet. We still have the final two pages, and by now they must know now that Sophie and Josh Newman are the twins described in that ancient text: twins with auras of silver and gold, a brother and sister with the power to either save the world . . . or destroy it. The girl's powers have been Awakened and her training begun in the elemental magics, though, sadly, the boy's have not.

We are now in Paris, the city of my birth, the city where I first discovered the Codex and began the long quest to translate it. That journey ultimately led me to discover the existence of the Elder Race and revealed the mystery of the philosopher's stone and finally the secret of immortality. I love this city. It holds many secrets and is home to more than one human immortal and ancient Elder. Here, I will find a way to Awaken Josh's powers and continue Sophie's education.

I must.

For their sakes—and for the continuance of the human race.

From the Day Booke of Nicholas Flamel, Alchemyst
Writ this day, Saturday, 2nd June,
in Paris, the city of my youth

SATURDAY, 2nd June

CHAPTER ONE

𝒯he charity auction hadn't started until well after midnight, when the gala dinner had ended. It was almost four in the morning and the auction was only now drawing to a close. A digital display behind the celebrity auctioneer—an actor who had played James Bond on-screen for many years—showed the running total at more than one million euro.

"Lot number two hundred aand ten: a pair of early-nineteenth-century Japanese Kabuki masks."

A ripple of excitement ran through the crowded room. Inlaid with chips of solid jade, the Kabuki masks were the highlight of the auction and were expected to fetch in excess of half a million euro.

At the back of the room the tall, thin man with the fuzz of close-cropped snow white hair was prepared to pay twice that.

Niccolò Machiavelli stood apart from the rest of the

crowd, arms lightly folded across his chest, careful not to wrinkle his Savile Row–tailored black silk tuxedo. Stone gray eyes swept over the other bidders, analyzing and assessing them. There were really only five others he needed to look out for: two private collectors like himself, a minor European royal, a once-famous American movie actor and a Canadian antiques dealer. The remainder of the audience were tired, had spent their budget or were unwilling to bid on the vaguely disturbing-looking masks.

Machiavelli loved all types of masks. He had been collecting them for a very long time, and he wanted this particular pair to complete his collection of Japanese theater costumes. These masks had last come up for sale in 1898 in Vienna, and he had then been outbid by a Romanov prince. Machiavelli had patiently bided his time; the masks would come back on the market again when the Prince and his descendents died. Machiavelli knew he would still be around to buy them; it was one of the many advantages of being immortal.

"Shall we start the bidding at one hundred thousand euro?"

Machiavelli looked up, caught the auctioneer's attention and nodded.

The auctioneer had been expecting his bid and nodded in return. "I am bid one hundred thousand euro by Monsieur Machiavelli. Always one of this charity's most generous supporters and sponsors."

A smattering of applause ran around the room, and several people turned to look at him and raise their glasses. Niccolò acknowledged them with a polite smile.

"Do I have one hundred and ten?" the auctioneer asked.

One of the private collectors raised his hand slightly.

"One-twenty?" The auctioneer looked back to Machiavelli, who immediately nodded.

Within the next three minutes, a flurry of bids brought the price up to two hundred and fifty thousand euro. There were only three serious bidders left: Machiavelli, the American actor and the Canadian.

Machiavelli's thin lips twisted into a rare smile; his patience was about to be rewarded, and finally the masks would be his. Then the smile faded as he felt the cell phone in his back pocket buzz silently. For an instant he was tempted to ignore it; he'd given his staff strict instructions that he was not to be disturbed unless it was absolutely critical. He also knew they were so terrified of him that they would not phone unless it was an emergency. Reaching into his pocket, he pulled out the ultraslim phone and glanced down.

A picture of a sword pulsed gently on the large LCD screen.

Machiavelli's smile vanished. In that second he knew he was not going to be able to buy the Kabuki masks this century. Turning on his heel, he strode out of the room and pressed the phone to his ear. Behind him, he could hear the auctioneer's hammer hit the lectern "Sold. For two hundred and sixty thousand euro . . ."

"I'm here," Machiavelli said, reverting to the Italian of his youth.

The line crackled and an English-accented voice responded in the same language, using a dialect that had not been heard in Europe for more than four hundred years. "I need your help."

The man on the other end of the line didn't identify himself, nor did he need to; Machiavelli knew it was the immortal magician and necromancer Dr. John Dee, one of the most powerful and dangerous men in the world.

Niccolò Machiavelli strode out of the small hotel into the broad cobbled square of the Place du Tertre and stopped to breathe in the chill night air. "What can I do for you?" he asked cautiously. He detested Dee and knew the feeling was mutual, but they both served the Dark Elders, and that meant they had been forced to work together down through the centuries. Machiavelli was also slightly envious that Dee was younger than he—and looked it. Machiavelli had been born in Florence in 1469, which made him fifty-eight years older than the English Magician. History recorded that he had *died* in the same year that Dee had been born, 1527.

"Flamel is back in Paris."

Machiavelli straightened. "When?"

"Just now. He got there through a leygate. I've no idea where it comes out. He's got Scathach with him. . . ."

Machiavelli's lips curled into an ugly grimace. The last time he'd encountered the Warrior, she'd pushed him through a door. It had been closed at the time, and he'd spent weeks picking splinters from his chest and shoulders.

"There are two humani children with him. Americans," Dee said, his voice echoing and fading on the transatlantic line. "Twins," he added.

"Say again?" Machiavelli asked.

"Twins," Dee added, "with pure gold and silver auras. You know what that means," he snapped.

"Yes," Machiavelli muttered. It meant trouble. Then the tiniest of smiles curled his thin lips. It could also mean opportunity.

Static crackled and then Dee's voice continued. "The girl's powers were Awakened by Hekate before the Goddess and her Shadowrealm were destroyed."

"Untrained, the girl is no threat," Machiavelli murmured, quickly assessing the situation. He took a breath and added, "Except perhaps to herself and those around her."

"Flamel took the girl to Ojai. There, the Witch of Endor instructed her in the Magic of Air."

"No doubt you tried to stop them?" There was a hint of amusement in Machiavelli's voice.

"Tried. And failed," Dee admitted bitterly. "The girl has some knowledge but is without skill."

"What do you want me to do?" Machiavelli asked carefully, although he already had a very good idea.

"Find Flamel and the twins," Dee demanded. "Capture them. Kill Scathach if you can. I'm just leaving Ojai. But it's going to take me fourteen or fifteen hours to get to Paris."

"What happened to the leygate?" Machiavelli wondered aloud. If a leygate connected Ojai and Paris, then why didn't Dee . . . ?

"Destroyed by the Witch of Endor," Dee raged, "and she nearly killed me, too. I was lucky to escape with a few cuts and scratches," he added, and then ended the call without saying good-bye.

NICHOLAS FLAMEL
was a real person.

Legend says he was the keeper of the philosopher's stone,

which he used to achieve eternal life.

The records say he died in 1418, but his grave is empty.

Sometimes legends are true.

DISCOVER THE SECRETS OF
THE IMMORTAL NICHOLAS FLAMEL!

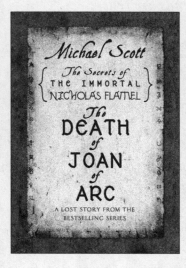
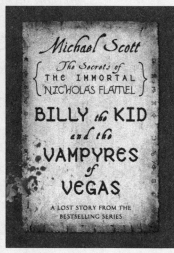